The
FORTUNE
HUNTER

Meagan McKinney

The FORTUNE HUNTER

KENSINGTON BOOKS

http://www.kensingtonbooks.com

Mac

KENSINGTON BOOKS are published by

Kensington Publishing Corp.
850 Third Avenue
New York, NY 10022

Library of Congress Card Catalog Number: 97-073785
ISBN 1-57566-262-0

First Printing: April, 1998
10 9 8 7 6 5 4 3 2 1

Printed in the United States of America

For
Celeste Eichling Neuffer
who showed me how to be rich and famous—
rich in friends and famous in the eyes of God.
I love you.

Author's Note

The current spiritualist movement began in 1848 in Hydesville, New York, created by a pair of young sisters named Margaret and Kate Fox. The sisters would produce strange knocks or "rappings" that seemed unexplained until it was theorized that the girls—illiterate and uneducated—had, in their innocence, somehow become conduits for communication with the spirit world. Local notoriety ensued which, nurtured by their eldest sister Leah, grew into a national sensation.

The Fox sisters—Leah included—became rich and famous. Much of the scientific community raised doubts about the girls' actual abilities to communicate with the dead—and some of the Disbelievers are quoted herein. But they compared their task to "punching a feather pillow"; one makes a dent but then it refills with feathers and air. Many were utterly convinced the Fox sisters were frauds but the public investigation into the rappings, as one historian put it, "only threw a publicity over the subject of the rappings, which . . . culminated in the conversion of more investigators to the belief of Spiritualism than had been known in the space of so short a time in any other city." The Believers, when faced with the calamity of exposure, were notoriously dismissive of any evidence. By ignoring any facts to the contrary, the Believers ended any possibility of argument. The Devoted's opinions are included here also.

Of special note is the romance which grew between the arctic explorer Dr. Elisha Kent Kane and Margaret Fox. Kane was from an elite Philadelphia family. His society did not mix with backwoods maidens from Hydesville but he was willing to overlook this point when he set eyes upon the young and beautiful Margaret. Kane was unusual in many ways. Not only did he fall in love at first sight with the young Spiritualist, he was also never taken in by her craft. Never public about his opinions of the rappings, his letters to Margaret leave no doubt of his contempt for it. He was her publicly-silent, and yet, most ardent, Disbeliever. Excerpts from Kane's letters clearly reveal how absurd he thought it. But all through his chastising, he continued to remain infatuated with Margaret Fox. His love seemed to endure despite being tormented by class-distinctions, the expectations of his mother who thoroughly disapproved of the Fox sisters, and his devotion to his occupation, the dangerous and extensive explorations of the arctic regions. Furthermore, he had to share her with her public. Jealously, he wrote, "Maggie Dearest: I am mad, angry, disgusted, at the hogs who have kept me from you on this my last day. What a life to lead—at the call of any fool who chooses to pay a dollar and command your time." His hope was always that he might lead Margaret away from the life in which she was mired; he ached to reform her.

Alas, the Fox-Kane love affair ended in tragedy. In 1856 Elisha Kent Kane died as an indirect result of his arctic travels. Margaret claimed to the day of her death that the good Dr. Kane had officially taken her to wife, but no wedding certificate was ever produced. In effect, she was left behind an abandoned, ruined woman.

Forty years after Margaret Fox of the famous Hydesville Fox Sisters began the spirit rappings, she confessed that she was a fake. Kate and she performed the rappings by cracking their toe knuckles and hiding the movement beneath extra long dresses. Strangely, however, few believed Margaret Fox. The victim of alcoholism and a notorious doomed love affair, she was viewed as a woman of no account. Her confession was tossed aside—in the typical dismissive manner of the Believer—because the public was now utterly dazzled by the latest newcomer to the spiritualist field, the great wit and show woman, Madame Helena Petrovna Blavatsky.

Chapter One

What is one to do when, in order to rule men, you must deceive them, when, in order to catch them and make them pursue whatever it may be, it is necessary to promise and show them toys? Suppose my books and The Theosophist *were a thousand times more interesting and serious, do you think that I would have anywhere to live and any degree of success unless behind all this there stood "phenomena"? I should have achieved absolutely nothing, and would long ago have pegged out from hunger.*

MADAME BLAVATSKY

The white-draped specter seemed to float along the floor of the parlor, her ethereal gown waving in the sudden, inexplicable breeze. August in Manhattan provided no cooling winds, but yet, as the ghost girl placed her icy lips upon the cheek of each member of the séance, the Exalted Czarina began to tremble as if chilled by an unearthly presence.

"Go home, sweet spirit. Phantasm, I now bid you to return to the other side." The Exalted Czarina waved her hands across the table where she sat. The phantom paused, then took a slow, elegant step backward as if pulled by otherworldly forces.

Beneath the Czarina's hands, the shawl-draped table began to levitate. The sound of gasps from the audience seemed to raise it higher and higher still, until it slammed violently to the floor. In tandem, the single gaslight in the parlor flared, then extinguished. Cries in the dark accompanied the confusion of gentlemen trying to relight the sconce. But when it was finally lit, the phantom was gone and the table was still.

"Bravo, Czarina! Bravo!" cried a reporter from the *New York Post*. He scribbled something on a pad of paper just as the man from *Harper's* took a shaky sip from his hip flask.

The Exalted Czarina stood. Her young pale face seemed even whiter beneath the pre-Raphaelite cloud of her dark unbound hair. "I must rest," she wept convincingly, her arm draped across her forehead.

The newspapermen shuffled to the door, scrawling and sweating with the same fervor.

"A front-pager if I ever saw one," exclaimed the man from the *Post*.

Another reporter walked up to the table and drew back the shawl as if he wasn't convinced. But he found nothing. Beneath the table were four heavily carved legs and a frightful emptiness in between. "I don't know. I really can't say how this all came about . . ." he murmured before wandering from the parlor.

The Czarina gave a huge exhausted sigh when the last gentleman in the group had left the room. It wasn't easy putting on a display for the press, but it was profitable. Once the articles were published of the night's incidents, she and Lavinia would have a whole wave of the public beating down the door in order to have a chance to speak with their dearly departed. At five dollars a head, it would certainly pay the gas bill and then some.

She leaned back in her chair. The room was in near darkness but if she felt the cold presence of spirits, she didn't show it. Indeed, she felt hot; it was, after all, deep summer in New York.

The Czarina glanced at the closed parlor door, then, telling herself it was all clear, she stretched, knotted her hair upon her head to remove it from the prickly heat of her nape and poured herself a tall glass of water from a nearby silver pitcher. She was just about to unclasp the heavy mantle around her shoulders when she spied a last gentleman still sitting in one of the dim corners of the parlor.

"The séance is over, sir. I really must rest now. It's quite tiring being in communication with the spirits." She stared at the dark form, waiting for him to take his leave like the others.

He stood and joined her in the dim circle of gaslight. He was a head taller than her and the Czarina found herself craning her neck to look up at him. He was well dressed in a black jacket and striped silk vest, and in the dim light his hair appeared as dark as his jacket. He sported a trim Vandyke, all the fashion now, but his gave him a most satanic look. It didn't set her at ease at all to see his eyes flash in anger.

"The séance is over, sir," she repeated.

"You mean the *show* is over."

Her eyes fixed on his face. It was a handsome face. The closely shorn goatee hid nothing. Yet his face was an angry one.

"This was nothing but a genuine communication with the Other Side . . . and it was exhausting for me, sir. You must take your leave as the others have done and allow me to retire."

"How genuine is a fraud?" His black brows came together in a frown. "Not very, I'd say." He touched his right cheek where the phantom girl had in her turn kissed him. "She has cold lips. I daresay they match the temperature of her heart."

"She came from the grave, sir. How else do you expect her lips to be?"

He gave her a sardonic smile. "And where is your famous sister, the Countess? Why was she not conducting the séance tonight? Are her lips as cold? The reporters were disappointed not to see her. As I was."

"She is tired. She has taken to her bed. The spirits take their toll on the body."

"She doesn't sleep well? Could it be that her conscience keeps her awake?" He raised one infuriated eyebrow and gave her a look that proved he thought her less than the dirt scraped from the gutter on South Street. "And how do you sleep, Czarina *Renski?*" he added with naked sarcasm.

"Very well, sir. Very well indeed." She looked nervously to the parlor doors. Suddenly their English butler Rawlings appeared there, and she couldn't hide the relief on her face. "Rawlings, please show Mr. . . . ah, Mr. . . . ?" She looked up at the scowling gentleman beside her.

"Mr. Stuyvesant-French. Edward Stuyvesant-French. Remember the name. You'll be seeing a lot of me in the next weeks, my girl."

"Our séances are rarely open to the public, sir. We only make it a policy to have the press here when the demand requires it."

"Then you shall have a private séance for me. I'll pay you well to convince this doubter."

"The spirits don't like to be in the presence of doubters and naysayers."

"How utterly convenient."

"Please, sir. I must go now."

"I'll send a note to you tomorrow with the coinage. You and your sister will have a séance just for me."

"If the spirits are willing, but for now, sir, good night."

Rawlings held the door. Mr. Edward Stuyvesant-French nodded curtly and left with the butler, his tall form dwarfing the older man.

The Czarina flew to the window. Only when she saw the man embark his black hansom cab did she lean against the sill and take a deep breath.

❧ ❦

"He's gone, then? How I hate that man. Why do you suppose we've caught his attention? He's been to every press séance we've held this week." The voice came from the veiled phantom girl who stepped out from behind a screen. Trailing in her wake was a boy no older than eight carrying an enormous palm fan, the source of the mysterious breezes.

From beneath the medium's table, hinges creaked and snapped

open and out tumbled a pair of tiny girls, ages four and five, who burst forth from inside two of the hollow, deceivingly heavy, carved table legs.

"Edward Stuyvesant-French is right," the Czarina said, staring after his departed hansom. "Even our famed levitation is nothing but trickery and children playing table legs, but why is it his business to prove it?"

"He's not a newspaperman. He's not a scientist. He'd tell us if he were. We've seen enough of those lately." The phantom girl lifted her white veil and peered out the window at the rain-slicked cobbled streets of Washington Square. "He's taking us personally. I don't like it. He scares me."

Hazel Mae Murphy, onetime resident of the St. Louis Home for Abandoned Children and of late the Exalted Czarina Renski of New York, suddenly laughed. "He scares *you*, Lavinia? Just look at yourself. The white greasepaint you wear is really done well. You even frightened *me* tonight and *I* know it's you."

Lavinia Murphy, also known as the Countess Lovaenya, Medium Extraordinaire of Fifth Avenue, touched her cheek and looked at the white smear on her palm. She smiled, her teeth a haunting shade of ivory in the moonlight. "Ice costs a fortune this time of year but it works marvelously in preparing for a kiss, don't you think? I thought Mr. Champignon of *The Herald* was going to wet his trousers when I placed my frozen lips upon his cheek."

"You are wicked, Lavinia."

"Yes. Wicked."

"I don't know how our dear Lavinia thinks of these things." Hazel turned around and looked at the children behind them. The two girls were already half asleep on their feet, and the boy looked to be ready to topple into bed himself. "You did well tonight, my loves."

"You did," Lavinia said, dropping to her knees and giving all three of them a kiss, this time with well-warmed lips. "I'm so proud of you three. You were splendid. Absolutely splendid."

The smallest girl leaned her head on Lavinia's white-draped shoulder. Lavinia stroked the child's hair and lifted her into her arms. "Tired, my little sparrow? Of course you are. It's way past midnight." She smiled at the boy when he took the other little girl's hand. "Jamie, take Fanny upstairs and I'll follow with Eva."

"That man . . . he's sure good and gone now?" Jamie, the boy, seemed to fidget as if something pressing were on his mind.

"So you noticed that awful man too?" Lavinia asked, giving Hazel a sideways glance.

"He's not going to find us out, huh? I mean, if he found us out, would we have to go back to the home?" Jamie stared at the two young women, devastation on his face.

"You're not going back to any workhouse." Lavinia stood with Eva now in her arms fast asleep. "Heavens no. We're not going to even think about that place again. It's 1881, remember, Jamie? I know they don't realize this in St. Louis, but slavery is dead. I hear that applies to orphans as well."

"You and Hazel are old enough that they can't make you go back there. But me and the girls, well, we might get caught. They might find out our name's not Murphy—"

"Well, it *is* Murphy. That's my name and you all shall have it because you're my family now and will be forever."

"I don't want to ever go back there." The boy seemed to grow noticeably paler even in the dim light of the parlor.

Lavinia placed a hand on his head and caressed his vulnerable cheek still plump with boyhood. "I'll never let them take you back there. Never. Hazel and I remember the place too well to ever let you or Eva or Fanny live there again. So no more nightmares, all right?"

The boy mustered a smile. "Promise?"

"I promise. I've done this much to keep us from starving on the streets—why wouldn't I do more if it becomes necessary?"

Content, he hoisted the other sleepy girl into his arms and

tottered out the parlor doors with her. Lavinia followed, but Hazel made her pause.

"What if that man does want to cause trouble?" Hazel asked, her face pale and frightened. "I couldn't let them take away Eva—" Lavinia put her hand up. It was hell on the conscience being a heroine, but she'd done too many dark and dishonorable things to ensure the survival of her "family" to let them be destroyed now. All she really wanted was Hazel to be married and provide a father for Eva. The other two children, she knew, would thrive in the resulting beams of their happiness. With a real father, only then would they have a true family to count upon; and only then would her guilt diminish. The children and Hazel deserved so much. The worst of Lavinia's guilt arose from the idea that they only had her to rely upon, and she was impossibly inadequate.

Her eyes glittered with resolve. "He won't be trouble. I won't allow it. I'll see him out of our paths even if I must handle him all myself."

"He seemed determined. Did you notice the jut of his jaw and the anger in his gaze?" Hazel added.

Lavinia refused to be intimidated. She left the room, saying, "His cheek was like iron when I kissed it. Still, an iron man only makes him a fine match for me, because, you forget, dear sister, after all we've been through, I am a woman made of steel."

Edward Stuyvesant-French slammed his fist upon the black marble mantel. The drawing room of his suite at the Fifth Avenue Hotel was luxurious to the point of asphyxiation. Heavy brown velvet draperies, maroon leather upholstery and silk tassels the size of wine bottles elegantly finished the room, and yet, the splendid surroundings irritated him. Everything seemed to irritate him.

"Can I get you something to help that snit you're in?" An older gentleman sitting in a plush Turkish chair dismissed Edward's mood in order to contemplate the breakfast tray that had just been laid out by the hotelier. "What you need, Edward my boy, is a good bellyful of Mandan whiskey—that'd take care of the vile brew that passes for coffee in this place, and it'd also wipe out this foul temper."

"They're frauds and I'm going to prove it," Edward vowed.

"Yes, yes, but what will that accomplish? Wilhelm won't care, nor will he believe you." The older man poured coffee into a fancy Limoges cup, then grimaced when he made to drink it.

Edward opened his mouth to retort, but the picture of his friend made him bite back a smile. Cornelius Cook, gentleman adventurer, was the size of a grizzly bear, his fabulous gray whiskers an astonishing contrast to the fragile china cup he attempted to hold to his lips.

Cook put the cup aside, obviously defeated by its femininity. He turned to Edward and resumed the conversation. "They're just a couple of chits trying to make a living. Why bother them? Put the past aside, old boy. That's what I say."

"As you've put the past aside?" Edward's quiet voice belied the heavy meaning of his words.

Cornelius glanced away, his expression distant.

"There are those who say he speaks with Alice in the Countess's notorious parlor." Edward made no attempt to gentle his voice. "And I say this kind of fraud is the most heinous kind."

"He doesn't speak with Alice. You and I both know Alice is gone," Cornelius said quietly.

Edward retrieved an object from his desk and held it up. It was a heavily figured gold locket tied with a wide velvet ribbon the color of a raven's wing. The gold looked almost despairing against the funereal black velvet. "She is gone," Edward said. "This is all that's left. My mother, Alice Stuyvesant-French, has been dead my entire life, and I say no cheap carnival trick is going to diminish her memory by attempting to resurrect her."

Cook stared at the locket swinging in Edward's hand and he

seemed pained by it. "But look, Edward, the Countess and the Czarina are just two young women playing at being spiritualists. It's Wilhelm Vanadder you want, not them. Leave the girls alone. Let them have their fun."

Edward spoke through gnashed teeth. "All that 'fun' has built them a town house and furnished it. Have you seen the diamond-and-sapphire ring on the Countess's finger? I saw it once when she took an afternoon stroll. It's enormous. Everyone talks of it. Vanadder gave it to her 'for services rendered.' He gave the ring to her, and it was Daisy's money that paid for it."

"Your father isn't dead, Edward, as much as you might want him to be, and it's not your sister's money until she inherits. As long as Wilhelm Vanadder is alive, he has a right to spend his money on whatever trinkets he chooses."

"He's mad, and worse than that, he's dragged my mother's memory into his madness." Edward's eyes flashed. He dropped the locket on his desk. "I won't have him trumping up these charades of going to speak to Alice when he's only going to that woman for a leg-over."

"You don't know that. The Countess might actually be holding séances."

"It's a sham, and you know it. Those women are nothing but two-bit whores, and if they were just that, I'd leave them alone, but they pretend to be more—and now they've dragged the wrong spirit into their telegraph."

"I saw the Countess just the other day at Stewart's." Cook patted down his whiskers which he did when he was thinking. "She, of course, didn't know I knew of her, or that I was watching her, but she struck me as very polite to the clerk, and very modest in her behavior."

"They claim he talks to Alice when he's with her." Edward looked hard at the man. "*Alice.*"

Cornelius said nothing. He merely fingered the dainty cup at his side as if it brought him comfort.

Edward stared at him. "How long have we known each other?"

"A long time, Edward."

"Thirty-five years. It is a long time. It's my entire life."

"So what has our acquaintance have to do with Vanadder and those two wicked females down on Washington Square?"

Edward's voice was harsh, yet hesitating. "Before my mother died, there was talk of another suitor besides Wilhelm Vanadder. There was talk that a good and decent man had been in love with Alice Stuyvesant-French, and that his spirit had been crushed when Alice was caught in scandal with Vanadder."

"There was no such man," Cook answered, his own voice steady but his face taut with irritation.

"Oh? Well, thank God for that. I was afraid for a moment that one noble soul might actually reside in this festering city."

Cook didn't respond; he never moved his gaze from the tiny cup. The scrolls of pink bellflowers that daintily spilled over the rim seemed to fascinate him.

"You know," Edward added quietly, "there was also talk of a deathbed promise, and the kind of love that can last beyond the grave. The gossipmongers said this decent man couldn't stand to lose his dear Alice, not even in death, so in her final moments, before the birth of the bastard who stands before you now, he promised her he would care for it. He would care for this loathsome child of another man who took his love away." Edward stared at Cook, stared until the man lifted his eyes and stared back. "In thirty-five years I never questioned your loyalty, Cornelius," he whispered. "I never had to."

"You've always had my loyalty. You know that."

Edward's gaze was piercing. "You've always been the one I counted on. Even when I was a newborn, and the Stuyvesants filed to reclaim my mother's money, you fought them on behalf of her infant son. And when the Stuyvesants won their suit and shunned this unwanted boy, you took me in and gave me a home. Then, when I was just barely out of boyhood, and vowed to make my fortune in the frontier, you went with me, braving the cold, huddling with the rest of the miners beneath the pathetic shelter of a leaking tarp, enduring the endless meals of beans and pemmican, all the while assuring the foolish young man I was that you had wanted to come along for the sheer adventure of it."

"And it was an adventure." Cornelius finally smiled. "When you discovered that vein of gold near Fort MacKenzie I was never so amazed in my life."

"You were more surprised when I named the lode after you." Edward tipped his mouth in a half smile. "And I recall you were dumbfounded when I gave you half the profits."

"I didn't need half the profits. Now that you named it the Cook Mine and made me the famous one, everyone is curious to know why Edward Stuyvesant-French has returned to his hometown New York dripping in money, but with no visible means of support."

"I don't need to inform them."

"You had nothing to repay, Edward."

"Oh?" Edward frowned. "Yes, of course. I had nothing to repay. This decent man, conjured up by the gossipmongers, didn't exist."

"No, he didn't," Cornelius reaffirmed adamantly.

Edward smirked.

The older man shook his head and appeared to long for the whiskey. "Let's return to the real issue here, shall we? You only want to prove your father's insane for attending these endless séances, but you forget, my man, Wilhelm Vanadder *is* insane and all New York knows it. What's there to prove?"

"That he should have control of Daisy . . . it makes my stomach turn. I should be her guardian."

"Your half-sister has a sad tale to tell, being bound to the chair as she is and having to deal with a tyrant, but I still don't understand how exposing a couple of spiritualists will get the effect you desire."

Edward turned to the mantel and looked at him in the gilded

neo-Greco mirror over the mantel. "I'm going to have Vanadder put away and I'm going to use Hazel and Lavinia Murphy to do it."

Cornelius lowered his cup, his eyes focused on Stuyvesant-French. "You mean you're going to have the old guy legally declared insane? In the courts?"

"If the authorities in England could put George the Third away, then I can find a way to put away my wretched father, Wilhelm Vanadder."

"You really hate the old goat, don't you?"

Edward stared at him, his eyes full of anguish and meaning.

Cook eventually glanced away, complicitous.

"It wasn't enough that he failed to recognize me as his own?" Edward rasped. "Then how about the fact that my own mother perished from the scandal of bearing his illegitimate child?"

"Your mother was society. Look at your name, for God's sake. I'll never understand how Vanadder was able to make your mother fall so far from the pedestal of her birthright." Cornelius's eyes darkened.

"I'm told my father was handsome in his day. He had a way with women that made even a Stuyvesant-French overlook the shiny patina of his new money." Edward looked down as if unwilling to show the expression in his eyes. "Mother must have been convinced he would marry her, he must have convinced her he would claim his son as his own. That's the only explanation that makes sense. Alice misjudged Vanadder's penchant for cruelty, just as Daisy does even now."

"No one ever has proved he was your father, French," Cornelius said, using Edward's nickname.

Edward looked up. He strode over to a tintype encased in a rococo silver frame. "Do you doubt it? Really?"

Cornelius hardened his expression. The man in the picture was the exact double of the man standing before him: the same strong jaw, the same lean, handsome face, the same merciless mouth.

Except for the trademark bowler and the old-fashioned Tweedside jacket that dated the era to twenty years before, it could have been the same man.

"He killed my mother. She never recovered from the shame of my conception. She'd been forced by her parents to reject his suit because she was a Stuyvesant-French and he was a nobody with a fortune. Then for one terrible moment she melted for him, and he must have taken great glee in rejecting her when she needed him so desperately."

"Cruel . . . so cruel . . ." Cornelius whispered helplessly.

"Yes," Edward answered, his lips in the same hard line as the lips in the tintype.

"But if you go after Vanadder, all will say you're just doing it to get his money."

"I don't need his money—"

"I know that, but that's not what others will think. They'll say you're doing it to inherit."

"What people will think is of no account. Declaring my father insane on behalf of his invalid daughter isn't the same as declaring him my blood relative. I'll gain nothing from this but the guardianship of my half-sister, but I will pull her from the clutches of his tyranny if I have to use every attorney this side of the Hudson River to do it."

"And if you have to use the Murphy sisters."

"Ah, them. Yes, they're key to the plan. I'll expose them as frauds and make Vanadder look mentally incompetent, or I'll go to my grave trying."

"I pity the poor sisters."

"They're not even sisters, these two little frauds. 'The Murphy girls' ran away from some orphanage in the Midwest, and they've been performing tricks ever since." Edward walked over to a stack of papers sitting on a partners desk. "Here I have their entire history. As they moved east they hooked up with several vaudeville troupes whereby they were kicked out of town after town for solicitation. Finally they showed up in New York and have made a fabulous success of themselves, until they had the great misfortune of becoming my means to an end."

Cornelius's jaw dropped. "You amaze me, Edward. You and your nefarious schemes—how on earth did you dig up all that information?"

"Pinkertons. They were the ones that traced Lavinia Murphy to the orphan asylum in St. Louis." Stuyvesant-French seemed to take great pleasure in recounting the black spots on Lavinia Murphy's character. "It seemed her parents died of cholera on the homestead. She was brought to the orphanage at age five where she remained for eleven years until she left in the middle of the night with another girl of her age, a young boy of four, and two babies. Tracking her whereabouts after that was simple. It's not easy for a pretty young woman to travel with three sisters and a brother and go entirely unnoticed."

"No, I suppose it's not." Cornelius became glum. "Solicitation, you say? At age sixteen? Why, I hate to think of it. When I saw the Countess at Stewart's, I must say it's difficult for me to imagine that strong young woman reduced to such circumstances."

"Now that I'm banishing all myths, Lavinia Murphy's about as much a countess as her 'sister' is a czarina." Edward crossed his arms over his chest. "Their whole business is ugly. Think of the hardened characters we're dealing with here."

Cornelius softened with remembrance. "But she certainly is pretty. Not quite the fashion plate with all that blonde hair. Still, I just can't imagine the woman I saw—"

"Don't tell me she's sucked you in, too, with her play of innocence?" Edward looked down at his older friend as if he'd just turned into an ostrich. "That's her ploy, you know. She has to appear innocent because a naive young miss is the best kind of medium to attract the spirit world, according to 'the experts.' " He snorted in derision.

"She just didn't appear to be a hardened character, that's all

I'm saying. She was very polite to the clerk who assisted her and she even carried out her own packages."

"Then she performs her fraud well." Edward thumbed through the stack of papers on Lavinia Murphy. "But I'll see her exposed. I've got great plans for her."

"That's her livelihood you're planning to destroy. There aren't a lot of ways for a young woman to make a decent living."

Another snort. "Decent? Look, I've told you, there's nothing decent about her. She's a fraud. A criminal. Let her make her money legitimately, I say, or let her make it on her back like all the rest of her kind. That's the only living a woman like her should make."

"You are indeed your father's son, Edward," Cornelius said, with melancholy in his voice.

Edward didn't answer at first, as if the notion had somehow paralyzed him.

"That I am," he finally said, his expression hardened as his gaze trained on the tintype.

Chapter Two

If anybody would endow me with the faculty of listening to the chatter of old women and curates in the nearest provincial town, I should decline the privilege, having better things to do. And if the folk in the spiritual world do not talk more wisely and sensibly than their friends report them to do, I put them in the same category. The only good thing I can see in the demonstration of the 'Truth of Spritualism' is to furnish an additional argument against suicide.

—T. H. HUXLEY

Lavinia looked around the parlor in the town house on Washington Square. It was her triumph. Each satin upholstered Louis Seize chair, each carefully chosen chartreuse Old Paris vase, had cost her her pound of flesh. But now she could gaze across her gleaming home and take reassurance from its opulence. Never again would she be wanting. She had gone from starving pauper to the upper middle class of a prosperous city in only four short years, and more importantly, she'd pulled Hazel, Fanny, Eva and Jamie right up there beside her. The children would never again know the kind of fears that had scarred her in her childhood: the terror of abandonment, the ache of starvation, the ice-cold knowledge that there was no one who cared for her in the entire world.

Lavinia knew she and Hazel would always keep those wounds inside them, but the children were healing. She saw it every time they laughed and chased each other around the tea table, and every time the girls left chocolate fingerprints on their silk dresses. They were comfortable, and, thought Lavinia defiantly, they were at home. At last, they were all at home.

But now all of it—the Princess of Wales pink velvet drapery, the properly worn Aubusson rug, the tarnished Norman-revival gilt mirror, and, more sickeningly, the security each object represented—was threatened. Threatened by a man with no motive and no apparent connection to her.

She eased herself down upon a satin tuffet, her mind enveloped with a vague dread. She would never be able to forget the night she and Hazel had left the orphanage. They'd had nothing but the proverbial clothes on their backs, and rags they were. Now she swished around her parlor in red silk slippers, her icicle blue taffeta day gown making similar whispers, its stunning train of deep scarlet catching all the red highlights in her pale blonde curls.

Indeed she had come a long way from the long hungry nights now burned into her memory. She'd once regretted the impulsive decision to take the children with them; their future was haunted with the specter of starvation. But Lavinia knew what it would have been like for them at the orphanage all too well; she spent eleven years there. As a child it would be endless toil and pitifully inadequate meals, and then, if the girls didn't get out in time as she had, a brutally short lifetime of working on their backs until disease or childbirth stole them away.

So she'd fought back. She'd persevered. She'd done things that a more fortunate, cared-for woman would never have had to resort to, but Lavinia always forced those regrets from her very soul. Her joy was that now she and her "family" had a town house in New York City, servants and a stylish parlor with an exotic canopied Turkish cozy corner that was the talk of the town.

And there were times such as now when all she could think of was how right she'd been to take the children. Eva, Jamie and Fanny were upstairs in their schoolroom with the governess learning things they never would have learned at the home. At the St. Louis Orphan Asylum, the only curriculum was Cruelty and Want. Indeed, the children's futures had worked out beautifully.

But now the letter had come.

She looked down at the missive in her hand, a note hastily—perhaps even angrily—penned across stationery emblazoned with the crest of the Fifth Avenue Hotel: *I request a meeting. Will call this afternoon. ESF.*

Lavinia could almost picture him, Edward Stuyvesant-French, that dark-haired ogre, sitting in the bar beneath the decadent Bouguereau nude. Plotting her demise.

Yet the reason he should want her demise still eluded her. Perhaps that was what terrified her the most. He was no scientist or reporter whose career depended on exposing such as her. No, he was going after her for other motives entirely. What they were, she couldn't begin to guess, but she could tell from Rawlings' reluctant shuffle up the staircase, she wasn't going to have long to wonder.

"Mr. Stuyvesant-French is here, miss." Rawlings appeared at the parlor doors, looking hesitant and afraid. "He's downstairs. What shall I do with him?"

She plastered on her most brilliant, most confident smile, and said warmly, "You will show him up, Rawlings. Of course."

The old butler stared at her for a long moment, his rheumy gaze darkened with worry.

"It'll be all right," she said with a wry, tremulous uptilt of her mouth. "I promise."

"You promise so much, miss. I think sometimes you're going to drop from the burden of all your promises."

"I haven't let you down yet, have I, old Rawl?" she whispered.

He smiled, but his gray head slumped. "I'll bring him up."

She watched him go, again remembering the old days. In the four years' journey to get to where they were now, she and Hazel had picked up Rawlings along the way. He was an ancient English puppeteer whose fortunes had gone awry with the theft of his puppets. They first met him weeping at the side of the road to Albany. He claimed to be sixty-five years old but Lavinia thought he might be more along the lines of seventy. Nonetheless, they asked the old man to join them in their schemes. Now he buttled for them, and, in addition, he did a fine bit of voice imitation and ventriloquism. He was able to throw his voice to any empty corner and make it sound as if the Queen of England were standing there. Rawlings was a priceless asset in the production of a communication with the dead.

She glanced down at the note in her hand and determinedly put it aside. "Let the lion loose, Rawl. I'll put him back in his cage," she whispered to herself as she waited for the demon to darken her lovely ivory-and-gilt parlor doors.

❦ ❦

Lavinia Murphy didn't look as he'd last seen her. Edward almost smirked when she glided up to him, all cold blue taffeta and concealing powder, a display of precise curls cascading down her back.

No, when he'd last seen her she'd been wearing white. She'd had the ethereal masquerade down to a science and she'd beckoned with every muscle in her lithe body. He well remembered that last time. She had worn frozen white but her limbs moved with the hot liquid of a ballerina. Her veiled face had seemed stiff, wiped clean of all expression, yet he recalled her hair was not the studied vain array it was now. Then, it had been wild and full, teasing just by its heavy length dusting her rump. It had swayed like the tail of a mare in heat and that was precisely why they came in droves to see the phantom girl. Hazel and Lavinia Murphy were two of the best paid spiritualists in New York because when one of them summoned a ghost, she was always a beauty.

And last night, when Lavinia Murphy gave her brilliant performance of the ghost girl, even Edward had to admit she'd managed to tap into his own male fantasy of the madonna-whore. As the ghost girl played out her wanton innocence, he knew the powers that could drive men to their knees. And for that, even now, he had to marvel at her.

"Mr. Stuyvesant-French. At last we meet. My sister told me about your attendance at the last séance." She neither held out her hand nor pressed it trembling to her bosom. She was neither the cold, calculating businesswoman, nor the sheltered miss. She was, in fact, nothing he could pin down, and, worst of all, a bit of everything most men feared: she had the composure of a business-woman, the expression of an innocent. And that was exactly why he couldn't wait to rip away the facade. No mere woman should have such power to manipulate. No flesh-and-blood female should possess such merciless knowledge of men.

"Countess." He nodded, his gaze locked with hers.

"What can I do for you, Mr. Stuyvesant-French?" she asked sweetly, her fluid hand motioning him to a nearby *bergère*.

"I've come to request a séance. A private séance."

She studied him for a long moment, and he swore then that her blue eyes appeared violet. For an instant, they seemed to have just enough heat from the color red to astound him.

He took a deep breath. *Fire and ice.* That's what she was, and he was drawn to it. Helplessly drawn. It angered him.

"Sir, we really don't give private séances without a recommen-dation first, and I'm afraid you have none." She carefully lowered herself to the lady's chair. She managed her wire bustle with more grace than Mrs. Astor. "If we were to make an exception in your case, it would have be under the most extraordinary circumstances."

"I have extraordinary circumstances." He flipped a silk purse onto the table between them. It was so packed with gold coins it dented the walnut top.

She stared at it, then at him. "As extraordinary as your circum-stances are, these aren't the kind of circumstances I meant." With a delicate, achingly feminine hand she pushed the purse back toward him. She had such revulsion on her face he half expected her to hold her nose. "My sister, I believe, spoke with you the night you were here last. She says you plan to expose us as frauds. The spirits don't take kindly to such talk, such suspicion, Mr. Stuyvesant-French."

He smiled. His hand rubbed his jaw. It was a boyish, rueful gesture which never failed to melt the weaker sex.

Lavinia Murphy didn't even thaw.

He decided to change tack. "The spirits you summon here, Countess, surely aren't the kind to cast stones upon a doubter. The phantom I saw the other night was not brought down from her perch in the clouds." He smirked. "Indeed, *she* would know a sinner when she saw one."

"I wasn't at my sister's last séance. I wouldn't know the soul she summoned from the grave that night."

"The girl was much like you, Countess. She pressed her stone-cold lips to my cheek, and now I find I long to feel those lips again."

Lavinia rose and went to the window. She provided him with a fetching pose of herself framed by the magnificient lambrequins of petal pink velvet; her profile soft and vulnerable, and taut with worry.

"We could not possibly do a private séance for you, sir. I believe you're not telling the truth. I have a gift, you see, given to me by the spirits. I'm able to look into a soul and see the truth that lies within. I cannot find your truth, so I must conclude there is none."

She was, after all, a cold woman, he thought as he stared at her. A cold woman, and, therefore, an exquisite challenge.

And when she stood by the window in just such a light, he could see red glints in her hair; secret tantalizing flames that were only there in certain moments, a heat that was only made more intense by the chill of her manners.

"Perhaps that's why I've come. To find the truth in my soul." He stood and walked to her. He stared until he felt his gaze could bore right through her.

"I'm afraid that's not the service we offer here, Mr. Stuyvesant-French. Now, if you had a dead relative, or a long-lost love that you wanted to summon, perhaps we could help, but—"

He took her hand in his. It shocked him with its warmth. She gave him an all-too-human startled gaze and he smiled in victory. She was in there, all right. Deep beneath the iceberg lay the kind of sweet, hot nymph that lured sailors to the rocks. Maybe it was true what people said about Lavinia Murphy. Maybe all the séances were nothing more than a cover for a high-priced prostitute. In any case, he was now a believer. Whatever her price, it could not be too high.

"Give me my séance, Countess. I leave the coins to you. I'll be back this evening at five and I expect to see my phantom girl then."

"The spirits tell me this is dangerous," she whispered, her eyes wary.

He lowered his head and pressed his lips against her palm. She seemed shocked by his actions, but he swore she fought the urge to curl her hand against the sensation.

"The spirits are right," he murmured, and with that, he nodded farewell and departed.

❦ ❦

"I believe it would be best if we simply ignore his arrival at the door, darken the house and wait until he goes away. I don't think this is a good idea." Lavinia watched in despair as Hazel counted the gold coins again.

"He left a hundred dollars. Look at this. A hundred dollars!" Hazel gasped, her eyes wide with awe.

"We must give it back to him. I really don't think we should do this séance."

Hazel finally looked up. "This isn't like you, Vinia. You're not one to worry like this."

"This man is different. He's not just some ape coming in here to make a fool of himself. He's—he's—"

"He's handsome," Hazel said grimly, staring down at the gold. "He's very handsome. Don't tell me you didn't notice. Hair as black as a raven's wing, eyes an unforgiving shade of green, and so confoundedly tall. . . ." She began dribbling the coins back into the silk purse. "You're right, of course. We'd best not do it. I'm more than a little frightened of him myself."

"I'm not frightened of him."

"Vinia, you don't back away this easily unless you're frightened."

"He disturbs me, he does not frighten me."

Hazel glanced at her. She left the questions unspoken.

"It doesn't matter what I feel," Lavinia added, "because we really can't fool with him. We've got Wilhelm coming in an hour and he's the meal ticket, remember? So let's forget about Mr. Stuyvesant-French. I say we return the coins by courier in the morning and take in the theater tonight."

"If you think that's best, Lavinia. Perhaps avoidance is the cure for this evil."

"I believe so," Lavinia offered, her brow still furrowed with worry.

❧ ❦

Wilhelm Vanadder was their best client. He was the one who, by his constant demands for séances, had provided the income to buy the town house. He came every Tuesday afternoon to speak with his dear departed mother and it was almost solely through Wilhelm that Lavinia had discovered being a spiritualist had its financial rewards. True, she was a fraud. Sometimes the guilt ate at her; some séances required more mental justification than others, but other times, strangely, the actual deception didn't bother her so much. People seemed to find great comfort in talking with the dead. She and Hazel provided an outlet for the most human of yearnings—to seek hope for the afterlife, to communicate with their loved ones. The only balm for her guilt was that her services were perversely therapeutic, even if it was all done with trickery and bad lighting.

But what she did find unbearable at times were the confessions. It seemed that a medium's place was not only to summon the souls of the long departed, but to comfort the souls of those very much still around. The Countess Lovaenya and the Czarina Renski had fabricated fantastic stories of their past whereby they had traveled to Paris and Romania and Nepal in order to educate themselves in the practices of the mystics—even though the truth was that they had ventured from St. Louis to Albany to Manhattan barely scraping together a living by performing cheap carnival tricks— yet in spite of the truth, the Murphy sisters had succeeded in their illusion of success. Posing as the fictional Countess and Czarina, the bridges to the spirit world, they had become the shoulders on which Manhattan cried; they were the bosoms upon which society confessed its most dark secrets. Wilhelm Vanadder was no exception.

He was due at four o'clock. Lavinia looked at the Russian ormolu clock on the mantel and saw that it was five minutes till.

She wasn't really up to seeing him. Edward Stuyvesant-French had rattled her. She wondered if she could hold up the necessary deceptions in order to get through the séance. But the bills had to be paid and hopefully Stuyvesant-French would take his coins back and not bother them anymore.

"Mr. Wilhelm Vanadder, miss," Rawlings announced as Vanadder was shown into the parlor.

"Wilhelm, how lovely to see you. A week is too long without your company. The departed have ached to speak with you." She glided across the pastel-shaded rug and held out her hand for Vanadder.

"My dear," he said, bending down to kiss her hand. He was a

large man and too many years of drinking and overindulgence had made him fat. Still, there was a handsomeness to his face and today as she stared at it something tickled at the back of her mind.

"Won't you sit down? You look a bit pale today, Wilhelm," she murmured, nodding to the elaborately carved table that sat in the middle of the parlor. Fanny and Eva were not going to perform. When Lavinia wanted to have an easy time of it, all she did was rappings. Just like the Fox sisters, she'd found that a good crack of a toe knuckle at the right time could mean an entire conversation to those anxious to believe.

"I must speak with Mother," he said anxiously. He dabbed perspiration off his forehead even though the day was quite cool. "I'm afraid my son has come back."

"Oh?" Lavinia raised one eyebrow. She'd heard plenty about Wilhelm's bastard son. The old man had never formally recognized the boy because of some petty reason and now the guilt ate at him. Every séance with "Mother" was another confession of remorse over the boy's illegitimacy. Once, "Mother" had even suggested he recognize the boy, but that had only induced a tidal flood of weeping. Apparently Wilhelm had already tried to make amends and the boy would have nothing to do with him.

She sat down next to him at the table and contemplated once more the burden of society's guilt. It sickened her to know these people's dirty little secrets. There were so many of them, and they were, indeed, so dirty.

"The Czarina couldn't be here today, Wilhelm. She was called to Woodvine in order to perform a séance at the camp."

Wilhelm attempted a smile. Though he had dark circles under his eyes and looked as if he were coming down with a bug, he appeared rather handsome to Lavinia today; memorable somehow. The very notion that she should be attracted to him struck her as strange, and being in the strange business she was she never discounted intuition. Indeed, she rushed to find a rationale and quickly attributed her attraction to the fact that he looked different today.

His cheeks were whiter than normal, and he appeared as if he'd lost weight.

"I've talked of giving my money to the camp," he said, catching his breath. "I've told you that, haven't I, Countess?"

Lavinia solemnly put her hands together. The spiritualist utopia in Woodvine was where she and Hazel had had their start. Certainly, because of that, she had nothing but praise for the place. "You have certainly spoken of it, sir, and a worthy idea it is."

"Well, I've changed my mind. I'm not going to give it to the spiritualist camp. I don't think I like Olcott anymore."

"May I ask why not?"

"He's a monkey, that's why. Darwin is right. I had a dream just the other night that, in truth, the Colonel was nothing more than a stuffed baboon in little white shirt and bowtie clapping two cymbals together. I couldn't give money to such a creature."

"No, of course not." She tried to appear sympathetic and interested but she and Vanadder had a version of the conversation at least once a week. He was constantly having a dream or a vision that altered his perception of a certain person. His will had changed so often she wouldn't be surprised to hear the next recipient was to be President Hayes.

"I'm going to leave all my money to my son. I've decided. That'll make him take notice of his old father." He crushed his handkerchief to his lips as if he were biting back pain.

"Still preoccupied with your son, Wilhelm?" she cooed. She then discreetly slipped out of her shoe and stretched her toes. The *New York World* had once said in a fit of disbelief that the Countess and Czarina needed trainbearers because their gowns were so suspiciously long. But she didn't even need an extra-long gown with Wilhelm. He was a believer through and through. And it didn't hurt at all that he was completely mad.

"How dare he denounce me when he's nothing but a bastard? There ought to be a law against such insubordination."

"His anger upsets you, doesn't it?" she affirmed, her mind hardly on the conversation. She could do it all by rote now anyway: he would weep, Mother would console. The heavy purse of coins would be tossed into the bureau's top drawer until Rawlings could take it to the bank in the morning.

"He never met me before he was thirty," Vanadder said, rubbing his left arm as if he had a twitch there or something. "Why should he hate me?"

She coughed gently into a hankie to hide her disbelief. "I think there is more in this relationship than you understand. It's clear that your spirit and his have been locked in a centuries-old battle. That would explain so much of his strange animosity." *Not to mention the fact that you abandoned him as a child and shamed Mother into an early grave.*

The absurdities at times were hard to swallow, but that was why she kept the elaborate Belgian lace hankie with her. An indiscreet laugh could always be choked.

"You're right, Countess. I felt that I knew him long before I met him. There—there was something in his face that looked familiar to me."

It was your face, you dolt. "Indeed?" she asked brightly. "Well, shall we summon Mother and see if she knows how your two spirits might have collided in generations past?"

"Yes," he answered distractedly. He worried on his left arm as if it bothered him more and more.

"Are you all right, Wilhelm? Have you hurt your arm? You do look a bit under the weather—"

"No. Continue. It's this blasted heat, is all." He dabbed his forehead even though Lavinia was batting around the idea of needing a shawl.

"Take my hands, then, and we'll see if we can reach the other side." She clasped his hands into her own. His felt like blocks of Hudson River ice. "Are you sure you're all right, Wilhelm? Perhaps I should summon the physician. He could look you over—"

"No. I must talk to Mother."

She stared at him once, then twice. Finally she took a deep breath and closed her eyes. "Through the powerful forces of animal magnetism, we call for Alice. Wilhelm needs to speak with you, Alice. Alice? Alice, if you feel my force, will you contact us?"

A loud rap came from under the table. As usual Wilhelm looked beneath it and he seemed satisfied when he could find nothing there. "Mother?" he asked softly.

Another crack beneath the table.

"Mother? Is it you?"

Another loud rap.

"I need you, Mother," he began to sob most pitifully. His arm seemed to be forgotten now but he sweat profusely. "I'm going to accept the boy, Mother. I'm going to take him back."

One single rap.

"I knew you'd approve. It was you, after all, who compelled me to make amends. But he won't talk to me, Mother. He hates me."

Two raps.

"No, he really does. He really hates me. He blames me for your death."

Two more raps.

"Now don't argue with me, Mother. I'm telling you I know the man and he hates me. He's all but said it to my face. In our last meeting he called me insane."

Two raps.

"He did. He really did, and he offered not one apology."

Lavinia released a sigh. His hands were trembling and she worried about him. He was not acting in his usual mad manner.

"Mother?" he asked, his voice suddenly dropping to a whisper. It was almost as if he were choking. "Mother? I want him to have the fortune. My son. He will be my son and I'll let him take care of Daisy."

One rap.

"Thank God you approve. I'm going to do it, then. I'm going to change my will. If there ever was a deserving man—" He stopped and tried to catch his breath. Something seemed to pain him in his chest and he rubbed it frantically. "I say, Mother, if there ever— If I'd known there ever was a man—a man like our son, then I should have declared him ours—long ago."

"Are you well, Wilhelm? Let me call the doctor." She stared at him even though to do so was to break the séance.

But he didn't listen to her. He was still enthralled with his conversation. "Mother? One last thing. I think in my will I shall demand he take my name. What—what do you think, Mother?"

Lavinia cracked her toe knuckle once but she kept her eyes on the man who held on to her hands.

"Thank God. I knew that would make amends. So I'll claim him, then. I'll do the right thing—make up for all the bad. He'll be Edward Vanadder, as he should have been all along. And you, Mother, will be happy in your grave at last that your son is no longer a Stuyvesant-French."

"Dear God, wh-what did you say?" she stammered, forgetting about her toes and Mother and his strange illness. An awful conclusion had suddenly assailed her. She could think of nothing at that moment but shock and astonishment.

Wilhelm abruptly stood up. He stared at her for an eternity of seconds until he finally gasped, "No—longer—Edward— Stuyvesant—Stuyvesant-Fren—" He inhaled a deep breath. His eyes popped out. He clutched his chest.

"Wilhelm!" she exclaimed, rushing to his side.

"No—I don't—I don't—feel—well—at all—" he said.

Then it was over

He fell backward, grasping at his chest. His weight crushed the gilt parlor chair beneath him, and his lifeless body slumped to the floor with a loud thud.

Chapter Three

INVESTIGATOR: Have you ever heard of a medium who was not exposed in the end?

ALFRED RUSSEL WALLACE: On the contrary, I have heard of very few who were exposed. Monck was not caught in the act of trickery. Monck was a guest on that occasion, and a demand was made that he should be searched, and he departed through the window.

—*Testimony at the Monck trial*

"He's most definitely croaked."

Rawlings made this statement as he, Lavinia and Hazel stared down at Wilhelm's body awash in the fading afternoon light of the lovely parlor. Vanadder's form was like a mound of refuse abandoned inappropriately among the tender florals of the Aubusson rug.

"Dear God, what are we going to do?" Hazel exclaimed, her eyes like saucers as she gazed down at the body.

"The poor man. I don't think he knew what was happening. I should have just ignored his wishes and called the physician." Lavinia dabbed her wet cheeks. She wasn't the weepy sort but there was no getting around the fact that having a man drop dead in front of one's eyes was upsetting. All she could think about was all the things she should have done, and hadn't.

"The physician wouldn't have arrived in time to save him in any case," Rawlings comforted. "But what we've got to worry about now is that he's found somewhere else. The scandal could be ruinous if they find him here," he added, ever the pragmatist.

"His carriage is downstairs waiting for him. What shall I tell the driver?" Hazel asked, panicky.

Lavinia blew her nose with the Belgian hankie, then put her emotions aside. "The first thing to do is we must send the driver away."

"I'll go down and dismiss him, miss," Rawlings volunteered. "Then shall I summon Monty?"

Lavinia tried to think. Monty had helped them every now and again when they wanted to really put on a production for the press. He was a young man they'd met on Bleecker Street when they were first selling fortunes. Monty aspired to perform in operettas and vaudevilles, and when he wasn't acting, he drove a hackney cab and regularly fleeced his passengers.

"Yes. We must get Monty here. Perhaps for the right price, he'd help us load Wilhelm in his cab and then he can take him back to his mansion once we've concocted a story."

"But won't they ask Monty why he's dead?" Hazel piped in.

"Yes, yes, but Monty's just a hackney driver. We'll tell Wilhelm's driver that it's such a fine evening that the old man's going to walk to Delmonico's after his appointment. Then Monty can say he picked him up in Washington Square because he wasn't feeling well and wanted to return to the mansion and would not wait for his own driver to be summoned. Monty can tell them he figures Wilhelm had the heart attack in his cab and that will leave our names out of it."

"Good idea. Very good. Now let's hope Monty can get here before *rigor mortis* sets in." Rawlings looked expectantly at the two horrified young women.

Lavinia stared at Wilhelm's body. *Rigor mortis.* A vile thought. She prayed Monty was quick. "Go, tell the driver to be gone, that Wilhelm will meet him at ten at Delmonico's. Then send a courier to the cabstand and see if Monty's available to come right away."

"Very good, miss." Rawlings neatly stepped around the dead body and left the parlor. Hazel just stared dumbfounded at the body, as if she couldn't quite believe it was there.

"He looks rather peaceful, doesn't he?" she whispered.

"His face looks as kind and rational as I've ever seen it." Lavinia dabbed again with the lace hankie.

"I wonder . . . do you think he's carrying a lot of money?" Hazel, the true gamine of the streets, always turned to finances.

"I'm sure he brought payment for today. He was always prompt in paying us, remember?" Lavinia succumbed to another bout of weepiness.

"He didn't pay you ahead of time, did he?"

Lavinia looked at Hazel. The very idea of going through a dead man's jacket was about as awful as him keeling over in her parlor. "He didn't pay me ahead of time. You know he never does."

"He's not going to be paying you much anymore . . ." Hazel said forlornly.

"I really can't think about that now, Hazel. The man had the great misfortune to die and if he did so without paying for us today, then I must let that one go. Certainly, we're above having to collect a small debt from a dead man." She sat down on a tuffet. "Besides, I have another matter that's more important than that. I have to tell you something. He said during the séance who his son was. It's all kind of befuddled but at least there's some sense to that animosity now. I have to tell you that it's—"

"Miss! Miss!" Rawlings stumbled through the parlor doors, clutching his own chest and short of breath. "Miss! Edward Stuyvesant-French is just now disembarking his carriage and walking up the stairs to the door."

Lavinia could feel the blood rush from her cheeks. "Did you excuse Wilhelm's driver?"

"Yes, and not a second too soon. Stuyvesant-French's carriage appeared just as the other was pulling away."

"We'll pretend we're not here." She wanted to put her hands

over her ears to shut out the loud clack of the front-door knocker. "Go tell him we are not at home."

"Yes, miss." Rawlings caught his breath, then rushed out of the parlor.

The silence was thunderous when they no longer heard the bang of the door knocker.

"What do you think they're talking about?" Hazel whispered to her.

"Hush . . ." Lavinia warned as they heard an angry voice.

"They told me five o'clock."

"I understand that, sir, but the Countess and her sister are not at home at present."

"Who is the gentleman they're entertaining upstairs?"

"The gentleman? I don't understand, sir—"

"You cannot mean to infer that these are Miss Murphy's gloves and bowler?"

Lavinia looked down at Wilhelm who, hatless and gloveless, was blissfully unaware of the turmoil around him.

"Oh, God, Wilhelm's gloves and hat were left on the credenza." Hazel began to fan herself with her hand as if she were warding off a fainting spell.

"If you won't tell me who the gentleman is who has usurped my séance, I'll go upstairs and see for myself," Stuyvesant-French's angry words boomed out.

What little blood was left in Lavinia's face drained to her feet. She heard Rawlings release an indignant oath, then they heard a slight scuffle in the foyer.

"I'm telling you, sir, they are not at home and you cannot go up there!" Rawlings announced, his voice filled with hysteria.

Lavinia clutched Hazel's arm. She looked around the parlor, then toward the small Turkish cozy corner for which they had become famous.

"Help me drag him over there!" she whispered harshly, taking Wilhelm beneath the arms.

"Dear God, he's heavy," Hazel whimpered.

They hoisted him onto the paisley velvet banquette, then Lavinia shoved various potted palms in front of the corner.

"Now sit there and hold him up—and—and giggle," Lavinia instructed.

Hazel stared at her, her eyes wide with panic and disbelief. "Giggle?" she squeaked.

"He won't dare interrupt you if he thinks you're in the middle of an intrigue. Then I'll get rid of him." Lavinia swept back a wisp of hair on her brow that had come loose during their activity. Glancing at the mirror, she pinched her cheeks and calmly walked to the door.

"Mr. Stuyvesant-French, how nice to see you again," she said while Hazel burst out with a lyrical laugh, her form hidden behind the palms.

Stuyvesant-French, his face hard with anger, looked over to the Turkish corner. The only things visible through the potted palms were the frilled bottom edge of Hazel's skirts and the side seam of a man's dark wool trousers.

The skirts shifted, there was a slapping sound and then another fit of giggles. Lavinia's eyes almost popped out of her head when she saw the trousered leg move. Hazel was improvising brilliantly.

"We have company, as you can see." She turned to him. "I must ask you to leave."

His eyes had narrowed to derisive slits. "Yes, I see that, Miss Murphy."

"You'll have to go." She breezed out of the parlor and led him back down the stairs to the foyer.

He paused on the landing. "I paid for a séance. What about it?—or should we quit using the polite terms and call these little encounters by their real names?" He glared down at her.

She bit her tongue to keep from getting angry. In all her times with Wilhelm she had done everything within her power for him to make amends to his bastard son. And now that bastard was in front of her, all but calling her a whore, and she wondered why she had bothered.

But the will kept a rein on her temper. She had a power this man would pay dearly for. She would tell Edward Stuyvesant-French of his father's last intentions only if he were polite. If not, the will could remain uncontested and Wilhelm could leave all his coins to the camp in Woodvine. It was no sweat off her brow.

"I must ask you to depart, Mr. Stuyvesant-French. I cannot perform your séance now, or ever. I'll have your money returned immediately."

"I don't want the money. I want an admission that you and your sister are frauds. Give me that and we won't have to go through the absurdity of a séance."

"Ah, the truth is out." Impatiently, she showed him the front door. Behind him, Rawlings stood looking like a ghost. "I am not a fraud and so have no need to admit to it. And I question your intentions, sir. Of what interest are my séances to you?" *As if I care,* she thought.

"Your séances are very important to me, Miss Murphy—"

"Countess, if you please."

"*Countess,*" he exaggerated snidely. "So I shall return tomorrow at this same time and will do so every day until you give me a séance."

She looked him right in the eye. If she weren't so frazzled and afraid, she might have even laughed. His father was lying dead in their Turkish corner with Hazel giggling away like a trollop, Rawlings looked ready to clutch his chest and add to the day's casualties, meanwhile Wilhelm's bastard son was at the door, threatening to expose her, all because he probably wanted to do some harm to his father.

And one thing was certain. His father was beyond harm now.

"Please leave, Mr. Stuyvesant-French," she said breathlessly.

"I'll be here promptly at five tomorrow."

"It's really not necessary." Her gaze wandered up toward the parlor where Hazel could still be heard laughing. "So many things could change by tomorrow."

"I'll be here at five." He tipped his hat, which he had never even removed; he released a sneer of a smile, then embarked upon his waiting carriage.

She closed the front door and locked it. She then picked up her skirts and ran upstairs, Rawlings in her wake.

Hazel was still in character when they retrieved her from the jungle of potted palms. They found her next to Wilhelm, frozen in a position of desperation, trying to hold Wilhelm's bulk upright while the laws of gravity slowly won and her small form succumbed to his large, flaccid one.

"Is he gone?" she begged, her face as white as the ghost girl's.

"He's gone," Lavinia said.

Hazel leapt up. She shook out her hands as if trying to remove imaginary bugs. "Eeeeek," she croaked, her feature contorted with revulsion. "Don't ever make me do that again. Promise? Never again!"

"It worked, didn't it?" Lavinia said as she watched Wilhelm's body slump once again to the floor.

"Now he thinks we're a couple of you-know-whats."

Lavinia absentmindedly nodded. "Yes, yes. Well, we've been called that before and even worse. I believe they even dared to print it in the newspaper. No, I'm not worried about that. Name-calling won't hurt the business, but a man dying in the company of spiritualists would. They want to *talk* to the dead, not *be* the dead. Remember that."

"Shall I summon Monty?" Rawlings interrupted.

Lavinia in a daze seemed to look right past him. "Of course. We must get him over here immediately. Thank you for reminding me."

Rawlings nodded. He had a way of pulling on the buttons of his waistcoat when agitated; an acceptable habit for an out-of-work puppeteer but not exactly proper for an English butler. Lavinia had tried to help him overcome it but to no avail. He was now working the buttons so hard, one suddenly popped off, rolled on the carpet and landed right beneath Wilhelm's expressionless face.

"I'll get Monty right away," Rawlings muttered, not even bothering to retrieve the button.

Lavinia stooped and picked it up.

"You were about to tell me what Wilhelm said before Mr. Stuyvesant-French got here. What was it, Vinia?" Hazel took her turn wearily sitting on the tuffet, her back to Wilhelm as if she couldn't bear to look at him.

"He's the bastard son. Mr. Stuyvesant-French."

Hazel's numb expression turned animated with disbelief. "You're kidding. Why, I guess I always thought of the boy as—well, as a boy. You know, all the wounded feelings and everything made me think he was a child. It's hard to believe that Wilhelm felt bad about hurting that—well, that terrifying man."

"That terrifying man is beyond wounded feelings. He's wandered into the realm of revenge and I'm afraid we're it."

"But why?"

"I think he wants to discredit his father in some fashion. He thinks to use us to do it." Lavinia lowered herself to the settee. "This is horrible to say—and do forgive me, Wilhelm—but our beloved Mr. Vanadder may have died not a minute too soon for us. When Stuyvesant-French gets the notice the old man is gone, I believe he'll leave us alone."

Hazel let out a sigh. "I do hope so. I really don't want to cross that man again."

"Me too," Lavinia answered, giving Wilhelm's body a final remorseful glance. "And if the spirits are on our side, this is indeed the last we'll ever hear from him."

Chapter Four

Now, Katy, although you and Maggie never go so far as this, yet circumstances must occur where you have to lacerate the feelings of other people. . . . You do things now which you never would have dreamed of doing years ago; and there will come a time when you will be worse than Mrs. Fish, a hardened woman, gathering around you victims of a delusion.

—To Kate Fox from Elisha Kent Kane (1853)

"**M**onty, have another cake. Shall I pour you some more tea?" Lavinia lifted the heavy coin silver teapot and gestured to his cup.

"No more for me, Vinia. *That* appetite is fed—now for a little dessert, eh . . . ?" He grabbed her, bustle and all, and pulled her onto his lap.

"Monty, you're a wretch. Look, you're wrinkling my gown."

"Then let's remove it, shall we?"

Lavinia eyed him, her features amused but placid. It was the day after the tragedy and still relatively early in the afternoon, but outside, through the open windows, the newsboys were already hawking the evening edition. Even through the second-story parlor window, she could hear them call out the headline: "COPPER BARON DIES—HEIRS UNNAMED!"

"You really do need to decide, Monty. Do you want me or these precious few gold coins that I offered last night when you came and hauled Wilhelm's body away?" From her corset, she extracted a small silk purse and swung it before his face like a pendulum.

He snatched the bag and counted the coins. He bit each one in turn, then, satisfied, tucked them into his waistcoat.

"Now release me," she instructed.

He grinned down at her. He was quite attractive when he smiled and he knew it. If Monty had just a bit more coin to spend for his clothing, some might consider him a gigolo. Even in his hack-driver rags, his shaggy hair streaked a dark gold from the sun and a day's growth of beard on his chin, he was still a lady-killer. Lavinia supposed it was his eyes. An earthy shade of brown, they held a permanent expression of licentiousness.

"Go on, Monty. Give up the game." She looked down at his hands resting easily on her waist. "I'm not going to keep you in the guest quarters and you know it."

"Vinia, it's not just that. I really am in love with you."

She rolled her eyes. "I've heard how bad the jobs have been lately. Rawl told me he saw you hawking a vaudeville that consisted of an orangutan and a man larger than a piano case. Really, has the acting career sloped you that much to your grave?"

"It's bad. I won't say it isn't."

She gave him a sympathetic look. She didn't want to keep him, but he definitely held a place in her heart. Some might think him nothing but a common hack driver, but she knew better. She'd seen him perform many a song in the seedy opera houses on lower Fifth Avenue. He had an achingly clear Irish tenor voice and a wicked sense of humor, and sometimes she really wondered why she didn't take him on as a lover. She would probably never find one more likable.

"I do owe you. I'll never forget it," she said, tenderly touching his rough, unshaven cheek. "We would have been ruined if you hadn't taken the questions—not to mention the body—for us."

"I know just how you can repay the debt." He leaned forward to kiss her.

With more than a little guilt, she drew away. "I've told you a thousand times, Monty dear, I'm not dangling after a man, not even one as charming as you."

"Doesn't that cold heart ever get lonely?" He sullenly toyed with the lace frill of her bodice.

"My heart's not the issue, it's my mind, and I made it up long ago. I'm not going to let a man interfere with business. To act the fool and fall in love is not for me at all. Nor is the idea of raising a bastard."

"There's always a visit to Mrs. Odenheimer to cure that problem."

"Yes, and the population of Manhattan would probably double without the services of Mrs. Odenheimer, but that's not the address I want my fantasies to lead me. No, I've made up my mind: No men." She pushed from his lap, straightened her gown and sauntered to the window.

"There's nothing I wouldn't do for you, Vinia. You know that."

"I do know that. You were the first one we called when we needed someone to trust." She turned her head and gazed at him. "But I just don't want you taken after me. I want us to be friends. I don't want to hurt you. You have to understand that as much as what you offer might tempt me, I find my rational side puts me beyond temptation. I don't want to be at the emotional mercy of a man. Any man."

"Are you begging for a proposal? Is that it? I'll marry you, Vinia. You know I will."

She smiled. "And let marriage take you from the thrilling life of the cabstand?" She waved her hand across the lavish parlor. "Dare I force you to marry me and accept these dreary surroundings? Why, Monty, I couldn't do it to you. How selfish it would be of me."

He walked to her, wrapping his arms around her waist. "You think I'm nothing but a gold-digger, don't you? But if you were in rags, starving on the street, I'd still gaze into your eyes and want you, Vinia. Ah . . . if I could make you love me . . . I'd marry you and I'd marry you even if you were a pauper. Love is helpless. So helpless. Remember that when it ever happens to you and you fall in love."

She gave him a peck of a kiss on the cheek. "I don't flatter myself that you've fallen in love with me, you've just fallen in love with the drapery. Besides, I'm not going to fall, Monty. So don't be disappointed. Quit wasting your time and go chase after another."

"You're a cold woman."

"No, not cold, just logical."

"I wish I were the man to take that logic away." He tapped her forehead. "All this thinking will go to the wind then, I wager."

"There's not a man alive who could do that."

"Miss! Miss!" Rawlings' voice intruded into the intimacy. Lavinia looked toward the parlor doors and saw the old butler standing there.

"What is it, Rawl?" she asked, completely unconscious of Monty's arms still around her waist.

"He's here. He insists you made an appointment with him for five."

" 'He'—?" she asked, her brow furrowing. "You can't mean Mr. Stuyvesant-French. He doesn't need to come now—" Her words fell silent. A shadow fell upon Rawlings and behind him appeared the tall form of Edward Stuyvesant-French.

He had the usual scowl upon his handsome face. It only deepened when his gaze took in the unkempt rogue who held her.

"Busy again, Miss Murphy?" he asked, startling Rawlings.

"Sir, if you please, you must be announced," the butler sniped.

"No, let him come in, Rawl. If Mr. Stuyvesant-French still feels a need for a séance, then let him have his séance." She glanced up at Monty and stepped from the circle of his embrace. "Please make yourself at home while I have my guest shown to the door."

"Let me know if you need anything, Vinia—I mean—ah—Countess." Monty looked over at Rawlings, then back at Lavinia.

But her eyes were locked on Edward's, as Edward's were locked on hers.

"I'll take my leave now. You know where to find me. If you need me." Monty nodded to Stuyvesant-French, then looked again to Lavinia. She hardly acknowledged his departure. "Remember what I said, Countess," Monty added, each word pregnant with meaning. Then he tipped an invisible cap and followed Rawlings down the stairs.

"I would have thought the séance would be unnecessary now. My deepest condolences for your father—that is . . . Wilhelm Vanadder was your father, was he not?" she asked, looking him right in the eye.

"There's no secret to my illegitimacy."

"Apparently not."

"Everyone in New York knows it was my mother who was the Stuyvesant-French, but I suppose when one hails from St. Louis, I imagine such information is hard to come by." He smiled and took a seat at the table.

She stared at him, forcing aside a bout of paranoia. So he knew about St. Louis. It was no tragedy. The world hadn't come to an end.

She sat with him at the table, only then realizing his rudeness. "In St. Louis, I believe it was the custom to seat the ladies first." She looked down her nose. "I've never known New Yorkers to think otherwise."

"New Yorkers seat the ladies first also, Miss Murphy." The derogatory glint in his eye gave her no doubts that he did not think she belonged to that club.

"Why do you want a séance, Mr. Stuyvesant-French? Do you want to telegraph the spirits, or do you want to prove me a fraud? If it's the latter, I must say, I don't see what there's to be gained by it now." Her patience was at an end. It was time to get done with it.

"He was insane and I'm going to prove it. If he believed the offal that you dish out, perhaps I can find a court who will think him insane too."

"But why do you need this now? He's dead."

"There's a matter of his will."

She smiled. A chilly smile at best. "You don't appear hard-up, Mr. Stuyvesant-French." She raised an eyebrow at his attire. He was a well-dressed man and certainly clothing was an indication of wealth—even now he wore a handsome striped green silk vest and a splendidly tailored wool jacket and trousers that matched in the new en suite style. But perhaps, like many others, his pocketbook didn't keep up with his appetites.

She met his gaze once more. "Ah, now I think I understand. Credit is a terrible thing. Especially when your tastes lead you to live beyond your means. You want to inherit and pay your debts. This all boils down to money, doesn't it? Of course it does."

"If I might remind you, praying to the great god of money has been your philosophy, Countess. It is not mine."

"What else could this be about if not money?" She almost smirked. The power was delicious.

"I don't need money. And I particularly don't need Vanadder money. I want guardianship of my half-sister and I want to make sure she—and she alone—is the recipient of our father's fortune because it is she who put up with him all these years."

"What makes you think she is not the recipient? Has the will been read? The newspapers say it has not been. We haven't even had the funeral yet."

"The lawyers tell me Vanadder had a penchant for changing his will. They've led me to believe Daisy is not the current recipient. I've already been told her presence will not be needed at the reading of the will."

Camp Woodvine. She rolled her eyes and sighed. It was time to be out with it and cast out the devil before he ate her alive. "Look, he mentioned his will often during our sessions. I think I know who's to receive your father's money, but I also know that at the last séance, he expressed that you should inherit as his son. I'll be more than glad to say that in a court of law. Bring the papers,

I'll sign them. You or your half-sister, I don't care who gets the money, as long as you will leave me alone and let me go about my business."

He seemed surprised by her confession, but whether it was the willingness of it, or the veracity, she didn't know.

"You confound me, Miss Murphy. I can see why the newspapers have called you fascinating. You play the guileless innocent very well. Your offer to assist me is, in fact, a touch of brilliance I didn't expect this evening. I've underestimated you."

"It's the truth." She looked right at him, unwilling to let him see her rattled. A smile played at the corner of his fine, handsome mouth, and she could almost find herself having fantasies about that mouth if it didn't twist in such a cruel fashion whenever he looked at her.

"You are good, Miss Murphy. I'm impressed. I now fully understand why you command the fees you do. Perhaps I should just pay you to summon the spirit of my father in the courtroom and he can speak his final wishes in person. That should convince even the most hardened skeptic, shouldn't it?"

"If that would solve your problems and cause you to leave us alone, I'll be happy to see what I can do about it."

"Would you, now?"

"You seem to doubt my sincerity." She bristled. "I know this may be hard to believe but I was fond of your father. I want to see his money go to the person he wanted it to go to. If you in your cynicism find that worthy of suspicion, then so be it."

He tipped his head back and laughed. The sound, the way it boomed from his chest, was quite pleasant. If it weren't tinged with malevolence, she might have even laughed too.

"Do me my séance, Countess." The smile suddenly wiped off his face.

She felt the hairs raise on her neck. It wasn't the specter of ghosts she worried about, it was the sight of his mirthless face. "With whom do you wish to speak, sir?"

"Let me speak with the spirit I understand Vanadder always spoke to. I wish to speak with my mother, Alice Stuyvesant-French."

"You choose a good spirit."

"I barely remember her."

She looked at him; she wondered if he possessed the all-too-human emotion of longing, but it didn't seem possible. No, this strong, rigid man could not ache inside for the connection with a mother. It was beyond belief that this grown man, this cruel-bent tyrannical soul, could gentle himself with thoughts of motherly love. But staring at him, she couldn't help but wonder if it could be so.

"She always asked that your father reconcile," she said softly. "Alice was a kind spirit. She taught him empathy."

"How did she do that?"

Her hands began to tremble. She took them off the table and placed them in her lap. "Alice told him what her sorrow was about."

"What would you know about such sorrow, Countess?"

She blinked. She shouldn't have. "You must remember that it was not me who spoke to Wilhelm. Rather it was Alice who spoke through me. I was merely the medium."

"What did Alice say to teach my father empathy?"

"She—" His stare caused fear to constrict her throat. The barely leashed emotion on his face was a terrible sight. She felt poised upon a precipice and there was no turning back, but she didn't know what kind of precipice it was.

"She told me about her pain." Lavinia closed her mouth and bit back further words. She didn't want to utter another sound but by the expression on his face she could almost imagine him lunging across the table to beat the words right out of her. "Rather, she told *him* about her pain. It was not easy for her to find her belly growing bigger each day. It was not easy to think of a fatherless child. She—she wept a great deal. Yes, I believe she said that too. She told Wilhelm how she couldn't bear the scandal. It was true she hadn't loved him, but in the end she had needed him and he'd abandoned her, and so every night before her death she told him she was forced to weep—you see, she wept upon— Well, you can imagine how terrible it was."

"No, I can't imagine," he bit out. Clenching and unclenching his jaw, he said, "Finish."

"There's—there's really not much more."

"Finish," he demanded, his eyes glittering. "What did she say to him? How did you tell him she wept? Tell me how she said she wept."

"She said—she said she wept—wept nightly upon her ringless hand until her death. Yes, I believe those were her words conveyed to me."

He was silent. So silent. She almost flinched when he spoke.

"You speak as if you're in a deposition, Countess. You hedge every word."

"I don't want to be accused of inaccuracies. Spiritual telegraphs are not always easy to interpret. I hope I was not inaccurate."

"No, you were not. The melodrama has been added but the bones of the story are true." He stared right at her, right through her. The stomped-down anger inside him seemed to make him momentarily blind.

"Can you see now that I have nothing to do with your relationship with your father? Will you leave me alone now?"

The gaze refocused and by its force alone seemed to lash her to the chair. "I was the child of that *blessed* union. I was the reason—how did you put it so theatrically?—oh yes—the reason she 'wept nightly upon her ringless hand.' A nice touch, Countess. One that fairly tweaks the heart."

"Please, just go. I have nothing to do with whatever angers you. I beg of you—"

The bitterness in his eyes stole her breath.

"You're a whore, Lavinia Murphy. And that you make your fortune spinning these stories, that you earn your coin on the backs of the tragedy of others, I say that you are worse than a whore."

"You've been hurt. Alice's pain has hurt you. I understand." Quietly, she said, "But I'll ask you to leave now, Mr. Stuyvesant-French. I must ask you to go."

"You're just a two-bit actress. You discover Vanadder sired a bastard and you fill in all the blank spaces with your own diseased imagination."

"I'll ask you to leave, Mr. Stuyvesant-French." She stood. Her heart pummeled in her chest. She hoped her position came across as compassionate, yet firm. He had to go. She feared him too much now to dare let him stay longer.

But he didn't move. Not even a muscle flexed in his face. His look of disgust seemed etched there in marble.

"You've sat there and pretended to be another, pretended to feel another's pain," he rasped, his voice harsh. "You made it up blow by blow and pretended to care all the while you're just counting the coins the act was going to make you. You really should do the more honorable thing and let the men just plow you, Lavinia Murphy. At least then I could respect you a little."

She didn't even realize she had raised her hand. It wasn't like her to resort to physical violence, but the insults he hurled were too sharp for her not to protect herself.

"Go ahead." He taunted her by just staring, his eyes piercing her with that—as Hazel had put it—that unforgiving shade of green.

"Go. Don't come back." Her words were short and breathy; her throat choked with unshed tears.

He got up from his chair. She expected him to walk out the door, but he took her arm and drew her from her seat. She was too frightened to do anything but comply.

"You taught him empathy? Perhaps I should teach you some."

"Please." She looked down at her arm. His grip was solid and unyielding, but so far painless.

So far.

"You seem to know all about the fear a woman feels when she's been given a child and abandoned. Perhaps you should feel the indignity firsthand. Perhaps, being the spawn of my father, I'm just the one to do it."

"Please," she gasped, more terrified of his expression than hurt by his grip on her.

"But then it's a conundrum, isn't it?" he said calmly, coldly. "Tell me, Countess, can a man rape a whore? More importantly, can a man rape you, the whore of whores?"

"Stop this. Stop this," she choked out.

"If I don't pay for the privilege, I suppose it must be called rape. But then I've paid you, haven't I? I remember distinctly the talk of a séance and my giving you a bag of gold coins. There has been no séance—but then séances aren't really what you sell, now, are they?"

"Why are you threatening me like this? What did I ever do to you?" she gasped, her entire body trembling.

"You haven't done it yet, but you will next Friday. Daisy Vanadder, my half-sister spends her days daydreaming out a window because she's crippled and bound to a chair. She's his legitimate child. His wealth should by all rights be hers."

"And it will be," she answered, on the verge of hysteria.

"No, it won't. Not yet."

"But why?"

He withdrew a set of papers from his jacket. He threw them on the table as if they were so vile they burned him. "Vanadder's will is to be read on Friday. The lawyers told me that Daisy's presence wouldn't be necessary." His eyes turned to steel. "But yours will be."

She looked at the papers, stunned.

He stared at her, loathing on his face. "You think you're going to get away with this, but you're not. I'll see him declared insane even though I must do it posthumously. I will see you out as a fraud, and I will see Daisy inherit."

"But don't assume I'm in the will. I've never heard him mention it—"

"Did he mention he wanted to leave his fortune to Daisy?"

"I never knew he had a daughter. I just knew his last words were—"

She shut her mouth, suddenly astounded at her own stupidity. It would be, at best, unwise to tell a mortal enemy something that would help him. She didn't want to see Wilhelm's crippled daughter not inherit anything, but she didn't know enough about the situation and couldn't begin to assess it correctly. Wilhelm had made it perfectly clear that Stuyvesant-French was to inherit, but the old man was working from a half-deck of cards. For all she knew, Stuyvesant wasn't here on behalf of poor Daisy; indeed, as with most, he was probably here on behalf of his poor self.

If Daisy really did exist and was the true and righteous heir, then Lavinia would be happy to help the daughter inherit, minus, perhaps, a healthy fee for working herself out of the will. Hell, if the girl was a cripple, Lavinia could see herself going all-out and lying to say Daisy was the name Wilhelm spoke in his final moments. That was certainly a more appealing option after the threats Stuyvesant-French had just made to her. All she knew right now was that she sure wasn't going to see the money go to him. The man had no conscience. Daisy, if she even really existed, would probably turn to dust before Edward Stuyvesant-French unclutched his hands to give his half-sister her rightful fortune.

"This is probably all a misunderstanding," she began, once more gaining her calm. "I'm pleased that Wilhelm may have left a small pension for me—if he even left me that, I might add—but as for you and your half-sister, I think you should wait until the full measure of the will is read before you jump to conclusions and make—make heinous threats toward me."

"You will never inherit the Vanadder fortune. I'll fight you to the grave before I see that money go to the likes of you."

And I'll see myself in the grave before I see it go to the likes of you,
she thought. "I don't want the Vanadder fortune. I know it's hard
for you to believe that, but I'm doing well on my own and don't
need a vast fortune. Besides, I'm a businesswoman and not ignorant
of the law. I can't see how I would have a legal hold on the
Vanadder fortune given that Wilhelm had a *legitimate* child. Even
if I am named in the will, I cannot in my wildest dreams think I'll
be a major heir when the will is read."

"We won't know that until Friday. That is when your presence
has been requested at the Vanadder mansion."

She took a deep breath but kept her gaze level. "Then I shall
see you there, Mr. Stuyvesant-French, and we will resolve this
matter then."

"Yes."

He studied her, his face a shadowy mask in the gaslight spilling
from the hall. Finally he said, "He never mentioned Daisy?"

"No."

"He never mentioned he wanted his daughter to inherit?"

"No." The words she left out of her answer could have filled
the Crystal Palace.

In closure, she walked to the door. She opened it and Rawl
almost fell through the keyhole. "Ah, there you are, old Rawl.
Wonderful. Mr. Stuyvesant-French was just leaving. Will you see
him out?"

"I'll get my results one way or another, Miss Murphy. Remember
that," Edward said behind her.

"You get more with honey than vinegar. Just you remember
that." She nodded to him. "I pray this will be your last visit."

"I'll see you Friday, Countess."

She couldn't have inflected a deader monotone. "Good evening,
Mr. Stuyvesant-French."

Chapter
Five

"You don't have to do it on my account, Edward." A small woman, petite and fragile as a Sevres cup, wheeled herself around from the palatial window. The drawing room overlooked the same Fifth Avenue as the Murphy town house, but the Vanadder mansion, much farther north of Washington Square, was cased in marble, not brownstone, and the surrounding lots were presently just cordoned-off masses of earth and debris of colonial farmhouses. The Vanadder mansion and a few notorious others aside, the north section of Fifth Avenue hadn't yet been sentineled with Richard Morris Hunt châteaux, although everyone in town knew they were coming.

"You know, Edward, I've been thinking all about it. I don't need the house and Father's money. It might be nice to just take a small cottage in the Adirondacks. Surely there's enough in trust for a cottage. And you know, the fresh air might really make me strong." The woman looked up at the man who stood beside her.

She had the same black hair, the same startling green eyes, but her skin bore the translucence of bad health.

Her brother stared at her, his normally harsh features softened. "This obscene marble ruin is rightfully yours, Daisy. It should be yours and it will be."

"But I don't really want it, Edward." Daisy helplessly gazed out at the expanse of creamy Carrera squares that tiled the drawing-room floor. She appeared so small in the room's expanse, just one tiny wheelchair-bound figure in an echoing chamber of beautiful stone. Even the draperies were unfeeling masterpieces, a hundred yards of fringed burgundy satin swagged beneath gilt cornices that were covered with fat Italian putti. The effect was stunning, costly and utterly tasteless.

Edward's gaze followed his sister's to the window treatments. Without checking his words, he murmured, "This room in particular has always reminded me of a bordello."

"Father spent a fortune on it."

"The only thing missing is Nero, drunken, nude and romping in rose petals."

Daisy suddenly looked at her brother. "Edward, how do you know what a bordello looks like?"

He peered down at her, his eyes lit with surprise. "For that matter, how do you know what a bordello is?"

"Why, I read, Edward, that's how I know."

Edward tipped her a sheepish grin. "I read too, Daze."

She just looked at him, her chin resting on her hand, her fingers tapping her cheek in bemusement. "I don't know if I quite believe you, Edward."

"I didn't come here to discuss my sporting habits, I came here to tell you about the will."

"Well, I don't want anything." She gazed at her hands now folded in her lap. "Father's gone now, may he rest in peace. He can give his vile house and money to whomever he pleases. It's laughable, me in this cold, windy place all alone."

"You'll marry one day, have children perhaps. The house should be yours."

She gave him a reproving look. "Marriage? Children? Are you being cruel, Edward?"

He knelt down beside the walnut-and-iron wheelchair. "I'm not being cruel. You feel you have no worth, Daisy, but it's only because of him and how he treated you—"

"And inheriting all this, I might actually find worth? What you really mean is as an heiress I might find a husband to love this crippled wretch of a woman. Oh, Edward, how could you think I don't see what you're doing? You pity me and you hated Father. By me inheriting all this wealth you think you take care of both of us, but I don't want your pity, and Father is dead. It's too late for revenge, Edward."

"I'm not doing it for you to find a husband, nor am I doing it solely for revenge. Believe me, I'm getting you his money because it's rightfully yours. He never treated you well, Daisy. He never gave you two minutes of his time. He hid you in here—kept you a prisoner here—as if he were ashamed of you. I won't let the cruelty continue now even beyond his grave."

"Then, even more reason to leave it all behind."

Edward stood. The muscle in his jaw bunched. "Sell this monstrosity of a house if you like. Take the money and go to Egypt for all I care. I just want it to be yours. It's a small pittance for want of a father, but it's something you can hold in your hands."

"Edward, do you remember when we were children? Do you remember way back when, that first time you snuck into the mansion? I must have been five. You were eight. Do you remember?"

"I do." He stared at her, his expression quizzical.

"And for all your Stuyvesant-French breeding you looked like a ragamuffin, cap askew, dust on your face where you climbed up the dumbwaiter, when you finally peered around the playroom corner after Nanny had gone to the kitchen."

"I knew I had a sister. I just wanted to see what my sister looked like."

"Father never told me about you. I suppose he figured I'd hear it through gossip one day, or maybe never. He didn't care."

"No. He didn't care."

"I couldn't believe your face, Edward. You looked so much like me, but you were so brave and strong, and foolhardy. Do you remember the walloping Nanny gave you with the broom when she'd thought some street urchin had thieved into the nursery? I truly thought she was going to kill you."

The corners of his mouth tipped up, then suddenly he chuckled. A miser with his smiles, Edward could make Satan grin back once he finally let go of a laugh. "You saved my life, sticking up for me like you did."

"You were a bad little boy, Edward, by any standard. Sneaking into other people's homes—"

"I got to meet my sister."

"And what a disappointment she must have been to you, stuck in this awful chair, with none of your strength, none of your heart, none of your passion."

"With all of it and more," he answered gravely. "You told that woman who was beating me to stop, and you made her stop, too. You did that, Daisy. You're not weak. You're strong. Stronger than I am in some ways."

"That little boy who stole his way into the playroom, he was only looking for a sister and nothing more." Daisy hesitated. She wouldn't meet his gaze; instead her eyes turned to the windows and bustling street beyond. "If— If I don't get anything out of Father's estate, well—sometimes I fear— I wonder, will that boy still be happy with just a sister?"

Edward took her two hands in his. An unnamed emotion gripped his features. He stared at her for a long moment and when she still would not meet his gaze, he knelt down before her, his head slowly resting in her lap.

"My mother's family prayed for a stillborn child," he said, his voice deep with emotion. "Sometimes I believe my mother died just to avoid having to look at my face, this terrible face that is so much like his. My presence on this earth has been cursed and damned from the beginning; I've been reviled by just about everyone, but not you, Daisy. Not you. Never you. You're the only one whose eyes ever lit up when I entered a room."

"No, Edward." Tears slid down her cheek. Slowly, she lifted one small fragile hand and caressed the dark head in her lap.

"The money has nothing to do with my feelings for you, Daisy."

"Sometimes I fear it. Sometimes I think the money will sap what little spirit I have left and leave me with nothing inside. I'll become just like my mother. I won't be a woman anymore, just a bank account, and whatever love I have to give will just die for want of it in return. He only loved Alice. He told Mother that every day of their marriage."

"He enjoyed being cruel. It was always an amusement to him."

"I hate his money."

"That is why you will take his money when I get it for you."

"Why, Edward, why?"

His gaze, burning with hatred, bore into the distance as if he were summoning the spirit of his father from the grave. "You shall have his money, Daisy. Because in this foul world where there is no justice, I will be the avenger. Daisy Vanadder, the neglected, shunned daughter of a madman, shall have the Vanadder fortune." He paused. "She shall have the one thing her father loved most."

Chapter Six

*Maggie, dear, you have many traits which lift you above your calling
. . . but you are not worthy of a permanent regard from me. You
could never lift yourself up to my thoughts and my objects; I could
never bring myself down to yours . . . Maggie, darling, don't care for
me anymore. I love you too well to wish it, and you now know that
I really am sold to different destinies; for just as you have your
wearisome rounds of money-making, I have my own sad vanities to
pursue. I am as devoted to my calling as you, poor child, can be to
yours. Remember, then, as a sort of dream, that Doctor Kane of the
Arctic Seas loves Maggie Fox of the Spirit Rappings.*

—Elisha Kent Kane to Margaret Fox, 1852

It was a five-carat sapphire circled in diamonds. Vanadder had told her once that the stones had come from his very own mines. He'd given her the ring the night she'd first telegraphed from "Mother." Even now Lavinia couldn't believe the beauty of the piece as she watched it sparkle in the slanted yellow light of early evening. She wore it often to proclaim her success. The ring gave her a confidence she didn't always feel. The gaudy piece was nouveau riche to the extreme but she found comfort in sporting such a tastelessly large ring. It had once even been written up in the *Sun* that some believed part of her powers of animal magnetism were given her through the ring.

And she thought *she* was a storyteller.

She shook her head and smiled wryly, the ring glittering in the long beams of fading sunlight. It did give her confidence. Whenever she was frightened or feeling alone, she would look at the ring. They could take everything from her: the town house, the clothes, even the luscious Princess of Wales pink velvet drapery, but if she still had her ring, they would make it. She wore a lifetime's fortune on one small finger.

"I'm ready."

Lavinia turned and watched Hazel enter the room. The young woman looked splendid in an olive green taffeta walking gown. The color highlighted the peaches in her cheeks and glossed the brown highlights in her curls. Passementerie of black arabesques rimmed the cuffs and the hem, and gave the outfit just enough sobriety to quell the wicked look in Hazel's eyes.

"You were just born to be an heiress, weren't you, you naughty girl?" Lavinia laughed.

"Not me. Eva's going to be the heiress in this family," Hazel countered smartly.

Lavinia raised one eyebrow. "And leave out Fanny?"

"What's Eva's is Fanny's. We took Fanny so that Eva would have a sister . . . as I have a sister." Hazel glanced at her, her expression warm and tender.

"You couldn't be more of a sister to me if you'd been born one, Hazel."

"I hope Eva says that to Fanny one day. Then we'll know we made the right decision to take Fanny with us."

Quietly Lavinia said, "We should have taken them all. Every last child. I'll regret to the end that I didn't."

"The church helped them. The place is closed now, remember? The orphanage is gone." Hazel's expression was almost wistful. "We have to forget that place."

"I'll never forget it." Lavinia gave Hazel a meaningful look, heavy with unnamed emotions. "And I know you'll never forget it."

"But I want to forget it." Hazel paused and tipped a sad smile. "That's the difference between us, Lavinia."

Lavinia pulled on her kidskin gloves. She'd spend the better part of fifteen minutes working with the ivory glove stretcher, and still, it was almost painful getting the tight black kidskin over the ring.

"Shall we have more baubles like that one when the day is out?" Hazel almost giggled.

"We're not going to take the money and you know it."

"Oh, but it will fun to have, if just for an hour."

"That's all it will be," Lavinia countered as she buttoned the wrist of the glove and followed Hazel down to Monty's waiting hack.

❦ ❦

Edward watched her enter the library. Lavinia Murphy was not the confident siren he'd seen as she'd first walked through her own notorious parlor just days before. Now, in her dark blue attire, she looked almost prudish, but the foul memory of that last encounter still lingered in his thoughts.

He couldn't believe the woman. Her entire existence was a fraud. That she paraded around the manufactured spirits of dead loved ones in order to dupe the grieving out of their coins was beyond immoral. He'd met a lot of hardened characters in his time but none that bore the facade of this Lavinia Murphy.

She'd told him about Alice. All he could remember was the anger. It had ripped right through him. Lavinia Murphy knew nothing of his mother, and yet she spoke of her as if they were old friends; kindred souls. He himself had no memory of Alice so it was impossible that this stranger, this thief of the unwary, could know anything about her. It had all been an act. Just another day's work. He'd been with prostitutes that had more heart, more integrity, than Lavinia Murphy did.

He'd grabbed her. He'd uttered some kind of threat that even now he was pressed to recall, but it had frightened her. He remembered he'd seen tears glistening in her eyes . . . those lovely blue-lavender eyes with their wounded expression.

He closed his own to shut out the picture. Her emotion, the empathy she'd exuded, was so well constructed it had almost seemed real; *she* had almost seemed real, as if she were made of warm tender flesh instead of rock, like the ring that even now glittered ostentatiously on her hand.

He looked at her again. She sat ever so primly beside her sister, her pocketbook clutched in her hands like a schoolmarm with books. She almost looked scared. And there it was again, that wounded expression that seemed to look upon the world as if it were only filled with enemies that were out to betray her.

He brushed his mouth with the back of his hand. He hated the taste. Guilt. It came to his tongue every time he thought how he'd grabbed her. She was so tiny he could have snapped her arm in two on the first try. He'd held himself back, but just barely because she'd made him roar inside with fury. Never had anyone summoned the image of his tragic mother as she had. She was a charlatan, and yet she'd made him hurt for his mother all the more by her fiction. And that was one more reason to hate Lavinia Murphy. To want to destroy Lavinia Murphy.

He watched her from his side of the library. She didn't look at him. Her lack of attention seemed almost scrupulous. But she couldn't ignore him forever. They were all there to read the will, and she'd have to butt heads with him eventually.

But until he forced her attention on him he could see she was just going to sit there by her sister, at best taking small glances around the room, and holding up that chin that defied the world.

Maybe he'd been too hard on her the other evening. He hadn't liked the mangy dog of a man he'd caught her with—the fellow looked like he was nothing but a street-sweeper—but her choice of company was her own. It had nothing to do with him. He had to just keep in mind that this creature who tagged herself as a spiritualist was nothing but a woman. A conniving, heartless little whore, but the weaker sex nonetheless. He knew her kind well from all the years of experience he'd had with the underbelly of society, and he was tired of her kind. The bastard Edward Stuyvesant-French, sullied with scandal, didn't exactly merit the cream of society, but he would one day. One day soon he was going to earn that lily white–souled woman who was out there waiting for him. He hadn't met her yet, but he knew her well. She would be just like what he knew of his mother, and what he knew of Daisy. She would have beauty, and goodness, and wit, and when she fell for the cad, this time the cad would deserve her; he would prove himself worthy. He was going to marry her and take her to his ivory tower and there he would live with her and thank God every day for his gift.

In short, he was going to do everything his father had not done.

He released a deep breath. Lavinia Murphy still sat opposite him, stiff and proper in her dark attire. She was nothing but a wretch, a soiled dove who made her living in a more shameful way than most. In spite of her beauty, in spite of the fact that he even found himself attracted to her, he still had to pity her. She would never be the kind of woman he admired; the kind of woman he was determined to have. He thought again on his harshness with her the other night, and again the guilt left a bad taste in his mouth. Maybe he had pushed too far in his threats. Maybe he should have treated her simply with the patronizing disdain with which a gentleman should bestow her kind. He should have remained cool and collected. He should have taken her equally frosty manners with the pity due her and left his own passions out of it.

Ah, but it had felt good to have that cold bitch hot with terror. Something inside him had just snapped when he'd grabbed her. He'd wanted a connection with her; he'd demanded it. It took near violence, but in the end, he'd forced the facade away.

He'd gotten a reaction at last.

❦ ❦

Lavinia sat solemnly in Vanadder's library, her bustled figure dwarfed by the mahogany bookcases and leather-topped tables. A coven of lawyers convened around the fireplace, shuffling papers, bickering over language. She stared at them and wondered if she had not been foolish to have refrained from bringing her own attorney.

She'd thought about having her own lawyer, but she didn't know any. Besides, she figured she'd needed a lawyer like a hole in the head. First of all, if the truth be known, she didn't want Vanadder's money; she didn't really need it and she knew morally it was not rightfully hers. Second, to inherit meant a battle, and she didn't want that above all, certainly not if it involved going against the steel wall of Edward Stuyvesant-French.

She had dimissed the attorney idea. Any lawyer worth his salt would see dollar signs the minute Vanadder's will was read, and she feared he'd make her fight for her "rights" even if she didn't want him to.

And she really *didn't* want the money. Not if it meant ruin and damnation, and Stuyvesant-French had threatened all that and more. She was doing fine in her business, she had a nice little nest-egg, there was no need to rock the boat. She wasn't a greedy person. Wilhelm might have been a lunatic but he surely wanted his fortune to remain in the family where it rightfully belonged. She couldn't interfere with that. Especially now that she had seen the real heirs.

Her gaze covertly turned to the two people at the opposite end of the room. One, the woman in the wheelchair, had a disarming pretty face. She was soft and kind-looking, and her eyes held such an expression in them that one couldn't ever imagine her being an enemy.

Oh, but how a face could change with another soul behind it.

Lavinia looked at the man standing next to the woman. He had the same eyes, and as they stared at her, Lavinia had the idea of what it was like below in the fires of all hell.

"Shall we begin?" Vanadder's personal attorney, Weisman, sat down at the large partners desk. He offered Lavinia and Hazel seats across from him but Lavinia declined. She didn't want to move closer. She didn't want anything to do with this procedure. Weisman didn't look competent. He had the graying apathetic face of a basset hound, and irrationally Lavinia blamed him for the mess. He was a man of no account if he couldn't counsel his client to do the right thing in his will. Especially, Lavinia thought, when the man's daughter was a cripple.

"We are here to read the last will and testament of Wilhelm Giddings Vanadder the Third. Misses Murphy," he nodded to her and Hazel, "Mr. Stuyvesant-French has asked that he and his sister, Daisy Vanadder, be allowed to attend the reading. I must know if you object. If you do, I will ask them to leave."

Lavinia steeled herself and looked at Edward. His gaze fairly bore into her.

Hazel leaned over and whispered behind her hand, "His sister can stay but I'd sure feel better if he weren't here."

"We have no objections, sir," Lavinia said. Hazel squeezed her arm, but Lavinia paid no attention to it.

"Fine, then we will begin." Weisman put on spectacles and began to read the document in front of him.

Lavinia felt the back of her neck prickle with the heat of Stuyvesant-French's stare. Weisman read, numbing her with Latin terms and parenthetical explanations and caveats. She was afraid to turn and look at Edward. He would be staring and his stare was probably the thing that was most likely to unglue her.

" '. . . and so concluding that I, Wilhelm Giddings Vanadder the Third, being of sound mind—' "

Stuyvesant-French let out a snort so loud Weisman had to pause.

" '—being of sound mind, leave all my worldly belongings including but not limited to my copper mines in the Dakota Territory, my mansion on Fifth Avenue, my accounts at Lloyd's of London, and the Bank of New York, to the Countess Lovaenya, for her devotion—' "

A chorus of gasps rocked the room. Immediately three of the

lawyers stood and began to object. Slowly Lavinia turned her head. The woman in the wheelchair just stared down at her clasped hands, a small frown wrinkling her brow. But Stuyvesant-French, he gazed right at Lavinia, his vengeful stare piercing her heart.

" '. . . and should anyone wish to question me about this will I ask that you contact me through spiritual telegraph via the Countess or her sister the Czarina Renski.' "

"Bravo! That puts it all in a much better light," Edward derided.

Weisman looked up from his reading. "Mr. Stuyvesant-French, will you please desist from interrupting—"

"The hell I will." Edward strode to the front. "This is a sham. You sat there and let Vanadder dictate this garbage while it is obvious he belonged in a lunatic asylum. You men have no ethics—"

"Sir, we cannot diagnose the insane. We're lawyers, not doctors."

"Then that explains it."

Weisman looked at once irritated and confused. His basset hound face came alive as if he suddenly realized he'd been insulted. "There are avenues by which you contest a will. I suggest you and your army of legal talent pursue these."

"I will, and the first of my actions will be to sanction you, my friend. He was not of sound mind, and yet you let him do this." Stuyvesant-French slammed his hand upon the library table.

Everyone jumped. Even Weisman.

"He had a God-given right to leave his money to whomever he chose and he chose her." Weisman pointed directly to Lavinia.

Hazel gripped her arm.

Lavinia thought she might be sick. "I've heard enough," she said softly and rose to her feet.

"He hasn't finished," Hazel gasped.

"I've heard enough. I've got to get some air." Lavinia hastily drew her gloves from the indigo silk pocketbook that matched her gown. No one even noticed her. Everyone was staring at Stuyvesant-French as he and his lawyers began arguing with Weisman.

"Shall I stay?" Hazel asked.

"No," Lavinia directed, pulling her to her feet. "We've *all* heard enough. Too much, I'm afraid." She turned around and stopped. The woman in the wheelchair just stared at her, not condemnation in her eyes, but acceptance. It shocked Lavinia. She was now certain the woman hadn't expected to receive Vanadder's money. It was unfathomable that the man would leave his crippled daughter out in the cold, but that was exactly what Wilhelm had done, and the woman knew it.

"Lavinia, perhaps we should hear this out—" Hazel whispered, but Lavinia paid her no mind. She was sickened and felt trapped. Everyone would perceive her as the evil influence in Wilhelm's life, and yet she was not. She'd been nothing but a pawn in his desire to find contrition, but now no one would believe that. The weight of his fortune bore down upon her and strangled her.

She fled into the enormous cavern of a foyer, struggling to attempt to pull on her gloves.

"We should know what they're doing in there," Hazel said as she tripped behind her.

Lavinia tugged on one kidskin glove. She tried and she tried but the thin, tight leather caught on the enormous sapphire-and-diamond ring Vanadder had given her.

"Damn!" she cursed, a furrow darkening her brow.

"Lavinia—" Hazel gasped.

A voice boomed behind her. "Miss Murphy, I suggest you take off the ring entirely. Some hands are meant to go ringless. 'If the shoe'—or the glove, in this case—'fits . . .' "

Lavinia looked behind her and found Stuyvesant-French standing in the doorway of the library, a derisive smirk twisting his handsome features.

She glared at him, at once ashamed and furious. Without speaking a word, she stuffed the kid gloves in her purse and fled the mansion.

🌺 🌿

On Fifth Avenue, Hazel trailed behind her, half running to keep up. "What are we going to do? All that money. Wouldn't it be nice—?"

"Don't even think about it. We're not going to take it." Lavinia picked up her skirts and almost ran to get away from that terrible address.

"I know," Hazel said, glancing backward as if she longed for the mammoth house behind and yet feared whoever might be leaving it to come after them.

Lavinia stopped and turned around. Relieved they weren't being followed, she dug several coins from her handbag and pressed them into Hazel's hands. "Take a hackney cab back to the town house. I want to be alone for a little while. When I return, we'll discuss everything. Maybe we'll even break down and speak with an attorney."

"Are you all right, Lavinia?" Hazel asked, her eyes wide and innocent like Eva's.

"I'm fine. I just need to walk. To get some air. To *think.*"

"I'll let you think," Hazel said quietly. "I'll meet you at home."

"Thank you, Hazel." Lavinia stared into the young woman's dark eyes. "We'll be all right. The man is frightening but we haven't done anything wrong, and that's the way we'll keep it."

"His sister seemed very nice. Very helpless," Hazel added grimly.

Lavinia nodded. "But she's not entirely helpless. Remember who her brother is."

"He probably only wants the money for himself. He'll take advantage of her. He's so awful."

"I've thought of that. That's why I want to move slowly. I want to make sure if we give up the fortune that it goes to who needs it most." She looked down Fifth Avenue and saw a black hackney cab with his flag up. She waved to it; it stopped in front of them at the slate curb. "I'll see you back at Washington Square."

Lavinia watched as the hack pulled away, Hazel's pale, fragile face solemnly staring back at her through the open window.

She walked down Fifth Avenue, glad to see the shadow of the Vanadder château recede with every step. To the right of the avenue, mounds of clay soil, garbage and the requisite cesspools of stagnant water that went with them, filled the land to the horizon. A few blocks north of Vanadder's mansion Irish shanties still stood on the old farmland but even they were being torn down to make the new greensward of what was to be called Central Park.

And it was a fitting landscape for all this treachery, she thought. On one side of Fifth Avenue were the marble palaces of the rich, and on the other the imminent doom of the poor. The metaphor chilled her.

She went for blocks, barely noticing how the dribble of pedestrians and shoppers turned into a storm by Forty-seventh Street. Lost in her own world, she was unable to notice the avenue of modern, tin-fronted department stores, the mud-spattered omnibuses, the tangled web of telegraph lines that crocheted the sky at the corner of Fifth and Broadway. All she saw in her mind's eye was the face of Stuyvesant-French bearing down on her, his fist crushing her with the weight of his malice.

A lady strolling alone was guaranteed attention and suddenly she realized she was being stared at by the many businessmen who thronged the avenue this time of day. One or two of them tipped their bowler hats to her, but most just leveled their eyes at her, their gazes taking in the sapphire ring on her middle finger. The finger that wasn't the important one; the married one.

She hastily retrieved her gloves and once more tried pulling them on. She continued walking, sure she would be all the way down Fifth and home by the time she ever got her glove over the ring.

"A penny for a posie? A penny for a posie, ma'am? Sir?"

Lavinia looked up and found a woman, grim-faced and haggard, slinging a baby on her hip while she held out a wilted bouquet of violets.

"Penny for a posie?" she cried out, her expression drawn with worry and hunger.

The baby began to wail, and helplessly the woman drew back toward the building. She desperately sang to the babe in order to keep it quiet so she could continue her meager business.

Lavinia didn't even realize she'd stopped. The crowds of passers-by swooshed by like a river, some trying to catch up with the rumbling, mule-driven omnibuses, some merely trying to signal a black-cabbed hackney, but suddenly the men in their bowler hats seemed to recede along with their rude stares. In the throng of swirling humanity, everything seemed to still except the despairing woman and her crying baby.

"A penny," Lavinia said to her, holding out the coin. Distract-edly the woman handed her a little posie of violets and then tried to thank her with a smile all while the baby screamed.

"How old is your baby?" Lavinia asked, unmindful of prying, unmindful of everything except the sudden, pounding, panic-filled notion that she was staring at herself. But for fate and circumstance, either she or Hazel could have been this sad, old-before-her-time, hope-less woman whose only wish in the world seemed to be to quiet her baby. But for fate and circumstance and the strength of an iron will.

"She's six months. Becky's her name," the woman answered in the hushed voice of those unsure if they're permitted to speak.

"Rebecca. Such a beautiful name." Lavinia held out her finger. The baby took it in her dirty hand. Suddenly Becky quieted and studied the treasure in her grasp, then she tried to put the finger in her mouth.

Hunger. Lavinia knew hunger all too well. But she'd not known it now for years.

She looked down at Wilhelm's ring. It was their insurance policy. The ring was the way to keep the town house and the pink velvet drapery. The ring meant starvation would never knock at their door.

As it was knocking at this woman's.

"Are you alone?" Lavinia asked softly—so softly she was sure the woman didn't hear her. But the woman did.

"Yes," she answered, her shame as thick as grime.

Lavinia looked away. Becky started to wail again and the woman rocked her, but there was no more comfort to give an empty stomach. Lavinia felt the baby's hunger like a knife to her gut. She might have been this woman with her hungry, wailing bastard. This woman's despair could have been her despair. And the victims would pile up, just two more bodies laying in the wake of a man's lust and greed.

"Here," Lavinia whispered softly, tugging on her finger. "Now you and Becky will never be alone again . . . because now you'll have this." She pressed the huge sapphire ring into the woman's callused palm.

The woman looked like she was about to faint. The baby's wails, the throngs of bullying pedestrians, all seemed to fade to the distance as the woman stared down at the costly jewel in her hand.

"Surely you don't mean to give me this?" the woman whispered.

Lavinia thought about her luxurious town house, her plush drapery, her content and happy home. But she suddenly realized it wasn't a ring that was their insurance policy, rather, it was her ability to fight. She had always been the one struggling against the tide, even Hazel hadn't the endurance she had. Lavinia's will and her strength was what would keep her home together—and Edward Stuyvesant-French be damned—those things couldn't be given away like a diamond-and-sapphire ring.

"I don't need it," Lavinia whispered. Her face opened up with a soft smile and she said, "I see that now. I don't need the ring. I'll do fine without it and"—she touched Rebecca's thin little arm—"and this little girl needs a home and good food, and an education; if you promise to give those things to her, then the ring and the money you can get for it is yours."

"I'll do it. Of course I'll do it." The woman's eyes nearly popped

from her head. She seemed almost hysterical. "But I don't understand, why would you give me this ring? Why would you do that
for me? I'm a stranger."

Lavinia stared at the woman as if she were looking at Hazel
holding Eva. She shook her head, smiled, and slipped the kid gloves
easily over her hands. How wonderful it felt to have the heavy,
awkward ring off her hand. "No, that's just it, you see. You're no
stranger at all. Not at all."

She touched Rebecca's downy curls. She bent and kissed the
child on her head, then she strode away.

She didn't look back at the woman who stared at her like she'd
just seen an angel.

Chapter Seven

Lavinia returned home without a word to Hazel. She retired to her bedroom and ordered a glass of claret and a bowl of ice from Rawl. The claret was for her mind and the ice for her sore feet; she'd walked half the length of Manhattan.

She'd just unhooked the first two hooks of her corset when Hazel burst into her room.

"Oh . . . you'll never guess what's downstairs waiting for you. You'll never guess." The dread in Hazel's voice made Lavinia guess right away.

"Not Stuyvesant-French?"

"Much worse. His carriage. His sister sent a note asking you to join her for tea at four."

Lavinia visibly slumped. She didn't want to meet the sister now. She hadn't strategized enough and she didn't want to show her hand just to comfort the woman because that would tip off her brother.

"I'm not going."

Hazel frowned. "You can't stand her up. She just lost her inheritance today, Vinia, *to you.*"

Lavinia put her hand to her head. Forget the aching feet, she now needed that ice for her aching head. "All right. Of course I'll go speak with her. I'll do my best to reassure her that she won't be left out in the cold, even if, God willing, her brother will be."

"That's the thing to do."

"Get me my purple dress, will you, Hazel? You know, the lilac taffeta?"

"Shouldn't you wear something a little more . . . well, somber?" she asked.

Lavinia looked at her own reflection in the mirror of her dressing table. There was the faintest suggestion of circles beneath her eyes and her cheeks looked much too pale. She looked beaten. But she wasn't beaten, and if a little rouge pot and an overly vivacious gown would make her look more of an opponent, then she would make use of those things, and more.

"Get me the lilac taffeta, Hazel. That's just in case Stuyvesant-French decides to take tea with us." She turned back to the mirror, flipped open the powder jar, and let the camouflage begin.

❦ ❦

"Does she wear a turban when she does her séances? Perhaps a blue satin one with a huge peacock feather on it? Oh, it sounds so very exotic to be a medium. *The Countess Lovaenya.* Just think of it. And she didn't look anything as I expected. She looked very nice and very pretty. Beautiful even. I'd think she was just your type, Edward—blonde and—and— How shall I put it? I think the term is . . . well endowed?" Daisy looked up at her brother, her eyes holding a naughty gleam.

"She's sure as hell well endowed now," he snarled after taking a long sip of brandy.

Daisy glanced around the tomb that served as a drawing room.

"I'll do fine with a small house in the mountains. I'm looking forward to it, actually. Besides, she seemed more suited to this place. It was almost eerie the way her elegance dovetailed with the background here. After all, she's a countess. Perhaps she was meant for this place."

He snorted. "God save us." He put down his brandy. In the foyer they heard the bell ring announcing a visitor, and he turned to his sister, adding, "You may dispose of the castle if you like, my lady, but this knight is going to slay all usurpers." He stood.

"If she can talk with spirits, do you think she can read our minds, too?"

He quirked his lip in disgust. "If she could, she'd be running out of here like the devil was at her heels."

"Oh, you are wicked, Edward. So wicked indeed." Daisy laughed.

§ ℰ

The butler toured Lavinia again through the foyer as he had done earlier in the day. But instead of showing her to the library, he took her to an astoundingly large room to the left of the foyer that must have been the mansion's drawing room.

They were waiting there for her. The lion and the lamb. She couldn't hurt one without damaging the other. She needed that ice now desperately.

"Countess, we're so glad you could make it." Stuyvesant-French was already standing when she arrived, so he merely walked toward her and led her to a ruby velvet settee.

If he was angry, he didn't show it. There was no sign of tension at all on his handsome face, just the slightest tic of muscle in his jaw, but that alone was enough to send her stomach plummeting down cliffs.

"Thank you so much for inviting me, Miss Vanadder," she said, taking the proffered seat. "Your brother thinks very highly of you. It's my pleasure to finally meet you."

"Edward has spoken of me?" The pleasant woman laughed as if that were the most absurd thing in the world. "Good heavens, I can't imagine what he said."

"He said he wants you to have what's rightfully yours and let me assure you that my sister and I want that with all our hearts also." Lavinia smiled. Daisy's affability was infectious. She only wished it extended to her pill of a brother.

"I've got the papers and you can sign all of this to Daisy right now if you like," Stuyvesant-French announced in a most grating manner.

Lavinia looked up at him, but Daisy drew her attention away.

"Tell me," the woman said, leaning toward her and whispering, "can you read people's minds, too? I've always wanted to do that. I suppose because I never had a lot of company here I always thought it would be deliciously naughty to read the servants' minds and hear all that gossip to which I'm not privy. You know, I've always suspected the housekeeper of having an intrigue with the stable boy—"

Lavinia laughed out loud. It was a gut reaction and she wished she'd been able to stop herself, but she hadn't expected to be so disarmed.

"Very amusing, Daisy. Now where's that tea?" Edward interjected, his tone as quelling as a piano dropped from four stories up.

"Shall I ring for Adolfo? No, no, let me go and see what happened for myself." Daisy smiled at both of them. "I know you two probably have a lot to discuss. I can't read minds, but I don't have to in this case. I'll be right back."

Lavinia bit back a cry of, *Come back here!* Helplessly she watched the woman wheel herself along the creamy marble floor. Daisy was out of the drawing room quicker than if she could have run.

Lavinia stared at her hands. She wished she still had her ring, at least for this one moment. She could then be secure in the knowledge that he could never clean her out entirely.

But that was no longer possible now.

Now she just had to have backbone.

"I had hoped your sister and I could speak privately," she said, her gaze lifting to his.

"I have the scoop on you, Miss Murphy. I know about the little incident with the law in Rochester."

She stared at him, wondering how someone so loathsome could be so terribly handsome. "What incident in Rochester?" she asked innocently.

"The incident whereby the citizens of that fair city ran you and your sister out of town for soliciting."

"We were not soliciting. We simply set up shop there to tell fortunes and they came to that mistaken conclusion without any proof."

"That's not what the authorities said."

"My past seems to be a hobby of yours." She lifted one eyebrow. That usually worked for the most serious of doubters. It didn't work for him.

"Come, sign the papers, Miss Murphy. Avoid the scandal."

"I have a lot of money now, Mr. Stuyvesant-French. More money than you have, if the Vanadder fortune is estimated correctly."

"You won't see a penny of it. What money will you use to fight me in the meantime while I contest the will?" He lifted an eyebrow.

She wanted to claw the expression right off his face. "I won't capitulate just because you threaten me."

"Oh? Instead you would steal money from a cripple?" He nodded to the doorway that Daisy had just exited.

"I don't intend to take a dime from her."

"Then sign the papers. You can understand that I'm the logical one to see that she is taken care of."

"And you're the logical one to rob her. Admit it, you have a lot to lose if you must share the fortune with a legitimate offspring."

He laughed. "Is that how you're reconciling this with your conscience? That you're protecting her from me?" He sat next to her on the settee. Too close. His thigh brushed against hers. "I'm not the greedy one here. I'm not the one who deals daily in fraud."

"Perhaps I should speak with an attorney. Then your law firm could speak with my law firm and we won't have any more need for these little tête-à-têtes."

He leaned close, so close she could smell that he'd been drinking brandy. And strangely, that very thing that normally would have repulsed her, aroused her.

It was just his closeness, she told herself. It was the aggressive posture of him leaning toward her that she must have mistook for some kind of sexual overture. His eyes gleamed with vengeance; she could see the message there very clearly, but still, she couldn't erase the sudden odd notion that this passionate hatred he held for her was separated by a mere fraction of an inch from sexual passion. And like a bad seed that had taken root, she now couldn't put it from her mind.

"I've given notice to *Harper's* that I'm going to expose you as a fraud," he whispered, as if by lowering his voice and letting it echo throughout the mausoleum of a drawing room she might be that much more intimidated.

It worked.

"Tomorrow night," he continued, "every reporter in New York will be in your drawing room at eight."

She just stared at him, mesmerized.

"I think it's time to sign the papers, Miss Murphy. Now. While there's still time to withdraw the challenge."

"I think you should leave your sister and I to work out the inheritance. You've no need to do this. I will be fair with her. I promise you."

"Oh? If you're going to be so fair with Daisy, why not sign the papers?"

"How do I know you're honest? How do I know anything about these legal proceedings? I'm not fluent in Latin, I'll remind you. I didn't understand much of what went on in that library today."

"It was very simple. Vanadder left you everything." He straightened and peered down at her. "If I expose you as a fraud, *Countess*, I kill two birds with one stone: I prove him insane, and therefore, his will invalid. Under New York law everything then reverts to Daisy. So I put it to you, do you force me to go to that séance tomorrow night?"

"If you go to the séance and do as you say you must, even if you prove me a fraud and have the will declared invalid, what do you get out of it? Daisy will get everything as Wilhelm's only legitimate offspring, and I really don't believe you want to do that. Actually I believe you just want me to sign your papers blindly no matter what they say, no matter whom they hurt." She drew back to the end of the settee but he was a large man and the settee was small; she couldn't get away entirely. "No, you really should give me a chance to work things out with your sister. That way—"

"That way you and the 'Czarina' can keep a cut of the take, am I correct?"

"Wilhelm obviously wanted us to have something. He left us a lot of money and we are human, after all, Mr. Stuyvesant-French. Such altruism you demand is something of which only an angel might be capable."

"Or a spirit?" He leaned toward her again, and his gaze captured hers as if he were a hypnotist. "What do the spirits think of my plan, Countess?"

"The spirits think you should leave this to me and your sister."

"Do the spirits relish a séance with me tomorrow night?"

"They think you might be proved a fool." She jutted out her chin and met his chilly gaze with one of her own.

He leaned back against the settee, his arms crossed over his chest, his gaze penetrating her very soul. The corner of his mouth lifted in a smirk. "Such defiance. It almost becomes you, Lavinia Murphy. All right, then, we'll do the séance."

"Here is the tea," Daisy said, gliding back into the drawing room, the butler in her wake. The man placed the heavy silver tray on a table and Daisy began to pour.

"Sugar or lemon, Countess?" she asked, a pleasant ring to her voice.

"Sugar," Lavinia answered numbly, her mind whirring with an overload of panic. She would need a supreme performance to get past the scrutiny tomorrow night, but she'd done it before, and she could do it again.

"Miss Murphy is going to do me a séance tomorrow night, Daisy." Edward declined the tea and still stared at Lavinia.

"Who's Miss Murphy?" Daisy asked, appearing genuinely confused.

"The Countess Lovaenya here. Her real name is Lavinia Murphy. That is, I believe that's her real name—but it's not her sister's real name, and her sister isn't really her sister—and Miss Murphy's not even a real countess. I'm not sure what's real about Miss Murphy and what's not, but we're going to find all that out tomorrow night," he finished smugly.

"A real séance?" Daisy's eyes became huge. "Are we to speak with the dead?"

Lavinia opened her mouth to respond but Edward interrupted.

"Yes, Daze. We're going to sit in a circle in the dark and convince Wilhelm to rewrite his will." He grinned and picked up his brandy glass, saluting Lavinia.

"Really?" Daisy stared at Lavinia. "Are you really going to contact Father?"

Lavinia took a deep breath. "If that's who you'd like to—"

"Not really," Daisy blurted out.

Edward interjected. "My only wish is to speak to the girl in white. Do you know of whom I speak, Countess. She had a faint resemblance to you."

"Really?" Daisy gasped, her eyes glittering with delight. "Does that mean you've experienced reincarnation?"

Edward groaned.

Lavinia might have even laughed if she wasn't so afraid. Daisy was so longing for fun she'd believe anything, and that was why it had all worked; that was why little Lavinia Murphy had a town house and pink drapery and sapphire rings.

"I hate to burst your bubble, Daisy, but your brother is mocking me. He's a disbeliever. He wants to prove me a fraud."

"I know," Daisy said easily, as if that detail and maybe more wouldn't stand in the way of a blossoming friendship. "But who is the girl in white?"

"She's a spirit. If she's willing, she sometimes makes an appearance in my parlor."

"Oh, I must see her," Daisy said in a hushed reverent tone.

"You will, Daisy. I have a feeling she will appear tomorrow night just to spite me," Edward threw in.

Lavinia shot him a quelling look. "I have no control over her. I can't say whether she'll appear or not. Besides, she only comes when the Czarina does the séance."

"Then the Czarina will preside tomorrow night. I want to see the girl in white. I've something to tell her."

Lavinia looked at Stuyvesant-French. She wanted to shout out her veto of that idea, but she could see now that he'd lit on their trail he would hold on to it like a hound with a bone.

"Fine. You shall have your girl in white." She stared at him.

He twisted his fine mouth into the semblance of a grin. " 'Have' is an overly broad word, Miss Murphy. Right now all I need is to see her."

Lavinia could feel her cheeks grow hot, but from anger or chagrin she didn't know. She took a sip of tea to calm her nerves, then she stood. "This has been enchanting, but I find I must take my leave. Miss Vanadder"—she turned to his sister—"it will be my pleasure to entertain you tomorrow night, and I hope you can attend."

"Oh, I wouldn't miss it! I've never done anything so exciting!"

Daisy pulled away from the tea table and rolled alongside Lavinia. "I would love to try and summon my mother— Do you think—?"

"Daisy," Edward interrupted.

Both women turned. Lavinia never had seen a man so utterly disagreeable.

"I don't think we should bother the Countess with our requests. I wager she's got enough on her hands right now." He gave that grin again; she hated him for it.

"Of course, of course. How foolish of me," Daisy said with a smile as she kept right at Lavinia's side. "I don't want to be a bother. I hope you still don't mind my attending the séance?"

"If it would amuse you, then you must attend." Lavinia gave a glance back at Stuyvesant-French. He nodded farewell, those wicked eyes gleaming at her beneath half-closed lids.

At the drawing-room door, she held out her hand to Daisy. "I'm so very glad I've finally met you. I can see why your brother regards you with such affection. I— I—" She stole another look at Stuyvesant-French who glowered in the marble background. "Well, I just want you to know— this will—Hazel and I, we want to work things out in a fair manner. You understand?"

"Is he making you do this?" Daisy whispered as if she were being mischievous.

"Your brother?" Lavinia asked weakly.

"Yes. Edward. You know, he can be so wonderful, but I can see how some might view him as having a rather dark nature, especially when they're in the way of what he wants." Daisy smiled and warmly shook Lavinia's hand. "I'll see you again, Countess. I'm not a fortune-teller, but I have a feeling we're going to be friends."

Lavinia looked down at the woman. Daisy's smile was so ingenuous she had to smile back. "I fear I don't belong in your world, Miss Vanadder, but if on some slight level we might remain acquaintances, I would like that."

"But we must become friends. I don't know why, but I really do feel it is fated." Daisy looked at her, a strange expression on her face. "But you're best the one to explain such notions, aren't you, Countess?"

"I can't explain much other than to say that I don't belong here in your world, Miss Vanadder." She looked around at the costly Carrera tiles, the gilt cornices, the heavy drapery of wine-colored plush. "You see I'm the kind of woman who's had to—to—earn—her living, do you understand? And, well, I've not had the luxury of—of . . ."

"The luxury of what?"

Lavinia didn't know what to say. She looked at the woman in the wheelchair and chided herself. Daisy Vanadder knew no luxury if she couldn't walk about the earth on her own two feet as most took for granted, yet Lavinia knew what she'd been trying to say was true. She didn't belong in this life of status and wealth. Lavinia Murphy's history could be summed up as one long painful crawl from the gutter, and this woman's had been so exquisitely sheltered that Lavinia couldn't see how they would ever find common ground. Except that they'd both known hardship, both from birth.

"I do hope we can be friends." Lavinia glanced again at Stuyvesant-French. He hadn't moved from his position standing in front of the settee, but he still stared at her. "If we're not, believe me, it's just fate and circumstance. As everything is in this life."

"Yes. Fate and circusmtance." Daisy smiled. "But they're not always bad, right?"

Lavinia tried to smile in kind, but it was without strength of conviction. "Perhaps," she said. She then gave Stuyvesant-French one last backward glance. Thoroughly chilled, she followed the butler to the front door.

❧ ❧

"She's gone, Edward. She's been gone for a full minute, and I daresay, her charming figure won't come waltzing through the door just because you've willed it to do so."

Edward snapped his gaze back to his sister. Daisy was smiling. Teasing him.

"For your sake, sister, I will force myself to retain my sense of humor."

"Pshaw. You've long lost that, darling Edward. She took it from you and that's why I think the Countess is under your skin."

"Don't be absurd."

"Absurd, am I? We'll see who the fortune-teller is."

"You've got a wicked streak in you, Daze. I can finally vouch for the fact we're related." He walked over to the marble mixing table and opened the crystal stopper on the decanter.

"Edward," Daisy said, gliding around the settee, "getting a visitor like that makes you think, doesn't it? I mean, we're such a sad pair, you and I. Here I am, the outcast, and here you are, the misfit, I wonder what she must think of us."

"She's a worse outcast and a worse misfit." He raised the glass to his mouth. "If truth be known, she's nothing but a two-bit . . ." He swallowed the rest as if he couldn't bear to say it.

"She looks at you, Edward." Daisy stopped her chair. "She looks at you like a woman looks at a man. Her expression is vulnerable."

"You mean calculated."

"She couldn't pretend that, Edward. I don't believe it."

"Acting is her second profession. You'd do well to remember that."

"Men. You're all cads." She heaved a sigh and began to head for the door.

"Where are you off to?" he groused.

She didn't even turn to look at him. With an artifically light tone, she said, "I'm going to instruct Addie to begin packing. I'm off to my cottage next week if I can manage it."

"Like hell you are. You're staying right here."

"I've no prospects, Edward. We've gone over this. I want to move. And now with the reading of the will, I must move."

"No more talk of that, Daisy. I told you, this house will be yours."

"I don't want it. Nothing will change then. It'll just be me here, entombed in this cold elegant space. No, give me a garden, Edward. Give me flowers and butterflies and then brisk autumn winds and winter snows. I want my cottage in the country."

"Everything's *going* to change, Daisy. It's going to change *here.*" He gripped his glass and walked to her, leaning one hand on the arm of her chair. "I've thought a lot about this. You're going to have friends, I'm going to see to it. We're going to open up the house and have parties. You're going to travel, you're going to *live*, Daisy, and I'm going to make sure you do, to the fullest extent possible. I'm here now, remember? I'm here."

She gazed up at him with such devotion and admiration in her eyes he almost seemed to flinch. "I love you, Edward. I love you for saying all that, and mostly for meaning it. Sometimes you're so wonderful I can't believe I'm related to you."

"You're my sister. My only sister."

"Yes." She patted his cheek. "Your very realistic sister. Let me say this one last time, Edward, then don't make me say it ever again: I'm going to live in the country. There are no prospects here for me, and I don't plan to fool myself into believing there are. I'm a thirty-two-year-old spinster, and spinsters belong in the country."

He shook the wheelchair to emphasize his point. "You will find a man who loves you. I know it. You must try."

She glided away from him a few feet, unwilling to let him deter her. "The men will come with the money if you insist on getting it for me, but as I've told you before, I don't want that kind of marriage. So I don't need that money."

"You're marriageable without the money," he roared between clenched teeth.

Her expression hardened. She looked away. "You can say one thing, Edward. You were the product of a terrible passion, but a passion nonetheless. I, on the other hand, am nothing but the outcome of a loveless marriage. I've endured being the damaged goods of that cursed union; all my life I've taken the blame for being the weak spawn of Father's loins; I could hardly live through it at times, but I did." She paused as if her throat were caught with tears. Finally, in a small harsh voice, she whispered, "Oh God, please, Edward, let me get out of here. Don't make me become my mother. Don't do it. Poverty and death is much preferred."

He stared at her. For a long terrible moment, they said nothing. Then she calmly wheeled out of the drawing room.

A sharp crack resounded like an echo. Stunned, he looked down to find spatters of blood on the virgin white marble. His blood.

Slowly, he released his grip on the brandy glass. With an angry mournful growl, he let the shards crash to the floor.

Chapter Eight

I laughed aloud at the absurdity, and flung the report aside with the righteous scorn of an honest nature that knew its own kin when it met them, and shrank from the foulness of a lie.

—Annie Besant (after she discarded the report from the Society of
Psychical Research exposing Madame Blavatsky as a fraud)

L avinia stared at herself in the mirror, white greasepaint across her face, cornstarch on her nose, her hair unbound beneath a veil of tea-colored netting.

She was the phantom in white; the ghost girl; her humanity covered beneath ancient rotting lace and the bluish tint of the makeup. But there was still no hiding her eyes. The damnable eyes. They stared back at her; betrayed her. They were desolate, frightened eyes. Eyes too quick and suspicious for a death mask.

"We don't have to do it this way," Hazel said, staring at her in the mirror. "You could do the séance, and I could be the one to plead a headache."

"No," Lavinia said, her hand trembling as she reopened the powder pot. "He's taunted me beyond endurance. I want to do this. I must do this."

"But what if we lose?"

Lavinia's hand paused. "Then we cash in the town house and move on. We can always start up again elsewhere. No one ever went broke in this business being exposed as a fraud. The only ones that go broke are the ones that tell the truth." She stood and turned to face Hazel. "Whatever happens, let's promise right now to stand by each other. Call it conspiracy, call it fraud, call it whatever you like, but there's our truth and then there's their truth, and we must stand by one another if we're to survive."

"It's me, Lavinia," Hazel said, a concerned wistful tone to her voice. "You don't have to tell me all this. I already know it. We've been through worse, remember?"

"But somehow, this time, it seems different." She stared darkly at the grease pots. "There seems to be much more at stake here. This time I feel . . . Oh, I don't know what I feel. Maybe it's just that I feel more vulnerable now. Before we had nothing to lose. Now we have so much."

Hazel didn't meet her eyes. She began to bustle around the room as if each little errand were of utmost importance, and Lavinia got the notion she was avoiding something.

"You don't think we should perform tonight, do you?" Lavinia asked.

"No, no. Whatever you think is best." Hazel straightened the lace doily on the mantel. Each crystal prism on the candlestick glistened from Rawlings' regular dustings with his white-gloved hands, but still Hazel found reason to lift up her hankie and polish one.

"What is it?" Lavinia didn't want to show the anxiety in her voice, but Hazel was indeed acting odd.

"No. If you think we must do this séance tonight, we must, and that is all there is to it."

"What's frightening you?"

Hazel glanced up, met Lavinia's gaze, then looked away. "I really can't quite put my finger on it. It's nothing to worry about, I'm sure."

Lavinia gasped. Her eyes popped out of her head. "Dear God, you're fibbing. You've never done that before."

"I don't want to— It's just that—that—oh, you don't have any experience with these things!"

Lavinia gasped again. The world seemed to be going mad. "What are you talking about? I'm the one who's contrived every-thing we've ever done!"

"I'm talking about men! He's attractive, Vinia. Attractive." Hazel's words faded in the wake of Lavinia's expression. "That's why you're scared this time." The last syllable was barely a squeak.

Lavinia didn't utter a sound. She just stared at Hazel as if she'd just nominated herself as a candidate for the Brooklyn Asylum.

Hazel gave a coltish toss of her head. She was prone to do such a thing when she was irritated. "I know you think you're not affected by a handsome man, and maybe you aren't, Vinia. But we're both women, and despite your attire, we're both human and—and—well, I know about these things, remember?" She crossed her arms across her chest in a defiant protective gesture.

Lavinia gave her one long stare, then she slowly closed her eyes and nodded. In a contrite tone, she said, "Of course I remember, and if I ever forget what happened to you there's always Eva to remind me of your plight."

Hazel tried to give her an encouraging smile. "I don't know what's the matter with me tonight. I'm not one to doubt you. We've come so far and all on your coattails. It's just, well, Edward Stuyvesant-French gives me the willies. He stares like he can see right through you, through all the lies. But you're strong, Vinia. I'm a fool to doubt your strength. Of course you will beat him."

Lavinia's gaze met Hazel's. "Yes, I'm strong. Just remember, I'm strong."

Hazel gave her a long helpless look. "You don't need to convince me."

Lavinia turned away, her insides numb from fear and self-doubt. She stared at herself in the mirror as if she might find sustenance there, and as she had done a thousand times before, she lost herself in the vision of the phantom girl. There, in the unseen world of the dead, she could let her fearful spirit soar, and she could once again hide in the illusion where shadow never meets with flesh and blood.

※ ❦

"When is this thing going to take place? I've a dancer, a sweet *petite rat*, waiting for me at the opera tonight and she wants to see me in the audience when the ballet performs in Act Three." Herman Langley, renowned newspaperman, the icon behind the daily *New York Comet*, snapped open his repoussé gold watch and noted the time.

"The Czarina will be here shortly. She sends her apologies, but she had a spell just before leaving her room." Rawlings bent with a silver tray in hand and handed out brandy.

"What kind of spell?" William Boatman asked, for once unmindful of the silver mines that bore his name.

"The kind of spell that all mediums experience whenever they become entranced with the idea of duping another convention of dullards." Edward Stuyvesant-French waved aside the offer of brandy and assessed the group of gentlemen gathered in the parlor.

"Huzzah, old man! I daresay, Frenchy's got a point there!" A skinny, mustachioed reporter from the British Isles raised his glass to Edward.

"The Exalted Czarina is no fraud. Why, I spoke with the spirit of my dear departed wife only last week." Another reporter, an older man from the *Astoria Gazette*, scowled from his seat in the cozy corner. His frown was barely hidden by the numerous palm fronds.

"How did you know it was your wife you spoke to?" Stuyvesant-French asked. "The spirit could have been manufactured right from the Czarina's extensive files and her even more limitless imagination."

"No, no. The Czarina got every question right. She knew my wife's name, her pet name, everything."

"And what was your wife's name, sir?" Edward asked.

"Margaret."

Edward snorted. "The Czarina and her nefarious sister could have found that out in a heartbeat. Just reading the obituaries would tell them who your wife was as long as you supplied the date of her demise. Did you do that?"

"Well, actually, yes, the Czarina did ask when Margaret died before she would consent to the telegraph, but even reading the paper wouldn't have given the Czarina my wife's pet name."

"What was her pet name, sir? Was it Margie? Or Peggy? Or Peg?"

The old man got very quiet. "It was Peg, but she couldn't have known that."

"A common enough nickname. It took no great thinker to guess it, and it certainly didn't take a spirit to tell it. If I should have yelled out the name Peg at the old Castle Garden I'd have started a stampede." Edward leaned his frame against the heavily draped window. "What else did our Exalted Czarina tell you?"

"She got everything correct. Every question I asked, she answered me." The reporter defensively crossed his arms over his chest and snorted. "There was but one thing the Czarina told me that was not true, and that was why I knew Renski was no fraud. I knew I was talking to Peg."

"What was that one thing, sir?" Edward asked, the corner of his mouth tipped in amusement.

"Peg said she liked it up in heaven because they gave her all the chocolate she could eat. After the Czarina Renski conveyed this message to me from my wife, I had my proof. I knew it was Peg."

"Most people are fond of chocolate, sir. I must say that's another generalization that could apply to anyone."

"Ah ha!" The reporter stood up and pointed his finger at Stuyvesant-French. "But you see, only I knew Peg! Only I knew Peg despised chocolate. It gave her the meanest rash you ever saw!"

Edward looked utterly confounded. "Then what you're saying

only gives fuel to the fire, my man. The Czarina guessed wrong. She is a fraud."

"And that is where *you* are wrong, sir." The man smirked. "I knew it was Peg I was talking to that very instant." He chuckled. "You see? Peg was always full of fibs." He laughed out loud. "Peg liking chocolate! The little minx. What will she say next?"

Edward's jaw dropped open. If not for the nudge on the shoulder, he might have just fallen right over in his chair.

"You cannot disabuse the faithful, son." Cornelius handed him his empty brandy glass and winked to the tray the butler had left behind. "And that is precisely why I drink."

"But this is ridiculous."

"Ridiculous? How so? The man just gave you proof." William Boatman put down his brandy glass and shook the *Astoria Gazette* reporter's hand.

All the men seemed to congratulate the fellow, much to Edward's amazement.

"I'm with you, French," Cornelius interjected. "The only spirits a man should believe in are this kind." He raised the new glass of brandy and downed it in one tidy gulp.

"These people are lunatics. Certifiable lunatics. There's no logic there whatsoever." A muscle bunched in Edward's jaw as he glanced over the group.

"No, but it's not logic that motivates them, it's need and desire and emotion. Those things are much stronger than logic. You can't fight it, French. Besides, the believers outnumber you by ten to one. That is why the medium's craft is so very compelling . . . and so very lucrative."

"This whole thing is just women grabbing for an imagined power. And they're pushed along by every dense thinker who wants to go along for the ride."

"Yes, but these dense thinkers are rich men, and women have been outwitting their kind for centuries, using one method or another."

"Exactly my point," Edward murmured between clenched teeth.

"The Czarina is ready. Gentlemen, will you have a seat at the table?" The butler motioned to the large table in the center of the parlor. The men took their seats, the reporter from *Harper's* and the man from the *Gazette* bickering over who would sit to the right of the Czarina.

"Gentlemen," the butler announced, "the Czarina Renski." He motioned to the parlor doors. All eyes followed.

❧ ❧

"Rawl, is he in there?" Lavinia whispered as she descended the rear staircase.

"I just left them," he answered. "May I say, you look ghastly as usual, miss."

She tossed him a grin behind the veil. "Thank you, Rawl."

They stood on the servants' landing hidden from the public part of the house. Above them, the stair rose three floors all the way to the attic; below, it went to the kitchens and rear service courtyard.

"I don't want to be out there long. We can't trust what that man might do. I just want to make an appearance." She looked at him. "Rawl, when you flare the gaslights this evening, I want you to watch me. I may have to cut the act short if Stuyvesant-French starts giving me trouble. Just keep an eye to the proceedings. If you see me getting into difficulties, flare the lights early, then out. That way I can make my exit."

"So you won't be doing the whole routine?" The old butler seemed almost disappointed.

"Not tonight. I can't risk taking extra time for dramatics. That awful man in there is too suspicious." She stood on her tiptoes to peer through a small brass plug in the wall where Rawl had been standing. The peephole was camouflaged on the other side by the brass scroll of a sconce. From her hiding place, she could see everything. The gathering of dark-suited men were now at the table. The Czarina—Hazel—had instructed them to clasp hands in the circle. Hazel lorded over them while she sat upright in her gothic-style armchair, her eyes vacant as she pretended to draw the invisible world of the spirits close around them.

Then Lavinia spied Stuyvesant-French. He sat at the round table nearest to the velvet screen as if he were anticipating the appearance of the phantom. The harsh planes of his face were lit with yellow gaslight and his eyes were fixed on Hazel in a cynical, penetrating stare. Watching him, Lavinia wondered if anything ever made that expression soften. He seemed so utterly cold, so thoroughly unyielding. She couldn't imagine a woman's hand running down that hard cheek. She couldn't picture him responding to a caress on that stone-carved face. There was no kind of touch that might make him turn and smile. His face never smiled because the soul behind it didn't know how to play. It probably never had.

She stepped back from the peephole and glanced at Rawl. It was time to cast out this demon from their lives or give in to it. Pushing on the wall panel next to him, she opened it silently, glad that Rawl kept the hinges scrupulously oiled. She slipped inside the wall space between the servants' stairs and parlor, and Rawl closed the panel. Then she heard him return to his station by the gas key.

The wall space was a coffin. Barely a foot deep, she crushed herself against the plaster keys of the opposite wall and placed a small handkerchief of ice to her lips. Tonight in the act, she wouldn't dare go as far as giving each man a kiss, but if Stuyvesant-French stayed in his seat, she might give a peck or two to the men closest to her.

But then, of course, Stuyvesant-French was the closest to her.

"I call the spirits who walk these floors to make themselves known to me. I call the spirits!" Hazel's muffled pleadings could barely be heard behind the thick plaster but Lavinia kept her ear to the wall. She had to appear at just the right moment or the synchronism of their performances would be off.

"I feel it, gentlemen. She's a female spirit—a young woman who died not far from this room. She wanders among us searching for her lost lover. She wanders among us, lost and forsaken—"

On Hazel's cue, Lavinia slid open the silent panel on the parlor wall. A velvet screen hid the panel from parlor visitors and obscured her maneuvering out of the wall. Once on the other side, she straightened her gown and listened for her cue.

"I feel her, gentlemen. She's in this room with us. I feel her even now. She walks among us, searching . . . searching . . ."

Lavinia waited for the breeze. The first strong gust hit her brow from the holes camouflaged on either side of the parlor walls. Behind one wall, Eva and Fanny worked an enormous bellows. Each little girl put her tiny weight atop the contraption and forced the air out, and the effect was marvelous, especially when Jamie was on the other side of the parlor working another bellows. The phantom girl always appeared in an unexplained gust of air. And to finish the ghostly choreography, the gaslights began to waver in a haunting rhythm, the effect manufactured by Rawlings' station at the gas key.

"There she is, gentlemen, there is the spirit I feel ever near us!"

Upon Hazel's words, Lavinia walked around the screen, her diaphanous gown billowing in the artificial wind, the breeze spreading the musty, dead smell of the lavender and vetiver water she doused herself in before each performance.

The chorus of gasps and cries were most satisfying. Indeed, she must have presented a terrifying sight, her sheer clothing afloat in the air, her light steps making her seem to be more floating above than stepping upon the solid floor.

"It's her! The girl in white! The one you summoned!" Boatman sobbed.

Lavinia made a mental note to kiss him first.

"What do you want, dear spirit? Who has called you?" Hazel asked.

But Lavinia's was not a speaking part. She simply stared ahead, her eyes seemingly blind to the earthly subjects in front of her. Walking forward, she drew toward Boatman, doing her best to avoid proximity to Stuyvesant-French. In the past, she'd once even dared to circle the table, but that was infinitely risky. She could get trapped at the other side of the room, far from the concealing screen and the sliding wall panel. Now all she wanted to do was place her icy lips upon Boatman's trembling cheek and back away.

"Spirit, what message do you bring from the other side?" Her man Langley demanded. He clutched Hazel's hand and the *Astoria* reporter's, his own trembling in the flickering gaslight.

From the corner of her eye, Lavinia saw Stuyvesant-French rise. She heard him hiss, "Yes, tell us everything," and her heart began to pound in her chest.

"You've broken the circle, man!" a gasp went out.

"You're going to cause her to disappear!" another man cried.

"Get back here!"

But Stuyvesant-French ignored the choking chorus of protests and took a step toward her.

She couldn't react. In her world, his physical presence wasn't noteworthy. So instead she remained still, her eyes unfocused, her blood thrumming with terror, her heart beating so hard she was sure it alone would give away her humanity.

The gaslights flared. In the sudden brilliance of light, she saw Stuyvesant-French walk to her. The men behind him shouted out their objections, but even when he grabbed a handful of her veil, she couldn't move, she couldn't do anything because it would give her away. She had to remain composed but all the while she prayed to Rawlings to come through for her.

Edward snarled in her ear, his hand threatening at any moment to pull off the veil, "Now, sweet phantom, kiss me before this audience and prove that you're really molded from cold death."

The gas flames jetted from the fixtures like Herculean torches. Stuyvesant-French's hand tugged on the veil. She heard the rip of netting and the scream of the men behind him.

Then the lights went out.

Utter blackness.

She stumbled backward in a dash for the velvet screen. The winds had stopped with the gaslights. No doubt, Eva, Fanny and Jamie were running for Rawlings' spot at the peephole.

"Kiss me, phantom," he grunted as he slammed her body against the unforeseen obstacle of a table.

She released a feral moan and clawed his face in the darkness. Behind them, men shuffled in the blackness, making noises that they were anxious to intercede between them, but hesistant, as if they feared what Stuyvesant-French might truly have caught in his arms.

"Kiss me, phantom. Just one more kiss from those cold lips," he whispered, a wicked amusement in his voice.

She pushed her hand to his face and tried to force him off her, but he shoved it to her side. Then his mouth came down on hers, stilling her, taunting her.

A cry died in her throat. Her emotions ripped like shattered silk. She hated him, he was the conquerer, he was going to take away everything she had, but yet she couldn't find it within her to despise his kiss. She expected it to be messy and imprecise, that his lips would grope in the shadow like an inept lover. Instead, his mouth moved on hers in the manner of a cat, a creature well versed in darkness, one that can find its prey in the dense night of all hell. In one split second, he had taken her mouth to his like a starving carnivore, his tongue licking and pushing inside her until she now shuddered from the power of it.

She was a fool. Just like Hazel had been once.

She let out a low guttural cry, then ripped herself away and ran to the back of the screen. She scrambled for the hole in the wall, but before she could hoist herself into it, his arm went around her waist and he pulled her back.

"Who would have guessed this lifeless spirit to be such a hellion?" He shoved her against the wall, his body leaning on hers, covering her completely. She was now trapped. Hopelessly, utterly trapped.

"They'll turn on the lights eventually. Hear them?" he whispered.

She could detect forms in the distant darkness, men bumping into unseen furniture, cursing for a candle.

"What will they say when I drag you out and expose you?" His breath was hot along her cheek where the veil had been torn away.

She struggled, but his arms were like iron manacles. She pushed against his chest, but it didn't budge. The fine jacquard of his vest was slick against her fingers, the garment just a distinguished cage for the wild beast that wore it.

Gaslight from the street slowly leaked through the heavily draped windows. Panting, she looked up at him and made out his features in the shadow.

"Do I win, phantom?" he asked softly.

Swallowing a sob, she said nothing, unable to find an argument.

"Shall you meet me in Washingon Square at midnight to discuss the terms of surrender, or shall I drag you from behind this screen when the lights come back?" He leaned closer into her, his head bent down so near she could feel the movement of his mouth as he spoke.

"I'll meet you at midnight," she conceded, her voice choked with tears. Inside she was numb. It all seemed like a nightmare now, a bad dream she wanted desperately to put behind her. Denial mocked her like an echo through her head. If only she hadn't challenged him. If only . . . If only . . .

"Look up at me so that I may make out your face in the dimness."

She tipped her head, her gaze barely following. There was no longer any need to watch him, to challenge him. He wasn't her nemesis any longer. He was her victor.

His hand rose to her face. Slowly he drew his knuckles against her lips. The touch was filled with wonder. It sent a shiver down her spine.

"This mouth is not cold at all. Not at all." His comment hung in the darkness like his outstretched fingers.

She didn't speak. There was no point. She was trapped and he was so much more powerful than her. If he wanted to mock her, to lord it over her, he could do it now, and she couldn't stop him.

"I'll see you at midnight, Lavinia Murphy." He pushed away from the wall and walked from behind the screen.

She was left behind in the darkness, suddenly feeling naked without his weight pressed against her. In shock she suddenly realized the men had acquired a candle and were attempting to light it. Without wasting another second, she drew herself into the hole in the wall, swept back her gown and the tattered veil, and closed the panel.

"My good man, there you are! When you went after the spirit we had thought to never see you again!" Boatman slapped a grip on Stuyvesant-French's arm and shook his hand.

"Where is she?" the reporter from the *Astoria* cried out when he folded back the screen and found nothing there but the wall.

"What was it like to touch her? Tell me the whole story and we'll do a front-pager on it." Langley rubbed his hands in glee.

All the men gathered around Edward. No one noticed Rawl enter the parlor and relight the gas lamps.

"She was unlike anything I've ever touched before." Stuyvesant-French glanced at Hazel. She stared at him as if he were an executioner.

"So you really did touch her—did you get a look at her face?" Langley began scribbling in a little leather book.

"It was dark." Edward's gaze locked with the Czarina's.

"When she disappeared, did she go in a puff of air or did she fall away like fabric?" Now even Boatman was doing an interview.

"She just left. One second she was there in my arms, the next, she was gone." Edward seemed to take great satisfaction when he saw the Czarina defeatedly resume her seat. "Now, gentlemen, I believe the medium who summoned this spirit looks tired. We must let her have her rest."

"But you will do an interview for the paper, won't you?" Langley demanded.

Stuyvesant-French assessed him. A smile tipped the corner of his mouth and he glanced at Hazel. "I'll be doing that front-page story, but the story isn't finished yet."

"Well, when—?"

Stuyvesant-French waved aside the rest of the questions. Nodding to the Czarina, he gave her a cursory farewell. The other gentlemen dribbled out of the parlor, each engrossed in the debate and interpretation of the phantom, ignoring the wilted form of the Czarina as she dejectedly placed her head in her hands.

Chapter Nine

A minute spot of white, no larger than a dollar, is first noticed on the floor; this gradually increases in size, until there is a filmy, gauzy mass which rises fold on fold like a fountain . . . until there is enough there to permit the Spirit, who has crept out from the Cabinet under the black cloth and has been busy pushing out the white tulle, to get her head and shoulders well within the mass, when she rises swiftly and gracefully, and the dark cloth is drawn back into the Cabinet. I always want to applaude it, it is charming.

—Dr. H. H. Furness (The Seybert Commission—
University of Pennsylvania)

"You touched her, then. You held her."

"Yes."

"And she was real?"

"All kinds of real. Her body was one hundred percent very much alive female right down to the way it quivers when a man pulls her to him."

After this exchange with Edward, Cornelius stared into the cold hearth, unmindful that there was no fire there.

"Do you want to go with me?" Stuyvesant-French asked while the valet held out his jacket.

"No. The fun and games are over. I think I'll just retire to my room at the Lafayette Club. See you tomorrow, French." Cook placed his bowler on his head.

Edward stared at him in the mirror while his man whisked the shoulders. "I told you I was there to trap her. Now that I have, you look as if the world were coming to an end. What's gotten into you?"

"Nothing. So you're meeting with her now? To cut the deal?"

"Yes." Edward smirked. "I still think you should come. Perhaps the fun and games aren't over."

"No, thank you."

"They're frauds and I proved it. I'd think you'd be congratulating me." Edward's expression turned puzzled.

"I know. I thought so, too." Cook paused. "I guess deep down we all have a small wish to believe in the unbelievable. Good night, French."

❧ ❧

"There he is." Lavinia stared out her bedroom window. She'd left the lights out in her room in order to be able to see the park. A tall man walked from a hack toward the center of the square. Outside the streets were quiet. This time of night there was no one else around except a street-sweeper on the far end cleaning the slate curbs.

"What are you going to tell him? How will you explain to him—?" Hazel didn't finish.

Lavinia took a deep breath. "There's no explaining anything to him. He won't listen. He doesn't care. I just have to think of what to say when I see him." She threw a black muslin shawl over her shoulders and pinned on her hat. The iridescent black feathers that adorned it were perfect. All she needed was some jet earrings and a hankie, and she'd look like she was going to a funeral. Her funeral.

"Be careful, Vinia." Hazel pressed her hand and walked her out. "Do you want me to come with you?"

"No," Lavinia answered. "I'm going to work this out. We may not like how it ends, but let's see what I can do in the meantime."

She gave Hazel a peck on the cheek and Rawl held open the front door. The door shut behind her. She crossed the street with the feeling that Rawl and Hazel watched her through the brownstone's dark windows.

"Miss? Miss?"

She stopped. A large figure stood near the square's iron fence. It was a man who had attended the séance. She remembered him. He was an older, well-dressed man who sported an unsual wealth of whiskers.

"Miss, I hope I didn't frighten you. I know you're going to meet him." The man stepped into the path. A hack rolled by on the street behind her. It headed toward Fourteenth Street, the clop of the horses' hooves, the jangling harnesses, shattering the night's stillness.

She shook her head in dismay. "This is hardly proper—"

"I know. But I need to talk to you." The man gave a nod toward the center of the park. "Before he does."

"Why?" She knew she should walk away. A lady would. But again, a real lady didn't wear white greasepaint for a parlorful of men, nor did they hold clandestine meetings in Washington Square with a blackmailer. Besides, she could see the man was almost desperate. There was an edge of suffering in his voice. He wanted something so badly that she was compelled to listen.

He brushed down his whiskers as if agitated. He moved onto the path with her as if he didn't want to be seen skulking in the greenery. "Stuyvesant-French is going to put you out of business, Miss Murphy. I can't stop him and neither can you."

"Perhaps, but why is this your concern?"

"I apologize. It isn't my business. Furthermore, I think you're probably a fake. French himself told me how he caught you in the parlor tonight." He hesitated and glanced through the manicured shrubs that obfuscated the center of the square where Stuyvesant-French was waiting. "I'm a fool. I always have been," he muttered, his gaze flickering with pain. "I know you're really just an actress, maybe worse." He looked at her and Lavinia was struck by the sadness in his eyes. Even in the inadequate gaslight of the street, she could see the deep hurt he held inside him.

"I'm sixty-five years old, Miss Murphy. For these past thirty-five years, I've lived my life alone. There's never been anyone for me. Because no one was like her. No one." He turned away.

She swore she saw the excruciating glimmer of tears in the corner of his eye. She wanted to ask him what he was talking about, but she knew he would explain if she just gave him the time.

"Edward looks just like his father, you see." The gentleman's mouth hardened in a bitter smile. "Vanadder lost his handsomeness, but only because he was rotten inside. He always was rotten inside. Edward is so much like him at times: cruel, calculating, unfeeling . . ." He met her gaze. The desperation in his eyes shocked her. "But it's a facade. Inside, he has her in him. Alice. My Alice." He grabbed Lavinia's arm. "Please. French told me you talked to her. That was why Vanadder came to you. I know you trick people. But I thought maybe some of it was theatrics . . . and that maybe some of it was real." He stared down at her. His expression was so forlorn and despairing, she could hardly bear to look at him. "Is it possible to contact the other side? Have you really ever spoken to Alice? It's been thirty-five years since I saw her last. Thirty-five years is so long. It's a desert. This life is interminable. Oh, but give me one minute with her, and I'll go another thirty-five. I just want to know if you ever did contact her. Just once. I'd give my fortune and then some to know that. You see, I want to ask her something. She died so young, there was so much unfinished business. I must know that I'll see her in the hereafter. I have to know that I'll see her, and—and—that if things could be done again—" His voice caught in his throat; the words dwindled to a whisper. "—that next time she'd choose me."

Lavinia's heart constricted. This was the worst part—the desperate, tortured people alone in their grief, reaching for lies that would comfort them.

But she couldn't lie to this man. She couldn't tell him that she knew Alice, that her spirit hovered just beyond the parlor doors, to summon as Lavinia wished just so that she could fill her coffers with a living man's money. She couldn't bring herself to dupe him.

But to crush his hope—while truthful—seemed ever so much worse.

A silhouette appeared at the end of the path where it ended in the center of the square. It was Stuyvesant-French. She knew he stood too far away to know what they were talking about; still, she could see how he crossed his arms over his chest, how his legs stood slightly apart. He was judging her. His height and strength came across even in silhouette. He towered in condemnation; he was a metaphor for her conscience. She hated him.

A man's voice in her ear brought her back to reality. The gentleman pleaded softly. "If you ever even *thought* you might have contacted Alice, perhaps we could try—"

"Do you think Stuyvesant-French does have his mother inside him?" She frowned. "He seems so much like his father. Wilhelm was good to me, but I saw his cruelties. I knew how he worked."

"He has Alice's goodness. I see it on occasion within him and it astounds me. But can you tell me if you ever—?"

She placed her gloved finger on the man's lips.

He silenced and waited.

Slowly, she spoke, her gaze darting toward the ominous figure of Stuyvesant-French in the distance. "I can tell you this: Wilhelm Vanadder had nothing but darkness in his soul. His son, I fear, has that same darkness. There is one thing I know about Alice, sir. I'll tell it to you, and then you must never ask me anything about her again. Do you promise?"

He nodded; his eyes lit with the hellish fire of hope.

She stared again at the tall man standing at the end of the path. Stuyvesant-French was going to ruin her tonight, take away all she'd worked for, destroy her to the point where she might never quite recover from it.

She looked up at the gentleman beside her, his gaze imploring. She swallowed and said softly, "I will not explain it. Nor can I give you logic and reason why I know it, but I will tell you this one truth about Alice Stuyvesant-French, and then you must live out your life like everybody else, never understanding what waits on the other side."

She took a deep breath. Inside she was dying for this man. She prayed she could help him. Gently, she said, "Sir, Alice made a terrible mistake. She died unhappy and even Wilhelm knew it. She should have picked you, sir, and I know Alice regrets it. I can't tell you how I know this, but I do know it. Utterly." She took a deep breath. "Now, please, go on your way and don't ask me any more questions. What I've said is true, and I mustn't say any more. . . ."

He pinched the bridge of his nose as if he were fighting back tears. He didn't speak for a long moment, nor did she. She pressed his arm to console him, then she made to walk away toward the devil who stood in the center of the park.

"Miss Murphy," the ragged voice sounded behind her.

She stopped but didn't turn around. She had to face Stuyvesant-French, and do it now before she lost her courage. She couldn't afford any more delays.

"Thank you," he said simply, his anguish still showing. "Maybe I can suffer through this life now."

She nodded, still not looking at him.

"Her son would not be who he is without his father," he called out to her. "Maybe it's all been for the best. He's a good man, Lavinia Murphy. Just look for it when you talk to him. Appeal to the angel of his better nature, and you'll see it."

The angel of his better nature. The words tore at her. She shook her head, but she didn't look back. She knew even if she did, the gentleman would be gone.

❧ ❦

Stuyvesant-French gave her no greeting. Lavinia walked up to him just as the clock in the Reformed Dutch Church tolled midnight. Her gaze met his. They held for several seconds, then he led her to a bench.

She spoke first.

"I'd like to find some way that we can both get what we want, and I'd like to believe you do indeed have your half-sister's interests at heart." She studied him. He'd changed clothes since their last encounter. His shirt collar appeared freshly starched and his jacket pressed, but the vest he'd worn earlier, the one she'd run her fingers down, was the same. She stared at it, then had to glance away. She didn't like remembering how he had felt beneath her hand, the dark silk smooth and soft over a chest hewn of iron.

"You're in no position to bargain, Miss Murphy." His gaze flickered over to the walkway where she'd had her conversation with the gentleman. She wondered if, in the darkness, Stuyvesant-French had been unable to recognize the man. She hoped so. The last thing she wanted to do was have to make up more explanations.

"You seem to have won this battle," she said, "but though you've caught me, I still have one last hand."

"You want to continue this battle?" He lifted one eyebrow. "The next time I'll drag you out from that screen and rip off your clothing if that's what it takes to expose you."

She took sustenance in how she was holding up. She wanted to fall weeping at his feet and beg for mercy; instead she sat stiffly, her feet tucked beneath her skirt, her voice calm to the point of frigidity. "Only you and I know what happened behind the screen, Mr. Stuyvesant-French. If you want to announce to the whole world what I really am, then you risk being cast aside as one of the disbelievers. You'd be in the poor position of having to prove what you say and if you think you'll ever catch me again, you're wrong. Then you've won the battle and lost the war." She gave him a level stare. "So, as I see it, you need me as much as I need you now."

He eyed her through half-closed lids. Suspicion was thick on his face.

"What are you going for? You want money, is that it?"

"Your father left me a fortune. I'll need a reason to walk away from it."

"The reason will be that you cannot win."

"I know. If I hold to the will, I'll lose by attrition. Still, you're asking me to walk away from it, and by my doing so, it helps you. I'm entitled to something."

"How much money?"

She paused. "I don't know. I need to think this through. If I'm to allow my reputation to be damaged, I'll need to plan for the future."

"If you want to plan for the future, why don't you just hook up with one of your keepers like the old gent I just saw you with?"

His aspersion wounded her but she hid her hurt well. She had to remain strong and cold. There were more futures than even hers riding on her now. "I also must have assurances that Daisy will be the recipient of Wilhelm's money. I'm not going to walk away from this with you getting the lion's share."

He caught her chin in one hand and held her face to his. "Your arrogance, Miss Murphy, never fails to astound me." His words were biting. "Yes, yes, we wouldn't want Vanadder's *son* to get anything. What a tragedy that would be. Much better the bastard should just earn his wealth on his own without putting his dirty fingers on his father's legacy." He took a deep breath as if to inhale his anger. "I don't need the Vanadder fortune, and I don't want it. I'm doing this for Daisy. You'll see that when the will is revised."

"Fine," she said softly, staring at him, helpless to remove her face from his hand. "In the meantime, I'm going to decide what I want for my cooperation. This may be my last opportunity to ensure my future. I'm going to think hard on it."

"While you're thinking, think of this." He smirked. "If you and I don't reach an agreement tonight, in the morning I'm going to have my lawyers begin contesting the will. After I begin that process, I won't care about your little blackmail scheme, *Countess.*"

"And if I'm gone? If I pick up with my family in the middle of the night and just leave? With whom will you contest this will? I might lose by attrition if I stay and fight you, but if I leave, you will lose, Mr. Stuyvesant-French, because no one will be able to find the heiress and the proceedings will go into limbo. Forever if need be. And Daisy—if you really do care about her—will get nothing."

He dropped his hold on her and leaned back on the bench. His gaze held contempt but also a small amount of begrudging respect. "You have thought about this, haven't you? You've mapped out every avenue."

"I've had to take care of myself in this life. I've had to earn my way and I don't want to give up what I've earned without something in return."

"I'm only making you give up séances, Miss Murphy. You don't have to give up the rest of your living."

She wanted to slap his face, but because she'd taken his scorn before, this time it didn't cut so deeply. "I don't earn my money in the manner of which you speak, and I don't plan on starting just because you're trying to damage my reputation as a spiritualist."

"But why make it difficult on yourself? Why fight me over this will when you can just set up house with one of those gentlemen you entertain in your parlor?"

"Because I'm not that kind of woman."

"Don't be absurd."

His conviction sliced her. Maybe if he were just another aged wealthy fool begging for a séance, she might not have taken it so hard, but Stuyvesant-French was no bewildered old man. He was the one who'd kissed her. And he was the one she'd kissed back, as horrible as the idea was.

Stuyvesant-French wanted nothing from her but the precious truth, but the truth was more costly than she could spare. Indeed, his words did hurt her. Because when this man—this truthseeker—

maligned her character with such confidence, even she found it difficult not to believe him.

"I want a future," she announced softly. "I'll not walk away without one."

"What kind of future could anyone provide you, Miss Murphy?" He smirked. "You almost sound like a maiden yearning for a proposal."

"Perhaps I am. A husband is a future. The right husband is much better than a living."

"I can't provide you with a husband, *Countess*. That kind of scheming is women's work, and it belongs in the parlor—or, as in your case—the bedroom."

Her own anger rose. "Mock me, but if you take away my livelihood, I'll have nothing and so will you."

He studied her. "What amount of money are we talking about here?"

"Money runs out. You'll be damaging my one means of making more. I need something more than money."

"What exactly do you want, then, Miss Murphy?" His expression grew thunderous.

"I want— I want another life if you're bound to take this one. If Hazel is no longer going to be the Czarina and I'm no longer the Countess, we need to be someone else, then."

"How can I do that? You think me a magician?" he scoffed.

She stared at him. An idea began to stretch and yawn inside her head. "I need to ruminate on this." She looked deep into the interior of the park square as if somehow she might find her answers in the night. "I'd like to get out of New York. We can't live here anymore if we're to be stripped of our identity. We need to go elsewhere. Perhaps abroad—"

"The money will take you anywhere you feel like going," he bit out, his face taut with frustration.

"But how do two young unmarried women travel respectably

abroad? We need new identities. We need to be someone else. Someone better than we are now."

"Indeed you do."

She ignored his sarcasm. "If there's an opportunity here for Hazel and I to elevate ourselves from the working class, I'm going to take it, Mr. Stuyvesant-French, in spite of your ridicule. I just need the time to figure out how to go about it."

He shook his head. "I'm not giving you time. You work this out now. What do you want?" When she didn't answer, he posed his question again, this time more brutally, "Tell me in a word, Murphy old girl, or this meeting ends and we will never have it again."

"I want a husband." The words tumbled out of her mouth and grew like some kind of haunched creature that had leapt onto the bench and now sat between them. She wanted to shove the confession away, to run and hide, but the creature was out, licking its jaws and laughing at her.

"Who would marry you, Miss Murphy?"

She expected such words. She deflected them with a swift recovery. "If not for me, then for Hazel. We have others we provide for, you see. If Hazel were happily and well married, then everyone would be taken care of, forever. I would then be free to find another occupation."

"I hate to be the death's head at the feast, Miss Murphy, but you and your sister and that parlor with the Turkish corner are what they call in more refined circles 'notorious.' No decent man would take an adventuress to the altar, not even your dear sister."

"That's why we must go abroad. We need to wipe away the past. Become someone new. Someone respectable. We need to travel beneath the respectability of an untarnishable name." Her gaze flickered down. She paused, then hesitantly looked at him. "Stuyvesant is a very respectable name."

His gaze slid to hers. He tipped his head back and laughed.

"Laugh if you must, but Hazel and I could travel quite well if you gave us an introduction."

"I'm going to give you some money and then I'm going to make you go away, and that's all the participation I'll do. Go abroad on your own if you like. I can't stop you."

"I want a future for us, not just money. If you take away our livelihood and give us nothing to replace it, what have we got then?"

He laughed again. "You've got money, stupid girl. Listen, I'll give you a sum and we'll tie this up tomorrow. If you're cautious with it, it'll take care of you in your old age."

"But a husband would do that better. If you can't find one for me, then I must have one for Hazel. I must."

He sat forward on the bench, his face right in hers. "If you think I'm going to provide you women with false identities in order for you to snare husbands, you're more daft than I thought. Neither of you are good prospects. Your reputations being what they are, you may as well resign yourselves to concubinage or a nice warm friendship with your banker which I'll be glad to set up once we have all the papers signed."

"If we went away, say to London, and you put the word out we were fabulous heiresses, then we could start anew with the past behind us. At least if you did the entrée, Hazel and I could go in as equals. We could make our own futures with that much."

"I would be duping people."

"I must insist upon a future."

"I will not do this. You'll have to be happy with a bank note."

"I'll need that too. I don't want to be introduced as a fabulous heiress without it being somewhat true."

He shook his head as if he thought he were hallucinating. "I have to further diminish your plans, Miss Murphy, but I'll have you know I have no social connections in London whatsoever."

"But you're a Stuyvesant."

"And illegitimate." The corner of his mouth tipped in derision.

"Give me a sum and give me an introduction. I'll do the rest. In London, they won't care about your birth. All they'll care about is your millions and they'll accept us. Why, haven't you seen the papers lately? I saw only two weeks ago that Lillian August is going to marry the Duke of Winchfeld. Everyone on this side of the Atlantic knows she's just some bumpkin from Denver. And remember, her father was abandoned as a baby on the docks here at Castle Garden—why, he doesn't even know what country he's from, let alone who his parents are—he's a nobody, just some man who struck it rich in gold, and now his only child is reaping the benefits of it."

He shook his head. "I'm not going to do this. You couldn't sell me on the spiritual telegraph, so you're certainly not going to fleece me on this husband fraud. But I'll tell you, Miss Murphy, you've got a hell of a gift for imagination. You astound me."

"It's a simple deal. We get the money and an introduction in London. I'll sign your papers when Hazel has a husband."

"I'm not going to do this. You'll take the money I give you and be on your merry way."

She stood and looked down at him. She'd never seen him as angry as he was now. A small smile lifted the corner of her mouth. She reached out and patted his taut, angry cheek. "You mean on your m-a-r-r-y way. We'll see you for tea tomorrow to plan the rest of the details."

"I'll just start the proceedings to contest the will."

"And then you'll come to tea at an empty house. We'll be gone—off to some other state where we can begin our mediumships anew."

"I'm not going to play matchmaker for two trollops."

"Heiresses, Edward. Heiresses." She stared at him. He stared at her.

Before he could say another word, she departed, taking the path at a hurried walk, anxious to give Hazel the good news.

Chapter Ten

"She is a person of genius," Henley had said to me, "but a person of genius must do something."
I could not accept this explanation. . . .

—W. B. Yeats, disputing Madame Blavatsky's failures

azel stared at Lavinia as she rose for the third time to assess the contents of the tea tray. It was four o'clock. Jamie was in his best suit, rebelliously fidgeting in the armchair while his fingers worked on his starched collar. Eva and Fanny flanked either end of the settee. They wore their best taffeta dresses and hairbows and looked for all the world like two French porcelain dolls.

"Jamie, please. Leave the collar alone." Lavinia walked to him and pulled down his hands. Truantly he sat on them, but then his leg began to swing.

"This is madness, Lavinia. He's not going to come." Hazel stared at her sister as if she were looking at a lunatic.

"He'll come. I know it." Lavinia straightened a teacup then strode to the window to look for a carriage. The street was filled with hacks but not the familiar black one.

"What if he doesn't come?" Hazel rose from her seat. The two little girls stared at her until she wanted to cringe. "We should make other plans. Now, while there's time."

"He'll come. We'll wait another hour."

"He might be going to the authorities." Hazel heard the panic in her voice. She whispered, "Vinia, we've got to keep our heads."

"This is the right thing," Lavinia whispered back. "This is a chance to give you and Eva a real home. And perhaps your husband will take to Jamie and Fanny. Who knows?"

"We stick together. Remember?" Hazel looked back at the children. Jamie was making faces at the girls and Fanny was giving it all back, much to Eva's delight. "You know I want the best for Eva, but I don't want a home without you. So let's make other plans, I beg of you."

A furrow marred Lavinia's brow. She stared out the window as if staring would produce all that she wanted. "That man hurt you, Hazel. He took what was only yours to give. You deserve another man now. Only the best. This way—"

"This way what? Do rich men not hurt women? They do."

"I'll find you one who won't."

"I don't need a husband. I've done without one this long. I've borne the shame. I'll bear it as long as I have to."

Lavinia finally turned to her. She took her hands and whispered urgently, "Forgive me for doing this, Hazel. I know my plans are madness, they always have been, but I've got to give you this chance. We were never able to find retribution for what happened to you. You know by the time we had the money and the means, Hinchley had sold the orphanage and left town. I'm angry about it every day. Every moment I look at our dear Eva, I feel rage in my heart. I wanted him to pay for what he did with you. I still would like him to pay, but in the meantime, they say living well is the best revenge. So we must live well and here's our chance to do it."

Hazel stared at her sister. Lavinia was always scheming, but in the past her plans had always benefited them. Her gaze slid to Eva. Her heart melted as it always did. Who was she to deny anything to this angel from heaven, all blonde curls and cornflower blue, silk taffeta bows? Eva had come under the worst sort of circum-stances, but from the first moment she'd gazed upon that tiny red face, Hazel knew there was a God to give her such a precious gift in midst of such cruel fate. "Oh, Lavinia, you know I could never cross you." She tugged a grin from the corner of her mouth. "I hope he does show. You know I would give my life to provide Eva with a real home and a real father."

"I'll get it for you." Lavinia frowned and returned her gaze to the street. "I swear I'll get it for you."

🌿 🌿

It was five o'clock when the carriage pulled in front of the Fifth Avenue Hotel. The wheelchair was out first, then the carriage driver gently retrieved his passenger out of the cab and placed her in it.

"I'm not going to stay, Herrington."

"Very good, miss." The driver wheeled her into the lobby.

"Mr. Stuyvesant-French, is he in?" Daisy inquired at the desk.

A nattily dressed clerk nodded. "Yes, Miss Vanadder. The bell-boy was just about to take a message up to his rooms."

"I'll go with you, if you'd be so kind?" Daisy grinned. "I confess I do adore the elevator here."

The clerk smiled. He gave her the note the bellboy had brought, then he took the handles of the chair from her coachman. "Very good, Miss Vanadder. It's my pleasure."

They arrived on the fourth floor. Daisy knocked at the hotel door and almost jumped at the nasty growl that greeted her.

"Who's there?" the voice boomed.

"It's the big bad wolf," Daisy answered lightly.

She heard footsteps, then the door opened wide.

"Dear heavens, you look terrible, Edward. I had no idea you were under the weather."

"I'm not under the weather, Daze. I just didn't expect company." Edward stood aside while the clerk rolled Daisy into his suite.

Daisy released a rather theatrical little gasp. She held out an empty glass that was left by the leather barrel chair. "You've been drinking. And so early in the day?"

Edward gave the clerk a dollar. The man quickly departed as if he were well aware of the hotel's guest and his infamous moods.

"She's really getting to you, isn't she?" Daisy wheeled her chair toward him. "Did you discover her to be a fraud? Cornelius said that was what you wanted to do."

"Anyone who tells fortunes is a fraud whether I expose them or not."

"Oh," she placed her hand to her forehead, "you are a killjoy today, Edward."

He grumbled something.

"And look at you. What's got into you today? The black death? You haven't shaved, you haven't even put on a tie or collar."

"I told you, Daze, I didn't expect company. I've had some thinking to do today."

"Thinking about what?"

"About you and Father, and what to do about the Vanadder will."

"I thought that was all decided. You were going to be Machiavellian, as I recall, and I was going to ignore you and do as I pleased." She smiled.

He cracked a wry little grin. "Well done," he murmured.

She tugged on his sleeve affectionately. "Order me up some tea, will you? And here, there was a message sent. I brought it up for you." She handed him the note.

He opened it, scanned it, then put it aside.

"Well, who's it from, Edward?"

"Let me ring for tea." He went over to a heavy-tasseled rope and pulled it.

"You're avoiding my questions, and being rather artless about it, I do say." She rolled over to the table where he'd discarded the note. "It's from her, isn't it?" she whispered as she read it. "Why, you cad. You stood her up. How dare you." She looked up at her brother.

"She's not worthy of your consideration, Daisy, so forget her."

"I liked her. She wasn't like the other women with which I've been acquainted. She seemed so real. This chair didn't embarrass her at all."

"Well, you won't be seeing her again, so don't think about her."

A knock came at the door. The sound of a commotion and several bickering voices came from behind it. Edward opened the door and there stood the clerk, the bellboy, the valet, and, finally, Lavinia Murphy, who stared at him as if she were staring at Old Nick himself.

"I told this woman that she could not see you without an appointment," the clerk huffed. "I caught her trailing the bellboy up here as he was attempting to announce her."

The bellboy remained silent, his head following the volley to Stuyvesant-French.

"Did you ring for me, sir?" the valet chimed in, oblivious to the tensions.

Edward ran an exasperated hand through his hair. "Send up some tea. And you, Mr. Johns, may take this woman back to the street where she belongs."

"Edward!" Daisy came forward. "How dare you be so rude. Come in, Miss Murphy. We were just about to have some tea."

Edward wrapped both his arms around his chest and glowered. The bellboy, the clerk and valet all leaned through the door as if they were lapping up the beginnings of a most delicious scandal.

"I came here to speak with you, Mr. Stuyvesant-French." Lavinia didn't move from the threshold. She was alabaster pale. Against the dark blue of her high-collared gown, her face looked as fragile as porcelain. "I just need to know if we have a deal or not. If not, I'll be on my way and you will not lay eyes on me again."

"You look upset, Miss Murphy. Please do come in. Have some

tea." Daisy paused and glanced at the men crowding the door. "Some tea, if you please." All at once they seemed to find themselves. They stumbled over one another to leave the threshold and close the door behind them.

"How do you find any privacy here, Edward? This place is more crowded than Vanderbilt's train station." Daisy motioned to a settee. Lavinia woodenly seated herself, but all the while her eyes were on Edward.

Daisy turned to her brother also. The two women stared until he seemed to want to throttle the both of them.

"I have no business with you, Miss Murphy. You had no right to come to my rooms," he snapped.

"Just tell me what your intentions are, then I may plan accordingly. That was why I invited you to tea. Now I need my answer regardless."

"What are your intentions, Edward?" Daisy looked at him wide-eyed.

His hands seemed to itch for her neck. "This is just between Miss Murphy and myself. It really doesn't concern you, Daisy."

"She's not pregnant, is she?"

"NO!" Edward and Lavinia both cried out, their faces frozen in horror.

Daisy clapped her chest. "Oh, do forgive the indelicacy of that last question. I don't know what possessed me."

"I don't know what possessed you either," Edward rumbled, his expression as black as night.

"Edward, it's just that this is all so curious. You do forgive me, Miss Murphy?" Daisy turned to her. "I'm just so confused as to why my brother is avoiding you."

Lavinia nodded. She clutched her little handbag with gloveless fingers. Daisy couldn't help but notice the sapphire ring was gone. She wondered why the woman wasn't wearing it, but after that last question, she dared not ask another.

"Just give me my answer, Mr. Stuyvesant-French, and then I'll leave you alone." Lavinia stared at him, but her shoulders were tense and her expression could only be described as one of open anxiety.

"Are you going to answer her, Edward?"

Stuyvesant-French looked at his sister. "I haven't decided yet."

"Decided to answer her? Or decided the answer to her inquiry? They're not the same, you know."

"You are being infuriating today, aren't you?"

Daisy smiled.

Lavinia remained silent. Just staring.

"I will not accept your terms, Miss Murphy. So you may take your leave." Edward locked gazes with her.

Lavinia stood. Daisy had never seen so beautiful a face so utterly despairing. "Then that is how it is to be. Very well. I'll go and you shall not see me again."

"Wait!" Daisy rolled between them. "What are you both talking about? I have the feeling this concerns the will, and if so, then it concerns me, so I'm going to demand an answer. Miss Murphy, what is my brother declining?"

"He wants to destroy my business in order for him to prove your father insane. I made him an offer that I would acquiesce my rights to your father's money if he could provide my sister and I an introduction abroad. He has declined this offer, so I will take my leave."

"Wait! Is this true, Edward?" Daisy's eyes were round as saucers.

"Indeed. She's nothing but a blackmailing adventuress, and we're best to wash our hands of her."

"But this is perfect! Why didn't you tell me, Edward?"

Both Stuyvesant-French and Lavinia looked at Daisy.

Daisy laughed. "Don't you see? Edward, you said you wanted me to travel, to make new friends. If I go with the Murphy sisters to Europe, I'll have two companions to go with me!"

Silence boomed through the suite.

Ominously Edward said, "Daisy, if you think I would let you travel with two such hardened characters as this woman and her sister, you've lost your mind."

"How do we know about their characters, Edward? We don't know them at all. So let's get to know them."

"You cannot fraternize with these women, Daisy, I forbid it."

"Oh, pooh." Daisy turned to Lavinia. "Would you and your sister like to pay a call tomorrow afternoon?"

Lavinia looked to Edward, then back at his sister. "If I could be so bold, Miss Vanadder, I'd rather you take our hospitality which your brother has so soundly rejected. May I give you my card and expect you at four?"

Daisy's face was all smiles. "Why, that would be lovely, Miss Murphy. I have to admit, ever since I heard about you, I've been dying to see your famous parlor."

"You're just doing this to thwart me, aren't you, Daze?" Edward's gaze was thunderous.

"That's part of it, Edward," she turned to Lavinia, "but I confess, the other part of it is sheer curiosity. I find I've few friends and lots of imagination. A visit abroad with two practicing mediums seems tailor-made just for me."

Lavinia suddenly gave a smile of her own. Her brow cleared. The worry seeped from her eyes. As if she could read the humor in the situation, she shook Daisy's hand and turned to her brother. "My invitation extends to you both. I hope to see you tomorrow."

"She won't be there and neither will I," Edward said to her, ignoring Daisy's chuckle.

"Tomorrow at four, then." Lavinia tossed a smile to Daisy. She left before the tea arrived.

It was like a play, one they were forced to act out time and again. At four o'clock Jamie was back in his suit, his fingers again tugging at the collar. Eva and Fanny were dressed in their taffeta and eyeing Jamie from opposite ends of the settee. The tea table was perfect, but still Lavinia was up and down making sure every cup, every sugar lump, every wedge of lemon was artfully arranged on the tray.

"Oh my God, I don't think they're going to come, Lavinia," Hazel burst out.

The doorbell rang downstairs.

Hazel's eyes widened. "Oh my God, they've come."

Lavinia gave herself one last primp in the mirror. She looked back at the children. They eyed her solemnly as if she were their captor. "Smile, children, smile! We must look presentable! Jamie, for the last time, I beg of you, leave the collar alone!"

Jamie's hands went beneath him. On cue, the leg began to swing.

Lavinia positioned herself in front of the mantel. Hazel perched on a chair. Rawl announced the guests.

"Miss Vanadder. Mr. Stuyvesant-French."

Lavinia's heart pounded. She didn't know why she was so nervous. Daisy Vanadder already liked her. She knew it. It was just that man. He hated her. She could see it when he walked into the parlor, his expression dark with disapproval.

"Miss Vanadder, I'd like you to meet my sister Miss Hazel Murphy." Lavinia brought Hazel toward the door. Daisy took her hand and rolled herself into the center of the room.

"Who are these precious children?" Daisy asked, turning to Lavinia.

"This is Fanny and Eva," Hazel said, going to them. Eva slid to the edge of the settee and into her arms. Fanny, the older girl, merely stared at the woman in the wheelchair.

"And this is Jamie," Lavinia added, glancing at the boy.

Daisy seemed entranced. She looked at Jamie, then back at Stuyvesant-French. "Edward, I daresay the boy reminds me of you at this age. Look at his brow. It's absolutely devilish."

"Is that fun to ride?" Jamie asked amid the ensuing laughter.

Daisy smiled. "My wheelchair? I suppose it does look fun. It must be pretty strange to you to see a woman rolling everywhere when she should be walking."

"Can't you walk?" the boy asked.

"Jamie!" Hazel cried, mortified.

Daisy took Jamie's hand in her own and glanced at the other women. "No, it's all right. He's curious, as he should be. Oh, I could tell you stories about Edward as a boy that would make this little fellow's *faux pas* look like nothing."

"True?" Lavinia raised one eyebrow and looked at the angry man standing at the doorway.

"Absolutely," Daisy said. "Edward, why don't you tell them about the time you threw a rock into the—"

"They don't need to hear about that, Daisy," Edward interrupted.

Lavinia smiled. It was a joy to see this man so uncomfortable. "Where are my manners? Please do sit down, Mr. Stuyvesant-French. We've a place for you right here on the settee." She motioned to the seat between Fanny and Eva.

He hesitated, then he moved forward rashly like a man trying to prove he was not hesitating.

The two little girls watched him as he lowered his large frame down between them. He eyed them suspiciously, his face not cracking the slightest smile.

What a picture he made, Lavinia thought, this dark, furious man, trapped between two little wide-eyed taffeta-bowed tea cakes. He couldn't have looked more ridiculous. Lavinia lapped it up like a dish of cream.

"Shall I pour?" Hazel looked to Lavinia.

"That would be lovely," Lavinia answered, slipping Stuyvesant-French a taunting little smile.

He scowled. She could have laughed, but his eyes promised retribution. Despite her amusement, his expression sent a tingle of warning down her spine.

"Shall the children be traveling with us, then?" Daisy asked after Hazel gave her a cup of tea.

Lavinia opened her mouth, but didn't know what to say. "I— Well . . . we couldn't possibly leave them behind."

Hazel added nervously, "We're all a family now, you see. The children were orphans. Lavinia and I are their only providers."

"We consider Jamie, Eva and Fanny our brother and sisters. We just couldn't part with them. We've even changed their names to Murphy." Lavinia looked at Edward and wanted to wipe the smirk off his face. She knew what he was thinking. It was what most of society thought, but, except in Hazel's case, it wasn't true. Fanny and Jamie weren't theirs; they had come from the orphanage. And they had all changed their names to Murphy, at least in practice.

"How wonderful you are to have taken them in," Daisy announced. "There aren't many single women who would suffer the gossips in order to care for a young child."

"We've managed through most of our difficulties." Lavinia turned her gaze to Edward. The smirk was still there. She knew he thought the worst. So damn him.

"Miss Murphy, how soon do you think you, your sister and the children would be ready to travel? I'm not encumbered. Anytime would be good for me. The sooner the better." Daisy placed her teacup on the table and folded her hands sweetly in her lap.

The idea of actually going abroad, of actually having the benefits she'd put to Stuyvesant-French, threw Lavinia off balance. She supposed in her mind she'd rather given up on the idea, especially since Stuyvesant-French had failed to come to tea yesterday. Now everything was working out so incredibly she couldn't believe it. And when she looked into Stuyvesant-French's baleful green eyes, she knew it was nothing but a fairy tale. He was going to wreck everything; she just didn't know how yet.

"We could go anytime, I suppose," she said cautiously, "but there is the matter of the will." Her gaze locked with Stuyvesant's. "The terms of our agreement haven't been mapped yet. These things need to be worked out to everyone's satisfaction."

"Of course." Daisy turned to her brother. "I'll book passage tomorrow, Edward. So why don't you take Miss Murphy to dinner tonight and come to a final agreement? I'm sure over a nice Bordeaux you could work out all the details."

"Like hell . . ." he began, until his gaze stopped dead in front of Eva's. The fearful little girl stared at him as if he'd just grown horns.

"Now, now, Edward. No naughty words in front of the children." Daisy smiled at Eva. The little girl tremulously returned it.

Lavinia put her hand to her mouth. Stuyvesant-French looked so utterly disconcerted as he stared down at Eva's innocent little face framed in the taffeta bow. She wondered if anyone had ever pulled him up as short as little Eva had just done with one innocent stare.

"In fact, I'd love to stay here longer and get to know the children better." Daisy waved at her brother and Lavinia. "You two run along to dinner. If I get in the way, I'll have Herrington take me home."

"You won't be in the way," Hazel assured her, but then she turned worried eyes to her sister. "But Lavinia, I'm not sure if you should go—"

"With Edward?" Daisy rolled to Hazel's side. "Why, he's a pussycat, my dear. Your sister will be in good hands."

Especially when those hands are wrapped around my neck, Lavinia thought as she glanced at Stuyvesant-French. In truth, it was admirable how he kept from frothing at the mouth; even now the anger gleamed in his eyes like burning jade.

"Ready for dinner, *Countess?*" He lifted one dark eyebrow.

"What a lovely opportunity. Let me gather my shawl." But still, her hand went to her throat as if his stare could choke her.

"We'll walk," French said gruffly to his coachman who waited in front of the brownstone. He took Lavinia's elbow and led her down the walkway toward Fourteenth Street.

"Where shall we go? Delmonico's? Everard's?" she panted, his anger and quick stride leaving her breathless.

"We'll go to my hotel suite. That's the only place to discuss this."

She stopped. He tried to take her arm, but she pulled back. "I won't go there. It isn't seemly."

"You weren't worried about that yesterday when you burst in without an announcement," he snapped.

"That was different. I just wanted a quick answer, and then I knew I'd be on my way. Besides, your sister and Hazel believe we're going to a public restaurant. This isn't seemly at all." She wondered if her voice gave away her panic.

Pedestrians were beginning to stare at them as they blocked the walkway. The sun had set early behind clouds and the ever-rising row of Manhattan buildings. The street was dark. Way down Fifth Avenue, she could see the man on his ladder just starting the lamps.

"You want me to call my lawyers and let all of New York in on our deal? Fine, then you'll have it at Delmonico's, and we'll see if you beat the gossips to London." He glared down at her. Several men passed by, obviously caught up in the drama being played out on the walkway. They whistled and hooted, but she hardly noticed them. All she could see was Stuyvesant-French and his rage. They were both bigger than life. She didn't need the lamplighter for that.

"I don't want any lawyers. I can't understand them. I want this agreement between us and only us." She clutched her handbag. She felt small and stupid defying him on the walkway as men were passing by on their way home from work. She was nothing but an insignificant woman, but she'd fought so hard to get what she had. She would fight longer if she must.

"Come." He took her arm. Gently, he led her northward along the walkway toward his hotel.

If he had acquiesced, she wouldn't know for sure until they were in his suite.

Chapter
Eleven

The Fifth Avenue Hotel had always frightened Lavinia. It was an imposing edifice where the male elite gathered to drink and have a dalliance. She supposed her name had been bandied through the halls once or twice. Many rich men were her clients and a few of them had made no secret of their attraction to her, but she had never fallen for any of them. She had stayed on her pedestal and rebuffed them all. Besides, none of them had ever offered her anything respectable. If her deepest wish be known, she might have considered a marriage proposal from one of them, but a proposal had never been forthcoming partly because most of the men she knew already had wives, and partly because she was not the kind of woman to whom men normally offered proposals of marriage.

Now she was finally at the notorious hotel with a man and under the strangest circumstances she had ever imagined.

"Dinner should arrive soon." Edward stared at her from across the suite's elegant parlor. He'd removed his hat and had even been about to remove his coat when he'd caught her horrified expression. If there was a gentleman inside him at all, he'd been persuaded to leave the coat on.

"We really don't have to have dinner," she said, nervously perching on the end of a leather chair. "If we could just iron out the details—perhaps sign a letter—one we both understand—"

"I'm only humoring Daisy on this. You understand that, don't you, Lavinia? May I call you Lavinia? No sense in formality now, eh?" He leaned back in the leather barrel chair and studied her. "My sister has a rebellious streak in her. She enjoys this little game she's playing with me now. She didn't like Vanadder, you see. Believe it or not, she doesn't even want his money. But she doesn't know what's good for her. Money can be everything. Especially if you have none." There was an iron quality to his voice, much harsher than she would have expected from a man of privilege such as he was.

"All I need is some kind of binding agreement." She leaned forward, almost in supplication. "Surely you can understand that. I just need a stipend and an introduction abroad. I'll do the rest."

"I suppose you could do a lot with an introduction and a fat bank account." His lips twisted with sarcasm and his eyes lowered to her figure. They became nothing but slits of probing, violating darkness. She didn't like the perusal at all.

"You're a beautiful woman, Lavinia Murphy. Men must tell you that all the time."

She turned away. She wished they could just be done with the business and leave. She'd had enough of him toying with her.

"I've heard men speak of you," he said slowly. "I didn't believe their talk until I met you. You do have a special power, but I think it has nothing to do with raising the dead—unless, of course, you've devised your own special cure for impotency."

"I really hate you, Mr. Stuyvesant-French." She didn't even look at him. "May we now continue with the discussion at hand?"

"I am discussing it." He stood and leaned his elbows back

against the mantelpiece. "I'm not going to be sucked into this hoax of passing you and your sister off as decent women just to please my sister. I want you to name your price, and then I want you to go the hell away."

"Your sister is clearly lonely. Where is the harm in giving her companionship during her travels? And if being in her company should elevate Hazel and me in the eyes of society, then what's the difference to you?"

"You soil my half-sister just by speaking her name." The venom in his voice cut her to the quick. "I forbid her to keep company with a couple of whores and their gaggle of illegitimate whelps."

Anger choked her. Somehow he always seemed to go right to her Achilles' heel. He had his own special way of destroying and that was why it was best to get this evening over with as fast as she could.

"Name your price, Lavinia. I'll give you a cheque this night and you can sign the papers I have at the desk over there." He nodded behind her. "Then you and I shall part company, and this nightmare will be over."

She stared at him. Inside, the will to fight began to crumple and die. It had been an absurd idea. She and Hazel weren't going to marry into respectability any more than this man's sister was ever going to walk. Suddenly she realized her head was pounding. She hadn't eaten much that day and her hands trembled. It was over. Finally over. She couldn't win against this man, and accepting that fact brought an unexpected relief. It should have made her glad, but she found she wasn't glad, she was just tired and defeated.

"I'll take a sum and I'll sign your papers, Mr. Stuyvesant-French." She rubbed her throbbing temple. "But then you will in turn promise to leave me and my family alone."

"My pleasure." He smiled. His teeth were white and rather wolfish. He was ungodly attractive when he smiled, and she could see that where women were concerned he was used to getting his way. "There's a smart girl," he murmured, "and do call me Edward. We're certainly friends now, aren't we, Lavinia?"

"Just show me the papers." She blinked back hot tears. She was broken but she vowed not to suffer the ultimate indignity by letting him see her cry about it.

"Fine." He rose and shuffled through some documents at his desk.

She rubbed her cheeks, discreetly ridding them of any watery tracks of betrayal.

"Here. You'll see everything's in order. It all goes to Daisy, as I promised." He placed a stack of documents on a small table by her chair, then handed her a fountain pen filled with ink. She began signing her name at the X a thousand times over, it seemed. When she was done she was almost blinded by it all.

"Here you go. I think you'll find I was quite generous given the trying circumstances." He handed her a cheque.

She glanced at it, not even registering the amount. All she could see was that it was from his personal account at the Bank of New-York.

It didn't really matter. If she were rich tomorrow, or poor, nothing would really change. The elusiveness of a decent life would still be as beyond her reach as the ghosts with which she claimed to communicate. "The Countess" and "the Czarina" would continue their trade but without the chance of ever becoming truly respectable.

"Where are you going?" he demanded when she rose and walked to the door.

"I believe our business is concluded." She placed her hand on the doorknob.

Suddenly he was beside her, removing it. "I promised you dinner."

"I'm really not hungry."

"But you must allow me to make amends for all the harsh words we've had. You understand, I had to protect my sister."

"Yes," she whispered, unable to look at him. She couldn't bear him to see into her eyes.

"Come, have dinner with me. We'll share that bottle of Bordeaux and, perhaps, find we can be friends."

She wanted to laugh. His statement was ridiculous.

"Come," he said softly.

She looked at him. The corner of his mouth tilted in a wry smile. His eyes had warmed. When he asked for something, it was hard to refuse him. She suddenly could see him as a little boy; he must have been a heartbreaker just like Jamie. She couldn't understand how Wilhelm could have turned his back on his son unless he, too, had glimpsed the cold soul she knew so well.

"Just one glass of wine. To seal our bargain." He took her hand.

The door knocked. Dinner arrived. The maître d' entered with two waiters and several carts, and they began to set up the meal by the window.

She told herself she would stay only because she was hungry. It wasn't because of the company. Every time she looked at Stuyvesant-French her blood rose. He'd treated her like she was nothing but a piece of refuse, without feelings, without flesh, that he could kick aside whenever he chose. The money he paid her was nothing compared to the fortune Wilhelm had left her. She owed him nothing, not even the courtesy of accepting his invitation to dinner.

But the maître d' assisted her to her seat at the table, and she sat down. The spread was fit for a king; there was duck in lemon rind, whitefish with capers, four different ices, and an entire table of salads. Sometimes Hazel and she would take the children to Albrite's Pharmacy downstairs and eat at the counter, but she hadn't actually eaten from the hotel's dining room. Unescorted women were not allowed there, and she had never been invited by a gentleman.

Edward slipped the men several bills, and they gathered the plate covers and trays and departed. He sat down to her suspicious stare.

"I don't like to be hovered over while I'm eating," he said lightly.

"Is that why you dismissed them?" She returned her attention to her filled plate. "You might have been hasty, you know. I've no desire to play serving wench."

"You mean there's a role you *don't* play?" He smirked.

Fuming, she bit into the duck and vowed to spend the rest of the meal in silence. But then she heard the sound of wine being poured into a glass.

"No, thank you," she spoke up, pushing the glass away.

"It's very good. Château Margaux. You may never have the chance to taste it again." He pushed the brimming glass toward her.

Her hand still didn't touch the wine. "I find it curious that your sister would want us to have this discussion at dinner. I can almost understand her desire to have traveling companions, but I do find it odd that she would put you and me together over a bottle of wine."

"This is her idea of amusement. She's got a wicked streak in her a mile wide."

"What is she being wicked about?"

"She knows I'm attracted to you." He chewed on his food, staring at her.

Lavinia quit eating. The slow, painful crawl of a blush heated her cheeks.

"Don't go losing your head, Lavinia. I've been known to be a glutton for attractive women. I'll even pay for the privilege if I want something quick and unencumbered. You know all about that."

"How you speak to me," she gasped softly, her eyes accusing.

He put down his fork. "You see? There you go again, the picture of indignant womanhood. You sit there, so silent, your expression, your very stance, damning me for my crudeness. God, can you blame a man for being attracted to such an actress?"

"You flatter me and insult me all in the same breath," she said. "It makes me wonder what you really want."

"I have what I want. Daisy is free of you. I'm free of you." His eyes became shadowed. "And now I've the chance to put things right between us."

"I don't think that's possible, Mr. Stuyvesant-French." She left her seat once again.

He pulled her back down. "Call me Edward. I insist."

"Let me go, *Edward.*"

"You needn't play a charade for me any longer. I caught you, remember? I saw you in makeup. I touched those ghostly rags you wore, I put my hands on your uncorseted waist. You can't claim innocence. I know you too well. Your job, Lavinia, has been to dupe men. To dupe them or to please them. I'd now like to be the recipient of the latter."

"Your own thoughts dupe you, then."

He laughed. "Do they? I think not. Spiritual affinity has long been associated with sexual affinity. You must be a master by now."

Her mouth went dry. A strange dropping sensation occurred in the middle of her belly; it was fear heightened by arousal. The evening seemed to be careening out of control and she hadn't even touched her wine. "Please, I really must return. Hazel—"

"Hazel is being amused by my sister, who, I might add, is quite the wit, hence this dinner." He nodded to her wineglass. "Drink it up. There's more where that came from."

"You really have mistaken my character," she said, her gaze darting to the door.

"Have I? And who was the man you met in the street the night you were to meet me in the park square? I saw you in silhouette talking to him most fervently. And then there was that chap— what was he, a hack driver?—whatever he was, I saw you in his arms the night I arrived unannounced in your parlor. Now you mean to tell me all these dalliances are chaste?"

"I'm not a whore without feelings or a soul, Mr. Stuyvesant-French. I am a woman who's had to fight—"

"And yet, are you not also a ghost? And a medium? And a mentalist? It's all so confusing." He leaned forward. His knuckles brushed her cheek. His hand was so warm she almost flinched from the shock of it. "And logic tells me there's one more role inside you."

"Could you love a woman and put a ring on her hand, Mr. Stuyvesant-French? Your father could not. I suggest you cannot, either, and I must stay clear of you, then."

A muscle bunched in his jaw. "There you go. You've now committed the ultimate sin by comparing me with Vanadder."

"He told me you're a lot like your father."

She knew she was on dangerous ground with that last statement, but she couldn't stop herself. She wanted protection, and nothing short of an assault seemed to be a strong enough defense.

"Who told you this?" His every word seemed to bite like those wolfish teeth snapping at flesh.

"The man I saw in the park the night I met you there. The man you saw me with." Her voice lowered to a whisper. "The man who loved Alice."

Rage seemed to bank in him like a fire. Green sparks lit in the depths of his eyes. His mouth hardened. "Did you toy with him?" His voice was almost as quiet as hers.

"I don't toy with any man."

"No. I'm asking you if that black little heart of yours told him lies."

"He wanted comfort."

"You've had no trouble refusing me comfort."

"His want was not a physical need, but a spiritual need."

With one arm, he pulled her to his lap and held her still by a grip that was a band of iron. She struggled but it was no use. He held fast. His words were hot caresses on her nape. "And what spiritual need could you fulfill without spinning tales? Tell me."

"I swear I didn't lie to him." Her hands tried to push at his chest but it only served to tighten the arm around her waist. She could hardly breathe.

"Cornelius Cook is a decent man. A tragic man. You had no right to feed upon his vulnerability."

"I didn't. I wanted to help him," she gasped, tears of fright choking every word.

His hands went around her face. He tilted her head up and studied her for a very long time. He was looking for the lies. The fraud. But there was none. He wouldn't find any. She was telling the truth.

"My God. You deceive so well. Your face, it's so very sweet. So very beautiful. Even I want to believe you." His voice was barely a rumble.

"You must believe me."

"What you do is wrong."

His arm nearly crushed her rib cage. He was so angry, she wondered if he might really hurt her.

"Please," she begged softly, her face so close to his she could have touched him with her tongue. "I told your friend nothing that a priest wouldn't offer to the bereaved. I didn't lead him on."

"What did you tell him?" His entire body was like a wound-up piece of leather ready to snap.

"I told him to believe in what I desperately believe in."

"What is that?"

Her gaze locked with his. Her vulnerability tortured her. She cringed by the confession. "I told him to believe in love beyond death."

In small unmeasurable increments, his arm released its vise around her waist. His mouth was so near she wondered if he might try to kiss her. She also wondered why she hadn't pulled away.

Slowly, he leaned his head on her shoulder. His breath was long and deep as if he were savoring the fragrance of her hair.

"Edward," she whispered, his name familiar yet foreign on her tongue.

"I know what you are." His hands found her waist and he pulled her into him, but his head still hung on her shoulder as if in a gesture of surrender. "I see your character so clearly, yet when I'm near you I wish and I pray otherwise."

Her heart drummed beneath her bodice. For one wild moment, she had the thought of running a hand through his dark, closely cropped hair. It would be so easy to touch him, to caress him. Her hand almost ached to begin it. But she knew only too graphically how it would end.

"Maybe your mind decieves you," she whispered helplessly.

"But I've learned not to be guided by my heart."

For some strange reason, her eyes filled with tears. "Some would say you have no heart."

His every muscle seemed to tense. "I am *not* my father's son."

"Show me."

She couldn't believe what she'd said. The last two words were a clear invitation. It was insanity, fooling with him. She knew only too well how deep his cruelties ran. But she knew, too, how deep her attraction was to him. With every passing minute in his company it grew and tantalized her with the promise of going beyond the physical and perhaps landing in realms that before she'd only fictionalized.

He lifted his head. His eyes were hard with the mix of lust and fury. He seemed to be battling with himself. His tongue ran over his teeth as if he wanted to kiss her.

She closed her eyes. Deep in her soul, she knew she wanted him. For the first time in her life, logic didn't matter, not now when everything seemed destined to defy it. Her only desire now seemed to be to succumb to her heart. Her only thought was the remembrance of his lips when he'd kissed her in the séance.

She wanted to feel them again. No one else would do. There was this man, Edward Stuyvesant-French, or there was no one.

Unforewarned, she suddenly found herself on her feet, being dragged to the door. The brutality of it was like ice water gushing onto burnt skin.

"Get out. Don't come back or I'll put my claws in you and tear you to shreds. And I'll give you not a moment of mercy." He breathed hard as if he were fighting some kind of animal impulse. He shoved her purse in her hands and pushed her toward the door.

"What?" Her tongue was thick and clumsy. Words were difficult. The shock was so great, she wondered if she'd just been awakened from a dream.

"I am not my father's son. I am not going to hurt you." He drew closer, but this time he didn't do it to seduce but to threaten. "Don't cross my path again, because if you do, next time I might not want to see whatever humanity you possess." He grabbed her chin. "Next time I might just look at this pretty face and have a go at the whore I think is inside it, your pain be damned."

She backed away. Through the open doorway, she spied one of the young waiters watching them from the hall, his body frozen with mortification, his face white as a sheet.

Humiliation drove through her heart like a stake, and it was a wretched companion to rejection. The tears came hard as she gave Edward Stuyvesant-French one last glance. The old disapproval had returned to his face. She sobbed and ran out of the room. She never looked back.

❦ ❦

Edward didn't hear the banging on the door. The gaslights were still on in the suite. He guessed they had given him away.

"French? Are you in there, French? The concierge said you didn't leave the hotel."

Edward lifted his head from his hands and went to the door. He opened it and Cornelius filled the doorway.

"What's gone on here tonight?" Cornelius asked, his face lined with a frown. "Daisy said she saw Lavinia Murphy return home. She said the girl's face was white and she took right to her bed."

"She and I are like oil and water."

"Did something happen?"

"Nothing with any consequence, if that's what you mean." Edward rubbed his jaw. His eyes gave away nothing.

Nonetheless Cook seemed visibly relieved.

Edward finally stood aside and allowed the man into the suite. He nodded to the untouched dining table. "Help yourself."

The older man picked up the wine bottle and surveyed the full glasses. "Not a drop missing, and yet you two had a spat?"

"She shouldn't have said anything to you the other night in the square."

The other man's spirit suddenly seemed to flag. "You knew it was me, then? I'd hoped you wouldn't see us."

"I didn't recognize you. She told me tonight it was you." Edward didn't look at him. "She told me what you asked her."

Cornelius dropped into a chair. In seconds he seemed to turn into a very old man. "I want you to forget about it, Edward."

"It's forgotten." Stuyvesant-French's gaze grew vengeful. "*She's* forgotten."

"Maybe it's for the best."

Edward took a deep breath. "I've got all the papers in order. Finally Daisy Vanadder has become one of the richest women in the city." He looked at the other man.

"She's afraid of being an heiress. You know that, don't you, French? She's fearful of the vampires that come to call when they smell money."

"The right man will find her."

"Daisy's so terribly alone. She has no friends to help her with her judgment. She's vulnerable. Very vulnerable, and she knows it."

"She has me to be beside her."

"You're her half-brother, Edward. You're a man. She can't discuss these things with you. She needs friends."

Stuyvesant-French gulped back a rage. "She isn't going abroad with the Murphys. I forbid it."

"But she has taken a liking to them—"

"It will not happen. End of discussion." Edward flashed him an angry glance.

Cornelius looked at him. He said not a word. Yet he couldn't help but sigh.

Chapter Twelve

In dreams commences all human knowledge; in dreams hovers over measureless space the first faint bridge between spirit and spirit—this world and the worlds beyond. . . .

—EDWARD BULWER LYTTON (1803–1873)

Lavinia rolled onto her side and stared at the robin's-egg blue walls of her bedroom, her eye following the Greek key pattern leafed in gold below the cornice. The right-angle waves undulated toward infinity, ending where they began. Always ending where they began. Her worst fear.

"Are you awake?" Hazel's whisper came from the corner.

Lavinia turned her head.

A frown marred Hazel's pretty forehead.

"Is it morning?" Lavinia asked.

"You've been sleeping like the dead. It's noon." Hazel rose from the chair and perched on the side of the bed. "Aren't you feeling well? Was it— How did your talk with Stuyvesant-French go?"

Lavinia buried her head in the pillow. Beneath her, her hair was a knotted mat. She hadn't bothered to plait it last night, and she regretted it already.

"If you don't want to talk, I understand," Hazel said quietly.

"I had a dream last night," Lavinia said, the expression in her eyes dark and distant. "Do you remember the time when I dreamed Fanny couldn't be found?"

Hazel became still. "You woke up screaming that she was trapped in the woodbox."

"Yes." Lavinia wrapped her arms over her chest as if she were chilled. "And then later that summer, do you remember? Fanny wandered off from the rest of us while we were in the park."

"We had everyone looking for her. I was terrified. Rawl and Jamie were frantic." Hazel's frown deepened. "She'd returned home and decided to hide in the woodbox. She'd been able to lower the lid, but it was too heavy for her to lift when she needed to get out. She would have died from suffocation and the heat if we hadn't found her when we did."

"I was so frightened," Lavinia whispered.

"But you were the one who ran home and looked in the woodbox. You were the one who saved her, Vinia. You and your dream." Hazel stood and paced the room. "You also had a dream that I was going to have a little girl. I did have a little girl, didn't I? And you told the midwife to cut the cord even though she was breech. You said you dreamt the cord was wrapped around Eva's neck. And it was."

"The dream I had last night didn't concern you or the children."

Hazel returned to her perch on the edge of the mattress. "Then why do you look so sad?"

Darkly Lavinia whispered, "I only remember fragments. It was hot. There was a wind that howled all around. Stuyvesant-French was with me. His hair was wet from the rain." She turned to her stomach and clutched the pillow. "There was a hammock in this strange place. A hammock. And . . ." She buried her face in the bedclothes. "I hate him. With every fiber of my being, I hate him, and I'm glad I won't ever see him again."

"Oh, Vinia," Hazel gasped softly. "You won't have to see him again. I don't care what promises his sister makes, we'll forget about them. I don't want what happened to me to ever happen to you."

Lavinia looked up from the pillow. "What promises did Daisy make? What are you talking about?"

"Daisy Vanadder sent this this morning." Hazel retrieved a heavy vellum card from the pocket of her dressing gown.

Lavinia read:

Miss Daisy Vanadder
Requests the Pleasure of Your Company
at Dinner
this Thursday Evening
Seven O'clock

In handwriting across the top was the scrawl, *Edward is* not *expected.*

"Daisy Vanadder is a lovely woman." Lavinia's expression softened. "We can't refuse the invitation. She wants friends so desperately."

"Yes, but her brother could show up in spite of her promises." Hazel chewed her lip.

"This will be just a quiet dinner. Remember, it's been barely enough time for her to go into mourning for her father. I don't think Edward will be there."

"She shouldn't even bother with mourning, the way that man treated her."

Lavinia nodded. "He was terrible, wasn't he? To both of his children."

"I'm surprised you have sympathy for Stuyvesant-French at all." Hazel watched her.

"I don't." Lavinia turned away. "The wretch, he probably won't even wear a black armband for Wilhelm."

"He likes shocking people, doesn't he?"

"You can count on it, but I'm sure Daisy will do the proper thing, especially now. She inherits everything, Hazel. I signed it all over to her last night. I couldn't fight him anymore."

"Oh," Hazel said, her expression worried.

"He gave us a cheque. It's in my handbag. No doubt it's a pittance, but I took it anyway. It's some compensation for all the trouble."

Hazel retrieved the handbag from on top of the bureau. "I'll put it in the bank this afternoon on my errands. How much is it for?" She dug out the slip of paper. A small gasp ushered from her parted lips.

"What is it?" Lavinia asked, sitting up in bed.

"Have you looked at this, Vinia?" Hazel asked, her voice rising.

"What has he done to us now?" Lavinia groaned.

"He's made us rich, is what. Just look at this cheque. Look at it!"

Hazel rushed to the bedside. Lavinia took it from her. Her eyes grew large as she read the distinctive handwriting.

"We're rich, Lavinia," Hazel said in between counting zeros. "I can't imagine why he did this, but we're really rich!"

Lavinia frowned. She read the cheque again just to make sure her eyes weren't deceiving her. They weren't.

"We can go to Europe now with Daisy, and on our own coin!" Hazel exclaimed.

"No, my bargain with Stuyvesant-French was that we'd leave his sister alone."

Hazel laughed. "Well, Daisy Vanadder and I had a long talk last night, and I can assure you, she won't be leaving us alone. She wants us to come to Europe with her and we have to. We'd have no other introduction without her."

"If we take that cheque we have to honor the intentions. He told us to stay away. We have to do it."

Hazel threw out her hands in supplication. "But I like her, Vinia, and I know you like her, too. Are we to shun her and hurt her feelings, all because of a silly condition set by her brother?"

It was Lavinia's turn to chew on her lower lip. "I don't know what to do."

"She'll be terribly wounded if we turn our backs on her—and just for the sake of accepting her brother's cheque? I don't think we can do that, Vinia."

"Oh, what a wretched mess. I truly hate that man."

"But what's a small dinner party? Edward Stuyvesant-French won't even be there. And remember, Daisy's in mourning. This is to be a quiet affair."

Lavinia moaned. "All right. We'll go to her dinner party. I know this is going to be the wrong decision, yet I can't hurt her feelings, either." She cast a worried gaze to her sister. "But remember, I warned you. He told us to stay very far away from his beloved sister. There'll be hell to pay if he finds out we're not keeping up our bargain."

"I'm not so worried about the dinner as I am about your dream." Hazel turned quiet. "If you could sell your dreams to the public, Vinia, they'd be the only authentic things we've ever sold."

"Unfortunately, dreams can't be sold." She closed her eyes. "If I ever have the desire to buy a hammock, just shoot me dead, will you?"

Hazel nervously laughed. "I'll stop you from buying it, I promise."

※ ※

Daisy surveyed the line of servants wandering in and out of the west-wing passage, their arms loaded with heavy canvas sheets. She pointed in the direction of the eight guest suites and said, "Cover everything. I don't plan to return for ages."

"What's all this?" Edward interrupted, taking the stairs two steps at a time.

"What does it look like? Why, I'm closing the house. That's what one does when one goes abroad, isn't it?"

"It is, but we haven't yet finalized—" He suddenly stopped and looked down at his sister. He studied her skirt and bodice of matte black crape. The only ornament to the outfit at all was the tiny jet beads that trimmed her collar and buttonholes. "I don't believe he merited this, Daisy," he said rather harshly.

Daisy glanced down at her clothes. "Father? No, I suppose he did not merit it—but New York expects me to mourn, so mourn I must."

"You are going to dress like that for six months—for him?" He made no attempt to hide his incredulity.

"I inherited everything, Edward, thanks to your machinations. How would it look for his only heir to not even attempt to mourn her father?"

His eyes darkened. "I didn't do it just to see you in dowdy crape and closing down the mansion. Do you still have silly ideas about that cottage in the mountains?"

"Oh, you can be so patronizing sometimes, Edward, did you know that?"

He seemed to bite back his retort. "I don't mean to patronize you, but I can't figure out what you're doing."

"I'm being wicked, that's what." Daisy smiled. "I'm closing down the house because I plan on being in London by this time next month. And as for the dowdy black crape, well, New York society requires it, but I don't think anyone will mind while we're at sea that I *not* dress myself in deep mourning, do you? And by the time I get to Europe, I may discard these rags altogether, what do you think?"

He tossed her a smile. "*Mea culpa*, but when do we leave for Europe?"

"I'd like to be on the HMS *Maritimus* by the weekend. She sets sail for London Monday."

"I'll book the necessary cabins today, if you like."

Daisy seemed to flinch as if she were hiding something. "Well, I've already booked all the necessary cabins. I even got one for Cornelius—do you think he would be so gracious as to come along?—I do love him so."

Edward touched her cheek. "I'm sure he'd be proud to escort you around Europe, as I would."

She pressed his hand to her face and sighed. "You're such a dear with me, why is it you let no one else see you this way?"

"No one else needs to," he said, a strange note of bitterness in his voice.

Daisy didn't answer.

❧ ❦

"This is marvelous. Incredible. I could eat the entire cake!" Hazel exclaimed.

Lavinia finished her dessert and looked across the table at the gentleman who sat there. His name was Cornelius Cook. They'd finally been introduced. He was Daisy's fourth for dinner.

"This is delicious, Daisy. Pierre, the chef, must be weeping that you're closing the mansion," Cook said, his hand lightly resting on a glass of port.

"I'm taking Pierre with me—along with several others I couldn't leave behind." Daisy winked. "This is really so exciting, isn't it? Going abroad."

Lavinia smiled. The evening had been sumptuous and lovely, but she still wasn't sure why they'd been invited. Daisy Vanadder had her hands full with her preparations to leave for Europe. Between being fitted for mourning, and travel plans, the woman didn't seem to need the additional worries of a dinner party—even this small one. It didn't quite make sense.

"Now I must unveil my surprise." Daisy took a sip of tea. She looked around the dining table at the three faces. "I've booked you a suite, Cornelius, on the *Maritimus*, and I've five other compartments, one each for you, Hazel and Lavinia, and one each for your dear butler, the children, and their governess."

Hazel's mouth dropped open. Cornelius Cook stared at Lavinia.

Lavinia squelched the notion to run from the table in horror.

Slowly she said, "You know we'd love to travel with you, Daisy, but your brother expressly—"

"Oh, pooh. Edward has nothing to do with this," Daisy countered. "Am I not an immense heiress now, dependent upon no one? And I would be so thrilled if you would accompany me. I've no family, you know. Nor real friends. Going with you and your family seems so much nicer than going alone."

"Yes, but we mustn't come along. We wouldn't want you to shrug your brother's guidance for us. Besides . . ." Lavinia swallowed. Her nerves were stretched taut. ". . . besides, part of Mr. Stuyvesant-French's settlement over the will was that we were to not even think of going abroad and bothering you."

"Edward's up to his tricks, is he?"

To Lavinia's great relief, Daisy didn't appear hurt at all. She laughed.

"You promised him?" Daisy continued. "Well, fine, I mean to see you hold by that promise. But that doesn't mean I cannot invite you to come along independent of my brother's wishes, nor does it mean you must decline the invitation that wasn't even made when you settled with him. None of that was part of the settlement, was it?"

"No," Lavinia answered hesitantly.

"The settlement didn't account for the possibility that you and your family might want to go abroad coincidentally on the same ship Cornelius and I are on, did it?"

"No," Lavinia clasped her hands as if she were pleading with her, "but your brother will throw us overboard if he should find out we're on the same ship—"

"I have to see that," chortled Cornelius.

Daisy gave him a quelling look. "Really, why is everyone so afraid of Edward? And what's he to do with this anyway? It's no fault of the Murphys if they should decide to take their newfound wealth on a trip to England."

"That's right," Hazel said, suddenly perking up. "Isn't she right,

Lavinia? I mean, we have the right to travel, don't we? And it would be so much easier to travel with someone who can make us introductions. You know we could never get that on our own."

"It's all very lovely," Lavinia said, exasperated, "but I just can't see how this would work."

"Is it that you don't want to go with me?"

A black silence surrounded the previously festive dinner party. Daisy seemed to wilt before Lavinia's eyes. She looked so defeated, Lavinia felt a lump of tears come to her throat.

"I'll understand if you don't want to come with me," Daisy continued. "I can see how it might offend   "

"Nonsense!" The word was out so loudly that even Lavinia was shocked. She shook herself. Swallowing the lump, she said with more composure, "Really, it's not you, Daisy. Believe me, it's not you or that chair. Or anything like that. You can't know how much Hazel and I would love to travel with you. We've never been to Europe. We know no one. And though I know you've been confined, your father was of such a stature that people are going to fall over themselves to hand you invitations—"

"—Because I'm rich—"

"—because you're rich, and—" Lavinia stopped herself again. Everything was getting so tangled up she didn't know how to extricate herself.

Daisy finally smiled. "Don't worry about it, Lavinia. I know the situation. When you live your life in a wheelchair, you can't pretend about things."

"But we don't want to be friends with you because you're rich."

"I know," Daisy answer quietly. "That's why I want you to come with me. Use my position as the Vanadder heiress to better yourselves. Why not? I don't even want the wealth, but Edward is forcing me to take it. So why can't I use it to help five orphans find their way in the world?"

"You know about all of us?" Hazel gasped.

Daisy nodded. "Cornelius heard about the orphanage from

Edward. I have to say it's quite ingenious of you to have become spiritualists. What a clever way to make a living. I almost envy it. It's so amusing."

Lavinia broke in, "But the other things Edward said about us were not true. We weren't soliciting in that town—"

Daisy held up her hand. "Say no more. I don't believe it, nor do I care. All I do care about is going to London on the *Maritimus* with all of you. Please say you will?"

Lavinia sighed. "Oh, you don't know how furious Stuyvesant-French will be. This is just the situation he forbade."

"Exactly," Daisy said impishly. "It serves him right. This will be a good lesson for him. He'll see he doesn't rule everyone around him."

"He won't take it well. He'll have us removed from the ship."

"Not if he doesn't see you until we're out at sea," Daisy countered.

"He'll find a way to get rid of us, you watch." Lavinia shuddered.

Cornelius laughed out loud.

All three women looked at him.

"Forgive me," he burst out, trying to sober himself.

"And what is so funny?" Daisy asked.

"Can't you just see Edward's face when he bumps into the Countess in the middle of the Atlantic?" A boisterous chuckle escaped from his lips. "It should rank right up there with the biggest maritime collisions of the century." He bit back another laugh.

"What's your answer, Lavinia? Won't you and your family come with me on the *Maritimus?* We'll all have much more fun if we can travel together." Daisy turned pleading eyes to Lavinia. Cornelius and Hazel stared too. Lavinia couldn't take it anymore.

"We'll take the five cabins on the *Maritimus*, but one of you had better jump in after me when I go overboard. The Atlantic Ocean is frigid."

Daisy grinned. She looked just like a schoolgirl plotting mischief. "Don't worry, Lavinia. The *Maritimus* is taking the southern route to Bermuda. The ocean is very warm, I hear."

Hazel muffled a giggle. Lavinia shot her a censorious glance. The butler came to show them to the drawing room. Lavinia's only consolation was that Daisy looked as if she were having the time of her life.

Chapter Thirteen

I thought these knockings, these table-turnings, these phenomena, if they can be produced in America, can they not also be brought about here? Indeed, tables tilted as strongly in England as anywhere else.

—The Spiritualist *magazine,1860*

E dward looked across New York Harbor toward Wall Street. He could still see the steeple of Trinity Church, but it was being overtaken by taller structures. The financial soul of America no longer belonged to patriots and farmers. Ever since the Civil War, the city belonged to the man who could master the ticker tape, men such as J. Pierpont Morgan, R. T. Wilson, Wilhelm Vanadder, and now, even him, Edward Stuyvesant-French.

With his own fortune, he was no stranger to stock options and investments. But making money was the easy part of life. It was all the rest that eluded him. Sometimes he felt that whatever was missing left an emptiness inside him that was as big and cold as the North Country where he made his first million.

"Manhattan. Isn't it lovely from here? Such a beautiful city. Why, I'm homesick already," Daisy said in her chair at the railing, the breeze blowing the feathers of her hat. "Tell me, Edward, is London as impressive?"

"More impressive." He smiled. "We're going to see places where before you could only dream about them. After London and Paris, we'll cruise the Nile. I'll caravan you to the Valley of the Kings, then we'll be off to India and Hong Kong. You've never seen anything like it, Daze. The world is out there just for your asking, and I'm going to give you all of it."

She shivered. Her eyes were brilliant. "Oh, I can't wait. I simply can't wait."

He sombered and looked out at the sound, Manhattan drifting away with every churn of the steam engines.

Daisy quieted, too, while she studied her half-brother's finely wrought profile. "Why so glum suddenly?" she asked.

He looked down at the brass handrail. He'd gripped it until his knuckles were white. Haltingly, he offered, "All of your excitement makes me think I should have returned to New York earlier. We should have done this years ago. Instead I left you with him."

"You had things to do, Edward. You had your own life to lead."

"Yes, my own life," he answered, bitterness in his words.

"I never thought you abandoned me, never."

"I should have taken you with me. Somehow I should have done it."

"You would have only turned into a tyrant. You would have ruled me in some manner the way Wilhelm ruled me. I would have had no power over my life at all." The expression on her face turned inward as if she held back a secret. "You know what, Edward? I've discovered this fortune serves me well. I may never have a great love nor a blissful marriage come from it, but the money gives me a measure of control over my destiny that I never had before. It's a luxury for a woman of my unfortunate situation to be able to do exactly as I please. No one can stop me from living now, Edward. Not even you."

He flashed her a gleaming smile. "Even I, your terrible half-brother Edward Stuyvesant-French, can't control you?"

She smiled back, guilt crossing her features as she glanced

toward the row of suites next to theirs that opened to the top deck. "Oh, my dearest, if you only knew. If you only knew."

※ ※

"I know I will always look back at this trip and recount how disaster could have been avoided if only I'd done certain things right—and the worst thing I've done so far is paying for that cabin in steerage for Monty." Lavinia paced the wine-colored carpet in her suite while Hazel glumly gazed down at the pattern of gold arabesque woven into it.

"We had to help him, Vinia. How could we have left him when he was so desperate? He rescued us from the situation with Wilhelm. We could never have gotten through that night and weeks afterward if he hadn't helped us. We owed it to him."

Lavinia wanted to weep. "I know we owed him, but he was running from the law—"

"He was running from a bookmaker, not the police." Hazel brightened. "Really, Vinia, it's all kind of funny. Destiny has played a trick with us again, wouldn't you say?"

"I adore Monty. You know I do. It's just that I feel strange having him pose as our servant. He's not our servant. This is going to cause ruin and damnation, you watch."

"But that man was going to kill him! You heard poor Monty last night. He couldn't pay the bet. It was the end for him. We had to save him."

"We should have just given him the money to pay the bookie off."

"And let him go back to his old ways? How could we have done that? Besides, did you see his face when we said where we were going? He'd give anything to act on the London stage."

"He should indeed be on the stage, not in the steerage posing as our servant."

Hazel gave her an exasperated look. "How could we respectably take him with us introducing him as our friend? We'd be ruined."

Lavinia slumped into a chair and sighed. "I know."

Hazel put her arm around her. "I guess it does seem to you that every road we've been on lately hurls us toward catastrophe, but I've a feeling about all of these things that have happened to us. I think that maybe we're being led to something good. Something right." She grew pensive. Her eyes had a faraway expression. "Lavinia, have you ever felt that you have a special kind of destiny? I've felt it. I feel it now." She stood and looked out the porthole where the skyline of Manhattan was sinking into a foggy evening twilight. "I think he's out there, Vinia, this man, this destiny. He's there waiting for me just across this ocean. He's as lonely as I am and I must find him." She turned to her sister. "We had to do this, Lavinia. Right or wrong, the road led us to where we are now, and as crazy as it seems I have a feeling that this is exactly where we're supposed to be."

Lavinia stood. She went to the bedroom to assist the chambermaid in unpacking the steamer trunks. Her only answer was, "We're here now; the ship has sailed. There's no turning back unless we're prepared to swim, so dress for dinner, Hazel. Daisy has us sitting at the captain's table, and I do pray Edward Stuyvesant-French has a nasty bout of seasickness which keeps him in his cabin for the length of the voyage."

❧ ❦

The first-class dining room was decorated in the Louis taste. Gilding and puce-colored satin blended artfully with the delicate florals of the velvet Brussels carpet. The room was designed to be purely a showcase for its patrons, the important men in their tie and tails and the even more impressive wives in breathlessly expensive jewels and gowns so elaborate the garments bordered on upholstery.

The captain sat at the end table which was draped in white damask and entertained only an exclusive eight. Lavinia's stomach lurched when she saw it. She half expected Stuyvesant-French to be there. She could already picture him upon seeing her. He would stand, point his finger at her and damn her to steerage with the likes of Monty, whilst the rest of the dining room would applaud.

But Stuyvesant-French was not there, only Cornelius who stood when he spied them. The captain was busy speaking to the steward, but when Lavinia and Hazel walked up, he stood also.

"How lovely you ladies look this evening." Cornelius beamed. He kissed Lavinia's hand and whispered, "And what name are you ladies choosing to go by on this excursion?"

Lavinia smiled. "Countess" and "Czarina" were titles they had decided best to shed. They were now going to go by the less famous—and infamous—name of Murphy. "We are mere plebes on this excursion, Mr. Cook."

Cornelius nodded, understanding her meaning. He gestured to the captain, an older man with an intelligent gaze and a neatly cropped mustache. "May I introduce you? Captain Stafford, the Misses Lavinia and Hazel Murphy."

The captain bowed to both women, then helped each with her seat. He poured them a glass of champagne and played the jovial host. "I understand this is your first trip abroad, Miss Murphy," he said to Lavinia.

Lavinia attempted a calm smile, but her insides were writhing. Any minute now she feared the ogre was going to appear with Daisy and chew her to pieces. Her only wonder was how embarrassing a spectacle it would be. "Hazel and I feel like Alice through the looking glass. This is such an adventure." She gripped her wineglass as if it were the holy grail.

"You're in good hands," Cornelius added. "Captain Stafford here has sailed the Atlantic more times than most whalers. He was just telling me how he circumvented the most astonishing iceberg—"

"Now, we mustn't worry the ladies with such talk," the captain broke in. "Besides, we're going south on this route. No icebergs to worry about at all. My favorite place, you know, Bermuda. It's a longer route from London, but there's no place as beautiful."

"I hear it's green all year round," Hazel said, obviously gathering her nerves after a sip of champagne.

"They have seasons, but not like London or New York. . . ." The captain nodded to the steward to refill the glasses.

Lavinia was shocked to see hers already empty; she realized she must dread this first dinner more than even Hazel.

". . . no snow, you understand," the captain prattled on, "but this time of year we hardly need to worry about that even if Bermuda did have such a thing!" He chuckled, and Lavinia followed with a nervous laugh.

"The water should be lovely, and the beaches are beautiful. Just as pink as the inside of a conch shell. You've never seen anything like them. Ah, here we are. My other guests." The captain stood.

Lavinia found her gaze glued to her charger.

"Your Grace, we're honored to have you and your brother on board with us," she heard the captain say.

Lavinia looked up. She realized the persons joining them were strangers. There was a man in his late twenties and another a bit older who looked to be the titled one.

The men took the proffered chairs flanking Hazel.

"May I introduce His Grace, the Duke of Kylemore, and his brother, Lord Buchanon." The captain pressed his hands; he appeared bursting at the seams with pride, and Lavinia guessed that the duke and his brother must be fairly eminent for the captain to gush like he did.

Hazel glanced across the table at Lavinia and mouthed the words, *A duke!* with her eyes nearly popping from her head. At any other time Lavinia might have been happy herself to be in such company if she weren't waiting for the Big Bad Wolf to have her for dinner.

"And these ladies," said the captain, "are the misses Murphy."

The duke looked down his nose at Hazel. She seemed suddenly frozen by an attack of self-consciousness; she didn't even glance at him.

"You're both such *interesting* girls. How is it that you're traveling alone?" Lord Buchanon was the first to speak.

Lavinia opened her mouth but she was unsure of the answer.

"They're not alone," Cook interjected, saving her. "The two Miss Murphys are protégées of Mr. Stuyvesant-French. He's on board accompanying his half-sister, Miss Daisy Vanadder."

The duke laughed. "And how is old Stuy? We haven't seen him for months—I believe the last time was in Capri, was it not? He and I played cribbage in a bar overlooking the Mediterranean, and I don't like telling you that he won a fortune from me."

Cornelius chuckled as if he, too, remembered the incident. "Edward's the same, Your Grace. He's as difficult as ever, but now that he's finally settled Miss Vanadder's affairs, he's mightily looking forward to—"

"Looking forward to seeing old friends," a voice boomed from behind her.

Across the table, Lavinia saw the duke's eyes light up. She suddenly realized that Edward was directly behind her. Worse than fearing she might appear unladylike, she didn't dare turn around to look at him because she didn't have the courage.

The duke rose to his feet and shook Edward's hand. His brother stood too. There was so much talk and back-slapping that Hazel went unnoticed.

"Here is my half-sister, Daisy Vanadder. Daisy, I'd like to introduce you to Buc and his wretched brother the Duke of Kylemore—or Kyle, as we call him back in the old country."

"I'm pleased to make your acquaintance, Your Grace," Lavinia heard Daisy say nervously.

"Edward, you rapscallion, how did you devise to become chaperon to three such beauties as this?" the duke announced.

Lavinia cringed. She could see from Hazel's expression across the table that Stuyvesant-French had finally looked at the rest of the diners. Hazel's eyes were so wide and fearful, she looked ready to duck under the tablecloth.

Finally Lavinia turned her head and smiled. "Why, Mr. Stuyvesant-French. How glad we are that you could join us for dinner."

Edward said nothing. He merely stared at Lavinia as if he were carved in stone. He seemed to view her like a mirage that he could blink away, but when she didn't disappear, he turned ominously to Daisy.

Lavinia swore she heard thunder.

"*Daisy*—"

Daisy quickly wheeled her chair between her half-brother and Lavinia. "Now, Edward," she said brightly, "don't ruin my surprise. Think how grateful dear departed Wilhelm must be now that you've taken Cousin Hazel and Cousin Lavinia under wing."

" 'Cousin'—?" he spit out.

"Oh, Wilhelm must be so very grateful," Lavinia heard herself say even while she wondered where she got the cheek.

"These are cousins of Vanadder's?" the duke asked.

The expression on Stuyvesant-French's face boiled.

"Well, not exactly *cousins*," Hazel offered, her gaze darting between Edward and Lavinia.

Cornelius blustered into the fray. "They're really rather second cousins, isn't that right, Edward old boy?"

Stuyvesant-French looked like he was going to punch Cook right in the nose.

"Actually the relation is completely on the Vanadder side. The Murphys have nothing to do with the Stuyvesants at all," Cook added hastily.

Daisy wheeled forward toward the duke as if to embellish the explanation further. "But that's what makes Edward such a saint. I'm the one they're really related to, and yet Edward, in his extreme benevolence, agreed to accompany all of us across Europe just because he's such a dear." She gazed up at her half-brother with a worshipful expression; Stuyvesant-French looked like he was going to go into apoplexy. In her wheelchair and mourning attire, Daisy was not the kind someone wanted to be caught screaming at in the middle of the dining room.

A muscle in Edward's jaw ticked.

"Will you help me to my place, Edward?" Daisy asked innocently.

Slowly he took the back of her chair and maneuvered her to the place of honor at Captain Stafford's right. He then had no choice but to take the last empty seat which was between Daisy and Lavinia.

"You have broken the deal. Give me the cheque back," he whispered through clenched teeth when no one was looking.

"Our deal was that I was not to take Daisy's offer to travel with her. We didn't. We've come on our own," Lavinia answered back as she coughed delicately into her napkin.

"You have no right to be here. I should dump you overboard like the baggage you are."

"I told them you'd try that, but as far as I know America is still a free country and I bought my own tickets. I believe that gives us the right to be here without interference from you."

"You bought those tickets with *my* money."

"No, it's my money now," she answered in a low singsong voice so that people would think they were exchanging pleasantries instead of cutthroat threats.

"I should have you arrested."

"On what charge, Cousin Edward?" She batted her eyelashes.

The muscle bunched again in his jaw. "If Daisy thinks she's going to suck me into this, she's wrong. We'll change ships in Bermuda."

"You may do as you please."

He looked at her. Their gazes locked. If they hadn't been in a crowded dining room full of society people, she didn't know what he might have done.

"You're going to pay for this, Murphy old girl. You're going to pay dearly."

Lavinia turned to the rest of the guests. Her mind followed the dinner conversation but her stomach remained in a knot. Even though he was sitting right beside her, she swore Stuyvesant-French did not take his piercing eyes from her the entire meal.

Chapter Fourteen

"I suppose they're fantastic heiresses, eh, Edward?" Lord Buchanon took a gulp of brandy and let the smoke from his cigar obscure the expression in his eyes. The men were in the ship's gaming room where no women were allowed. After dinner, the captain had offered a tour, but Daisy had cried off, pleading a headache. The two Murphys went with Stafford. Now the four other gentlemen enjoyed a game of poker and a glass of spirits.

"It's all Vanadder money. I wouldn't know," Edward said, ignoring Cornelius's reproachful stare.

Buc glanced at his brother. The duke studied the cards in his hand, hardly paying attention.

"The blonde one, she's very pretty," Buc commented.

The duke finally spoke. "You mean the brunette one, don't you?"

"The younger one? Yes, she was pretty too but the blonde—"

"The brunette had green eyes, I think. Am I right, Edward?"

Edward looked at Kyle over the rim of his brandy glass. "Hazel-brown eyes. That's her name, by the way. Hazel."

"Hazel," the duke repeated. "It's sort of a common name, isn't it?"

"It fits her," Edward said under his breath.

"Edward," Cook interjected, "don't you think we should change the subject?"

Edward grunted.

Cornelius shifted in his chair.

Kylemore suddenly looked suspicious. "So what is it about these ladies you don't want us to know?"

Edward opened his mouth.

Cornelius shot him a quelling glance. "We're just very protective, aren't we, Edward? Besides," he added for the benefit of the others, "escorting around three beautiful heiresses, why, we're both wrecks wondering how we'll manage it."

"Indeed, I can imagine it's a very difficult chore," Buc said with a smile on his face.

"We meant no offense," Kylemore said, his gaze pinned on Cook.

Cornelius nodded. "Oh, we're not worried about you, Kyle old boy. We read about your engagement in the *New York Gazette*. The news made it all the way across the Atlantic. Besides, you've already inherited the estate; you've no need to procure an unsuspecting rich American girl to fill the family coffers, but Buc here, well, he's the younger son and with that notorious penchant of his to run through money like water, surely you can understand our reluctance to throw the ladies out unforewarned—"

"Are you calling me a wolf, Cook?" Buc, always good-natured, even smiled. He then raised his glass to the group. "Can you blame a man to being attracted to the things his brother already has? Of course you can't, gentlemen. So allow me to toast the American heiress. She's the one thing the Duke of Kylemore does not have, especially one who is blonde and possessing a certain specific generosity to her figure that a man would like to . . . ."

Edward started from his chair.

Buc paled and silenced.

Every man in the room stared at the gentlemen at the poker table. Slowly Edward eased himself back into the seat.

"Has Buc here hit a nerve, Stuy?" the duke asked when the room had turned to normal and the others in the room were no longer staring. "I apologize for his boorishness, but a man would have to assume since the ladies are going abroad under your chaperonage that they were unattached."

"They are," Edward said tightly.

"But perhaps Miss Lavinia Murphy is less unattached, am I going in the right direction?"

Edward rubbed his jaw. Looking around for the steward, he seemed to be avoiding the answer.

Cook saved the day. "Edward has three ladies under his care right now. He has to make sure no one behaves in an untoward fashion. You understand."

"We understand," said Buc. He gave Edward a covert glance. "There's a ball tomorrow night. It wouldn't be untoward of me to ask Miss Lavinia Murphy to place my name on her dance card, would it?"

"You may do anything you like so long as it falls within propriety." Edward folded his cards and stood. "I think I'll take a walk on deck. The sea air is just the right thing before bed."

"I'll go with you, French," Cornelius said, folding his hand as well.

Kylemore stood. "We'll see you tomorrow, then, at the ball? Will *all* the ladies attend, do you know?"

Edward nodded. "Yes, I expect Miss Hazel Murphy to attend."

Kyle flashed a grin. "Very well, then. See you tomorrow night, gentlemen."

❧ ❧

"The man should be called out for making a comment like that," Stuyvesant-French said to Cornelius as they stood at the rail. The sea churned beneath an etched-glass moon. Above, the stars scattered across the dark velvet sky like a coat of crushed diamonds.

"Buc's attracted to Lavinia. Do you blame him? If I were younger, I might have a go at her myself." Cornelius threw his cigar overboard. The ashes created a shower of orange that fell like fireworks into the black water.

"She's not good enough for you, Cornelius."

Cook looked out across the ocean. "The same logic should apply to you, my friend."

"It does," Edward answered.

"So then why not let her go to Buc? You shouldn't care what he does."

"I wouldn't let Daisy near him."

"But he's an earl, for God's sake—albeit an impoverished one—still, Lavinia Murphy's way beneath him. Yet you take umbrage—"

"I just don't like women being spoken of the way he spoke of her."

Cook looked at him, disbelief on his face. "This, from the man who once wagered for a barmaid in Dawson and kept her for a year—"

"The woman we're speaking of now is not that woman."

"Lavinia Murphy is different, is that what you're trying to say?"

"Exactly."

Cornelius studied Stuyvesant-French. When he seemed satisfied in what he saw in Edward's face, he said, "Yes, she is different." He returned his attention to beyond the railing. Suddenly he began to laugh.

"What is so funny?" Edward snapped.

"Now surely you haven't missed the irony in Buc's courtship with Lavinia. Think of it. Buchanon's an earl. If they married, Buc would make Lavinia Murphy a countess. A *countess*. Won't that be a shock to all the New Yorkers who thought she already was one!"

Edward chuckled. He did it again. Soon it turned into an out-and-out laugh.

Cornelius had just got out a handkerchief to wipe his eyes when a figure appeared on the other end of the first-class deck. "There she is, Edward," he said in a whisper.

Stuyvesant-French turned his head and took in the cloaked woman standing by the railing at the far end. She didn't look at them. Instead her attention was pointed to the moonlight.

"Look at the hour. I've got to retire, French. These old bones need rest." Cornelius slapped him on the back and left him at the rail. "Good night."

Alone, Edward turned back to the figure. He seemed torn between retreat and advance, so he just stood at the rail, his gaze fixed on her, until she finally turned, and looked at him.

§

"Good evening, ghost girl."

Stuyvesant-French's words were soft, but there was menace in his walk as Lavinia watched him saunter over to her. She hadn't realized it was him and Cook at the rail until Cornelius had taken his leave, and she found her gaze locked on her nemesis.

"Good evening, *cousin*," she said even more softly, the hint of a laugh in her voice. "I thought you and the rest of the men had retired to a game of cards."

"I wanted to check on Daisy." He glanced at the cabin door from which she had come. "I see you're right next to her. Your cabin must be quite luxurious. What a shame you'll be put off ship when we get to Bermuda."

"I thought it was you who wanted to flee in Bermuda."

The corner of his mouth lifted in a smile. "I changed my mind. Why should Daisy and I be inconvenienced? There might not be a ship out of Hamilton for days."

She turned back to the moonlit water. It was not her intention to spend time with Edward Stuyvesant-French. All she had wanted was a breath of salt air and a short walk on the deck. But perhaps it was just as well she have out with him. It was better to do it now than in the middle of a crowded dining room. "I must say you held your temper well at dinner. I expected a tantrum, truly I did."

"I don't have tantrums, Lavinia, I have revenge."

She looked at him. He unnerved her. "I'll agree it must have been a shock to see Hazel and me at the table, but we didn't plan this trip. I meant to keep my promise to stay out of your hair, but Daisy wanted us along so badly. She's growing fond of the children, you see. She really has a way with them. I think she'll make a wonderful mother someday."

"You would know more about that subject than she would."

Lavinia got the implied insult but she no longer had the energy to correct him. "That's all I can say, except good night, Mr. Stuyvesant-French." She took a step away, but he touched her arm, and she paused.

"You had a conquest tonight, Lavinia. Lord Buchanon was quite taken with you. Buc talked of little else at the gaming table tonight other than your . . . charms." He didn't hide the sarcasm in his voice.

"You sound as if you find it hard to believe that I might possess charms," she answered.

"Oh, you have charms."

"But I still can't make you like me, can I?"

He looked away. "I'd rather *I* like you than Daisy like you. I don't want you on this trip with her. You're not her kind."

She burned at the insult. "Perhaps, but we are on this trip so I think you might accept that. Besides, Daisy needs friends. Look how her father's treated her. She's starving for companionship."

"I brought her along so that she might find that. I want her to have friends, even find a beau. I didn't do this to help you two criminals set up shop in London."

She shook her head. There was nothing to say. He was always

going to think the worst of her, she would never change his opinion, and though it still hurt her, she was ready to give up on it. "You know, Edward, you've called me a lot of things since our acquaintance, all of them intensely insulting. I admit I'm not a saint. I've made my living on the edge of the law, perhaps, but it was only because I had to do it that way. I am not a whore, nor am I a criminal, but even more than that, I am not an ogre. I don't want to hurt your half-sister. I didn't fight the will. I gave her the money to which she was entitled."

"Then why don't you just get off the ship in Hamilton and leave her alone? She doesn't need your kind circling around her."

Anger flushed her cheeks. "My kind, Mr. Stuyvesant-French, has done the best she could. My profession might not be a worthy one, but it isn't easy being a female alone in this world. It wasn't easy feeding four other mouths when I was only a girl of sixteen. I had to make money to survive, and I did, and I demand the respect of that accomplishment, if no other."

"Why did you run away from that orphanage? Was life there really worse than what you've done since then?" he asked, his stare piercing.

If she hadn't been angry, she might have dodged the question, but the words came out like quicksilver. "A child thinks she's going to grow and get big and strong and one day fight the demons who are beating her up every day. But when you're sixteen and you find a man can pin you to the floor, you realize you're better off running away." Her expression darkened. She remembered the day so clearly. The name still burned into her mind: Burton Karpp. He'd run the orphanage for as long as she had memory, and he'd made her entire childhood a living hell. One day he'd hit her when she'd spilled some slop water in the foyer, and though he'd bruised her face, he told her how pretty she was becoming, and he explained in graphic detail what she could do for him if she wanted to better her existence.

Hazel had already been used by a man—Burton's nephew viewed the orphanage much the way Burton viewed it—it was for exploitation. Seduction hadn't bettered Hazel's existence, it had nearly destroyed it. So they'd gathered up Eva, brought along Fanny and Jamie to be a sister and a brother for her, and they'd never looked back.

Lavinia turned her face so that he couldn't see the vulnerability in her eyes. Quietly she said, "Now I never need run from another man again, Mr. Stuyvesant-French—including you—and I thank you for it."

He stood silently watching her. She wondered if her explanation had moved him, or just embarrassed him as she was embarrassed. It wasn't like her to blather about the past, but she was so utterly sick of his contempt. She didn't deserve it, not to the degree with which he viewed her.

"I guess I should say good night," she said.

"Wait." He looked at her, his face half cast in shadow. There was a hard, pensive gleam in his eye. "I want you to know I've done this for Daisy."

"You love your sister. You've already proved it."

"I want her to meet people. Maybe I've been too hasty in discounting you and your sister's help. If I agreed to give you women an introduction, would you in turn do your best to see that Daisy is not left out of things? In the wheelchair—well—I can see how she might be socially overlooked."

Lavinia gave him a soft smile. "Are you calling a truce?"

"I don't like the word 'truce,' why don't we use the term 'business agreement'?"

"I'll accept your business agreement. Mr.—*Edward*," she forced herself to say. "You and I have the same goal. I want Hazel to find someone special as much as you desire Daisy to."

"And what about yourself? You don't see yourself finding a prize catch in London?"

She shrugged. "After Hazel and the children are taken care of, I wouldn't turn the offer down. Have you someone in mind, Edward?"

He released a sardonic grin. "Are you asking me to play matchmaker for you also, Lavinia?"

"A rich, titled man would be nice."

"Buc is titled."

"Yes, but he's the younger son, and the pup makes it all too obvious he's only interested in my money."

"Trust me, Lavinia, that's not all he's interested in." He seemed to grow irritated. "I'll do what I can. In return you'll make sure Daisy is included in all your outings?"

"A pleasure. I know you don't believe this, but Daisy fits us very well. We're alone, and she's alone, and we know all about sticking together."

"She's not entirely alone. She has me to protect her. And don't ever think I won't."

Her gaze held his. She smiled. "I know you will, Edward. I know you might not believe this, but in some ways, Daisy is most fortunate."

The expression in his eyes changed. He almost seemed to soften. "If you need someone to rely upon—"

She laughed. "You mean there's a chivalrous streak inside of you? No, no, Edward, please don't look out for me. Just find me that rich, titled gentleman, but if you don't, that's all right too. As you've realized, I've learned to take care of myself."

"I think I've found one for Hazel already."

"The duke?" She lifted an eyebrow. "His eyes never left her through the entire dinner."

"Kylemore's engaged."

She wondered if he could see her shoulders slump in the dark.

"But his fiancée is utterly disliked," he continued. "I don't think anyone would weep if he ran after your sister."

"A betrothed man isn't much of a prospect. What's she like— this fiancée?"

"She has a soul made of ice, but she is beautiful."

"He must carry a fascination for her, then."

He looked hard at her. "Don't underestimate such things. Fascinations have made fools of many men."

"Yes. You forget *I* above most women know that only too well," she said, her voice near a whisper.

"I think you might find Buc a prospect in that field. It seems you're just his kind of girl."

"You don't know what kind I am, so how can you say that?"

Her honesty seemed to throw him off. He didn't answer, he just looked at her in the dark with a stare that made her shiver. She wrapped herself farther in her cloak.

"The question really is, am I your type, Lavinia? Does a man you cannot dupe merit your attention?" he taunted.

Her mind reeled with pictures from her dream. The hammock, the heat, the wind. She shut her eyes to it all.

"You know what I think of you, Mr. Stuyvesant-French. You're just waiting in the shadows to trip me up," she answered lightly.

He took her by the shoulders and forced her to look at him. "I ask you again, what do you really think of me?"

She took a deep, leveling breath. "You're not my type. You're too tall, too dark, too humorless." She lifted her hand to point to his face. "Your features aren't pleasing, either. The eyes, well, your eyes aren't good at all. Neither is your nose, it's too nonconforming." She pointed her index finger lower to his mouth. "And this, well, this has a penchant to give away the mean streak inside its owner and . . . and . . ."

It had to be a mistake. It had to be. But somehow, she found her fingers had touched his lips.

Then she swore that he kissed her fingers.

She told herself again it wasn't happening. He wasn't running his hard lips against her fingertips, her knuckles, her palm. It couldn't be, because that would mean she hadn't pulled her hand away, and then that would mean she was being seduced. And worse, she was doing nothing to stop it. She'd rejected such moments with Monty a thousand times. It had to be that she rejected them now. It had to be.

"Have you no mercy—?" she whispered just as his mouth met hers in a deep, needful kiss.

He leaned against her until her back was brought against the railing. A stiff Atlantic breeze kicked past but she hardly noticed the chill. She couldn't when he kissed her so thoroughly. His mouth heated her from her tongue to her toes. He pressed between her teeth and she instinctively opened to him, to take in more of his delicious taste.

Her heart pounded against her chest. She should have been frightened, or at least respectably repulsed, but she was neither. Not when Edward placed his hands between the part in her cloak and wrapped them around her waist. It was pure possession, but it fired her insides and made her belly fill with want.

He moved desperately over her, his mouth nipping and sucking her lips and tongue. She weakened and drew farther into him, the voyage only leading to the terrible discovery of her loneliness.

She wanted this. He worked on her like a drug and now all she wanted was more. The female animal inside her longed for him, and the need merged with her heart that cried out for sustenance after the long, endless drought of her life.

"Is this just play to you?" she finally gasped, her voice low and afraid, her hands balled into protective little fists that pressed against his front. "Oh, please say it's not so. Say you want what I want. Say you have a heart like me, Edward."

"But have you one?" he rasped, tearing his mouth away. "Sometimes I think you must be some kind of dark spirit the way you work on me."

"I'm just a woman. Able to succumb to sins of the flesh. Afraid to succumb."

The back of his hand swiped across his mouth. She wondered if he could taste her. The scent of bay rum, sea salt and maleness clung to her so thickly she thought she could run her tongue over her lips and lick him off of her. She still needed to catch her breath and she noticed he, too, was breathing hard.

"What is this thing between us? What does it mean?" she asked, innocently wanting explanation.

"It's called carnal fascination," he said, closing his eyes as if it would help him catch his breath. "After all, what else could it be?"

The words crushed her. Inside she knew she had a woman's heart that wanted love and tenderness—and meaning. Most of all meaning. She would get none of those from him. She was probably nothing more to him but a strumpet with which to while away the time. If there was a worthy man inside him, he would give himself only to a special woman. Not her. The very notion was ridiculous that he was as lonely inside as she was; so, too, was the idea that the kiss had somehow eased their aloneness if only for seconds.

With tears in her eyes, she was glad for the darkness. "Perhaps Lord Buchanon is not such a sorry prospect. The strength of my bank account would at least afford me some consideration for my feelings."

"There's that damned nobility of yours, acting up again. Where do you get it from, Lavinia? It confounds me so, like numerous other things about you."

"Let this confound *you*, Edward. Consider our previous 'business arrangement' intact. I shall look after Daisy's social well-being, and you will introduce Hazel. But from this moment on, that's where any accord between you and me ends. I don't want you to even speak to me unless there are others around to mediate." She gave him a long, withering stare, then drew her cloak around her and walked away.

From the corner of her eye, she could see him bow in her wake. "Whatever you want, *Countess,*" he said acidly under his breath.

She moaned and vowed never again to go out of her cabin to take the sea air.

Chapter Fifteen

" '. . . and Cinderella found her prince, and they lived happily ever after.' " Daisy closed the book. She gazed down at the two little girls sleeping on the couch. The governess was just about to put the children to bed when Daisy had knocked on the door. She'd begged to read them a story, and Abigail had consented. After kissing them good night, the woman left to retire to her adjoining room.

Gently Daisy fingered a lock of hair on Eva's forehead. So precious. Both little girls were. Eva and Fanny looked like fallen cherubs draped over the horsehair upholstery of the couch, fast asleep.

She wondered about them, where they came from, whose they were. Edward said he believed the children all were Lavinia's bastards, but none of them looked the slightest bit like Lavinia, except perhaps Eva who was blonde—but then again, many young children were blonde.

She pulled the comforter over Fanny who was curled against a needlepoint pillow. The little girl wore a white flannel nightgown with pink satin bows; she was the picture of innocence. Daisy's heart melted. She suddenly didn't want to know where these children came from. Their stories were probably ugly, filled with tears and abuse. In the few days she'd known them she was already becoming protective of them. If she truly knew their sad, unloved beginnings she wondered if her heart wouldn't break altogether.

From behind the couch she heard the cabin door swing open. She looked up and found a man in the threshold, his eyes filled with surprise.

"You're not the governess," he said, a grin on his handsome face.

Startled, Daisy didn't know what to say. The man stared at her with a proprietor's gaze, but she couldn't recall ever seeing him, or even being told about him.

"Who are you?" she asked, unmindful of any formal introduction.

"Montagu Baillie—Monty to my friends—and who are you? Have they taken another hire-on? Because I'm not giving up my room in steerage to bunk with the stokers, no sirree." He walked into the room and flipped his bowler onto a chair as if he lived there.

"Excuse me, Mr. Baillie, but you're in the Murphy children's cabin. I think you have this mistaken—"

"I have not." He winked and took a tiny wax paperbag from his vest. "See this here? It's licorice and I've brought a bit for each of them to stick under their pillows. I do it all the time back at the town house. They're practically my children, you know."

"Practically?" Daisy lifted one eyebrow. One thing for sure was that none of the children looked like this cocky Irishman.

He laughed. "They're not mine, I swear it. Though I'd take 'em as me own if Lavinia would only agree to marry me."

"She hasn't?"

"I've asked her seven times." He shrugged. "She'll be giving me the cold shoulder long after hell freezes. I don't think that woman could summon her feminine tenderness for any man." He popped a piece of licorice in his mouth and eyed her. His gaze studied every feature of her face, and then went lower, where he brazenly perused the top half of her figure that was not blocked by the couch. "So what about you? You're a fetching one. Is there a jealous husband in the wings, or is this my lucky day and you've come aboard alone?"

Daisy's cheeks went fiery red. She wasn't used to a man staring at her figure, nor asking her such personal questions. "I'm not married," she said quietly.

"What's your name?"

"I'm—well—" He didn't know who she was, and suddenly she found she didn't want to tell him. It was a novelty to have a man flirt with her. It was a little frightening, but strangely exhilarating. She knew that all of it would cease the minute he found out she was the heiress Daisy Vanadder.

"Well, who are you? Have they hired you on? What, to be a parlormaid or something?"

She gave him a wry sad little smile. The game was up. She couldn't pretend to be someone else when she was trapped in a wheelchair. "I would make a poor parlormaid, I fear."

She rolled out from the other side of the couch. By his expression, she could see he was shocked. Her face flushed red again.

"You're Daisy Vanadder, aren't you?" he asked, his gaze pinned on her.

"Yes," she answered.

It was finally his turn to be flustered. He looked around the cabin, but the words didn't seem to come to him.

"I should have told you," she offered, still wanting to be friends.

"My comments—I shouldn't have said—"

"No, don't," she burst out. It was rather silly of her to tell a rake that he shouldn't apologize for his behavior, but she'd found his attention so flattering that she just couldn't chastise him for it. "You didn't know who I was. I should have told you immediately. It's just, well, it's just that I suppose I was being a little naughty. Will you forgive me?"

He looked down at her, his gaze not moving from the wheel-chair. "I've a bit of a reputation for being a ladies' man. I'm the one to apologize. I acted a bit untoward there."

"No, no." Daisy looked at him. For some reason, she found a lump in her throat. It was depressing that he should apologize for finding her attractive, that he should find the need to apologize for treating her as any other young woman, but she was out in the world now, and she knew she was going to have to get used to such reactions. Still, they hurt. Her heart was a romantic one, and she found him attractive. His apology had served only to make her hate the chair she was in, and the woman she was.

The practical side of her finally took hold. She thought him handsome and now that he knew she was a fabulous heiress, no doubt he would be her slave forever. But he would never again look at her face the way he had just moments earlier. Instead of finding her pretty, he would now only see dollar signs. It was time to put him out of her mind.

She glanced over to the two girls still asleep on the couch. The corner of her mouth dipped in a pensive frown. "I really must retire but I can't abandon them on the couch. They need to be put to bed."

"I'll do it." He stole another glance at the wheelchair. It seemed to disturb him, and she wondered if he thought her ugly now. The idea was unbearable.

"If it's not too bothersome," she said lightly, but her eyes stayed lowered so he wouldn't see her wounded expression.

He walked to the couch and scooped Eva in his arms. The child awoke for a moment, fixed her gaze on him and let out a radiant smile.

"Monty, where's my present?" she whispered sleepily.

"You'll get it under your pillow in the morning like you have

all the other times, you little greedy baggage." He kissed her forehead and walked to the bedroom. He did the same with Fanny.
When that was done, he entered the parlor, hesitation on his
face.

"I suppose that's all, Mr. Baillie, except to say thank you." She
gave him an overly bright smile which she hoped would cover all
the pain she felt inside. Extending him her hand, she said, "I hope
we meet again."

He glanced down at her hand. A long pause ensued, then he
said, "Can you not walk at all?" It was as if the question so burned
in his mind he'd forgotten all else.

Self-consciously, she placed her hand back in her lap. "I can
stand up."

"But not walk? Not at all?"

She was compelled to answer him, perhaps because he seemed
so genuine. With a wry little smile, she said, "If I hold on to the
edge of a table I can move about a little bit. My physicians say I'm
just weak-willed, at least that's what Father told them to think.
Sometimes I think maybe they're right. Maybe I am just weak, and
I could walk if I really wanted to." A frown lined her forehead.
Suddenly embarrassed, she looked away.

"I don't think you're weak."

She glanced at him, then glanced away. He was a truly attractive
man. Black Irish, she thought his kind was called. He had dark
hair, vivid blue eyes and quick white smile. He was very handsome
and obviously handy with the ladies. With her inexperience and
her vulnerabilities she had every reason to want to stay clear of
him, but strangely she didn't want to. His attention seemed like a
drink for a thirst in her soul.

"I'd better let you get back to your cabin. If your brother or
Vinia catches me here with you, it'll be my hide." He cracked a
grin.

"What do you do for the Murphys? Have you always worked
for them?"

"I was a hack driver when they decided to go abroad. I figured they needed looking out for, so here I am."

"I've never heard of such a thing. You're a servant, and a *man*servant at that. Besides, I thought Edward was playing chaperon."

"Oh he is, is he? Talk about the wolf guarding the henhouse."

"You think so too?" Her brows knitted together. "I've thought a lot about my half-brother's attraction to Lavinia. I really believe there's something there. When he looks at her . . ."

He smirked. "Yeah. I know all about that look. But if he's gotten anywhere, then he's a better man than me. I gave up."

She suddenly remembered what he'd said earlier about his asking Lavinia to marry him. The embarrassment returned. "I'm sure you would have made her a good husband." She glanced in the direction of the children's bedroom. "I know for certain you'd have made them a good father."

He looked her in the eyes, an amused twinkle in his own. "I've a secret for you." He laughed. "I don't always give these kind of confessions but I'd have made a terrible husband, and Lavinia knew it. I was only after her money. My kind always is. Remember that when you go out into the world. I'm sure with all the Vanadder wealth, you'll be hounded by bouncers and fortune hunters to the ends of the earth."

"I know," she said softly. Then she added, "And yet, you can't be completely right about Lavinia's disregard for you. She must have some liking for you or she wouldn't have let you come aboard ship."

He grinned again. "Let's just say that she owed me a favor—the strange details of which I won't go into—and now the slates are wiped clean."

"But she must like you. I can't imagine anyone who wouldn't like you."

The sincerity, and, perhaps, naiveté, in her expression must have touched him. He bent down and locked gazes with her. "Vinia likes me but she knows me, too. She'll warn you off soon enough." He fingered the iron rim of one of her wheels. "I'm headed for the stage, you know. I think I've got a chance in London town."

"You're an actor, then? How exciting."

He laughed. "You think so? Most look down their noses at me, including those two Murphy witches."

"But it's like living another person's life. Who wouldn't want to do that?"

He looked down at the wheelchair, then up again into her eyes. Solemnly he touched her cheek with the back of his hand. "You know, I could get to like you, Daisy Vanadder. But maybe that's why I'd best do you a favor and leave you alone." A long moment ensued. He straightened and a coldness seeped into his face. "May I show you to your cabin?"

"It's right next door. You needn't trouble yourself." She looked at him. Every time his eyes met hers her heart sped; she wondered if this was what it was like to begin to fall in love. In the novels she'd read, they'd certainly written about it being like this.

"It's no trouble at all." He took her chair in hand. At her door, he said, "You might not want to tell anyone you met me. I don't need Lavinia angry. I know what she'll think, and she'll be right."

"What will she think?" Daisy asked, suddenly wondering if she had done something improper. She had no experience being alone with men. She worried she might have said something she shouldn't have.

"She'll think I want to get my claws in you because of your bank account, and I don't see any reason that she would be wrong."

"Does it *have* to be that way?" Her words were more bitter than she wanted to show, but all she could think of was her mother. Her despair had been like staring into black water. The money had been a curse; it had repelled all genuine love and encrypted her mother in loneliness. Now it was the same curse being handed down to the daughter, and Daisy could see no escape except to make sure she lived her life devoid of expectations. "I sometimes wish I didn't have the money, you know." She looked down at the wheelchair and swallowed the lump rising in her throat. "But I suppose it's better to be crippled and rich than crippled and poor."

He said nothing. Knocking on her suite door, he waited until the maid answered. By Evaline's expression, the old woman was shocked to see her mistress in the company of a man.

"Good night, Mr. Baillie." Daisy turned to look at him. With a quavering smile, she said, "I do hope one day I might at least see you again on the London stage."

"It will be your good fortune if that's the only place you'll see me." He tipped an imaginary hat, then walked away down the first-class passage. He didn't look back once.

Depressed, Daisy watched him go until Evaline wheeled her into her suite and closed the door.

Chapter Sixteen

The blue-gray Atlantic spread out from the ship like a desert of liquid dunes. Edward stood in front of the leaded-glass windows of the first-class lounge and stared out at the water, his thoughts as far away as the horizon. Even the seagulls had abandoned ship. There was now nothing between the *Maritimus* and Bermuda except a seemingly endless stretch of saltwater swells.

"Stuyvesant-French, come and have a drink with me, will you?" The duke walked up behind him. Edward turned as if he'd been startled.

"That engrossed, were you?" Kylemore commented.

Edward gave him a wry, self-deprecating grin.

"Aunt Celene is aboard, did I tell you? She was too tired to join us for dinner last night but she's ordering everyone about this morning." Kylemore signaled the waiter. "She's still pretty sharp for seventy, though. We can't keep up with her."

"Don't tell me she went out west with you and Buc." Edward chuckled.

"You must be joking? Celene, out west? Why, Colorado is too tame for her. No, she stayed behind in New York and ran the city in our absence. I don't know what the mayor will do without her." Kyle ordered a brandy and looked to Edward.

"Coffee," he said to the waiter, then glanced at Kyle. "A little early for the hard stuff, isn't it?"

"Ah, but you're looking at a doomed man, Stuy." Kyle leaned back on the damask-upholstered banquette. "You forget I'm to marry when I return to England. I haven't much time left."

"How is Delia?"

"As beautiful as ever. The perfect ornament. I don't know why the thought of this marriage has me so glum."

"Particularly when I thought you British had whomever you liked on the side. In fact, I was told—by you, I believe—that it was the height of rudeness in London to mention any similarity in looks between people—"

"Touché. Touché, you bloody . . ." Kyle's words were drowned in the brandy glass that had just been handed to him.

Edward grinned. "You can't be suffering that much. Delia Carmichael is more than pleasing to the eye."

"But not the soul. Not the soul."

"Why bother with the soul?" Stuyvesant-French's mouth twisted. "After all, you and Delia will unite the House of Kylemore with Carmichael Steel. There isn't a more powerful combination that I can think of. Wealth and title, isn't that what it's all about?"

"I confess I need her money. The dukedom is in sad shape. The lands are beginning to be parceled off. I could save the entire country with all that Carmichael steel turned to gold, but still . . ." He looked Edward in the eye. "Still, when I meet a girl as pretty and demure as the one I met last night, I can't help but think a lifetime is too long to be damned by the wrong choice."

Edward gave a black laugh. "Demure? Hazel Murphy? Give me a turban and a crystal ball, and I'll show you demure that Barnum couldn't top."

"What are you talking about?"

Stuyvesant-French rolled his eyes. "Never mind the details. If you like Hazel Murphy, go court her. You have my permission. In fact, you're the prize choice for her, just what she came on this fishing trip to catch—a nice fat duke. Her coin isn't Carmichael Steel, but she should have enough to spruce up the old family plot, and don't I know it."

"You're a sad excuse for a chaperon, Edward, do you know that? Why, you're practically throwing the girl at me, and you know I'm engaged."

"All I'm saying is that she's no fragile posy of violets. You just don't know her like I do. She'll be fine."

The duke leaned back and studied him. "No, I don't know her like you do."

"There's nothing like that going on between Hazel Murphy and me, I assure you."

"Yes, I know. Why would you take the sister when you want Lavinia so badly?"

Edward bit back a rising anger. "You don't know that."

"No? That's not what I saw on the deck last night."

Edward rose but whether to flee or call the blackguard out, he wasn't even sure himself.

Kylemore waved him back down to his chair.

Slowly, the tension eased and Edward sat again. "It's not what it seems. That's all I have to say." He stared at the duke with murderous eyes.

Kylemore sighed. "I really don't want to know. All I do want is to find out more about Miss Hazel Murphy."

Edward leaned back in the leather chair. "What do you want to know?"

The duke shrugged. "I'm not sure. I'm hardly acquainted with her, but she seemed sad somehow. A little lost, perhaps. Maybe it's the knight in me, I don't know. I'm drawn to her."

"She's had a tough beginning, I suppose." Edward still stared at the duke. "She and her sister started out in an orphanage in Missouri. Murphy's a common name and could have belonged to a thousand Irish immigrants any given day of the year. That's about all there is to say of Hazel."

"Where's the money coming from, then?" Kylemore sat on the edge of his seat as if enthralled.

Edward squelched his discomfort. "Let me just say they recently inherited from a benefactor who wishes to remain anonymous. Then Daisy insisted they accompany her to Europe, and here we are."

"I see." Kyle leaned back against the banquette again. He looked at Edward as if he didn't quite believe he was telling him the entire truth.

"Have you any further questions?" Edward asked, wishing the session were over.

The duke grinned. "Of course. Thousands. But there are some things about the young lady I must find out for myself, if you pardon me."

Stuyvesant-French shifted in his chair. "I don't like the sound of that."

"So are you the chaperon, or are you not?"

"I am." He stared at the duke. "What's the fascination anyway? Hazel's rather quiet. Not like her sister at all."

"Yes, but have you noticed, they have the same eyes?"

"Hardly." Edward smirked.

"Of course, the two women don't looked the same. To start with, their eyes aren't the same color, but still, the expression's the same. The same wonder, the same sadness."

"I don't see that at all," Edward said, not bothering to hide his annoyance. "What are you thinking, Kyle?"

"I'm thinking it's a bloody shame to grow up in an orphanage. It must have been terrible. It must have left scars, even if they're invisible scars. They both have them, I think, because I can see it in their eyes. Especially in Hazel Murphy's eyes when she looked at me from across the table."

Edward gazed down at his coffee cup. It was porcelain with HMS *Maritimus* painted in gold along the rim. The conversation was definitely taking him in directions he didn't want to go. He didn't want to feel empathy. His own life had been hard, and he didn't want to fall to his knees in Lavinia Murphy's wake just because she'd had bad things happen to her too. He'd crawled out of the gutter and all he'd wanted in this life was to leave it behind him. He'd developed a huge sense of entitlement in being a self-made man. He now desired a woman of refinement and grace on his arm. The privileged Delia Carmichael was more along his taste than that two-bit carnival act named Lavinia Murphy. "I think you think too much, Kyle," he said gruffly. "You're seeing more than is there."

"You want to know what I see in little Miss Hazel Murphy that I don't see in Miss Delia Carmichael?" Kyle took a quiet, belligerent sip of his brandy and made Edward long to order one as well. "What I see, old boy, is a prettiness, a gentleness, a forlornness. What it is is she's a mystery. And that's why I suppose I'm attracted to her."

Edward wanted to take the fancy painted coffee cup and smash it against the wall. It galled him to think Kylemore could perceive in Hazel what drove him crazy in Lavinia. It was like watching his life acted out in front of him. He wondered if all men were destined to become fools for the Murphys. "Let me give you some advice," he growled to Kylemore. "You'll never solve her. So just walk away while you have the chance to exchange her for Carmichael Steel. Believe me, it's the better deal."

The duke studied him from behind the brandy glass. He said nothing. In the end, Edward ordered his own brandy and the two men sat in silence for a long time.

"Is that the door?" Hazel called out, nearly taking Lavinia with her when she tried to raise her hand.

"Ouch!" Lavinia cried. She peeked at Hazel from behind the mop of rags that Hazel was tying to her head. She'd just washed her hair and begged Hazel to tie her hair into rag curls. Fanny and Eva had snuck down the first-class passageway to Hazel's suite along with her. Jamie was already in the cabin, belly to the floor as he read a penny dreadful they assumed he'd gotten from the ship's library.

"I'm sorry," Hazel soothed, extracting her fingers from Lavinia's scalp. "It's just that I swore I heard the bell at the door."

"You did, miss," Abigail announced as she sailed her prodigious black-uniformed girth to the door.

Lavinia pulled her wrapper closed and fled into the bedroom. Hazel, who was already dressed, just stood by the settee, staring at the cabin door. The children were oblivious as Jamie began to read aloud:

" ' . . . *and then the noble savage Touch the Sky drew up his hatchet to scalp the white settler . . .' "*

"Yes?" Abigail's voice boomed out across the open door as she look imperiously at the steward.

" ' . . . *screaming, the only words that echoed across the empty prairies was the cacophony of helpless "No! No! No!" . . .' "*

"Thank you very much," the maid announced before closing the door. In her arms was a long glossy white box tied with a shimmering purple silk bow.

"What's that?" Hazel whispered as Lavinia crept from the bedroom.

"It's for you, miss. I haven't a notion what it is." Abigail handed her the box and went about her business. The governess was very good at that, even though she kept her gaze trained on Hazel.

"It looks like a flower box, no?" Lavinia said, touching the bow. "Who's it from?"

"The card must be inside." Hazel's fingers trembled as she untied the box.

" '. . . the red man laid open his victim's scalp with all the gentle grace of a lion at the kill. . . .' "

Hazel threw open the lid. Nestled inside sheets of glimmering tissue were two dozen roses. "Look," she whispered, taking the stems in her arms.

"They're beautiful," Lavinia gasped as she touched each tight bud. "Who sent them? Why, there's no card, no name with them at all. And they're so red, they're exactly the color of—"

" '. . . blood! *The prairie ran red as Touch the Sky took his trophy and raised it skyward, victorious. Today he knew he had finally become a man. . . .*' "

"Eccch," Lavinia screeched, finally swooping down on Jamie. She snatched the novel and gestured to Eva and Fanny. "What are you reading to them? This is going to give them nightmares. You know better."

"Mr. Stuyvesant-French gave me the book. He said Mr. Juddediah Coltrain is his favorite author." Jamie looked down and shuffled his feet beneath Lavinia's damning gaze.

"Mr. Stuyvesant-French got this for you? When did you see Mr. Stuyvesant-French?"

"I saw him after luncheon. He was just leaving the lounge. He had a snootful, too, if I don't say, but he was friendly, more friendly than I'd ever seen him. He went with me to the library room and picked out this book just for me."

Lavinia looked down at the slim novel in her hands. It was cheaply bound in paperboard with the title *These Pristine Sons of the Wilderness*. She rolled her eyes. "You are to take this back—no, no, *I'm* going to take this back to the library and you're never to read Mr. Coltrain's adventures again, do you hear me? I won't have you fill your mind with this kind of horrific stuff."

"But Mr. Stuyvesant-French reads it—"

"Even more reason to forbid you. Now promise me, no more of these horrid westerns. I'm sure the library is full of books that will uplift you instead of forcing you down in the gutter with this nonsense."

Jamie kicked the carpet twice, then mutinously sat on the settee. Fanny and Eva watched with widening eyes.

"He's just a boy, Vinia. He's going to want to read such things," Hazel said softly.

"Not this. Not from *him*." Lavinia stared at all four of them. "What? Are you all turning against me?"

"Of course not." Hazel gave her a rather curious look, then she rounded up Fanny and Eva and said, "Come along, girls. We'll see if Abigail has a vase for these lovely flowers." She turned to Lavinia, her arms full of red roses. "I borrowed some toilet water from Daisy. It's there by the chair. Would you be a dear, and take it to her? I might be late to dinner if I'm to put the children to bed."

Lavinia nodded and watched as Hazel and the girls disappeared into her sister's bedroom. Jamie and she faced each other alone in the parlor.

"It's not fair!" Jamie growled, scowling as deep a scowl as she'd ever seen on Stuyvesant-French. "Just because you don't like it doesn't mean I can't."

"He just gave you this book because he knew it wasn't appropriate and he knew it would anger me." She lifted her chin. It wasn't like Jamie to be this defiant. She wasn't sure how to go about diffusing his emotions.

"You don't know! You don't know anything!"

She began to scowl on her own. "What has gotten into you? I'll get you another book, but not this one."

"I don't want another one. Mr. Stuyvesant-French told me I'd like that book and I did. I want to read that one." He crossed his arms in front of him. "You're just mad because he was nice to me and he's never nice to you."

She took a sharp intake of breath. With a glare on her face, she said, "He isn't nice to anyone but Daisy. Believe me. He just gave you that book to infuriate me."

"Did not."

"Did too."

"Did not! He told me all about it in the library and he wouldn't have known the story unless he'd already read it."

She opened her mouth but the logic was hard to refuse. "All right. I concede he might actually like this author's work, but you have to admit at the very least it was not appropriate for you to be reading it aloud to Eva and Fanny."

"Give it back and I'll read it just to myself. I promise."

"No." She clutched the novel to her chest. "I'm going to my cabin and getting dressed for the evening, and before I go to dinner, I'm returning this to the library with the admonishment that you are too young to read such violence."

"Fine." Jamie gave her a last glare, then he stomped out of the cabin to his own.

"How do you like that?" Lavinia exclaimed to no one. She glanced down at the lurid artwork on the paperboard cover of the novel and her mind filled with all the terrible deeds she'd like to do to Stuyvesant-French. He'd done it as a trick, she knew it, and she was going to call him on it as soon as she saw him that evening.

She took a calming breath. Walking to the table, she picked up the violet-colored bottle. Embossed in gold on the label, it read:

Mrs. Wirth's Violet Tonic and Beauty Aid—Cures Colic, Kidney
Disfunction and Liver Ailments—Will Impart
A Glow to the Sickly Complexion

She lifted the wax stopper and nearly passed out. Mrs. Wirth's tonic was nothing more than gin with a couple of crushed violets pickled in the bottom of the bottle. Daisy had better be warned to place it behind the ears and not take it as a cure or she might find herself tippling the swill with the rest of the drunks in Five Points.

She jammed the stopper back in but the wax crumbled in her

hand. Cursing, she threw the worthless stopper away and made a note to herself to find a cork stopper from her dressing table. But that task was quickly forgotten when, novel and toilet water in hand, she cracked open the cabin door and peered out into the public passage.

Empty.

She had only to turn a corner and walk a dozen yards to go to her own cabin door, but her embarrassment would know no end if she should be seen out in just her silk wrapper and with her head full of rags.

The passageway was slick beneath her slippers. She wondered how the staff kept the teak floor gleaming, especially when she'd never once seen a servant tend to it. Shutting the door behind her, she peered again down the hall. All quiet. She just had to rush to the corner, check the other side and hurry to her cabin before she shamed herself.

Her slippers skated on the slick floor when she took the corner. On the other side, she glanced at the end of the hall. There was no one. Relieved, she hugged the violet water and novel to her chest.

But then, she looked up again, and there he was. Stuyvesant-French appeared at the end of the hall as if the devil and his arcane humor had summoned him himself.

She choked. The dilemma now was, did she run forward to her cabin and allow Stuyvesant-French a better glimpse of her disgrace, or did she back away and scurry to Hazel's cabin, and perhaps find another cad around the corner?

Frozen, she moved in neither direction. Down at the end of the hall, Stuyvesant-French stopped, then squinted as if he didn't quite believe what he was seeing.

"Lavinia?"

"Oh, your timing as usual is just fantastic." Annoyance bubbled up inside her. She wanted to scream.

He took several steps forward and paused again. This time she could see his forehead wrinkle as he studied her. "Is that really you, Lavinia? What in God's name have you on your head?"

"Oh, never mind that! Go back where you came from. I need to retrieve my privacy."

"What are you up to? I'll not countenance any fortune-telling on this trip, not while I'm in charge." His voice turned thick with suspicion. "Don't tell me you're back to your old tricks? What are you? Playing someone's homely dead dowager?"

She bit her lower lip until she swore it bled. It wasn't bad enough that he saw her in her wrapper, but she had nothing on her head but the flapdoodle rags that were knotted through her hair. Humiliation tweaked her insides. "Go away, Edward. I was trying to flee to my room in order to protect my modesty, so just back up and allow me passage—" She glanced down and nearly gasped at the novel and beauty tonic in her hands. If he should see those, she'd die. Just die.

"What are you putting behind your back? What's that you're hiding in your hand? You're up to some kind of witchery, aren't you?"

He strode forward; she scooted back, her slippers taking to the buffed teak like it was ice.

"Go away, Edward. You're embarrassing me. Someone might come. Allow me to get to my cabin."

"Not until you show me what's behind your back." He paused in front of her. Suddenly he tipped his head back and laughed. "Why, Lavinia, you're blushing!"

"Oh, I hate you. Will you go away?" She frowned but it didn't ward him off much while her cheeks were flaming.

"Let me see what you have there."

"No." She tried to remain calm, yet she knew her face was the color of a cherry.

"If you won't show me of your own free will, then I—" He grabbed her shoulder and reached behind her. She wrenched away from him but suddenly she found herself engulfed in the scent of gin and violets. The capless bottle she held behind her had tipped in the struggle. Already the slick floor was awash in Mrs. Wirth's beauty tonic.

"Leave me alone, you baboon!" she cried. She broke free, but her feet slid out from beneath her. Grasping to keep her balance, she caught hold of his vest, then he slipped. Together they landed on the passageway floor with her sprawled on top of him chest to chest.

"Now look what you've done! I hope you broke your arm, you fiend!" She ground her fists into his front and tried to rise.

He locked his arm around her waist, and he held her in a most unladylike pose on top of him. His eyes lit with glints of wicked amusement. "What are you wearing on your head, Lavinia? What are those things? Are they rags?"

"Yes," she hissed, struggling to get off him but to no avail, his arm was like an iron band.

He grinned and fingered a rag knot with his free hand. "Why, now you almost look like the little orphan you say you are."

"Let go of me," she said, her voice as sharp as a knife.

His gaze moved downward. The silk wrapper had parted, leaving a generous glimpse of her corset and the two swells of flesh that pushed out from the top. The grin changed from amusement to something else entirely. He ran his knuckles down her throat tantalizingly close to the point where her flesh blossomed. "Ah, but then again, from this view, you don't look anything like a little lost orphan."

She closed her eyes and moaned. Men were nothing but animals. Especially this one. "Let go of me before someone comes into the passageway and sees us." She tried to roll off him, but his arm didn't budge.

"What is that smell?" It was his turn to frown. "I feel like I've been hit by a cartload of whores." He wrangled the bottle from her grasp. His lips moved as he read the label, then he sniffed it.

His eyebrows rose. "Good God, I hope you're not making a habit of this!"

She scowled. "It's well known that even the best of society women use Mrs. Wirth's tonic to brighten their complexion."

"Well, I don't know about brightening the feminine complexion, but it'll sure make your nose red if you ingest enough of it." His eyes narrowed. "What other little skeletons are you hiding from me?"

"If you don't let me up this instant, I'll scream for the steward and claim you dragged me from my room in the attempt to take liberties." Her voice held an edge of hysteria.

"Juddediah Coltrain? What? Did you sneak this away from Jamie just so you could read it first?"

She was sure her head was going to explode from trying to hold back her temper. The man's cheek was beyond anything. "I wasn't sneaking it away from him. In fact I expressly forbid him to read such wretched literature—and how dare you give it to him without my permission?"

"It's not so bad. If I were a boy, I'd love it."

"You can have it back, then." She slammed the book into his upper chest.

He caught it and laughed, easing his hold on her waist.

She scrambled away as quickly as she could, her wrapper soaking up all the Mrs. Wirth's tonic that had streamed onto the floor. Incensed, she cried out "Oh, look at me! Why did you have to be here, of all people!"—too exasperated to get to her feet.

He propped himself up on his elbow and studied her. He must have thought her pretty amusing because he still chuckled. "If you tolerate a little beauty advice, Lavinia—given that you seem desperately in want of it—might I suggest that next time you lighten up on the cologne?"

Her eyes flashed with annoyance. "You're not exactly smelling too fetching yourself, Mr. Stuyvesant-French, but then maybe I'm being unfair. It takes a special kind of man—if you catch my meaning—to wear the scent of violets as well as you do."

He sat up and grinned ruefully every time he took a whiff of his suit that was now drenched in Mrs. Wirth's. "Very witty of you, Lavinia, but now that I'm supposed to introduce you to Europe, perhaps you might at least attempt to hide your penchant for cheap perfume and cheap fiction."

She boiled. "It was your cheap fiction and your sister's cheap beauty tonic, so just pass along the insults to her."

"Thank God you dropped it, then. I've got to get Daze to the perfumeries of Paris before her nose gets used to this wretched stuff."

She stared at him. He was seated on the floor, his back to the passage wall and she was right opposite him, her own back against the other wall. They looked ridiculous, like they'd just done a round in the boxing ring. And the smell was unbearable.

Without warning, she suddenly began to laugh. He frowned at first, as if he didn't quite trust her, then he, too, let out a chuckle that finally ripened into full-fledged laughter.

"You look absurd!" she burst out between howls.

"Not nearly as bad as you, my dear, with those damn rags flopping on your head!" He slid lower down the wall and gripped his stomach as if the laughter were beginning to give him a bellyache.

She laughed so hard she almost forgot where she was. It wasn't until a man loomed over both of them that she even realized they were still in the passageway.

"Excuse me, but is this first class or a third-rate gin joint?" Cornelius Cook looked at both of them, then delicately held his nose. "I can't take it anymore. Someone tell me, is that liquor or violets I'm smelling?"

Shaking, Lavinia got to her feet. Her laughter quickly subsided into mortification. "Oh dear, don't look at me."

Cook, ever the gentleman, looked away as she closed up her wrapper damp with Wirth's tonic.

"What is going on here, French?" he asked as Lavinia slid away.

"Don't ask," Edward said, rolling his eyes. He gave Lavinia a parting glance, then he got to his feet.

Hastily, Lavinia fled to her cabin. After she'd shut herself in, she could still hear the two men talking and laughing outside her door. Embarrassed to her toes, she was nonetheless grateful the one to see them was Cook. Instinctively she knew he could be counted on to be discreet.

If only Stuyvesant-French were that trustworthy.

Chapter Seventeen

If you only knew what lions and eagles in all countries of the world have turned themselves into asses at my whistling and obediently clapped me in time with their large ears.

—H.P.B. (Helen Petrovna Blavatsky)

"I say, steward, we'd like some more claret, and whatever is that smell? Why, it's violets—violets everywhere." The duke, holding his nose, motioned to the wine steward to refill all the glasses at the captain's table. Kyle turned to the dinner guests and said with a grin, "If I didn't know better, I'd think the stench was coming from our friend Edward here."

Stuyvesant-French scowled.

"Perhaps that's the latest trend out of Paris," Lavinia said wickedly.

"What? Violets replacing bay rum for men? I think not," Buc answered, clearly offended by the idea.

"Oh, but if it's true, then Mr. Stuyvesant-French is on the cutting edge of fashion, and now I do feel dowdy in the presence of such a Beau Brummell!" Lavinia took a deep sip of her claret, eyeing Edward through her glass. He glared at her, and she deserved it. She herself had not been able to remove the cloying scent from her, even after her bath. The humiliation had to be double on him, but it was so terribly amusing to watch this brooding, controlling man attempt to brush aside the conversation that referred to someone at the table reeking of cheap violet water.

The captain's guests from the other night were all there: Daisy, Buc, his brother the duke, and Cornelius who, as Lavinia had thought, made no mention of the escapade in the ship's passageway. Lavinia found one empty place at the table, and she remembered some gossip from earlier in the day that the duke had an aunt aboard ship who was to join them. She wondered about this woman because Daisy had said the aunt was known to be quite the eccentric.

"There's another mystery aboard ship," Daisy suddenly announced with all the elation of a schoolgirl telling her chums a secret. "Miss Hazel Murphy has a most mysterious admirer. He sent her roses this afternoon—and he left no calling card at all! Can you imagine that?" Daisy giggled. She looked so pink-cheeked and pretty in her wine-colored velvet gown Lavinia didn't know why she bothered with Mrs. Wirth's silly beauty tonic at all. "Your Grace," Daisy added, "what do *you* make of such a thing? It's most intriguing, is it not? *Most* intriguing."

"Yes," Kylemore said, his gaze never wavering from Hazel.

Hazel looked at him. Though they were a table apart, she blushed. Her emerald taffeta dinner gown made her cheeks look even more pink.

"Roses, violets. Good heavens, the floral motifs are getting out of hand. Let's stop it right now." Buc winked at Lavinia.

She smiled, then her gaze met with Edward's.

His was quelling at best. He suddenly made no attempt to hide his belligerence. "All this talk of secret courtship is for fools. What self-respecting man would send roses to a lady and not own up to it?" He surveyed everyone at the table, his expression full of ill-concealed contempt.

"Well, you certainly put us in our place, Mr. Stuyvesant-French," Lavinia said, her voice tight and unforgiving. "Thank you for proving that you're above such frivolous—"

"My darlings! My lovelies! How absolutely wicked of you boys to snatch these delightful female confections to dine with you!" A woman appeared at the head of the table like a whirlwind. She was perhaps seventy, her hair a lustrous shade of silver with which she sported a rather adventurous set of bangs and, much to Lavinia's astonishment, she wore the reformed dress of twenty years ago. Her bloomers were of changeable purple-green silk and her overdress was of deep maroon damask. But in spite of its costly materials, it was an outlandish outfit, and the best part was the parrot green satin turban she wore on her head, pinned with a ruby the size of a knuckle.

"Are you going to greet your frail little old auntie?" the woman demanded of Kylemore until he dutifully rose and pecked her on the cheek.

Buc stood also and said, "May I announce, the Dowager Duchess of Kylemore."

The woman stood back from the table and suddenly appeared aghast. She looked at Lavinia and Hazel, then looked again, until she finally burst forth, "Countess! Czarina! I would know you both anywhere! Why, your portraits are the talismans of Camp Woodvine! How fortunate of me to be on the same cruise with two of Manhattan's finest mediums!"

Edward began to choke. Daisy grinned like a child smearing chocolate icing in her hair. The captain merely stared at the duchess as if he'd not yet quite gotten past her costume, and Cook looked as if he were courting a hernia in an attempt not to laugh.

"What are you talking about, Aunt Celene?" Kyle piped up, looking almost as confused as Buc.

"Camp Woodvine, you silly boy! I've been there a dozen times if I've been there once, and when it comes to spiritual telegraph, these two ladies are almost more famous than the Fox sisters!"

She waved Kylemore into attending to her chair. Once seated, she leaned toward Lavinia and pointed to her ruby. "I spent a year

in the Himalayas, in a secluded Tibetan valley, and this was given
to me when I completed my education with the master Koot Hoomi.
Oh, I don't presume to be an Adept, such as you, but I would so
cherish a séance before we dock in London."

Lavinia opened her mouth, but no words came out. This time
it was her turn to blush. Diners from almost every table in the
room were looking at the strange older woman who'd burst upon
the captain's table. What was more, all eyes seemed to be glued
on the duke and his brother who didn't seem to know what to do
with themselves now that their aunt had dropped this bombshell.

"Perhaps you have Miss Murphy mistaken for someone else,
dowager," Edward broke in, staring at Lavinia with an imaginary
noose-hold.

Lavinia kept quiet but the woman's memory was as sharp as a
razor. "Rubbish! I know the Countess Lovaenya when I see her,
and what an honor it is, my dear." She reached across the table
and patted Lavinia's hand. Hazel said nothing. She merely sat at
the other end and stared at Lavinia, a stricken expression frozen
on her face.

"Yes, Your Grace," Edward interrupted again, "but if I may jog
your memory, I think you'll find that Miss Murphy here is no
medium, but rather nothing but an ordinary—"

Celene drew back from Edward as if she had trouble seeing him
up close.

Stuyvesant-French, taken aback by the dowager's reaction, suddenly seemed to lose his train of thought. "Is there anything wrong,
Your Grace?"

"Whatever is that scent you're wearing, Edward dear?"

His lips drew into a thin, hard line. "It's the scent of damnation,
but that's beside the point. What I was saying—"

"What you were saying is that you think I'm an old woman
with a failing memory—but you know I'm right, don't you, my
dear boy? These are the women I think they are, aren't they?"

Lavinia closed her eyes. There was no point in denying it. The dowager had all but lined up witnesses to identify them. Edward would never get them out of it.

"Is that really your trade?" the duke cut in. He looked right at Hazel.

Unable to help herself, Hazel suddenly burst into tears. She glanced around the table, looking at Cook, Captain Stafford, and lastly to the duke. Before Lavinia could stop her, Hazel rose from the table and ran from the dining room amid gasps from all the diners.

"Everyone stay here." Kylemore glowered at his aunt. "And I especially want a word with you this evening before you retire." With that, he threw his napkin upon the table and went after Hazel.

"Really, I should be the one to go to her," Lavinia said softly as she rose from the table.

"He's already gone. Let him have a word with her. Maybe Kyle can convince her to return." Buc held out Lavinia's seat for her to return to it.

"Yes, sit down, *Countess*," Edward invited through clenched teeth. Daisy looked at her brother as if he'd gone mad, but Edward shrugged off the admonishment and returned his stare to Lavinia. "Go on. Have a seat. You were never one to decline a captive audience. I suggest you don't disappoint now."

Feeling like weeping herself, Lavinia lowered herself to the chair. She felt as if every eye in the room were on her, but worse was the pair of green eyes that pinned her from across the table. "Really, Mr. Stuyvesant-French, I do believe I've a headache coming on." She rubbed her temple for effect and looked to Daisy to help her find an exit.

Daisy remained mute, almost as if she were held captive by the proceedings, but the duchess had no loss of words.

"Steward, bring us a bottle of *Dom Perignon* while we await the return of the duke and Miss Murphy. Why, that should cure your headache just fine, Countess. It always does mine." She laughed, and Lavinia wondered if the older woman knew just how much trouble she had caused.

"Yes, that should cure it," Edward growled before he shot Lavinia a quelling glance.

"A cure or a curse?" Lavinia said under her breath.

But she took the proffered champagne glass anyway.

"What's this all about?"

At the duke's voice, Hazel lifted her head and stared nonchalantly out across the dark ocean. She heard him walk up behind her. Unable to look at him, she discreetly wiped her cheeks and kept her grip on the ornate brass railing of the top deck.

"This is nothing. Nothing at all," she said. "What your aunt said is correct. My sister and I are mediums—or at least we were before we decided to go abroad and find some respectability. But that's all gone now, so I suppose it's a relief." Her forehead creased and her eyes had a faraway expression. "I guess some charades are easier to play than others."

"What is Camp Woodvine?"

"It's in upper New York State. It's a spiritualist camp my sister and I have attended. We learned our craft there."

After this explanation, the duke grew so quiet Hazel was finally compelled to turn and look at him.

"Is it true, then?" he said, his voice hushed.

"Yes," she whispered, desperately wishing she could answer something else.

He became silent again and just watched her.

The stiff evening breeze had loosened several strands of her hair and she brushed them out of her tear-filled eyes. "Well, aren't you going to recoil at the scandal of it all? Or at least laugh at me? Or insult me? Or offer to pay for my services?"

"What exactly are your services?"

She couldn't tell by his voice whether he was titillated or horrified. Swallowing a sob, she said, "Never mind. I wasn't much of a fortune-teller anyway. You see, I received these roses today from a secret admirer, and isn't it silly? Here I am, still unable to identify—"

Her words were lost in a kiss. His lips covered hers as if God and fate were pushing him there. The kiss was quick and tender, yet deeper than Hazel had ever thought possible. When it was over, her hand went to her mouth as if she might hold in the taste of him.

"I'm engaged, you know," he said gruffly.

"I know."

"She's perfect for me."

The tears streamed down Hazel's face. "Of course."

"Then why do I look into your eyes and feel like I've just been hit by the moon?" he whispered, his gaze locked with hers.

"Maybe it's some kind of spell. Maybe these things really happen," she choked out.

"Can you really talk to the dead?"

She neither nodded nor shook her head, rather, she stared at him and uttered, "My sister and I are very good at what we do. We had to make a living, you see. At one time we were so desperately poor. So desperate . . ." She turned away again.

He said to her stiff, unyeilding back, "Look, I don't know how this is going to end but—"

"I do," she interrupted. "It's going to end unhappily, at least for me, so if you don't mind, I'd prefer you stay away. Once in London, I'm sure we'll never cross paths again."

His expression became dark and pain-filled. Looking out across the water also, he said, "She's perfect for me. Perfect. Do you understand?"

"Whether she's perfect or not, it has nothing to do with me."

Softly, she added, "I only know that I'm not perfect. So if you'll excuse me, I think I'll go to my cabin. Suddenly, I'm very tired."

"Don't avoid me. It's a long trip to London and we've still got a couple of days in Bermuda. It was improper of me to have kissed you. I won't do it again. I won't seek out your company when you're alone, just don't avoid me, promise?"

She glanced at him. Her eyes held back new tears. "Can I do that? Am I that strong?"

"I won't take advantage of you."

"No," she whispered enigmatically. "I've already been taken advantage of once. I won't let it happen again. Good night, Your Grace." With that she fled to her cabin and threw herself upon her bed in a fit of sobs.

The duke returned to the dining room grim-faced and distracted. No one made mention of Hazel's absence. Lavinia had the instinct to know that Hazel probably wanted to be alone right now. Besides, she herself was so full of champagne, and without the benefit of dinner, she wondered if she would embarrass herself when she stood.

Meanwhile, the dowager had kept them enthralled with tales of her travels. The woman had been everywhere. No longer with husband or children to burden her, her life had been filled with one exotic adventure after another. In helpless dismay, Lavinia watched as the steward refilled her glass again, while Celene prattled on.

". . . and in gratitude, the Mahatma presented me with a white tiger cub not even six months old that promptly set about chewing to shreds everything in my possession. I was forced to return him to India with my deepest regret that I could not adequately provide for the dear thing. 'Punjab,' as I called him, is now living in the summer palace on the coast."

"Remarkable," Cook exclaimed.

"Fascinating," Daisy interjected, her eyes sparkling with awe.

Lavinia looked across the table at Edward. The story seemed to have vaguely amused him but he was too busy scowling for her to know for sure.

"Shall I tell the chef to await dinner any further?" Captain Stafford twitched his mustache nervously and looked at the duke.

Kyle shook his head. "Please go ahead with serving."

The captain nodded to the crowd of servants milling around the table with nothing yet to do. They hopped to work, setting out the first course.

"So when shall we have our séance, Countess?" the dowager asked between bites of foie gras.

Lavinia shrugged to Edward as if to say, *The cat's out of the bag now, so what else can I do?* "Anytime is fine with me, Your Grace, but whom do you wish to contact?"

"Is this really happening? Are you famous?" Buc asked her, his face awash with astonishment. "I thought you were an heiress."

"Perhaps she's both, my dear boy," Celene answered for her. "Her bank account has nothing to do with her spiritual powers." Then the dowager did the most astounding thing: she winked.

"I must confess there was a time when I practiced séances but I'm putting that all behind me now because I'd like to see my sister married and my family taken care of." Lavinia groped for the right explanation. It still wasn't coming to her.

Edward finally stepped in. "What Miss Murphy is trying to say is there was some spiritualist activity performed in New York of which she was a part, but that she now considers herself retired, she would like to think no more of it."

"But she can't!" the dowager exclaimed. "Why, if you're taking the ladies to London, Edward, think how popular they'll be if they can perform spiritual telegraphs! The peerage will love it!"

"Yes, Edward, I think the duchess is right," Daisy said. "Hazel and Lavinia's craft is fascinating. Society embraces spiritualism here in America, why not England too? They'll adore them in London."

"Daisy," he said under his breath, "I'm not running a dog-and-pony show here, and I will not go about introducing you this way."

"But I didn't go abroad just to be stuck in someone's parlor drinking endless cups of tea. If that's how it's to be, then I should have just taken to my cottage and stayed in the States."

Edward ground his teeth in exasperation. "No, Daisy, that's not what I meant. I don't want this to be dull, but I also don't want your grand tour to consist of tagging along with a bunch of performing gypsies—"

"Gypsies! Is that what you think we are?" Lavinia got her back up. Perhaps it was just the champagne giving her courage, but she still managed to look indignant.

Celene joined her. "Indeed, Edward, these ladies aren't gypsies. What's gotten into you?"

"I don't care how they label themselves," he said angrily, "but I for one am not going to Europe in order to perform séances for the peerage!"

"Of course not, you silly billy," the dowager cooed, her voice as patient as if she were speaking to an unruly toddler. "You can't perform séances anyway, because it's a known fact that women make the best mediums, isn't that true, my dear countess?"

Lavinia wanted to laugh, but she had the prudence to hold it back. "Well, I have heard the notion that young women are more in touch with the Other Side. Perhaps it's their ability to give life themselves that gives them the gift. I'm not sure."

"No, no. I now recall that I once read about a medium outside of Shropshire," Buc threw in. "The *London Herald* said that this particular young girl was so adept at contacting the spirits because she was such an innocent and completely uneducated—unlike her male equivalents. They described this young girl's mind as an empty slate upon which the spirits could write their messages. You see, this very lack of intellectual power cleared the channel for the messages to come through, and come through they did. The young girl had people waiting for her services in a line all the way to town!"

"Buc, my dear boy, what an astounding story. How quick of you to recall such an article. A blank slate—what an intriguing theory." Celene grinned. The ruby in her turban glittered with fire. "Indeed, the best mediums should be empty-headed young girls upon whom the spirits can direct their bold conversations. Wouldn't you agree with me, Countess—you, being so talented communicating with the spirits?"

Lavinia took a deep breath. She then couldn't help herself. She giggled.

"Oh, this is rich," Edward grumbled. "The countess here's about as naive and brainless as a stalking panther. Buc would make a much better medium."

"Huzzah!" The dowager laughed.

Buc frowned. "But don't you see, Edward? It's this very female quality of lack of mental ablity which is exactly the conduit needed for the spirit world. It makes perfect sense to me," he said, giving Lavinia a patronizing glance.

"If it does, old Buc," Edward said, "then you go right ahead and ask the spirits to write their messages all over the countess here. And after she's through with you, if you've a farthing left, I've a bridge in London I'd like to unload."

"Oh, Edward, such cheek. If only I were fifty years younger . . ." Celene rose from her chair and bussed Edward on the cheek. All the diners in the room whispered and stared, but the dowager seemed used to the attention. In some ways, Lavinia was beginning to think it was her due. She was such an amazing woman. People should stare. They'd never see one such as her again.

"I don't know which of you gentlemen is right, but here is dinner, and just in time, wouldn't you say?" Captain Stafford rubbed his hands together and smiled at his guests. The waiters served. It wasn't until the party split after dinner that any more conversations took place.

The women went to the ladies' parlor, a room to the left of the first-class dining room, done in the ubiquitous Louis style. Between sips of cordial, Lavinia fielded a barrage of talk from the dowager.

"I just can't believe my astounding luck at meeting you, Countess. Why, I've been to Woodvine, New York, so many times I can't remember all the trips. Everyone who considers themselves even a dabbler in the spiritualist movement has heard of it."

"Hazel and I haven't made a mecca to Woodvine in some time. I'm sure the Believers have forgotten about us by now."

"Nonsense! You're a goddess there. An absolute goddess. You must tell me your secrets." Celene acquired a glass of blackberry liqueur and curled her legs upon the settee.

Lavinia almost envied the dowager's reformed dress. In a waterfall bustle and tightly swagged hips, she herself could do no more than perch on the slippery red-satin edge of her seat. "You flatter me with this talk, but I fear I'm not the great talent you believe me to be."

"Oh, but you are. I admire you so."

Daisy had demurred from the group, preferring to sip her sherry in the outskirts of the conversation, but now she blurted out, "I have to admit, Lavinia, as most do, I find it utterly wonderful that one might correspond with the dead. It's fantastic, I know, but I want to believe it. We should be able to do it—if the soul truly lives on—but how does it work? I can't figure it out in the least. It boggles me."

"I really can't explain it. . . ." Lavinia whispered, unable to meet Daisy's gaze. It was one thing to fool a crowd of paying men, it was another to dupe one's friends, and she truly considered Daisy Vanadder her friend.

"I've heard it defined as animal magnetism, mesmerism, hypnotism, electro-biology. The Fox sisters had their rappings, Daniel

Dunglas Home had his levitations, but séances, ghostly visions, spirit telegraphs, all of these things—these peeks into the other world—must be linked by one common phenomenon. But what is it that's at work here, I wonder?"

"What it is, darling girl," the duchess quipped, "is called 'utter nonsense.' "

"What?" Lavinia gasped in unison with Daisy.

"Well, it's all a fraud, isn't it? I mean, you aren't a true countess, are you, Lavinia?" Celene asked quite innocently.

"But I—I'm so confused. I thought you'd been to Woodvine. I thought you were an admirer." Lavinia was unbalanced. She wondered if she'd read the dowager correctly, or maybe all the talk of spirits had become skewed because she'd imbibed too many spirits. She quickly set down her cordial glass.

"But I *am* an admirer, dear child." Celene smiled. "If women had no power within the occult, men would continue to consider a female only useful as a means to wash his linen and bear his offspring. But there's so much more to our sex, now, don't you think?"

Daisy looked as confused as Lavinia. "So is it a phenomenon or not?" she asked.

"Why, of course it's a phenomenon!" The dowager frowned. Her gaze met with Lavinia's. "For a woman to fill an entire auditorium with her followers, what else would that be but a phenomenon? You see, in my day, to congregate in order to hear a woman talk was unheard-of. But now it happens frequently, in almost every town in this nation. We've found it, you see. This one special power, this presumed ability to communicate with the Other World."

"So are you saying there is no communication?" Daisy blurted out.

"What I'm saying is, Does it matter?" Celene gave Daisy a soft grin, the kind that made all the wrinkles in her pretty face fall away. "Oh, I don't imagine it's real, do you? It's too outrageous and illogical. But as long as there are men around to believe in it, then we'll have our flock of followers, and, too, the keys to the kingdom."

"I think we have an emancipated woman in our group, Lavinia," Daisy finally said, a grin softening her own features.

"Yes." Lavinia half smiled, half frowned. "So you don't believe in the spiritual telegraph at all, then?"

"It's only as good as the thespian who performs it." Celene gave her a mischievous wink like the one at dinner. "But what delicious power! Don't change a thing! I support it one hundred percent!" She raised her glass in a toast. "To the spiritualists, my dears."

Slowly Lavinia picked up her glass. Unsure at first, she hesitated, then, with a laugh, she raised it up high. "To the spiritualists!"

Chapter Eighteen

It came upon them like a small-pox, and the land was spotted with mediums before the wise and prudent had had time to lodge the first half-dozen in a madhouse.

—Augustus de Morgan, 1863

Edward arrived at the door of the ladies' parlor to find Daisy, Celene and Lavinia huddled like witches over a cauldron. None of this excursion was going as he'd planned. Celene's appearance was the final straw. The dowager had been more notorious in Europe in her day than Byron, Shelley and Keats combined. No amount of disapproval had stopped her. Now in her vintage she'd attained a kind of living-legend celebrity that would be quite useful in getting Daisy introduced to the most exclusive social circles, but the hitch was that Celene was incorrigible. And from the looks of Daisy's rapt expression as the dowager again related some wild tale of her youth, Edward could only cringe.

"Is the old girl ready to go home?" Buc asked when he came to the door.

Edward smirked. "Celene is in there preaching to the choir. Look at the three of them. She's the icing on my cake—as if this trip hasn't been difficult enough."

"Celene will never change. You know that." Buc nodded to the steward to announce him.

The women looked up as the steward announced them. Daisy wheeled herself to the door and Lavinia waved the steward aside as she herself helped the dowager to her feet.

"Have you taken good care of her?" Buc asked as Lavinia brought him his aunt.

"Indeed, she took care of me," Lavinia said with a gracious smile.

Buc held out his arm for his aunt. In a lowered tone of voice, he asked Lavinia, "Will you wait for me so that I might escort you to your cabin?"

If she saw the hint there, Lavinia did a good job of hiding it. "I'm right next door to Miss Vanadder. Please don't trouble yourself—"

"It's no trouble. I'll be right back."

"She's right next door," Edward interrupted, suddenly annoyed. He'd always liked the young turk but all his palavering was suddenly getting on his nerves.

Buc looked as if he wanted to say something which was liable to get him a punch in the nose, but being the refined peer he was, he merely nodded to the ladies and departed with his aunt.

"You should have let him escort you, Lavinia," Daisy said as Edward took hold of the back of her chair.

"Perhaps I should have. . . ." Lavinia gave Edward a covert little glance. "He really is handsome, that one. I could do much worse."

Edward pushed his sister along, but took a sideways look at Lavinia. He remembered the man he'd seen embracing her that night he'd entered her parlor unannounced. He'd never forget the man's face, nor his rough clothing. He'd looked like a street-cleaner. Even now it boggled him that Lavinia Murphy would involve herself so easily with the underbelly of society, yet remain cold and unfeeling in everything that concerned him. Without wanting to show his sudden irritation, he said, "But you've already done worse, Lavinia. I remember a certain louse-ridden mongrel I saw you with one night in your parlor. Whatever happened to him? He was a plush prospect for an unmarried girl like yourself."

"Oh, you wretched man," Lavinia said lightly, sliding her slippers along the glossy teak floor of the passageway. "Monty's no mongrel. He's a dear. He really is. He's the one I should marry— and I just might, too, once Hazel's settled."

Edward was stabbed by the old annoyance again.

Daisy grew quiet. She stared ahead and inexplicably seemed at a loss for more conversation.

"Look at this floor. It's truly a hazard. You can almost skate on it," Lavinia said while she slid past Daisy's chair. "You know, there is such a thing as too much maintenance."

"It almost reminds me of the marble floors in the mansion." Daisy looked up. With a smile she said, "You know, I hated that foyer. It was just like a stone cave. The only thing good about it was the expanse of smooth floors. I used to fantasize about racing along on it in my chair, and I might have, too, if I found someone who would have run behind me."

Lavinia suddenly stopped. "Well, let's see how fast you can go here."

"What?" Daisy exclaimed.

Edward rolled his eyes. "I think Miss Murphy has imbibed one too many tonight."

"No, really," Lavinia said with laugh. "This is just the kind of thing Jamie would devise, but it'll be fun." She took the chair handles from Edward, then leaned over Daisy's shoulder. "Are you ready?"

Daisy nodded.

Edward interceded. "No, you two are not going to do this. I forbid it."

"He forbids it," Lavinia whispered to Daisy.

Both women turned their heads and looked at him.

Then they were off.

He took a step forward to stop them, but there was no way to do it without losing all decorum. He watched with a sickening lurch to his insides as the women sped along the long first-class passageway, past the carved teak and brass double doors of all the illustrious suites holding all the illustrious passengers. Daisy cried out in joy, and Lavinia laughed helplessly as she tried to stop the locomotive once they neared the corner. Lavinia's slippery leather-soled shoes were no match for the floor. There was hardly any friction to slow the two ladies down. In a desperate effort, Lavinia finally sat down on the floor still holding on to the handles of the chair. In the nick of time, the chair slowed to a respectable roll and just barely touched the wall opposite the corner.

"Do it again! Do it again!" Daisy cried out, tears of laughter in her eyes.

Edward walked up to the spectacle. He stiffly held out his hand and brought Lavinia back to her feet. She was a disgrace: her bustle was torn, her hair was now mussed, and she had a smudge of wheel-grease down her right cheek, but her eyes sparkled like a child's.

He then looked at Daisy. He'd never seen his half-sister laugh so hard. In between gasps for breath, all she could say was, "Let's do it again!"

"I think that's enough for one night," he said. "You're going to wake the other passengers."

Lavinia swallowed her giggles and made an attempt to make herself presentable, but she suddenly noticed the rip in her bustle and the laughter started all over again.

"Oh, Edward, don't be a pill tonight. There was a time when it would have been *you* pushing this chair," Daisy chuckled.

"Untrue," he answered stiffly.

Daisy turned her head to Lavinia. "Oh, but you should have seen him. My brother Edward—the urchin of the streets—no one caused more mayhem than he—"

"You're telling tales, Daisy." Edward glowered.

Daisy continued mindlessly. "But now he's such a hopeless stick-in-the-mud. As if that's compensation for his sad beginnings."

Lavinia looked at him.

He refused to meet her gaze. His gut felt as if it were tied into one tight knot. He took his sister's chair in hand and rolled her to her door. He presented her to Evaline as soon as the maid answered.

"Good night, Lavinia. Good night, Edward. I had a wonderful time—and I can't wait for the séance!" Daisy waved and blew kisses until Evaline had closed the door.

Edward turned. Lavinia still stared at him. She stood in the corner of the passageway. Amid the laughter in her eyes was a new emotion, a kind of empathy, and it angered him. He didn't want to see the parallels between them; he only wanted to see the differences. And he wanted her to keep away. One day he was going to find the woman of his dreams. She would be good and gracious; flawless in character, not like this little witch who could entice a man to his grave just to get to his wallet.

He glanced down and noticed she held in her hand the piece of the torn lilac damask of her bustle. The smudge was still streaked across one smooth cheek.

He reached for his handkerchief and held it out to her.

"What's that for?" she asked warily.

He took three steps and wiped the white linen across her cheek.

She looked down at the mark on his handkerchief. The giggles returned.

"Shameless," he said.

She laughed only harder. "Truly, but Daisy never had so much fun." She walked past him toward her own suite at the end of the passage. Without really wanting to, he followed her.

"I don't need an escort. I already told my good Lord Buchanon," she said.

He took her hand and stopped her at the door. Staring down at her, he knew there was something he wanted to say, but suddenly the thought seemed to be gone. All he could do was stare and wonder what it would be like to put his arm around her tiny waist and crush her hard against him.

"Oh, Edward," she sighed, "you *do* smell of violets."

Unbidden laughter started in his chest. He grinned, and it was all over. She joined him and laughed too, until he couldn't fight the urge anymore, and he bent and locked his mouth on hers.

"No," she moaned, twisting away from him.

The laughter was gone. The frustration and anger returned. "I don't want you to do that séance," he said. "I don't care what Celene asks of you. It makes a mockery of you, of me, of Daisy. I don't want you to do it."

She looked at him. The sparkle was gone from her beautiful eyes. "I know exactly what you want and don't want. Don't fool yourself."

"Then behave."

That secret smile that drove him wild touched upon her lips. " 'Behave,' " she repeated, "but you don't want me to behave at all. In fact you'd prefer I do the opposite, such as open this door and let you into my cabin."

"I want you to behave in public. In private . . . you may do as you like."

"Do you want me to open the door and let you in, Edward?"

He knew she'd had too much to drink. By all accounts it would be unforgivable for him to take advantage of her now, but there was something about her, the way she smelled perhaps, all powdery violets and delicate femininity, that did something to him. He reacted to her from the very core of his being. At times he wondered if he'd ever know why she was so special, why she was the one who made his emotions so raw, so violent; he wondered, too, if he would ever know how to control it.

Her lovely face tilted up to him. Sweetly, she asked, "Do you want to come into my cabin, Edward?"

He bit back the urge to kiss her. "Yes . . ." The word was whisper-soft. His gaze locked with hers.

She hesitated. A small frown furrowed her brow. He wanted to lift his palm and wipe it away. He wanted to make her laugh like before, and then kiss her and make her act as if she was going to die if she didn't have his lips against hers.

"What would you think of me if I did let you in?" Her voice lowered. A dark emotion passed over her eyes like a cloud.

"I'd be grateful for the comfort, the pleasure, as I always am with women."

"You mean, women like me," she whispered.

He knew the wounded expression was there in her eyes before he even saw it. And God, she had beautiful eyes. They were the same color as the dusky blue shadows in the folds of her lilac evening gown, but full of feeling and warmth. He glanced away, then wondered why he felt guilty.

"I had a dream about you, my dearest, ever-so-stern Edward. Before we left New York."

A smile touched her rose-colored lips, lips he wanted so badly he had an ache in his belly from the want.

"It was a very vivid dream. I still remember the details." She reached up and touched his cheek with the back of her hand.

He pressed against it and closed his eyes. Her stroke was like velvet.

"It's not going to come true, is it?" she whispered. "It was too strange a dream, too fantastic, but in this dream of mine I proved to you what kind of woman I am. I proved I'm not one of the faithless wantons you've had a hundred times before."

"But there are times when even a faithless wanton has her value." He turned his head and kissed the inside of her palm. It was smooth and hot. It smelled of her. "Why not cast out these demons now, tonight? Maybe once satiated we could be a little more civil with each other. Hell, I might even grow to like you, Lavinia."

"I'd serve at least one useful purpose then, wouldn't I?"

He felt the rejection like a slap. "Don't turn away . . ." he whispered.

She met his gaze. Slowly, her other hand came up, and she

held his face in her hands, then pulled it down to hers. To his shock, she kissed him, full on the mouth, her lips slightly parted, her tongue moist and tentative and yearning.

"Again," he rasped, but she drew away.

"You think I kiss anyone like that, but I don't. I reserve it for you, Edward, only for you. . . ."

He refused to hear the hurt in her voice. He didn't want her to be human. He wanted to press his mouth against her eyelids and drag his tongue across the porcelain-pink of her cheek, then he wanted to bury his head in her throat until he moved lower to possess that lush feminine bosom that would captivate any healthy male. He wanted to take her, to have all of her, to wallow in her, but have no attachments later. Accusations and torn feelings weren't in the cards when a man dealt with women like her. But maybe that was why she was different. And maybe that was why she damned him by pulling away, as she always damned him.

"Why must this be so difficult? You give it to any cur on the street—I've seen you do it, in your parlor you were locked in the arms of that one man who hadn't washed his face in a week—but then you hesitate with me." His fury was getting difficult to pound down. She was driving him crazy.

"Maybe I'm playing coy." She smiled bitterly. "Oh, but I couldn't be, could I? Because I'm just some common adventuress. I'm like every other woman you've had." She drew near, her words grew throaty. "But then, I don't think you were so afraid of those other women."

His expression was carefully blank, but she was right. He was afraid of her. There was something about her—he might even have to concede there was something to all her supernatural trickery—because she was getting under his skin like no other woman. He wondered if his fear was that—once entangled—he might never get himself loose from her. He would be hers forever.

"When I have Hazel settled, I'm going to look for a husband for myself. What kind of candidate would you make, Edward?"

"Don't be absurd."

"Buc has a title."

"I have more money."

"The English peerage is known for forgiving past indiscretions. My séances probably won't bother him a bit."

"You'd be nothing but a novelty to him."

"And to you?"

He was taken aback. Slowly, he said, "To me, you wouldn't be a novelty."

"No?"

"I understand you too well, Lavinia. I've had women like you all my life. Little conniving thieves, willing to sell themselves for their latest desire. That's the only kind of woman available to an impoverished bastard like I've been. But now I've earned my way. Now I think I deserve something better."

"But that's me." She looked at him. Her words were so honest, so fragile, they made him hurt inside.

"What you are, what I am," he said gently, "are more of the same than I'd like to think." He put his arms around her tiny waist and pulled her against him. "But does that make us like two magnets drawn to each other, or repulsed by each other?"

She stared up at him. Her body became almost fluid as her curves pressed against his planes. "I feel both. That's why the emotion runs so deep. That's why it cuts me."

He gazed down at her, all dishonesty gone from his face. In a hushed voice, he confessed, "Sometimes, late at night, I've pictured you lying with me. You're naked, beneath me." He held up his hand. "Your hair is twisted in my fingers." He closed his eyes. "I imagine every part of you, how the musky scent of lovemaking lingers on your skin, how weighty your breasts are in my hands. I can see every part of you in this fantasy of mine, but not the expression on your face. The acceptance, the joy, I can never quite see that. Never."

"It was there in my dream, Edward."

His gaze met hers. "Then make the dream come true. Tonight."

She extracted herself. He felt the cold rush of emptiness in his arms. He hated it.

"*You* make the dream come true, Edward. *You* see the spirit—the soul—inside me, and it will come true."

He swore there were tears in her eyes before she turned away.

And he wondered if the anguish on her face mirrored his as she opened her cabin door and abandoned him in the passageway.

Chapter Nineteen

"'Were she ten times a witch, provided she were but the least bit of a Christian—'" Cornelius looked at Edward. "Am I getting even close to the truth?"

Edward leaned against the railing. The weather was getting warm as they closed in toward Bermuda. Stuyvesant-French, like many of the other male passengers, had already traded his gray wool jacket for white linen. Now he turned his face to the sun and tiredly closed his eyes. "I don't want to talk about it. I don't want to talk about *her*. It was the bane of my existence to meet those Murphy women."

"Buc asked me how much Lavinia's worth."

Edward popped open his eyes. The muscles along his jaw tautened. "You didn't tell him, did you?"

"Of course I told him—what little I know about it." Cornelius nodded. "Yep, he's just like a pup on a leash barking after a cat. He can't wait to get his jaws on her. Why, with that Irish estate of his all fixed up, just think of the magnificent séances Lavinia could hold in his parlor."

Edward said nothing.

Cornelius turned to the railing and looked out to sea. He didn't even bother to hide his grin.

※ ※

Daisy reached for the edge of the bureau. Evaline was in the other room of the suite, instructing housekeeping how she liked the linens to be pressed. The woman's commanding voice rode over the squeaks of the wheelchair being temporarily forsaken.

She groaned from the effort. Daisy raised herself to a standing position, then looked at herself in the mirror over the bureau. Her face was pale and tense beneath the dark frame of her hair, but standing, she could have been mistaken for a normal young woman. She looked like anybody else. If she hid the grimace, no one could tell how much her legs hurt, nor how weak and unreliable they felt beneath her.

She fell back into the chair. Out of breath, she could barely wheel herself from the bureau.

"Was that you, miss?" Evaline asked as she popped her head into the bedroom. "I thought I heard something. I feared you might have fallen."

"No, I'm fine." Daisy gave her a covert look. She didn't want her maid to know she was practicing. It was all part of the little game she played with herself. She vowed to practice standing every day until she could do it without effort. After that, she might even try a step or two. One day, she dreamed of seeing Montagu Baillie on the stage, and she would give him the standing ovation that she knew he dreamt of.

"I've got to go belowdecks and straighten out a few things with the laundress. Will you be all right? I promise to be back in a flash." Evaline gave her that worried look that was beginning to wear on Daisy's nerves. It was the kind of look a woman gave a fragile china teacup that was perched too close to the end of a shelf.

"You go on and take care of whatever you need to. You know I'll do just fine." Daisy brusquely rolled herself to the bookshelves and took out a volume of Sir Walter Scott. She hated being coddled and well Evaline knew it.

"I'll be back." Evaline gave her a curious look. "Are you sure you're feeling well today, miss? You look a bit more peaked than usual, and rather out of breath."

"I'm fine," Daisy said, breezily flipping through the novel.

Evaline gave her another study, then, with the housekeeping maids in tow, she left the cabin.

Daisy sighed and placed the book back on the shelf. She didn't feel much like reading when walking was what she wanted to do.

She rolled to the door. Maybe some fresh air would help her. It might invigorate her, give her more energy to practice standing. Too, a stiff wind just might blow away all the dissatisfaction in which she suddenly found herself mired.

Monty saw her before she saw him. He was out on the first-class deck straightening the teak lounge chairs that the Murphys used. The weather was fine. It was just the kind of day to lie in the sun and read. Other servants from other cabins bustled about, placing Black Watch plaid blankets along the chairs and attending to the tea carts. Monty didn't mind playing steward. He was the consummate actor. He didn't mind playing anyone as long as it wasn't himself.

Daisy Vanadder was alone. Typical of her social stratum, she hadn't even noticed him. On the first-class deck, he was nothing but a movable body in servant's clothing. He was another ant in the anthill. Believing herself to be unobserved, she greeted the few passengers that were out taking the sun, then she rolled herself to the end of the deck toward the bow, where she was out of view of first class.

Covertly he followed her to the tip of the ship where the wind blew relentlessly. He watched her, fascinated by her determination and purpose. Something was going on. There was an expression of hope on her face that he found compelling. She was definitely up to something. But what it was, he couldn't guess.

He placed two down-stuffed pillows on a chair and wandered toward her. He was spying, but he didn't care. She intrigued him, this rich girl trapped in the wheelchair. In her, he saw things within himself. He was trapped by an inauspicious birth, she was trapped by weak legs.

He watched as she hesitantly gripped the brass railing. She let go, as if she were afraid, or at least unsure. Her hands returned to the railing, and she gripped harder, and then harder still, until she lifted herself an inch from the chair.

Exhausted, she fell back. Her head hung for a moment, then her hands went up again, and she pulled and pulled until her strength gave out again.

The third time was the charm. Not that she had gotten herself to her feet, but as she pulled, he approached her.

"Practicing?" he asked in his usual cocky manner.

Shocked, she let go of the railing.

He caught her by the wrists. Putting her hands right back on the railing, he said, "Soon, maybe, I'll teach you to waltz." Then he put his arm around her waist and pulled her to a standing position.

Her face went from bright red to deathly pale. She held on to the railing as if her life depended upon it.

"Is it too difficult?" he asked. "Does this hurt you?"

Mutely she shook her head.

His arm held her against him. He couldn't help but look at her. Even the spinsterish chignon couldn't hide the fact that her black hair was glossy and tantalizingly thick. Her eyes sparkled green as the seawater below, and her lips were curvy and full, and probably had never ever been kissed.

"You know, you really are pretty. You're the prettiest girl this side of the ship and you'd best beware of wolves like me. This is exactly the kind of situation you should avoid." His hold on her grew tighter, more intimate. He looked down at his shabby-jacketed arm wrapped around her. He bet he could span that dainty little waist with both his hands.

"I *was* practicing. You must have read my mind," she gasped.

"I'm no mind-reader. I'm just observant of a pretty girl who comes up on deck." He smiled.

"I'm going to stand when the great actor Montagu Baillie takes his bow at the Royal Theatre." The ghost of a smile passed her lips. "You must think me such a fool."

"Are you that devoted a fan?"

"I have to find a reason to stand. I'd rather rise for an ovation, but I've conditioned myself to accept that I might instead stand at your wedding to Lavinia." She looked up at him, her expression so open and yet wanting it twisted his heart. "She's spoken about reconsidering your proposal. Just last night she mentioned you. I don't think she knows we've met."

"She isn't going to marry me. I know her well enough to know that."

"But you don't know. She speaks of you so fondly."

"And you? How do you speak of me?" He lifted one eyebrow.

She grew very quiet. "I don't speak of you at all. I don't dare." She glanced away. "But if I did, I'd say you're rather brazen . . . but charming. Terribly charming." She looked at him.

He touched a lock of her hair. "Charming, eh? But what has that to do with the price of tea in China?"

"Everything if you're an unmarried woman with few prospects."

He stared down at her. "Look, I told you you're pretty. Even better, you're rich. You've got to buck up and give yourself some worth. You won't be wanting for beaux as soon as your brother gets you out and about in London. So start thinking more highly of yourself. It's something that you just have to practice—like standing."

"Do you practice it?"

He grinned. "Indeed. There isn't a more vain actor in all of New York than yours truly."

She laughed. The sound was like the clink of fine crystal. He could definitely see himself wanting to hear more.

"Shall I help you practice this standing routine?" He glanced down at her figure that leaned most improperly, but most delightfully, against his. "I don't think it quite the thing that we go on standing here with me holding you like this without any purpose, do you?"

"I like you holding me like this." She looked him right in the eyes. It unsettled him. Her stare was too honest for a dyed-in-the-wool actor *cum* fraud such as he was.

"Really, I can't just hold you like this. It's not quite the thing to do with an unchaperoned young woman."

"But I've never felt so confident before. Maybe that's why I never could get the hang of standing. I never had anyone to hold me."

He studied her. In the harsh morning sunlight, most women looked their worst; she, on the other hand, appeared almost ethereal. Her fine profile was at once tender and as implacable as marble. Her expression was cut out of haunting loneliness. He found himself so caught up in her, he was hard-pressed to look away.

"What do you see?" she asked in a gentle voice, her cheeks flush with embarrassment. "I've never had a man stare at me so."

He shook himself and wondered what had come over him, but then he looked at her again, and he knew. "Shall you come here every morning to practice?" His voice was hardly above a whisper. It was the kind of voice a man used for intrigues and assignations. He knew too well what he was thinking. Worse, he knew what he wanted, and he knew how wretched he could be at getting what he wanted.

"I'd like to come here," she said hesitantly, looking around the empty bow. "No one can see me here. Are you up on deck this time of morning?"

"I am," he said, a faint twist of guilt inside him as he helped her back into the wheelchair, and then up again into his arms.

❧ ❦

"More flowers. More roses. This room looks like a cemetery!" Lavinia stacked the long glossy white boxes in Abigail's arms.

Hazel looked helplessly about the parlor at the numerous vases filled with every hue of bloom that could be had from the modern florist's shop belowdecks.

"And not a card among them!" Lavinia exclaimed.

Hazel began to laugh, then just as abruptly began to cry. She fled the room to the shocked stares of Lavinia, Daisy and Celene who were having their afternoon tea.

"Whatever was that about?" Daisy whispered.

"Oh, that terrible man. I've a good mind to teach him a lesson." Celene put down her teacup.

Lavinia watched her. "The duke?"

"Of course, it's Kyle! Who else would it be?" Celene answered.

"Is he just toying with her? She knows he's engaged." Lavinia perched on the arm of Celene's chair.

"He's like every man. He wants to have his cake and eat it too. Carmichael Steel is just too big an offer to refuse, but now Hazel's caught his eye and it's time to be a man—and he finds he just can't be. The cad." Celene shut her eyes, her expression disturbed.

"Well then, what are we going to do about it?" Daisy asked, looking affronted herself.

"We're going to pack up all these confounded flowers and send them to his suite, is what." Lavinia stood and began snatching stems from their vases.

"Huzzah! Now you've got the idea, Lavinia. I'll have you in reformed dress yet!" Celene began to help her.

Lavinia shook her head. "I may turn up my nose at most female endeavors, but I beg of you, don't make me give up fashion!"

They rang for the steward and piled the boxes in front of the door. Aghast, the steward was forced to call two others to help him deliver the goods to the duke.

When the flowers were gone, Celene shut the door. Then all gazes turned to the bedroom. Hazel wandered out with eyes red and shame-filled.

"Forgive me," she said, dabbing her nose with a handkerchief. "I don't know what possessed me. I'm frightfully silly."

"We don't know what you are talking about, my dear." Celene took her arm. "Now sit down with us and let me pour you a strong cup of tea. That takes cares of every problem for me."

Hazel suddenly noticed the change in the room. "The—the flowers?"

In unison, Daisy, Lavinia and Celene said, "What flowers?"

Suddenly they all broke out into laughter. Even Hazel.

"You know," said Celene, "I think every man on this ship is dangling after one female and professing love to another. Why, even old Cornelius, we've been friends for centuries and I've never been able to get his thoughts away from Edward's mother."

Daisy looked at her. "Celene, you're ten years older than Cornelius if you're a day."

"And what does that have to do with anything? My heart's still beating, isn't it?"

All the women nodded.

"Then it can still fall in love, can't it?" Celene sipped her tea and perused them.

"Oh, don't tell me even Cornelius isn't cooperating?" Hazel said. "Then we're doomed. All of us. The only one who's avoided making a fool of herself is Daisy here."

Daisy said nothing. She just sipped her tea with a shaky hand.

But Lavinia said, "I haven't made a fool of myself. Don't paint me as dangling after a man."

"And if my darling Edward were to sweep you off your feet and profess his love for you, you would decline?" Celene's eyes glittered almost as much as the emerald that she'd stuck in her turban that morning.

"He'd have to do more than profess his love." Lavinia held out her ring finger.

"Ever the businesswoman, aren't you, love?" Celene laughed.

"No," Lavinia answered truthfully. "It's just that I've learned to understand my adversary. Edward Stuyvesant-French can be counted on to be wicked, and charming, and witty, and he can always take your breath away. But for everything else, I've learned to get it in writing."

There was a long silence, then Celene cried out, "Lavinia! If I weren't old enough to be your grandmother, you'd be my hero. God save you and the Queen!"

All four women suddenly laughed. They raised their teacups, and by the time the toasting was over, the whole pot of tea was gone.

Chapter Twenty

The *Maritimus* reached Bermuda by the end of the week. Lavinia walked across the port and relished the solid ground beneath her feet. Overhead, the sun held a tropical warmth that soaked through her thin silk day-dress all the way to her skin. Breezes shook the scrub of palmettos surrounding the docks and tossed playful billowing clouds across the morning sky. The ship's passengers had two precious days in Hamilton, then they would sail to Penzance.

"It's beautiful here," Hazel exclaimed as she looked across the street to the ragtag patchwork of pastel-washed houses. Groves of banana trees filled in the alleys, and several women, their hair tied in lime-green-and-red tignons, sold pineapples from a stand.

"Shall we get the children some lunch and then explore?" Lavinia said, taking Eva and Fanny by the hand. Jamie lagged behind, his attention taken by two boys riding through town on a mule.

"The beaches here are supposed to be as pink as pearls," Daisy said as soon as Evaline drove her down the ramp toward the Murphys.

"I know! Let's have a picnic!" Hazel cried out.

Eva and Fanny jumped up and down in excitement. Even Jamie looked happy about it, something which Lavinia was glad to see. Jamie had been sullen with her ever since she'd taken away that awful Mr. Coltrain's book.

Lavinia sent Abigail for the lunch. They acquired a pony and cart from a local stable and put Daisy at the reins. Once Abby was back with provisions, the group took off for the nearest beach.

"I miss Celene," Lavinia said to Daisy along the way. "We're not the Four Musketeers without her. I wouldn't have thought Kylemore was related to anyone here in Bermuda."

"Apparently the Duchy of Kylemore owns most of the island, but I bet Celene would have had more fun with us in the pony cart than she's having now at some kind of stiff luncheon at a grand estate." Daisy tugged on the pony's reins. "Serves Edward right, too, for not coming with me. He's been a grouch for days now. I couldn't get him to budge from his cabin." She broke the pony into a trot and they turned onto a long, shell-paved path that drove them to an isolated stretch of beach.

The afternoon was delightful. Fanny and Eva played barefoot in the surf, dripping steeples of sand into fantasy castles. Daisy simply lounged on the blanket and watched the girls, giving them architectural assistance where necessary. Beneath the rich sunshine, even her pale skin became suffused with color.

Hazel took a long moody walk down the beach to where they couldn't even see her and Jamie found a niche in the rocks behind them where he did some reading.

Lavinia simply took satisfaction in orchestrating the event; she helped Abigail set out lunch, she dug moats for the little girls' castles, and she meticulously kept Stuyvesant-French from her thoughts. Ever since their last conversation by her cabin door, she hadn't seen him; it was almost as if he were avoiding her—or she him. Whichever it was, she was just glad to be rid of him. He only made her unhappy. At least that was what she told herself as she watched a storm out in the ocean creep closer and closer to shore.

"Do you think you ought to fetch Hazel?" Daisy called out, her voice barely above the wind. The sun had gone and the clouds came ashore in ominous striations of black-and-white.

"I think we'd best get back," Lavinia told Eva and Fanny. Abigail came immediately with all the shoes and stockings. From way down the beach, Lavinia spied Hazel. "We're leaving," she called out, waving her arm wildly. Hazel seemed to sense the urgency because she hurried her pace.

"Oh, Lavinia, it's the most charming place," Hazel said breathlessly as she rushed up to her. "There's an old house at the end of the beach. It looks abandoned but I saw wood piled by the side door. The house had such a magnificent porch—just like the kind you find at Cape May—with a big old hammock at one end."

"A hammock?" The word nibbled at Lavinia's mind. Fragments of dreams came back to her, but with so many other things pressing, she didn't have time to dwell on them. "Would you help get everyone settled in the pony cart? I've got to retrieve Jamie. He hasn't returned yet."

Hazel immediately went to help Abigail, and Lavinia took off for the rocks where she'd last seen Jamie.

The boy was oblivious to the drama of the changing weather. She found him burrowed between two boulders, his nose deep in the pages of a book.

"We're leaving, Jamie. Come help me with the girls and Daisy—" Lavinia frowned. She took a step closer. Jamie's guilt-ridden expression told all.

"You promised me," Lavinia gasped.

Jamie shut the novel he was reading. Defiantly, he said, "Mr. Stuyvesant-French told me it would be all right to read this one. And you don't know anything because you're just a girl!"

Lavinia grabbed the book. She looked down at the cover. Blazoned across it was the name Juddediah Coltrain and the latest title, *These Copper-Tinged Lambs of God.*

"How could you! You know how I feel about this! It's nothing but blood and violence!" The wind whipped angrily at her cheeks.

"You don't know. You never read it. Besides, you can't tell me what to do anymore!" Jamie's dark Irish eyes flashed with anger. He ripped the book from her hands and ran toward the shell-covered path.

Depressed, she returned to the beach to help with the pony cart. Daisy was already aboard with Fanny and Eva. Hazel had returned and once Abigail had packed the picnic paraphernalia, Lavinia led the pony back to the path.

Lightning cracked overhead. The pony became skittish and drops of rain began to plop onto the sand.

"Jamie!" Lavinia called out once they were on the shell path. She figured once he'd had his temper tantrum, she'd find him waiting for them on the path, but he was not to be seen anywhere.

"Could he still be in the rocks reading?" Hazel cried as she steadied the girls in the cart.

"No. I already found him there. We had a squabble but I just assumed he'd be waiting here for us." Lavinia looked every which way down the path, but it was empty. There was nothing to see but rocks and beach and five nervous faces staring down at her from the cart.

"Jamie! Jamie!" Hazel called, then Daisy joined in.

"Jamie!" Lavinia cried out as the rain fell harder, pouring from the black clouds.

"Where do you think he ran off to?" Daisy asked as she held on to Eva and Fanny.

The pony reared and Abigail grabbed the picnic basket before it bumped out of the cart. "Shall I go look for him, miss, while you and the girls get home?"

Lavinia wiped the rain from her face. Her linen gown was soaked. Daisy and the girls huddled together as if they were getting cold. "No, take everyone back to the ship. I'll find him and join you there."

"I'll help you," Hazel volunteered.

"No, you help Abby. He's got to be here. He's just mad at me. He'll come out now that the storm's here." Lavinia searched the deserted stretch of beach. "He must come out," she said before she handed the pony's reins to Hazel and watched them lurch away in the rain.

☙ ❧

A search party had already gathered on the docks by the time the sodden pony cart pulled up to the *Maritimus*. Edward gathered Daisy in his arms. He gently put her in her wheelchair. Evaline was waiting with blankets and a water bottle.

"But I've got to wait for Lavinia," Daisy called to her brother as she was pushed up the ramp by her maid.

Edward rubbed the rain out of his face and stared at Hazel and the two little girls. They looked like three shivering wet kittens. Abigail, soaked as well, handed the pony cart to a waiting steward with instructions to take it back to the stable.

"Where is she?" was all he said.

Hazel gave the little girls to Abigail who ushered them up the ramp. "She's still out there. We left her there because we couldn't find Jamie."

"For God's sake, the boy came back an hour ago. He's all dry and reading a book in the lounge." Edward shook his head. "I'll go after her."

"Maybe she'll come back on her own. I'll wait here for her." Hazel stared at him in the sheets of driving rain. She didn't make a move to go on board the ship.

"Don't be ridiculous. It could take an eternity for her to give up searching and return to town," he snapped. "I'll get a horse and be back within the hour."

Hazel gripped his arm. Her expression was filled with foreboding. "No, wait. Maybe Kylemore can fetch her. Or Buc. Have they returned?"

"No, they haven't. And why should they fight their way back to this ship in weather like this?" As if to add to the point, a thin netting of lightning hit the sky above in tandem with a deafening crack. He looked at her as if she'd lost her mind. "Let me go now, so time won't be wasted."

"No, you can't go!" Hazel's face was a mixture of horror and supplication. "Look, I know she'll come back. She'll be fine."

"What's wrong? Why don't you want me to go get her?" He gently shook her, then removed her hands from his arm.

"You can't go." She wiped the rain from her eyes. As if to implore him, she said, "It's the hammock. I saw it! I know this sounds crazy but Lavinia had this dream . . ." Her words drifted to silence. She stared at him as if questioning her strength to go against fate and the storm. Nearby, the wind knocked a shutter off its hinge and it tumbled down the cobbled road, adding to the cacophony.

"Enough. Let me get her before the tide comes in and we find her in the morning drowned." He directed her to the ramp. "You can tell me the story when I come back."

Defeated, she stepped up onto the ship's ramp. He sprinted across the docks to the stable where they'd rented the pony cart. She turned to watch him in the rain. With no one around to hear her, Hazel whispered dejectedly, "But by the time you come back, it'll be too late."

Chapter
Twenty-One

It appears to me that the whole question narrows itself into this small compass. The proof must be absolute, and not based upon inferential reasoning, or assumed upon the supposed integrity of seals, knots and sewing, for I have reasons to know that the power at work in these phenomena, like love, "laughs at locksmiths."

—William Crookes, *in a letter to* The Spiritualist

"Jamie!" Lavinia cried out. Around her, the wind screamed, the surf slammed at her bare ankles. A mile behind her on the beach lay her stockings and boots where she'd discarded them at the beginning of the picnic. They were all but forgotten now as she combed the beach frantically looking for Jamie.

Her imagination drove her onward. She was convinced that every terrible accident that came to mind was what had happened to Jamie. He'd fallen from a rock and hit his head. Even now he might be facedown in a pool of water, having breathed his last.

Swallowing her hysteria, she ran farther along the beach to the gray shadow of a house that loomed at the end. Maybe he'd gone there. Maybe when the storm grew fierce, he'd found shelter on the deep porch. When she got there, she was convinced she would find him, huddled in the corner, the water dripping off him in rivulets.

"Jamie! Jamie!" she called out when she arrived at the porch stairs. Already the ocean waves ate at the first step. Behind her, the storm rumbled ashore in great black currents of clouds, wind and lightning. She yelled his name into the darkness at the top of the stairs. "Jamie! Jamie!" she cried, taking the steps two at a time.

But no one answered.

Exhausted, she slid down onto the porch floor and leaned back against the clapboards. The porch was deep and dark, sheltered from the storm by a wall of thick-slatted shutters. It was the perfect choice for a boy to hide from a storm. Her fear escalated as she wondered where he could be.

She didn't care about Juddediah Coltrain now. Jamie could read all the Coltrain he could stomach, if he would just show himself. She looked around the dark porch, her eyes adjusting to the dimness. It was empty. No afraid little boy tucked in the corner just as she remembered he did when Burton Karpp would go on a rampage and take the crop to the children. Jamie was so good at hiding then because it was so important to hide, but not now. Now it was important to be found. That's why they all left the orphanage together, so they would have someone to care about them. So they wouldn't have to endure five-year-old little boys cowering in the corner, fearful of a man with a whip.

Tears of frustration pooled in her eyes. Her bare feet were cut and bleeding from her search through the rocks. Her linen gown was in tatters and her hair lay in a long dripping hank down her back, but she didn't care about any of it. She just wanted to find Jamie. They were in a place they'd never been before and he was alone. He might be lost. He might be hurt. With a sickening groan, the wind pummeled the side of the empty house; waves crashed on the beach just inches from the low brick piers that held up the house. The terror of her last thought made her crazy. *Jamie can't swim.*

She suddenly sat up straight. It might have been the wind but she swore she heard a voice call her name. With a start, she heard it again, then again. Scrambling to her feet, she dashed down the porch stairs and ran back into the storm.

"Jamie! Jamie! Is that you?" she sobbed into the darkness.

Through torrents of rain she saw a figure way down on the beach.

"Jamie . . ." The name died on her lips. A crack of lightning flashed overhead, and she made out the figure. It was a man on a horse. The storm had terrified the animal and with every new boom of thunder, the horse reared and pawed at the air with its hooves.

"Jamie," she whispered, desolate. The man and steed came closer. In another flash of lightning, she found he was galloping toward her, his mount white-eyed and frothy from terror.

"Lavinia!" he said, sliding from the steed.

"Edward! Oh my God, Edward!" His name came in fits and sobs. "I can't find Jamie! I can't find him anywhere! He's drowned. I know he's drowned. Please help me find him. I beg of you. I beg of you!" She grabbed him by jacket and began to pull him as if to bring him with her in the darkness. The cold rain slapped her skin with all the sting of icicles, but she was ready to brave the storm and anything else now that she had help in finding Jamie.

Suddenly she found herself wrapped in his arms. The surf was deep and strong around their feet. She shivered violently, releasing all her pent-up dread. "Oh, Edward, we must find him!" She broke down in a fit of tears. His hand went to her waist and he held her to him; she buried her head in his chest.

"Jamie's fine," he said through the pounding wind. "He beat you to the ship. When I left him, he was warm and dry, his attention buried in a book." Edward met her gaze and his own softened. "If he could see you like this, I think he'd be feeling much worse right now."

She wondered if her legs would collapse beneath her. *Jamie is fine.* She could hardly believe it. Alone, in the storm, her imagination had come alive. She'd pictured him in all sorts of trouble, and frantically she'd searched to find him in time. But, like the devil he was, he'd just stomped off in a fit of temper and returned to the ship.

"Thank God, thank God," she whispered weakly, suddenly feeling the exhaustion and cold.

"The captain said this is going to be a bad storm." Edward yanked on the reins to steady his frightened mount. "Come," he said, taking her hand.

She followed him.

He tied the horse to one of the heavy stair balusters of the empty house and quickly ushered her onto the porch.

The wind rattled the shutters, but this time, she noticed how quiet it was on the veranda away from the full wrath of the storm. Her relief at knowing Jamie was safe made every limb feel like lead. She'd barely moved from the railing before Edward lost himself in the interior of the porch, retrieved an old whale-oil lamp and lit it.

She looked around and could see that the veranda floor had been recently whitewashed and the wall of shutters was a dark bottle-green color. The louvers clacked and trembled against the force of the wind, a sign that the storm had no intention of letting up soon.

In the flickering light of the whale-oil lantern, she looked at Edward. He was staring at her. He seemed to mentally catalog every aspect of her appearance, from her tear-reddened eyes to her sopping-wet gown and bare feet. He looked away when she caught him staring. A muscle bunched in his jaw, hinting that he was forcing himself to play a game of manners he did not feel.

He set the lantern down on a wobbly table next to a hammock that swayed from the winds that pounded the house. He was as wet as she. Water dripped from his jet black hair, his linen suit looked like it needed to be wrung out by the washwoman. He peeled off his ruined jacket and draped it over a pair of bentwood chairs that flanked the door. Every muscle of his chest was apparent through his wet batiste shirt. It was her turn to look away.

"Thank you," she said softly.

He didn't answer. He was clearly trying to remain aloof, but it was impossible given the storm beating outside and the utter aloneness of both of them as they hid from the fury of the night.

"I was going crazy out here," she added. "I couldn't find him. Not anywhere. Not anywhere." Sudden, helpless tears of relief streaked down her face. She was overcome with unspeakable gratitude, but, stupidly, all she could do was let her tears add to the sodden mess of her appearance.

"I told you he was fine," he said, hardly looking at her.

"I know. It's just that for a few moments I thought something terrible had happened to him. This storm—it came so fast and so violently—" She tried to calm down, but she couldn't. The tears fell no matter what she did; catharsis for her fears.

"It's all right," he said, his gaze holding her. "It's all over now."

She tried to gather herself but couldn't. The emotion poured out unchecked. "The children and Hazel, they're all I have, you see. I couldn't lose Jamie. Not Jamie. He used to try to stick up for me at the home. Imagine that. Me, sixteen, and him only five with a streak of chivalry in him as wide as the ocean." Her voice broke. She was beset by trembling. She wrapped her arms around herself, but to no avail. Her teeth began to chatter.

He pulled her to him. She went gladly. His proximity had always been so threatening before, but now, to have that hard warm chest pressed against her own seemed the remedy for pneumonia.

"One lost little boy can do this to you?" He thumbed her damp cheek. "I wouldn't have guessed the Countess Lovaenya would fracture so easily."

With his arms around her, she suddenly found herself warm again. A calm she couldn't seem to find on her own overtook her. "I just can't lose any of them. They're all I have," she whispered.

"You have all of them safe on the *Maritimus*. In fact, they're probably more worried about you since you haven't returned to the ship."

"They won't worry," she said cryptically. Her gaze darted around the veranda. Behind him, the elaborately fringed hammock loomed like a pyre. She'd never been to Bermuda, much less this house, but it was all familiar: the howling wind, the shaking walls, the swinging empty hammock. Empty for now.

He wrapped his arms more tightly around her as the wind clipped the roof. "They have every reason to worry. This is a bad storm."

"They won't worry. They'll know I'm with you." She stared at him. Her trembling quieted beneath his penetrative gaze. He understood what she meant; she could see it in his face.

The corner of his mouth tipped in a dark smile. "But they should worry. Unlike Jamie, my streak of chivalry isn't worthy of a small stream."

She gave him a smile of her own. "You came here first and foremost to help me, Edward. Anything else that may happen is simply fate and circumstance."

"Fate and circumstance is on my side now."

"It always has been."

She reached up and instinctively touched his cheek. He reacted to her caress half with a flinch, but she didn't take her hand away. She'd never seen him without his normal scrupulous grooming. His beard-roughed cheek was an entirely new facet of him, but she found herself wildly attracted by it as never before. Damp and unkempt, he seemed more reachable now than the cool, polished man she knew. The way he looked now, she wondered if it were actually a peek behind his armor. "I'm glad you came for me. This is the way I would have wanted it. . . ."

He looked down at her as if he weren't sure of her words. "I only came because I knew you'd be worried about Jamie. I didn't want you to worry—"

"—because, perchance, you have feelings for me." A frown furrowed her brow. The futile search for Jamie had led instead to her destiny, and she wasn't so confident about it yet. She glanced again at the hammock. The details of her dream flooded back to her, sending a rush of anxiety.

She tilted her head back. Her gaze entwined with his. The hour had arrived. It was time to either embrace her destiny or run from it as fast as she could. She gathered all the courage left to her.

"If you admit it, Edward, no one else will know," she said in a whisper. "It won't change anything tomorrow. I'll still be the woman you claim to despise, and you will still be the tower of ice in gentleman's clothing. But here and now—just tell me for posterity—what are your feelings for me?"

Unwanted tears filled her eyes. Her emotions were raw. The terror over Jamie had wrung her out; now she had Edward here, and they were both so cold, and the rain was coming down so hard. She was vulnerable like this, with him, but it was time to decide it between them, and the decision lay at his feet, not hers.

She brushed away her tears. Gathering herself, she said, "You continually deride me and seduce me all with the same words. I've a right to know why you toy with me. Am I just another conquest? I think it must be more. Sometimes I look at you, Edward, and I feel as if my soul has known you for a millenium. But then, I'm a woman. A woman wants to feel these things." Her voice dropped to almost nothing. "I'm well aware they mean little to most men."

He didn't respond. He looked down at her, his eyes hooded in shadow, his face rigidly cleansed of all expression.

Despair hit her like the winds against the house. Monty had warned her that love would be like this, that it would weaken her, leave her with no pride and no choice. But he'd never told her how powerful her need for it would be, nor how it would sneak up to her and taunt her like a ill-remembered dream, or a hammock swinging from a dark corner.

"There's no risk to telling me, Edward," she finally said, tears choking her throat. "I'm not a young girl who needs to be duped with promises. I'm a worldly woman who knows better than to try and hold a man to a confession he made while we were alone and in the dark, surrounded by wind and rain. You'll never bear the shame of confessing your feelings to one such as me. No one would believe my kind anyway, remember? So tell me. Just tell me why you came for me."

He closed his eyes. An agony seemed to rip into him until he could no longer take it anymore. "You're a woman whose very life makes a mockery of the truth. You dress in ghostly clothes and playact the dead. You swindle money from gullible men. Yet the damnable part is that I find you desirable. *Most* desirable."

His hand rested at her throat. His gaze fixed there, at the pearl buttons that began under her chin and ran all the way down to her waist.

She looked down and her cheeks heated with something that was not embarrassment but perhaps should have been. Wet, the cream-colored linen of her summer jacket was transparent. The thin, clinging fabric outlined all the ridges of her corset; she could even see the tiny satin bows that adorned her chemise.

She leaned against him, surrender seeping into her bones. The steel hooks of the hammock creaked as the wind rattled the walls. Everything in this grand scheme was planned. There was no running away.

"You say I'm like every common woman you've ever been with, and maybe you're right, Edward," she said. "Maybe I'm finally able to see that you're right and accept it now."

"But you're not like them. I've walked away from all the rest. But from you . . . from you . . . You're like a vine creeping up a brick wall, finally tumbling it. I can't seem to find a way to keep what I feel under control."

"You master everything, Edward."

He seemed to hold his breath. "Yes, I'm a man who masters his attractions, they do not master me. . . ." He stared down at her for a long, painful moment. "Oh, but the devil of this one. The devil of it."

As if drawn by a will outside herself, she tilted her head back and offered him her mouth. His arm turned to iron around her waist. He slowly locked her against him, then bent his head and placed his lips upon her own.

His kiss was like an opiate running through her veins. It made her deaf to the wind's ceaseless pounding, blind to the ominous flickers of lamplight that foretold dangerous pursuits. All she wanted was him, more and more of him as his mouth moved hard against her own, as his hand slid up her rib cage to cup her breast.

He buried his head in her throat, dragging his teeth over her ear, tonguing the pulse points of her neck. She shivered but this time with ecstasy, not cold. The possession was sweet. Though she knew she would prove to be a novice at lovemaking, she was educated enough about the process to know the basic elements. What was to follow should have terrified her, but she couldn't be afraid of it when she was with him. Kissing him, touching him, holding him meant too much to her to check herself with fear.

"Do mine," he nuzzled as he began to release the pearl buttons of her jacket.

Hesitantly she put her hands on his chest. Her fingers fumbled over the buttons on his shirt, releasing half of his in twice the time it took him to do all of hers.

He held her hands to the gridded muscle of his torso. Shy at first, she was reluctant to spread her palms, but she quickly became greedy. She found him beneath the damp linen shirt and reveled in his feel. He was slick with sweat, and hard. Impossibly hard. A man's unyielding toughness.

The differences between them should have chased her away, but, instead, they drew her to him like a magnet. His chest was the antithesis of her own; where he was taut with muscle, she was generous with flesh; her own smooth skin that now threatened to overflow the top of her water-shrunken corset was in marked contrast to his roughened with hair. But they were the perfect complements, he and she. Edward and Lavinia. And she wanted more as he pressed himself against her and strained the breaking dam of her corset.

"How do you like to do it, Countess?" he said against her neck as he pulled her hand to his trousers.

Her fingers brushed the bulge. She pulled back as if stung.

Shock coursed through her as she realized they'd gone over the line. There was no return now. There could be no thoughts of turning back.

"How do you like it?" he asked again, his fingers finally at the hooks of her corset.

"I—I don't know," she whispered, her breath coming quick and shallow. She wanted this, wanted *him*, but it was like falling from a cliff, there was no climbing back, no holding on. "I must tell you—make you understand—"

"Tell me. Everything. We'll do what you like first. Then we'll get to me." He stared down at her. His eyes were as she remembered, an unforgivable shade of green. They were beautiful to her, even in the dim light of one lantern, and when he looked at her with such want within them, she knew she couldn't disappoint him. He demanded her; she would give to him totally.

He ran his tongue over her mouth. With aching slowness, he pulled away the sides of her corset. Her bare breasts spilled from their damp linen cage and he caught them both in his waiting hands. She gasped; he smothered the sound with another deep heated kiss.

Sensation rained on her like a cloudburst, drowning her until she couldn't think, couldn't breathe. He unhooked her skirt and drove his hands beneath the masses of petticoats and drawers until he cupped her bare buttocks in the same sensual manner of her breasts.

"Take these off," he said sharply, tugging at her skirt and under-clothing that caught at her hips. Finally losing all patience, he crouched and pulled all her clothing to the floor until she stood above him as nude as the *Venus de Milo*.

He kissed her between the legs. It was brief but, to her, all-consuming. The slick feel of his tongue made her wonder if she had the strength to keep standing.

"More?" he whispered wickedly.

She gazed down at him, mute, her mind unable to erase the vision of his dark head moving over the golden mound of her womanhood.

"Go to the hammock, then, if you're ready," he said, rising to his feet.

She backed up, nearly stumbling over her torn, discarded clothing. Modesty assailed her; she couldn't stop herself from pulling her arms over her breasts.

He studied her pose, then cracked a grin. "I like it. A touch of virginity. You really are brilliant . . . so brilliant." He drew her arms to her side and whisked back the damp hanks of blonde hair that fell over her breasts. Groaning, he kissed her on the mouth almost brutally before he buried his face in her chest and covered each nipple with his mouth.

"Please . . ." The word came from a deep animal place inside her. She wanted him to stop, but she desperately needed him to continue. In the end, she threw her head back. In surrender, she could say no more.

He straightened and pushed her back until her legs met the heavy cotton ropes of the hammock. Grinding himself against her hips, he forced her hands to return to his chest. She could barely look at him. His face had a lean intensity to it she'd never seen before; his eyes were shadowed, yet gleamed hot with lust. A small rush of fear shot through her. He still wore his clothes. Beside him, nude and vulnerable, she had reduced herself to being nothing but a toy for him to do as he wished. It was her worst nightmare, this loss of control, of status. As long as he still had the shield of trousers, he would be the master, and she would be nothing. Just another of his serfs, one who'd cast herself into utter wantonness.

"Do you want to get on your knees, or do you want me in you?" he whispered against her breast, his tongue reaching for her nipple.

She didn't answer. Her lips were swollen from his demanding kisses and her mind confused by his questions. She thought she was adept in her understanding of what went on in the bedroom, but now she could see that all she had really been adept at was avoiding it.

"All right. I'll decide," he said, kissing her and unbuttoning his trousers in the same smooth motion. He shrugged out of his shirt and put his hands on her shoulders so that she would lower herself to the floor.

She stood motionless, unable to comply. In the back of her mind, she knew what he wanted, but she couldn't do it. Not this way. Not first like a fifty-cent back-alley whore. Numbly she watched him. He kissed her mouth again as if trying to persuade her. Then he gazed down at her, a strange light in his eyes.

"I've dreamed of you, Lavinia," he rasped. "The manipulative little baggage that you are, surrendering to me while I stand over you and toy with the strands of your beautiful hair."

"I w-won't . . ." she stuttered, grasping one thin strand of sanity.

"You will," he answered, taking her soft mouth with his own, "one day," he promised as he pushed her back on the hammock and covered her.

They kissed again until her mouth was as wet as the place between her thighs. He moved and touched off the swinging motion of the hammock, an erotic rhythm that sent her bumping against him, increasing her need for resolution.

Her hand ran down his back. It was smooth, laced with muscle, broad. He was twice her size. She should have been smothered with him on top of her, but all she wanted was him closer, and closer still.

She cupped his buttock. It was one rigid curve of muscle. His trousers lay on the floor, neatly discarded. At last he was to be hers, and she his.

"Spiritualist, will you contact me on the other side just like this?" he asked, his straight white teeth grazing the plump side of one breast. "You must promise to, Lavinia, for you're such a sweet piece of meat, and I don't want to miss it, not even beyond the grave."

She stared at him. Lightning flashed across the porch, blinding her. She could see only him. He was transfixed in her vision like a tintype. He whispered something dirty, something she didn't quite understand, but her body did only too well. Her nipples tautened, and he seemed pleased, especially when his hand slipped between her legs as if to check the ripeness of an exotic fruit.

"Now," he asked her, his expression gluttonous and only slightly mocking.

"Now," she said, placing her mouth on his; knowing it would hurt; knowing but not caring. Her want went beyond pain.

She lost her breath. He drove inside her while his hand pushed up her knee, deepening the angle. His possession was unequaled. He had everything of her now. Everything. She felt the burn of tears in her eyes.

"Goddamn it. What kind of trickery are you playing now?" he gasped, his tone like a shower of ice.

She looked at him. She said nothing. There was no explanation. There probably never would be, for any of this night.

His gaze slammed into hers. He stared for a long time, the expression in his eyes going from disbelief to curiosity to awe. His eyes turned once to the hammock, then went back to her. "The hammock—" he whispered, a frown darkening his brow. "Hazel warned me not to come. She spoke of a hammock. *This* hammock. You knew, didn't you? Somehow, you knew. All this time, you knew. . . ."

"Yes," she barely breathed out.

He looked at her as if she'd lost her mind, or he'd lost his. "How could you know—how could you?"

"I have dreams. Sometimes terrible dreams. But sometimes dreams of this." Tears dripped down the sides of her face. He was still inside her, hard and powerful. She ached for completion. The situation was unbearable.

"Why?" he asked, his voice barely audible above the gale.

"Because I want you. I want you. . . ." She placed a kiss on his mouth. It should have been the hot kiss of a seductress, but instead it was the gentle kiss of first love, tasting of tears.

She didn't think it would bring him back. She had fears he might even withdraw and laugh at her ineptitude, but he didn't. The kiss seemed to move him, change him. He arched his back and took her nipple in his mouth, this time tenderly, as if trying to coax her back to the place she needed to be. Her desire expanded. Unmindful of time and place, she entangled her hands within his short cropped hair and gratefully allowed him to bury his head in her shoulder.

He moved carefully at first as if he were unsure of how to tread. His pace increased with her every moan of encouragement. The way he rocked against her was delicious agony and her loins coiled with the whispering promise of pleasure.

"God, are you tight," he groaned, his eyes shut as if with pain.

"Does it hurt?" she whimpered, unsure how it could when she was melting like chocolate in the sun.

"Sweet Jesus, no. I just can't last. I can't last." He looked down at her, at her knotted hair, the way her breasts crushed against him, then up again at her pliant, surrendering mouth. He seemed to lose even more control.

He gnashed his teeth as if he were battling all the forces of nature to continue. His last groan sent her plummeting. The rocking winds, the swaying hammock, his hard hairy body pounding into hers, all converged to that heaven between her thighs. Her ecstasy was sublime. She came in throbbing waves so strong she was convinced her body had fair swallowed him up. But he was there when she opened her eyes, his own pleasure gripping him in its pulsating jaws. A grip so strong, she knew she'd sell her soul to keep it there, and keep him hers forever.

Chapter Twenty-Two

He looked like a French painting, nude and asleep in the hammock; a portrait by Jacques-Louis David, something dramatic, neoclassical, maybe even hinting of past violence; a canvas from which one could not look away.

Lavinia couldn't bear leaving. She stared down at Edward as the first thin rays of dawn fingered through the shutters. His hair was tousled, his long legs were stretched languidly out across the ropes. She knew every part of him now: the way the cruel edges of his face softened in slumber, how substantial his shoulders were to her delicate hands. Her eyes moved to his thighs where the hair became became more sparse until it bushed out again, creating the perfect frame. No small fig leaf would hide all of that. Her own thighs, sore as they were, still grew damp when she looked at him. If she was his trophy, then he was hers, all six foot three inches of hard, bone-crushing muscle and domineering personality.

She hooked the last of her corset. It was a miracle she could stand, but perhaps that was the secret of men. Of Edward. He could be so threatening and loom so large, but then in the most delicate of intimacies, he could be gentle, a gentleness made that much more compelling by the harshness of his nature.

With shaky hands she put on her discarded linen jacket, pressed out the wrinkles with her hands, then began buttoning it. Her chemise was somewhere in his pile of clothes, but she couldn't look for it without shuffling around and maybe waking him, and she didn't want to do that. Because then would come the embarrassment, the explanations, the excuses. Already she could see herself putting her hands to her ears to not hear it. It would be too painful, and unnecessary. She didn't expect anything. She knew he wouldn't give it to her. All she wanted now was to sneak back to the ship before daylight resumed, and somehow to try to reconstruct her dignity.

It was going to be a difficult thing, especially since she'd learned how easily, how happily, she could let him take it away. Her eyes grew dim and she cringed at her wantonness. Last night he'd taken her two more times after the first, and she knew when she awoke that as soon as his eyes were open he would reach for her again, and she would go to him.

But now it was morning. She had her life waiting for her on the ship. She needed to leave. She needed to regain her dignity. Desperately.

She gazed out the porch door to the beach. It was half of what it was yesterday. The sand dunes cut three feet below the shell path that led to Hamilton; the storm surge had eaten the rest away. But the sun was clipping a horizon that was without a cloud. A soft wind carried seagulls already up and diving for their breakfast. It would be a beautiful day. If the *Maritimus* suffered no damage they'd be on their way to England on schedule.

Unable to stop herself, she glanced back at him. He still slept, oblivious to all her agonies.

Softly she stepped to the hammock and looked at him one last time.

If he asked her, she would marry him. She'd spend her days standing up to his hellish temper if only to have her nights like the last. Even in the poverty of a cotton-rope hammock, she wanted him. The longing that should have been satiated by all that had conspired was now even more acute because now she knew what she was missing.

If he asked her, she would spend the rest of her life with him. If he asked her. *If.* The terrible "if."

Bending over him, with lips aching to touch his own, she whispered, "I love you. You may not ever know it, but I'll always be yours."

Barefoot and with her bustled skirt in tatters, she crept away, holding back tears she knew would come later. There would be no forthcoming proposal. He might be attracted to her; she might even have pleased him with her performance last night, but it wasn't enough. She wanted him to love her in return and he didn't even like her. Her insides wrenched at the hurt. To him, she was nothing but a Barnum sideshow. She could read anyone's fortune for a dollar, yet not for a million could she tell her own.

He'd called her a fortune hunter. History wrote many a tale of those who went in search of such things only to return home empty-handed.

And empty-hearted.

Fortune was a cruel word, really, she thought as she gathered her skirts and crept down the porch stairs, her face already showing her tears. It could mean so many things. A treasure. Or one's destiny.

Her eyes darkened. She never wanted to speak or hear the word again. It was too excruciating; too full of hope and ruined dreams, and bitter tales of loneliness.

She could hunt the world over and never would she have the fortune she had last night.

🌿 🌿

Edward blinked against the glare of bright sun. Instinct from the days at the mining camp where every claim was staked out in bloodshed made him instantly awake, instantly aware.

Lavinia was gone. He knew it before he even reached for her. He sat up. Her clothes were no longer scattered on the floor.

He rose from the hammock and leaned out the porch entrance. One set of bare footprints led to the shell path going to Hamilton. She'd fled.

He rested against the shuttered wall and released a deep breath. Guilt lay on his tongue like a bitter aftertaste. As if wishing it were all a dream, he grabbed the damp wad of his trousers and busied himself with his own exit as if that might cause it all to be erased.

But everything reminded him of the night before. Even his trousers. Numbly, he slid himself into them, but the linen was only half dried and caked with salt. He grimaced. The fabric against his skin was unpleasant, but worse was the fact that every muscle in his body felt like he'd just endured a drunken brawl in the seediest tavern on Mott Street. He was stiff and on edge. A hot bath would ease the soreness, but not even five fingers of whiskey was going to take away the pictures in his mind.

He snatched his shirt off the floor. A feather-light piece of cotton fell from beneath it. Her chemise. The innocent pink satin bows that adorned its neckline mocked him. *Edward, the despoiler of virgins,* it said to him. And he was that. His gaze slid to the hammock. The evidence was all there. Small drops of crimson forever branded on the white cotton ropes.

The chemise was so delicate he could see through it. It was lovely, just like she had been last night. Unable to help himself, he crushed it to his face and inhaled. He found her there. She clung to the sheer fabric, her scent sweet and yet dark to his senses, like the deep smell of a summer garden at night.

He lifted his head. Outside, way down the beach, he heard a party of men shouting names. They were probably sent from the *Maritimus* to look for them.

Quickly he buttoned his shirt and stuffed the chemise in his jacket pocket. He would take it with him. He wanted it. Later, maybe, he would return it. Or maybe he would just hold on to it, look at it, smell it, remember. All he knew for certain was that there was more where the chemise came from. And though its owner didn't yet realize it, he was going to have it or go mad.

%§ §

Lavinia softly opened the door to her suite and tiptoed inside. The cabin was on the west side of the ship, away from sunrise, and still dim. She was glad. She didn't want any harsh light exposing her. She'd barely avoided the steward who was taking a silver tray to someone belowdecks.

"Thank God! We've been so worried," Hazel sat up on the settee. She was still fully clothed with only a lap blanket around her. She rushed to Lavinia's side and hugged her. "Oh, I was terrified. When Mr. Stuyvesant-French told me Jamie was here already aboard ship, I got so upset. I knew you were out in the storm and looking for him and—" Hazel's voice broke. Tears glistened in her eyes. "What would have happened to us without you, Vinia?"

"What would have happened?" Lavinia gave her a weak smile. "Why, you would have gone on to make a fabulous match with some rich peer, and the children would have forgotten all about me once their very expensive ponies arrived at the castle stables, that's what."

"Oh, you wretch, how you can joke about this is beyond me." Hazel's eyes clouded. Her expression turned even more serious. Quietly, she asked, "Did Mr. Stuyvesant-French find you? He was quite the gentleman to go after you in the storm."

Lavinia walked farther into the room, turning her back to Hazel so that she wouldn't see her face. The last thing she wanted to do was talk about Edward Stuyvesant-French and his gentlemanly nature. "He found me just in time. I was going out of my mind searching for Jamie. I couldn't find him . . . anywhere." She lowered herself to a velvet tuffet. The exhaustion had caught up to her. She wanted breakfast and a bath, and good long nap. And she did not want to talk about Edward.

Hazel gave her a long stare, one that assessed and concluded in a matter of seconds. Suddenly nervous, she bustled about the room, tugging on the bell pull for the maid and laying the lap blanket around Lavinia who still shivered in her damp clothing.

"This dress is ruined," Lavinia said, pulling up her hem. Her bare feet were swollen and scratched. She wouldn't walk without soreness for days. "I never did find my shoes and stockings on the beach. I guess they're out to sea now."

"I guess," Hazel said weakly, meeting Lavinia's eye, then quickly looking away. Suddenly, as if she couldn't take it anymore, she blurted, "Oh, Vinia, this is none of my business, I just want to know that you're all right. I—I told Edward about the hammock in your dream. I'm sure he thinks me quite crazed, but I was scared when I knew you two were going to be out in the storm. . . ." She frowned. ". . . And then I knew there was that hammock on that porch. . . ."

Lavinia rubbed her eyes. She was numb inside. Completely numb. Somehow circumstance and fate had conspired to put her on that porch with Edward, and though she knew she would cherish her night with him all the way to the grave, she now had to confront the dangers of it. The first was the fact that she was no longer a virgin. Not that it mattered much. In her line of work it was assumed she was not, but still, she'd crossed the line and now there was no selling herself as an innocent.

The second danger was pregnancy. Edward had threatened her once with the agony which his own mother had endured. Lavinia didn't relish the idea of having to inform him that she might be carrying his bastard.

But worst was the third. She'd fallen in love with him. He would be able to get her into his bed very easily now, with mere whispers and promises. If she succumbed, it would only be a matter of time before she would be carrying his baby, and then she would have to live at his mercy. She might have to beg him to return her affections; she might have to beg him to love their child. And it might not work. Orphanages all over the world were full of the abandoned product of failed love affairs. Of course, she would keep her child. She would love it and care for it. There would always be enough money. Worse things had happened to children.

But no worse thing ever happened to a woman than to be rejected by her lover.

Lavinia put her head in her hands and swallowed the lump of dread in her throat. She didn't know how Edward was going to react now that they were back on ship, resuming their old patterns. All she knew was that everything was up to him because she had fallen in love, and now her emotions would live or die at his very whim.

"Vinia, can I help? Can I get you anything? You seem so—so worn out."

Lavinia raised her head. She turned her world-weary eyes to her sister. Hazel's face was pale and her forehead seemed permanently marked with a frown. Unable to help herself, Lavinia said, "I'll be fine. Fine. After all, you've survived, am I not right, Hazel? So I can survive, right?"

Hazel dropped to her knees and wrapped her arms around Lavinia. "I survived. Yes, I survived, but only because of you, Vinia. Only because of you. . . ." She began to sob. "Oh, you must let me help you now. It's my turn to help you."

Lavinia clutched her. "But you can't. There's nothing anyone can do. I've given him my heart, Hazel. I can't get it back. I'll never get it back," she said darkly.

"Then he must give his heart to you!" her sister cried.

Lavinia brushed away her own tears that now ran down her cheeks. "I fear the situation is much worse than that."

"How?" Hazel gasped, staring at her.

Lavinia could barely choke out the words. "You see, Edward Stuyvesant-French might not have a heart to give."

Chapter
Twenty-Three

Other possibilities were that the whole thing was a result of the cavortings of Mrs. Piper's unconscious mind, "using its preternatural powers of cognition and memory for the basest of deceits," which [William] James thought fairly probable but, if true, distressing.

—RUTH BRANDON

"Tell me she wasn't out in the storm all night! Oh, that's just too dreadful!" Celene *tsked* to Daisy as she and Cornelius took tea on the first-class deck. The dock at Hamilton was busy as the captain prepared the ship for an early departure. Every now and again they heard shouts on the wharf as stevedores loaded the *Maritimus* with supplies.

"It gets worse," Daisy answered. She gave Cornelius a warning glance. "Edward went out in the storm to fetch her. They were gone all night. Now he's not willing to talk about it, and Hazel said Lavinia's taken to her bed with a headache."

Celene's face went rapt. "How utterly delicious. Cornelius, load up your shotgun. We just might have a wedding on our hands."

Daisy sighed. "Not even a shotgun is going to make Edward do what he doesn't want. Cornelius knows that better than anyone."

"Edward loves her," Celene said enigmatically. She turned her eyes to Cornelius. "Am I right?"

Cornelius shrugged. "He's become obsessed with her, I think.

There's no doubt he wants her, but he talks of her as if she's less than a servant. He hates the séances. Worse than that, he hates the idea of being in love. It suffocates him. I've never seen him grow close to a woman except Daisy here. He puts women like her on a pedestal which he can admire from afar—it's so much more safe that way. I think he distrusts females. It goes back to his mother's death and her ultimate subjugation by Wilhelm."

"Yes, such a tragedy. There was talk of it even in London at the time. No one could believe the cruelty." Celene scowled. "What we need to do, then, is make sure Edward doesn't live up to his legacy."

"But how do we make Edward do anything? He's too strong-willed. And he's as mean as a rabid dog when you cross him. He gets that from his father. I know it only too well." Daisy folded her hands in her lap.

"The thing we must do is pull them apart, before Lavinia has a chance to fall further into shame." Celene, deep in thought, tapped her lower lip with a silver teaspoon. "Buc has a fancy for Lavinia. We must put them together at every possible chance."

"That won't be easy," Daisy said. "Lavinia wants them to avoid Kylemore and his male friends. The duke made a play for Hazel, apparently. She got quite upset about it since he was engaged. They think it best to snub the duke now."

"Kylemore is not likely to marry his Miss Millions now that he's gotten a gander at Hazel. I've never seen the man so thrown. He'll marry Hazel, you watch." Celene smiled wickedly at Cornelius. "I'll put a hundred in gold on an engagement before we dock in London. What say you, Corny?"

Cornelius dug out a slip of paper and wrote down his bet. He neatly handed it over to Celene. "Double says she publicly slaps him in the face and never speaks to him again."

Celene waved the wager. "You're on," she said, tucking it into her dress pocket.

"Oh, you two, you're no help at all," Daisy sighed.

"Yes, we are, my dear." Celene patted her hand. "We're going to make Hazel a duchess and Lavinia Mrs. Edward Stuyvesant-French. The only one left to bet on after that will be you. Now don't you disappoint your Auntie Celene and remain a spinster. To start, I want to know what kind of man you're looking for so that I can throw him to you and bet on him at the same time."

"Me?" Daisy flushed and glanced between Cornelius and Celene. "I— Well—I really don't want anyone." Overhead the ship's bell sounded out eleven rings. Daisy started. "Is it that late? Oh, I've got to go."

"Where are you off to?" Cornelius asked.

"Where?" Daisy glanced around as if seeking an excuse. "Well, I told Evaline I'd help decide my attire tonight—and, well, I really must go. I can't keep her waiting."

"Let me help you," Cornelius said, standing.

"No, no, no. I've got it. I can do it all by myself, I promise. Please stay with Celene and enjoy your tea." Daisy gave them several nervous glances, then she said her farewell and wheeled herself down the deck to the door of her cabin.

When she was gone, Celene took a sip of tea and said, "That child is a dreadful liar. She really needs some tutoring in that regard."

"Yes," said Cornelius, staring at Daisy's closed cabin door. His shocked expression was only made worse when they saw Evaline, with the laundress, walk past Daisy's cabin door, clearly oblivious to any appointment with her mistress.

"She's having a rendezvous. All she has to do is enter her cabin through the deck, exit it through the passage door, and meet with her lover."

Cornelius ran a thumb across his mustache. "Edward doesn't know anything about this, I imagine."

"Even better."

Cornelius looked at her, exasperation in his eyes. "He watches over her. Daisy's naive, you know. She's rich and crippled. The perfect target for unscrupulous gentlemen."

"She's also beautiful and kindhearted and witty. Doesn't anyone ever see those things?" Celene looked at him. "She needs to live. She wants to live. Sometimes that means getting hurt. But let her have her hurt. She just might find the happiness she deserves."

"How do you know all these things, Celene old girl?"

"I'm twelve years older than you, Cornelius; I've lived a good, long, hard life. So what do you think I've done all this time? Anchored myself to a chastity belt—or flourished?"

Cornelius stared at her. "You've gotten hurt, then."

"Just like you, my dear. I know about the Vanadder scandal and the mysterious gentleman at Alice's deathbed."

He said nothing. His eyes had a distant expression to them. Slowly, he nodded "I've lived a good long hard life too, Celene."

"Then maybe we're a perfect match." She covertly slipped her delicately veined hand into his bearlike one, and nodded in Daisy's direction. "Let them have their passion and pain. They're young. That's what they want, what they need. Me, I'll settle for friendship and a comfortable chair with a good reading lamp. What say you, old man?"

Cornelius smiled. Then he looked down at their entwined hands and chuckled.

"Are we so undesirable that we're chasing the women away? I say, I've never felt so invisible in my life." Buc settled down on a leather chair in the barroom. It was only four in the afternoon but the place was filled with men and cigar smoke and loud, jostling laughter.

"At least I know why Hazel avoids me. But you, Buc, you've really got a problem with Lavinia." Kylemore brooded over an untouched brandy.

Hesitating, Buc finally said, "There's been some talk of Edward looking in her direction—do you think that's why she ignores me?"

Kyle looked at his brother. "I've known Stuyvesant-French ever since that first year I toured out west and got stranded at the Antelope Hotel in the Dakota Territory. He and that damn fool Cook were mining a stake up north, they were stone broke and dirty. I'd never met a man as intense as Edward Stuyvesant-French and I don't know if I ever want to again. Hell, I knew he was going to make something of that claim if he had to squeeze the gold out of the rock with his bare hands." Kyle looked around the bar to make sure no one was within hearing distance, then he leaned forward as if to emphasize his point. "All I can tell you is Lavinia Murphy had better be one fine skirt to make him roll over. He just doesn't fall like the rest of us, Buc. He's not that human."

"Do you think she might have fallen for him?"

Kyle lifted his eyebrows. "Maybe, but then all the more reason you should chase after her. Save her from the heartache, my boy. It's the right thing to do."

Buc nodded. "I was thinking of sending her flowers from the shop downstairs. Have you seen it? They've got a cold-box running on ammonia. It's most ingenious and modern."

"Yes, I believe I've seen it," the duke said dryly.

"What do you think? Roses?"

"No, most definitely *not* roses."

That seemed to throw Buc off. He sat back stumped. "I just thought roses would get her to notice me, but you know, there was this little posy of violets I thought fetching. It kind of reminded me of her."

"All you can do is try. It might come back like a boomerang, but there's no dishonor in trying."

Buc looked at his brother curiously. "You sound like you speak from experience, Kyle."

Kyle finally attached his lips to the brandy. "Trust me on this. Get her the violets."

Lavinia tried to ready herself for dinner. She'd bathed, repinned her hair three times in two different styles, tied and untied the heavy gold tasseled cords of her wrapper in an attempt to put on her chemise. But one thing always stopped her.

Seeing Edward. She didn't want to see him. Sometimes she thought if she never saw him that it would be for the best, but then the very thought would cause her to throw herself upon the settee and fight back tears of despair. No, she had to see him again. In her mind, he was becoming the very reason she breathed.

Regret burned at her soul like acid. If only Jamie hadn't run away yesterday. If only she hadn't had the dream. If only she hadn't looked at Edward on that porch and cast her lot with the inevitable. If only she had fought her desires, if only she were more experienced, if only he were less handsome, less manipulative, less . . . *Edward.* Oh, *if, if, if.* She squeezed her eyes shut.

Finally, calm once more, she rose from the settee and took one more chance with her dinner dress. Though she wanted to hide in her cabin for the rest of the cruise, she knew she had to appear tonight. People would talk if she didn't. Daisy knew she was gone all night, so did the servants and the captain. She had to go forth and pretend she was ever so grateful to be saved from the dire situation of the storm, safe once more in the bosom of the *Maritimus.* She had to do it if just for Hazel. Lavinia still had hopes for her making a brilliant match and pulling the children up in society with her.

A gentle knock sounded at the suite door. Lavinia called out, thinking it was the maid, but no one answered.

"Yes? Who's there?" she called again, this time going to the door.

Again, silence.

With trepidation, she cracked opened the door. But no one was there. She opened it wider and looked down either side of the passageway. It was empty. She had just convinced herself she had imagined the knock when she looked down at her feet and found a posy of violets wrapped in a fat French ribbon of green silk.

She bent down and picked it up, her heart filled with wonder. Closing the door, she brought the violets to her nose and inhaled the sweet scent. With a laugh mixed with tears, she suddenly knew who sent it. It was his version of Mrs. Wirth's Violet Tonic all over again.

A light came to her eyes. Maybe she was worried and anxious for nothing. Maybe he did like her. Maybe . . . maybe he could even love her.

Her breath caught. The very idea seemed unbelievable, but she wanted it so badly she couldn't disabuse herself of it. Maybe Edward could feel. Maybe he wasn't cold and uncaring. Maybe he cared for her. Maybe . . .

Her legs suddenly felt like she was walking on clouds.

She held the posy to her nose again and laughed out loud. Not only was he the most wonderful lover, but he had a sense of humor as well. Violets. What a perfect choice. She wanted him to give her violets forever.

※ ※

Edward stood and looked out his cabin porthole for the fifth time. Jamie and Cornelius had appeared in his parlor an hour before, both in search of male companionship. The two had long since taken up a game of checkers to forget about him and his bearish mood, but there was no real way to ignore him. Not when he blustered his way back and forth across the parlor, looking out the porthole at nothing.

Finally, in desperation, Cornelius looked up from the board and said, "I find a good long walk dispels this froth you're in, French."

"I'm not in any froth," Edward sniped.

Jamie looked up as if just waiting to see what Cornelius would say next.

"Well, if you won't take a walk, then just go and talk to her. Clear the air. Otherwise you're going to have to tell the steward to replace the carpet before we ever get to London."

Edward looked at Cornelius as if he wanted to cut him down. "Whatever gave you the idea this was about her?"

"About who?" Jamie chimed in.

"Lavinia," Cornelius offered before Edward could stop him.

"What about Lavinia?" Jamie asked. He turned guilty eyes to Edward. "I already told her I was sorry I left her at the beach. I promised not to read any more of Mr. Coltrain's work. Is she still mad at me?"

Edward rubbed his jaw. "She's not mad at you, my boy, she's — well, she's put-out with me, I think."

"Why? She told me you were quite kind to her when you found her in the storm." Jamie looked back and forth between both men.

Cornelius felt the need to intervene. "That's right. He was nothing but the soul of kindness to your sister. Aren't I right, French?"

Grimly, Edward nodded.

"Shouldn't you go about your business? We can stay here by ourselves and finish our game." Cornelius looked to the door.

Edward glanced at Jamie, then he snatched his jacket and slammed out of the cabin.

❧ ☙

Lavinia heard the knocking again, but this time the sound was more like pounding; more like the Edward she knew. Still in her wrapper, she rushed to the door and flung it wide, knowing he would be there.

He was. Edward stood in the passage, his jaw clenched tight, a vague wariness in his eyes.

"Come in," she said, her heart beating wildly. She stepped back and held the posy of violets behind her.

He walked into the room, never taking his eyes from her.

She closed the door. "Would you like to sit?" She walked to the settee, still hiding the violets in the velvet folds of her wrapper.

He took the armchair nearest the door.

She stared at him, suddenly nervous and shy.

"I'm sure you know why I've come. I want to talk about our night together." His words seemed to cause him difficulty, but his eyes never wavered from hers. "Sometimes when I think of what happened between us—it doesn't seem real—*you* don't seem real."

"But I am real, Edward," she said softly. "Only too real. You know that."

A shadow of guilt darkened his expression. "It never crossed my mind I'd find you . . . untested. Given your avocation, I think any roughness on my part should be overlooked."

"It never crossed my mind. I wanted you too badly," she whispered.

He finally looked away as if he couldn't bear her to see what was in his eyes. "And yet, I sit here confounded by it all because the strangest part of the entire night was that you knew it was coming. You knew it all along."

She knelt before him. "I had a dream about it. It was vague, I didn't know all the details." She quavered a smile. "I probably didn't know much sooner than you did what was coming."

He rubbed his temple. "But it doesn't make sense. If you were a virgin and you knew what was on my mind, why didn't you tell me?"

"Tell you that I was an innocent? That I'd had a dream you'd make love to me in a storm just as that one, in a hammock just as that one? Would you have believed me?"

His expression hardened. "Probably not."

"You would have laughed. The mockery never would have ended."

"Yes, but you still should have told me to stop. I would have stopped, regardless of what I thought of you. I'm not a rapist. I would have stopped if you'd wanted me to."

"But that's just it, don't you see?" She touched his knee and stared up at him.

"Why?" he asked, taking her face in his hands.

"Because," she said, giving him a secret smile, "I wanted you. I still want you."

He opened his mouth as if he felt compelled to say something, but then, as if compelled by something stronger than words or thoughts, he leaned down and kissed her, his lips as demanding as she remembered.

Her heart soared. He did care. The *ifs* and *maybes* be damned, he did care.

He broke off and rested his forehead on her own. "Even now I don't fully understand. I was sure you'd be angry. I suppose in hindsight our night together was fated, but I figured any woman would be upset by the loss of her innocence. And yet, maybe I misjudged you again. Perhaps an arrangement between us can work out. I'd like that, especially if you're going to be levelheaded about this."

"Ridiculous." She almost laughed. "I'm not levelheaded at all— just disarmed."

"Disarmed?"

"How could I be angry at a man who sent me this?" She brought the violet posy out in front of her and twirled it back and forth in her fingers. "I laughed and cried all at the same time when I saw this at my door. You're forgiven any indiscretions, Edward. I can't hate a man who pleads with such humble treasures such as this."

He looked down at it, his eyes widening almost imperceptibly. "You—you treasure this?"

"If you'd sent me diamonds I would have thrown them in your face in disgust of your bravado." She gazed lovingly down at the violets. "But these small innocent flowers, the gesture was so self-deprecating and thoughtful. I'll never forget you smelling of violets, Edward. I'll think of you and violets forever." She looked at him, her heart in her eyes.

"I'll have to remember to give you violets in the future." His gaze flickered down at her, then immediately looked away, as if he were uncomfortable.

"Do my confessions embarrass you? I'll try to be that levelheaded woman you want." She put the tiny bouquet to her nose. "I want us to get along. I realize now I've wanted that very much."

He looked at her again, his gaze unable—or unwilling—to focus on the flowers. "I want that too. That night on the beach, I found our harmony far preferable than the discord."

"Is that what you meant when you spoke of an arrangement?"

"There's no going back. I can't return your virginity. So I suggest . . ." He hesitated. "Well, I wonder why we shouldn't take more pleasure since we've removed the pain."

She lowered her head and placed the bouquet in her lap. Feeling disoriented, she realized she hadn't used her logic as well as he had. Her heart had been thinking of confessions of love and even— dare she hope!—a more permanent arrangement blessed by the church. But she knew all too well that in between noble proclamations and a walk down the aisle, there was a huge abyss into which many women fell, aptly named *mistress*. "I never really thought about our relationship in terms of an arrangement. I suppose I just thought it would evolve—like our passion has—but I know how you are, Edward. You like everything neat and orderly." She looked at the bouquet in her hands. It might be the last time she ever held one. Her disappointment was keen but there was no way to dispute the logic of his words. She had given up her innocence to him willingly, even gladly. He had no moral obligation to bind himself to her in holy matrimony, nor did he have to worry about an outraged father who would protest her unmarried state. Becoming his mistress was the most reasonable outcome of their liaison. Still, deep in her heart, she knew she wanted more. But wanting it was a far cry from having it. She didn't want this to be a game of all or nothing. She loved him.

"I'll think about an arrangement, if that's what you want," she answered quietly. She stared down at the posy, so sweet and innocent, and her heart swelled. He did have feelings for her. It had been a risk for him to place the violets at her door. He'd had to poke fun at himself and dip his toe in a cold lake of humility. If he'd been willing to do all that for her, in time he might be willing to do more. She would be foolish to cast him aside all in the name of propriety.

He kissed her again, this time more heatedly. His tongue drove deep inside her mouth and she moaned. She was helpless where he was concerned. His smallest gesture sent her to the edge. The want built inside her and took over, a dangerous thing when she was used to self-control, but she didn't care. He pulled her onto his lap, and he continued kissing her until she found herself gladly willing to trade even her very breath for another kiss.

"You won't regret this, Lavinia. It'll be good for both of us. I promise I can be very discreet." His lips moved over hers, then he slowly untied the gold tasseled cord that held her wrapper. Her instinct was to stop him, but then she reminded herself she was no longer a virgin, no longer an innocent. He'd had all of her before. There was no reason not to give herself to him again.

He parted the thick velvet wrapper and looked down at her chest. She bit back a suddden bout of shyness along with the urge to press the sides of the wrapper closed and scramble from his lap.

He shoved the wrapper aside even more and greedily stared at his treasure. His palm captured one bare breast and he seemed to enjoy the wealth of it as it spilled out of his hand. "Glorious," he whispered against her throat. "I swear you are glorious."

"Abigail said she'd help me dress at six. I'm not sure if you can stay. . . ."

His mouth nuzzled the swollen tip of her nipple. "We don't need much time."

She shuddered. He yanked the robe away until the arms caught at her elbows, then he covered her breast with one hand while his other reached between them.

"What if we're caught?" she whispered, her breath coming in short shallow pants.

"Then we're caught," he answered, a possessive gleam in his eyes. He unbuttoned his trousers. Then he wrapped his arm around her hips and lifted her to him.

She fell against him, full to bursting with need and fear and carnal desire. His hips thrust like the rocking of a ship. She didn't think she could keep up with him until his head lowered and he captured her nipple in his mouth. Then she soared. Her own fulfillment seemed only another bump or grind away and soon she herself was quickening the pace, anxious to get more. *More. More.*

"Edward," she gasped, pulsing against him in the blind throes of her pleasure.

He didn't respond. Instead he shut his eyes and groaned, her hips locked in his ever-tightening grip. He pounded into her until she thought she'd be pierced through to the other side, then he sank back against the chair, panting and staring.

"You see?" he whispered wickedly. "We didn't need a lot of time."

She pressed her cheek against his own and savored the feel of him still inside her, filling her loneliness. His smell was a mixture of bay rum mingling with the darker tones of aroused male. He seemed so near to her, so intimate with her, she hadn't even realized his shirt was still buttoned and his four-hand knot wasn't even loosened. "What you do to me," she murmured, falling against him, her nudity meeting with the fine wool of his jacket.

He stroked her hair and the velvet shambles of her robe still draped on her back. "I'd like to do more."

"Now?" she gasped, feeling a whisper of life inside her.

He laughed. "Well, maybe in a few minutes, if there's time— you said your maid was coming."

"Abigail!" She shot up and scrambled off him, her gaze riveted to the door. "You've got to go! She's due any second to help me dress for dinner!"

"Promise me we'll talk of an arrangement when we arrive in London?"

"Yes," she whispered, retying her robe.

He stood and adjusted his trousers. He then walked to her, took her chin in hand and met her eyes. "Promise me a waltz after dinner? Me and only me?"

"Yes," she said softly, melting again for him.

He kissed her. She clutched him to her as if she could never let him go. "I love you, Edward," she whispered when he finally lifted his head. She watched as a muscle bunched in his jaw. He seemed to want to say something, but instead he kissed her again, this time fiercely, with all the renewed passion of a youth.

She watched him go. He hadn't returned her sentiments in words, but she wondered if he didn't feel them anyway. Especially when she took up her posy of violets again. The little flowers went beyond all speech, just like their lovemaking.

She met his parting glance. She held out his innocent little bouquet and smiled in gratitude. She loved him; in time he would love her, too. It had to be, because the one thing she could say for certain was that he'd been as affected by the sight of the violet posy as she.

His love would follow. It was only a matter of time.

Chapter
Twenty-Four

L avinia looked at herself in the mirror. She wore her best
dinner gown, a dark spruce-green taffeta that made her eyes
look almost violet. It was low-cut and off the shoulder. Her
hips were tightly bound in a swag-front skirt and the back cascaded
into a demitrain that swayed delicately as she walked.

Nervously she clasped and unclasped the collar of pearls around
her neck. She wanted to look her best, but not overdo it. All she
could think about was the old line that said, "A whore wears all
her jewelry at once to mask her insecurity." Indeed the pearls were
definitely too much. She dropped them in her leather jewelry case
and fastened two pearl drops to her ears. The effect was much more
subtle and respectable.

"You look lovely, miss," Abigail cooed behind her in the mirror.

"Do I?" Lavinia stared at herself again, unsure. She wanted to
look good and to have Stuyvesant-French gaze at her in admiration,
but doubt had her in its grip. Everything seemed to show—her
guilt, her nervousness, even the small red abrasion Edward's mouth

had left on her right breast. Her gown and corset covered it well, but she was convinced everyone could see it right through the taffeta.

"Don't forget your gloves, miss."

Lavinia took the black leather gloves from her and squeezed her hands into them, all the while glancing nervously at the woman. Abigail had arrived on the heels of Edward's departure with hardly a minute between the two. The maid's appearance only added to Lavinia's flustered state. The maid obviously had not seen him, but Lavinia still couldn't shake her mortification over what had gone on during those few minutes alone. She'd once again behaved like a trollop and even now all she could think of was when she was going to be able to be with him again.

"Heavens, your color is high this evening, miss. If I didn't know better I'd think you were in love." Abigail smiled at her indulgently.

Lavinia quavered a smile in return. She was absolutely in love, but whether it was the fine state Abigail thought it was, had yet to be determined.

❦

"My, my, Edward is late," Celene commented to Daisy at the captain's table. "Is something wrong? I wondered why Cornelius was the one to escort us tonight."

Daisy toyed with the roast on her dinner plate. "He sent me a note of apology and said he would only be a little tardy. The valet was late running an errand for him. I'm sure he'll be here any minute now."

Celene covertly nodded across the table. "Have you seen Buc's performance tonight? Why, he just bleeds slavish admiration for Lavinia. I adore it."

Daisy glanced across the table where Buc was leaning quite pronouncedly toward Lavinia who sat next to him. Lavinia answered all of Buc's polite conversation, but time and again her attention was drawn to the ballroom's doorway as if she were expecting someone. "Edward won't like this, I imagine," Daisy whispered to Celene.

"She's not encouraging him in the least," Celene answered. "In fact, it would serve him right to have to stand by and watch her waltz in Buc's arms."

"Do you think Buc would make a better match for Lavinia?" Daisy pondered. "I know he's a shameless fortune-hunter, but sometimes I think he would be best for her. Edward will never soften. I wonder that a rational woman like Lavinia would even consider such a hothead like my brother."

"Opposites attract, my dear, or haven't you heard?"

Daisy looked down at her plate as if to hide a certain emotion in her eyes. "I've heard of such things—I've heard such an attraction is impossibly—no, *terribly* strong—but wouldn't Lavinia be happiest with a man who gives her tender care? Wouldn't she rather have a man's own entire heart even if he does have his flaws? Even if he is not all one would want for her?"

"You sound as if you're arguing your own case, Daisy darling." Celene's expression was one of puzzled sympathy.

Daisy shook her head and straightened in the chair. "Nonsense," she said softly.

"I see," Celene answered, her gaze never wavering from Daisy's haunted face.

Until Lavinia's voice rose above the din at the crowded dining table.

"It was *you?*" she cried out in shocked amazement.

❧ ❦

"Oh, I hear thunder." Celene put her hand to her forehead in a fainting gesture. "Do you see his face, Daisy, Corny? Oh, surely the heavens are ready to release all their fury at this exact moment."

Cornelius and Daisy stared at the entrance to the ship's ballroom. Edward stood there, a black scowl on his face as he looked across the ballroom to where Lavinia and Buc waltzed. Lavinia was laughing at Buc's every comment and Buc looked as if the Queen herself had just proclaimed him the Royal Consort.

"He's going to call him out," Celene exclaimed.

"That's the method of revenge for our generation, Duchess." Cook stared at Edward. "No, I'm much more afraid of a small plop in the ocean at midnight when no one would notice a man overboard."

"How can Edward even think to get angry over Buc's attention?" Daisy interjected. "He's never had a kind word to say about Lavinia. If he's in love with her, then he should declare himself or keep quiet."

"You're certainly the rebellious one tonight, Daisy. Since when do you chastise Edward?" Cornelious asked in a confused voice.

"Since— Well, since—" Daisy scowled and there was a marked resemblance to her brother. "Since I realized only a fool would pass on a chance for love."

Celene and Cornelius looked at her, dumbfounded.

Finally Cornelius stood. "Edward is obviously in no mood to play chaperon, so I'll take up the reins. The duke has had four consecutive dances with Hazel and I fear a crowbar is going to be necessary to pry them apart, but I'll do my best. Excuse me, ladies, while I cut in on Hazel and attempt to spare her reputation."

"Look! Edward is heading for the table. And that music has stopped! Oh dear! Buc's returning Lavinia here to the table. Cover your heads, darlings! We're about to hear an explosion." Celene held her breath.

"My, what a wonderful dancer you are, Lord Buchanon. I suppose that's one of the things you learned at Eton?" Lavinia asked pleasantly while Buc seated her.

"No, my dear. Talent on the dance floor is one of the things a gentleman finds he's capable of only when given the right companion." Buc handed her a champagne from a passing waiter's tray, then seated himself next to her. Neither of them seemed to even notice that Stuyvesant-French was bearing down on the table like a runaway steam locomotive.

"Lord Buchanon, you are too modest. I adore that in a man, along with a humble posy of flowers." Lavinia suddenly turned her gaze to Edward. Upon hearing her last sentence he stopped dead where he stood. "Oh, look who's finally arrived! Mr. Stuyvesant-French is here!" Lavinia exclaimed. "Why, I thought someone was missing from our table." She gave him the kind of smile seen best on a hissing cat. "Please join us. I don't know how we overlooked your company."

With barely a murmur of greeting, Edward took his place between Celene and Daisy but still never took his eyes off Lavinia.

Lavinia suddenly laughed. It sounded brittle even to Celene's bad hearing. "Buc has just been entertaining me with stories from his boyhood. He had the most delightful education at Eton. I'm terribly impressed."

"Maybe I should rescue Edward instead of Hazel," Cook whispered to Celene.

Celene clapped her hands together. "Indeed," she whispered back. "Our friend the duke is finally returning our charge from the dance floor. I think even he knows when he's gone over the line . . . unlike our dear Edward here."

Cook snorted.

"Eton. Just think of it!" Lavinia announced. "The most exclusive of institutions. I can't get over it."

"Well, do get over it," Edward almost snarled.

Lavinia gazed across the table, her face as cool as a glacier. "You, of course, Mr. Stuyvesant-French, received little formal education, did you not? I thought I'd heard a story from Cook here that you ran away from home at an early age and took the burden of education upon yourself. How quaint. You must be so proud how you've turned out. You manage most social *intercourse* quite adequately given your lack of formal skill."

"Are you calling me a boor, Miss Murphy?" Edward asked ominously.

Lavinia stared at him. "Why would that be necessary when you so assiduously embrace the role of one?"

Edward started to rise from his seat, but the duke and Hazel arrived at the table. Kylemore saw to it that Hazel found her seat, then he took the one to her right.

"A fair night for a dance, wouldn't you agree?" Kyle said cheerily to everyone.

Edward greeted the comment with silence, Lavinia downed her wine, and Cook shook his head. "You're monopolizing our charge, Kyle," Cook said across the table to the duke. "I think it best for the rest of the waltzes that you concentrate your thoughts on your fiancée, don't you agree, old boy?"

Kylemore smirked, then gave Hazel a meaningful look. "I plan to monopolize even more of Miss Murphy's time. I find one night at a ball is not enough time by her side."

"For an engaged man, I'd say those are fighting words, Kyle," Celene broke in, a lively glint in her eyes.

"I intend to fight, then." Kylemore raised his glass to Hazel. "To ever more waltzes with you, dear maiden."

Hazel colored.

Lavinia stood. "I hate to leave such a gay party, but I suddenly find I am beset by a headache." She turned to Buc. "Would you be a dear and escort me back to my suite? I find I really must retire early."

Edward began to rise from his seat again. Celene's hand on his arm made him stop.

"Darling girl, of course we'll excuse you," Celene announced, "but only on one condition: that you agree to perform a séance tomorrow night. I can't go another day in suspense. Now, don't disappoint me."

Lavinia looked taken aback. She glanced at Hazel who suddenly lost some of her color. "Really, I don't know if I'm up to it now. . . ."

"Miss Murphy is no longer performing vaudevilles, Celene," Edward growled.

"Oh pooh, Edward. The decision is Lavinia's not yours." Celene turned to Lavinia. "Will you agree?"

Lavinia looked at the faces at the table. She seemed to hesitate when she saw how taken aback Kylemore appeared. It was almost as if she were most wary of upsetting him and, thus, Hazel's future, but then her gaze rested on Edward's scowl and she suddenly brightened. "I'll do it. Tomorrow night in my suite at eight o'clock."

"Shall the Czarina accompany you?" Kylemore asked hesitantly, as if he weren't quite comfortable with Hazel's other role.

"If she wants to, she shall. I'll leave that decision up to her. In the meantime, I must say good night." She took Buchanon's arm and walked away without even one frosty glance toward Edward.

"Steward, take this away and bring me a brandy," Edward said under his breath, shoving his wineglass to the edge of the table.

"Why, Edward, I never knew you to be such a drinker," Celene commented breezily. She turned to the steward. "You'd best leave the bottle," she instructed slyly. She then gave Edward a little wave and smiled ever so brightly.

❧ ☙

The walk through the first-class passage to her suite was longer than the Sahara Desert. Lavinia had never been so tired, so despondent, so depressed, and yet never had she been so obligated to hide it all behind a facade.

"I had a wonderful night this evening. I'm sorry to see it end all too soon." Buchanon paused at her door. "Nothing would please me more to find your headache suddenly gone and you anxious for a walk on the deck."

Lavinia rubbed her temples. "I wish it were gone, but we'll have to take that walk another time."

"Another time, then." Buchanon stared down at her.

He was handsome. His features were regal, his eyes a clear azure blue. He was tall, strapping, reasonably well heeled. Titled. Good God, what more could a woman ask for?

Edward.

Her head pounded even more. "Well, thank you, and now I'll say good night."

He took her hand and brought it to his lips. "I'm glad you liked my violets. You can't know how glad."

Her despair deepened. "It was sweet of you to think of me."

"I've thought of you a lot on this cruise."

"Have you?" she asked distractedly.

"I wonder if you and your sister will visit Kylemore House once we get to London. If Kyle hasn't asked yet, I'll be the first to issue the invitation. It's beautiful there in the spring with the hyacinths and hawthorne blooming. Say you and your sister will spend a weekend there with me?"

She looked up at him and wondered how she would have the strength to erase the frown she knew must be on her face. "I'd be honored, but I'd hate to impose."

"Nonsense. Celene lives to entertain at Kylemore and curses us weekly for not having more guests out there. We'll make a grand party of it and invite everyone to meet you. In no time you'll find yourself in the thick of society."

"You're too kind, Buc," she answered.

"I want you to like me."

"I like you," she whispered. Her head felt like it was going to crack open. "Now I really must say good night."

He kissed her hand one last time. His lips should have been delightful on her palm. They were nothing but unremarkable. The current that ran through her whenever Edward kissed her was not there in any form.

"Good night, Buc." She left him in the hall and closed the door.

Something was different in her rooms. Even in the dim gaslight she could tell something was definitely changed. She went to the wall and turned up the flare. Suddenly she could see what had changed. Violets. They were everywhere. On her settee, stuffed in vases, tied up in French ribbon and strewn across her bed. Abigail must have seen to their arrival after she'd left for dinner. It was why Edward had been late. These were his violets, killing her with an overpowering sweet stench. Mrs. Wirth's tonic was a finer scent than Edward Stuyvesant-French's foul posies.

In a sudden burst of mad laughter, she began to gather them in her arms. The florist must have sold him every violet in the ship's cold locker. It was a fortune in flowers; the violets were everywhere, even crammed into folded squares of white linen and tucked into her drawers.

She snatched them all up until her arms were overloaded with dark purple blossoms. Irrational triumph drove through her and she opened the deckside door of her parlor. As if exorcising him from her very soul, she ran to the railing and tossed all the violets overboard as far as she could throw them. Then, alone, without any more violets, she stared up at a crisp Atlantic moon that seemed to stare right back at her and laugh.

She was no longer a virgin. She'd been twice taken by him, twice loved, twice lied-to. The cold tower of her pride had melted beneath him and now she had nothing to protect her. She'd have to build the tower again, but this time it would be twice as hard. She was no longer untouched, unsullied, unmoved by a man. Her newfound weakness had been pointed out to her with all the swift brutality of a punch to the gut. Indeed, she was no longer a virgin, an innocent, but her heart still was. Which was why it hurt so terribly.

"I hate you, Edward Stuyvesant-French," she whispered before her eyes filled with tears. With a curse to the laughing moon, she ran back into her suite and slammed the door.

Chapter
Twenty-Five

On the Art of Producing Phantoms:

[Fine white netting] could be compressed into a space no larger than an ordinary tin blacking-box to furnish a full evening suit for the largest spirit. Enough more can be carried into a hollow boot-heel to dress up a couple more with an abundance of clothing. In the other boot-heel can be carried an assortment of netting-masks with which to transform your own face half-a-dozen times. In the envelopes supposed to contain letters you have the water-color faces for completing the forms, when their relatives are in attendance

—Revelations of a Spirit Medium
E. J. Dingwall and Harry Price, Editors (1891)

Lavinia spent all day building the ice tower around her and planning the séance. She called in Rawl and Monty and Hazel. They met in her parlor on the *Maritimus*, and it was just like old times back in the Turkish cozy corner. Together they worked like a well-greased machine, each knowing their respective roles. She was glad it went so well. This particular séance might be her last. She wanted to make a production of it.

"Is everyone clear on what we're to do tonight?" she asked.

Monty grunted a response, Hazel nodded, Rawl only stared.

"Rawl?" she nudged. "Is there something wrong?"

"I just don't know why we're going to do this one. It's bound to make everyone upset," he blurted out.

"Really?" Lavinia raised an eyebrow. "And do we need care about that?"

Rawl glanced down. "No, I suppose not. If you don't care who gets upset, then I don't."

"Fine. We give a farewell performance tonight, then Monty

can go on to the stage; you, Rawl, can retire to just playing butler; and we don't even need the children for this one, so it should be quite simple."

"Jamie will be angry he's not allowed to participate," Hazel said, a moody frown on her face.

"Jamie is getting a bit too chummy with Mr. Stuyvesant-French. I don't think it prudent to include him." Lavinia released a wistful grin. "Besides, it's time the boy had a better education than what we've provided. Being able to levitate tables and read minds is hardly useful for a boy who's off to Eton next fall."

"Eton?" Hazel gasped.

"Well, why shouldn't we try to get him in there?" Lavinia countered. "If Buc can go, why not Jamie? The boy's never even laid eyes on a schoolhouse, and yet he could run circles around Lord Buchanon."

"But who will vouch for him? We have no connections—"

"We will," Lavinia said, cutting her off. "I'll be seeing to it personally."

"Buc?" Hazel exclaimed. "But everyone thought you and Edward—"

Monty kicked her so hard she jumped.

Lavinia pretended not to notice. "Rawl, if you would just rest your voice, we'll see you back here at eight. Monty, I think you'll be able to find a suitable divining rod belowdecks. Here is the last of the pulverized phosphorus." She handed him a small jar. "Now remember, wash the gauze seven times, use the entire jar of Balmain's Luminous Paint mixed with varnish and benzine. I think you'll find whatever you need belowdecks if you slip the shiphands a coin or two."

Monty nodded.

"All right, if that takes care of everything, I guess we're through."

Monty and Rawl went to the door; Hazel stayed on the settee. Lavinia showed the men out and returned to the parlor.

"Is there something wrong?" she asked Hazel. "You know, if you don't want to participate, I don't mind doing this alone. We don't need need two mediums. In fact, I thought Celene might even get her amusements playing medium at one of these events since she's educated herself for it." Lavinia lowered herself to the settee next to Hazel.

Hazel looked at her and tried to put on a smile, but it fractured into a bout of tears.

"What is this?" Lavinia asked, fighting back tears of her own. The last thing she needed today was Hazel's depression. Lavinia feared she would sink inside her own and never find her way to the surface again.

"He wants to marry me. He asked me last night. I thought of waking you, but your light was out and you seemed so out of sorts since the night of the storm, I just couldn't do it." Hazel threw herself down to the seat cushion. "Oh, what am I to do? Do I trust him and say yes? I love him, but what if we get to England and he finds he can't break it off with his fiancée!"

Lavinia stroked Hazel's head. Coldly she said, "You are not to see him again. How dare he ask you to marry him when he has a fiancée waiting for him in London."

"He told me he would cry off wedding her."

"Is that what he said? Perfect, then you tell him—no, wait— I'll tell him that you'll be happy to accept his courtship when he is no longer affianced." Lavinia rose and went to the bedroom. Woodenly she reached for her hat and pinned it to her head. She was going to tell the grand Duke of Kylemore in no uncertain terms that the Murphy women were not to be toyed with.

"But if I refuse him now, he might not ask me again."

"Then he would expose himself for what he is, a coward."

"But then I'll be—I'll be alone." Hazel wept bitterly into her hands.

"Alone but better off for it," Lavinia whispered to her. "You'd do better to marry no one than latch on to a coward."

"Kylemore might not like the séance."

"Then don't participate."

"Oh, why must everything be so difficult?"

With tears of ice in her eyes, Lavinia whispered, "Because we've let men into our lives." She abruptly straightened. "Now I really must get the script for Rawl together and I'll need a quiet hour to do it, so let me take you to the children's cabin. In the meantime, you can quit worrying about the duke; he can't disapprove of you if you're not participating."

"Lavinia, has this been worth it? Our lives seemed so perfect before Wilhelm died. Now I feel miserable all the time. If love is like this, I think I don't want it." Hazel took out a hankie she had stuffed inside her dress sleeve. She dabbed her eyes.

Lavinia looked at her. She couldn't help but secretly agree. Their lives had been near to perfect before Edward's and Wilhelm's wills interfered. "It'll get better, Hazel. If things work out the way I plan, you might be a duchess by the end of the year."

"And you, Lavinia?" Hazel asked, her eyes red and tearful.

"Me?" Lavinia frowned. "Well, if things work out for me, I'll just stay the same, thank you. . . ." The end of the sentence went unspoken.

. . . and with no bastard in my belly to remind me of its father.

❦ ❦

"It's getting colder. I think we must be getting nigh to Britain," Cornelius said to Edward as they walked the first-class deck.

"Have you seen Daisy of late? I missed her this morning." Edward seemed distracted as if his thoughts weren't on his words.

"Why, I haven't. I went to call just last morning and her maid said she's been disappearing from the cabin every day at the same time to take the air here on deck." Cornelius looked around. "But that's strange. I don't see her now. This is all very mysterious."

"Yes, and I don't like it," Edward grumbled.

"Oh, but what kind of trouble could she get into on a ship in the middle of the Atlantic? Maybe she's meeting Jamie to exchange the latest Coltrain adventure. Leave her be, Edward. Let her have a life away from your chain, will you?"

Edward grunted. A muscle bunched in his jaw.

"What this is really about is the séance tonight, isn't it? Or is it Buc and his attention to Lavinia?"

Edward turned on him. "Lavinia may have him and his infernal violets. I invite her to marry that penniless peer. In fact, she should get the captain to bind her to him while on board ship. That way, when she steps onto the docks at London she can start the long process of bleeding herself dry in an attempt to keep him out of debtors' prison."

Cook's mustache twitched as if he were trying to hold back a laugh. "You don't think very highly of Buc, do you?"

"His motives are wearing thin."

"Lavinia can see his motives."

Edward's eyes turned a stormy North Atlantic green. "Perhaps."

"She's an intelligent woman. She couldn't be in the avocation she's in, nor do as splendidly as she has, if she weren't."

"Lavinia is intelligent. You won't get an argument out me."

"But?" Cook raised one eyebrow, ready for the tirade.

Stuyvesant-French didn't disappoint him. "But Lavinia's angry, and Buc offers something that she might decide is worth acquiring: a title."

"Then turn her head. Make her forget her anger. Make her forget Buc."

Edward looked away, past the railing and far out to sea where gray fog blurred the horizon. " 'Make her forget Buc.' " He snorted. "I've worked my whole life to make sure I had more money than Vanadder. Now I have all the money and I find that's where I begin and end—at the bank-teller window. So how can I turn Lavinia's head if drowning her in gold isn't the way she wants to go? Perhaps she already knows the desires within her own heart.

Perhaps she dreams that 'Countess' might one day be truly and legitimately etched upon her tombstone."

"Morbid metaphors, but I see where you're going, Edward. . . ."

"And?" Edward turned to him, pain in his eyes. "Where's the sage advice I always could rely on?"

Cook shook his head. "This concerns women, Edward. You know better than anyone that my advice is no good on that subject."

Stuyvesant-French returned his gaze to the hazy cold sea. "I can't go to that séance tonight. The idea of her conjuring up such productions sickens me. But how can I stay away? I haven't been able to stay away from her since I met her."

"Why don't you ask her to marry you, Edward?" Cook said gently. "Slap a ring on her hand and drag her to the captain yourself. Tell her you love her. Maybe it's that simple."

"Was it simple like that for you?" Edward's words held a cruel edge.

"No, it was not simple," Cornelius answered evenly. "But she loved another. Lavinia does not love Buc. Yet."

Edward rubbed his jaw.

"I believe she loves you."

"Does that one know anything of love?" He scowled as if chastising himself. "But what does it matter anyway? She doesn't want to love me. She doesn't trust me. She has reason not to."

"If you ask and she refuses, then all you can do is walk away." Cornelius's words turned to a whisper as if he could barely say them. "It can be done, old friend. Weaker men than you have suffered such blows and lived to tell."

"I see myself becoming prostrate at the feet of spiritualism just to receive a nymph's cold kiss." Edward looked out past the rail. Finally he dug inside his coat and retrieved a gold locket tied with a large black velvet ribbon. "This is Alice's locket, Cornelius. Vanadder gave it to her. Inside is a tintype of him." Stuyvesant-French's voice became thick. "I look at it every day and wonder why she left it to me. It was she who tied the black ribbon to it. It was she who mourned him."

"She gave it to you perhaps because it was the only thing your father bestowed upon her—besides you." Cornelius's expression turned dark. "It was right that you have it."

Edward reached his arm back and made to hurl it overboard.

Cornelius lunged and grabbed his arm. "What are you doing?" he gasped.

"I'm ridding myself of it," Edward said. "A vile thing, this locket; a monument to all the lies, all the treachery. It used to spur my anger and make me strong. Now all I feel is disgust. People can be so impossible. So weak. I can't stomach it any longer. I want no part of it."

"Then give it to me! I want it."

Cornelius's confession seemed to shock Edward. "But how could you? It was from him. *Him,*" he cursed.

"It was hers. She kept it; therefore, I want it."

Edward dropped it in Cornelius's outstretched hand. "Weaker men than me have survived," he whispered woodenly.

Cornelius put a grim hand on his arm. "Come. Let's not think about this anymore. That's how you get through it, you see? You don't think about it. So let's just take a walk and get some fresh air. Perhaps if we're lucky, we might come upon Daisy."

Edward nodded. Together, the two men walked toward the bow.

Chapter
Twenty-Six

"You seem eager to do this now. Where's that frightened little woman who feared she was too weak to stand?" Monty grinned and held Daisy even more tightly against him.

She turned her head and gazed up at him. His chest was to her back and his arms were like great muscled fortresses around her. She had no fear of falling with Monty. Together they looked out across the bow of ship toward a rift in the water. A pod of more than fifty pilot whales swam toward the horizon, their water spouts and tails breaking the monotony of stone gray swells.

"I wish this ship would just sail right past London and go around the world forever and leave us be," Daisy said softly.

Monty rested his chin against the top of her scarf-covered head. "Let's see, if we throw Captain Stafford overboard, maybe the crew would just keep on sailing without someone to order them to stop."

Daisy giggled. "We couldn't let the poor man drown. Captain Stafford is quite the gentleman. What we need to do is lock him in your cabin and just *tell* the crew we threw him overboard."

Monty contemplated the idea in mock seriousness, but then he shook his head. "It won't work."

"And why not?" she kidded.

"Because then I'll have to forfeit my cabin to Stafford and that was the last berth to be had on ship."

"You could stay in his quarters . . ." Her green eyes darkened with emotion. She turned her head and looked up at him again. "Or you could stay in my cabin with me."

His gaze locked with hers. "If Edward Stuyvesant-French heard you talk this way to me he'd have both our heads."

"I don't want him to run my life. I want to do it myself," she said, jaw tightening.

"Then you'd best look out for yourself and not fall for a bounder like me." He tore his gaze away and looked out to sea.

Slowly, she looked down to where his arms were crossed over her chest. His hands were tucked on either side of her rib cage and the bottoms of her corseted breasts just barely grazed his thumbs. With tears in her voice, she said, "I don't think I can go on without you. Who will hold me like this? Who will laugh with me? There's no one. No one."

"You'll find someone better than me. Your brother will see to it. Look, it's for the best. You need someone more appropriate than me."

She lolled her head on his shoulder and tipped back to look at him. "But I don't want anyone but you, and I fear you don't want me because—"

"It's not true," he snapped.

"—because—"

"I said it's not true." He looked down at her, his handsome face lean and serious. "In that chair or out of it, it's your smile I long for every morning. If you have flaws, I can no longer see them because I'm too utterly dazzled by the woman who makes me laugh every day here at the bow. So whatever you're about to say, whatever you think, I tell you it's not true."

"Don't leave me in London, Monty. I want to see the world with you."

"The world you would see with me is not very pretty. It's filled with cheap gin and dark alleys and base desires. I want to leave it behind as much as you believe you want to go to it."

"I don't care. I'll see it by your side if only I can come along."

"I can't give you the things you're used to. Don't you understand that?" he said between clenched teeth.

"Yes, I understand it, but what *you* don't understand is that you can give me all that I'm *not* used to such as warm arms to hold me up, companionship on a cold autumn night, friendship . . . and even more should you desire it—"

"Are you offering yourself? Are you that much of a fool?" he asked, a slight Irish accent clipping his words as if he forgot himself.

"Am I a fool?" she repeated, lifting her hand and touching his cheek. She shut her eyes to it as if the feel of him was exquisite.

"Oh, Daisy, don't do this." He groaned.

"Take me with you. My needs are more than you think, but ever so simple. All I want, all I need is you." She leaned against him.

He shook his head as if he were telling himself one thing but wanting something else entirely. Finally with one hand holding her up and the other tipping her face toward his, he let loose his wants, and he kissed her.

Daisy moaned with joy. Her hands began to tremble on the railing.

Not able to hold back, he kissed her more deeply and quickly seduced her cautious, inexperienced mouth into opening for him.

She was a delicate blossom slowly laying open her nectar for him, and he was drinking it with all the greed of a man dying of thirst. He told himself he had to quit, he had to pull away and spare—not her—but himself of the rejection that was destined to come.

But he just couldn't make himself stop. She was too pretty, her mouth was too hot and too sweet, her body, swaying with the ship, moved too erotically against his. And when she grabbed his arm that held her and pressed it to her as if holding it next to her very heart, he knew it was going to be his heart that was destined to shatter. Even now the thought of her wed to the rich, deserving man he knew she would one day have, made him ache inside.

"They don't kill men anymore for kissing women, do they?" he panted, a nervous chuckle running through him when he finally had the strength to tear his mouth away.

"If you were to die for that kiss, I would have to go with you as punishment for disappointing you." She gave him an intimate little laugh. "I'm not used to kissing. I fear I'm not very good at it."

"Then we have to try it again, eh? Let's make this one worth dying for," he whispered before his lips pressed down on hers again.

"*Jesus Bloody Christ.*"

Monty felt the presence of the man even before his mind registered the words. Daisy froze against him. He pulled his head up and found himself looking eye-to-eye with Edward Stuyvesant-French.

"Daisy?" Stuyvesant-French ranted, a wild expression on his face. He took a step forward from where he stood at the end wall of the first-class cabins but an older man who stood next to him held him at bay.

"Stay out of this, Cook," Edward spat. His gaze riveted again to Monty. "What in hell's name are you doing with my sister?"

Daisy went limp in his arms. Monty thought at first she'd fainted, but she was only trying to take a step forward as if to hold herself out to her brother in supplication.

"Easy, easy," Monty whispered to her. She looked up at him, her eyes filled with fear and, yet, hope. She loved him. He knew it in that instant and now she was either going to sacrifice herself for him, or he was going to do the first decent thing he'd ever done in his life and prevent her from it.

"Is she your sister, then?" Monty released a cocky grin. Slowly he eased Daisy down into her wheelchair. He refused to look at her eyes.

"You damn well know she's my sister," Edward sputtered furiously. "She's Daisy Vanadder and not likely to go kissing some gutter-licking hack driver minion of Lavinia Murphy's."

"Really?" Monty ached to challenge him. He'd never liked the bastard anyway. Stuyvesant-French's previous threats to Lavinia had made him want to punch him; the fact that Edward had gotten Lavinia's notice when Montagu Baillie's attentions to her had gone unwelcomed all these years rankled him, too.

But he couldn't release his aggression now. He had to do the right thing. Edward Stuyvesant-French was well within his bounds to punch his eyes out. It was his sister Monty was kissing, and his sister Monty was going to be thinking of with longing and regret in the wee hours of the coming night.

"Daisy," Edward turned to her, "have you been meeting this man? We've heard you disappear every day here on deck. Is this why? To have an assignation with him?"

"Yes," Daisy answered defiantly.

Cook gasped.

"I don't believe it," Edward spat.

"We met here by accident," Monty cut in. "She was here and I was here and we got to talking is all. Then she told me she had difficulty standing, so I help her out of the chair. That led to a kiss." He slicked himself up and pasted on the actor. "Really, would I pick a fight with you? I'm all too glad to apologize for my mistake— if kissing a pretty girl is a mistake."

Stuyvesant-French seemed to stumble on Monty's disarming words. He merely stared at the man as if burning a black hole into Monty's chest.

"Daisy, perhaps you'd best come with me." Cook walked up to the wheelchair and took control of the back. Daisy sat numbly within it, her eyes never wavering from Monty's.

Monty shrugged coldly. Portraying the uninvolved rake in front of Daisy was the most difficult role he'd ever played. "No harm done. No need to make a scene. I'll go my way, the situation forgotten. But maybe from now on you can keep a better eye on your sister here. Keep her away from the likes of me, eh?"

Stuyvesant-French nodded. His eyes were poison green. "Don't you ever go near her again."

"I—" Monty bit back his resentment. Again he told himself he was doing the right thing. But he couldn't look at Daisy. Not even when he began to take his leave.

"No!" Daisy cried out, wrenching control of her chair away from Cook. She went up to Monty and took his hand in hers. "Don't say such things. Not even for Edward. Say you don't mean them!"

"Daisy, stay out of this," Stuyvesant-French warned.

"I won't!" she sobbed, pressing Monty's hand.

"See what you've done!" Edward grabbed Monty's worn wool jacket by the collar and shook him. "I won't have you toying with my sister's affections."

Monty ripped Edward's hands from him. His only jacket was now torn and he cursed it. "If we're going to come to blows over this, so help me, I'll give as much as I'll get."

"Truce! Truce!" Cook blandished.

Daisy pressed Monty's hand to her cheek. "Please don't say you won't see me again. I told you Edward does *not* run my life. You needn't listen to him."

"Bloody hell, you'll listen to me and like it, Daisy. What do you know of his kind? You think I'm going to stand by here and watch you defiled by this penniless parasite?"

"Stop it, Edward! Stop it and go away! I love him!" Daisy choked back the rest of what she wanted to say as if the last admission had even shocked her.

"You've lost your mind," Edward gasped, glancing between his sister and Monty.

Finally he pinned his gaze on who he obviously thought was the culprit. "What have you done to her?" he demanded Monty.

Monty shook his head. He couldn't bear any more. Let Edward Stuyvesant-French draw and quarter him now; the agony he was putting Daisy through was unbearable. "Go to hell," he cursed, unable to say more.

Stuyvesant-French released an epithet of his own. He stepped toward Monty, but Daisy had let go of his hand, and wheeled herself between the two men. In an ice-cold voice, she said, "Stay out of this, Edward. Go back to your cabin and stay out of my life. Monty and I will decide what's to be done, and not you."

"You don't know his kind—"

"Yes, yes, a thousand times, yes!" she cried out, tears in her eyes. "I know I'm naive, I know I'm inexperienced, but I also know when I'm in love and I love him!"

"You can't marry him, so why bother with him?" he demanded.

"And why can't I marry him?" Daisy countered. "I'll tell you the first reason why—it's because he hasn't asked me, but if he does, Edward, I plan to accept his offer."

Stuyvesant-French ran an exasperated hand through his hair. Cook stood by, his face white as a sheet.

Monty knew it was time to inject some sanity in the conversation. He opened his mouth, but Edward almost lunged at him.

"You will not ask her!" he ranted. "Because I'll tell you this now, her money is held in trust, and I am the executor, and if she dares to run off with you, you cur, she'll be penniless. Penniless! I'll see to it personally that she is cut off. So now how fetching does my sister look?" Edward's expression was hard and cruel, and Monty could finally understand why he was considered such a terror.

Daisy began to weep into her hands. It was all in the open now. Monty knew her brother's words must have cut her to the quick, but he couldn't help but wonder if it wasn't for the best. He could now walk away branded as the cad, she could get on with her life and follow her brother's obviously prudent direction, and the world would be all the better for it.

"What say you now, cur? Are you going to propose or not?" Stuyvesant-French's voice was like a lion trying to hold back his roar.

Monty stared down at Daisy. She didn't look at him. Shame and tears covered what little he could see of her face. His heart twisted, but he was helpless. He could offer her nothing. Nothing.

"Go on. Propose," Edward bellowed.

Monty took a deep breath. His fist itched to meet with Stuyvesant-French's jaw, but he stopped himself.

"There, there, my dear girl," he heard Cook whisper to her. He wanted to go to her himself and console her, but he was the true reason for her suffering. He had nothing to offer her. The best thing he could do for her would be to just walk away.

Just walk away, he told himself again and again as he turned and took those first painful steps.

"What? You're leaving? Without a proposal?" Edward taunted behind his back.

Just walk away.

Monty wondered what kind of an actor he was destined to be when he couldn't erase the anger from his face.

Just walk away.

He found himself on the stairs leading down to steerage. Again he wondered about his talent for the stage when he couldn't remove himself from the pain that threatened to shatter his insides. As an actor he should be above emotion, for that was the only way to master it and emulate it. But it was choking him. He never thought he'd feel for a woman like he felt for her; her every tear was like acid etching his heart. Yet he had to do it. She deserved better. She and all her goodness merited a knight in shining armor, not some underemployed no-talent actor who'd spent the better part of his life parasiting off the pocketbooks of wealthy women. He had to do the right thing and leave her alone. He must.

Just walk away.

Chapter
Twenty-Seven

It haunts me to see you perched over a twopenny song with "Margaretta" in great big print underneath ... what a life to lead—at the call of any fool who chooses to pay a dollar and command your time ... I believe the only thing I ever was afraid of was, this confounded thing being found out.

—Noted Nineteenth-Century Arctic Explorer
  Dr. Elisha Kent Kane in a Love Letter to Margaret Fox

Lavinia gazed around the parlor table at the familiar faces gathered there. Celene was to her right, her expression rapt as she waited for the séance to begin. Buc and Kylemore flanked her. Buc appeared unsure of the goings-on, as if he were almost afraid the experience might prove him a coward. Kylemore looked grim and circumspect, and he covertly stole glances around the room as if he were anxiously awaiting Hazel's appearance.

Stuyvesant-French sat directly across from her. He looked almost as grim as Kylemore. If not for the sarcastic twist of his lips, he might have been mistaken for taking the proceedings seriously.

Daisy sat next to him in her wheelchair. Her face looked as if she'd forgotten how to smile. When she'd entered with Cornelius and her brother, her greetings had been swiftly and uncharacteristically glum. Now Lavinia watched as the young woman stared at the candle lit in the middle of the table, her face wiped clean of expression, and Lavinia couldn't believe Daisy's resemblance to her brother. Brother and sister shared a dark side. It was possible they even possessed the same lighter side as well, but whereas Daisy had always been free with her smiles, Edward handed his out with all the generosity of a Scrooge. Lavinia hadn't seen enough of them to compare.

"Are we ready?" she asked the group of pale, watchful faces gathered around her at the table.

"May we s-speak with whomever we choose?" Buc stuttered.

Lavinia slowly shook her head. "It's not up to me, it's up to the spirit who answers."

"Oh," Buc answered, as if it made sense.

Hazel made a dramatic appearance at the bedroom door. Her hair was loose and flowing down her back in Pre-Raphaelite fashion. She entered the room wearing a simple gown of white gauze that reached well past the floor. The extra-long hem concealed the source of the Czarina's celebrated "spirit knockings," more mundanely produced by Hazel's double-jointed toes.

"Does the Czarina need a trainbearer to help her with her gown?" Stuyvesant-French commented, scorn dripping from his words as he watched Hazel trip to her seat.

Lavinia gave him her most poisonous glance. "If there are doubters among us, I ask that they leave the room now. The spirits are loath to waste their presence among disbelievers."

"Oh, it's not wasted on me," he answered bitingly while Cornelius assisted Hazel into her chair.

Lavinia looked again toward the bedroom door. Monty entered with four long ropes on his arm. Without introduction, he went to the wall that held two pair of bronze ship's lanterns which illuminated the cabin. He extinguished all of them, then stood sentinel at the cabin door.

In the lone light of one flickering candle, Lavinia nodded to Monty. Solemnly, he went to the table and waited for her next instruction.

"Ladies and gentlemen," Lavinia began, staring at all the occupants of the table, "tonight the Czarina will conduct the séance.

She will attempt to speak to an occupant of the Other Side, but, in order to do this, she must have cooperation. Those who attempt to flee or disrupt the proceedings will not be tolerated; therefore, if anyone would like to take this opportunity to depart, I ask—no, I *encourage* them to do so." She scanned the faces at the table. No one moved. Buc was the only one who even glanced at the door.

"All right, then. We will proceed." Lavinia nodded to Monty.

He stepped forward with the first rope and tied it around Cornelius.

"What's this?" Cornelius gasped. He looked down at his chest where he was being bound to his chair.

"I must remind you that no one may flee or disrupt the proceedings." Lavinia nodded to Kylemore and Monty began to tie him next. "In order to accomplish this, I find it most useful to tie up my male guests. Call it an insurance policy."

"This is absurd." Edward stood.

Cornelius just stared, his expression almost comical as he glanced bug-eyed down at the rope around his chest.

"You're free to leave, Mr. Stuyvesant-French." Lavinia pointed to the door.

He hesitated.

She held her breath. If he left, the point of the séance would go with him. She could continue without him, of course, but it would be a Milquetoast performance. Her plans for him were magnificent, and though she risked his fury, revenge was too sweet a temptation, one made that much more desirable by the lessons she meant to teach him about women scorned.

"Shall you stay, or shall you leave, Mr. Stuyvesant-French? My patience wears thin." She locked stares with him. The expression in his eyes took her breath. *Oh, if looks could kill*, she thought.

Without a word, he lowered himself to the chair. He never took his gaze from her. Monty came up behind him and laid the third rope across his chest. Edward's mouth lifted in one corner. He was smirking, she thought. Taunting her.

Nervously she prayed the rope held.

Buc was the final man to be lashed to his chair. With a small grunt of a protest, he, too, allowed Monty to tie him up.

"If I may be so bold as to ask: Why aren't the women being subject to this humiliation?" Cornelius asked lightly.

Lavinia placed her hands on the table and used them to circle the single candle that provided the light. "I've found in my experience that the most disruption women cause during a spirit encounter is their predilection to fainting spells. They are not inclined to dash about the room and search the curtains as many men are."

"Have you something to hide in the curtains, then, Countess? Czarina?" It was Kylemore's turn to speak. He looked across the table at Hazel, who pointedly did not look at him.

"Rest assured, Your Grace, Hazel and I have nothing to hide," Lavinia countered. "And should you have the opportunity to dash around and look behind the drapery, one thing you are certain not to find hiding there, my dear Kylemore, is a fiancée."

Kylemore grimaced a smile. "I bow before your wit, Countess."

Lavinia went back to the facade of studying the candle. Across from her, Hazel nodded almost imperceptibly.

"Shall we begin?" Lavinia looked at the faces at the table. She bowed her head and clasped the hands on either side of her.

Hazel's voice rang out. "We summon such passing spirits as those who may hear our call. We summon the good spirits that surround us. We implore the occupants of the Other World to contact us if they may, and beg that they give us a word from beyond the grave. . . ."

A loud knocking sound vibrated from the rosewood table around which they sat. Lavinia knew it was only Hazel's toes cracking against the table leg, hence causing the table to appear that the sound was actually emanating from within it. Still, it was a creepy feeling to lean against a table that seemed to vibrate of its own volition.

"Speak to us, spirit. Tell us your great knowledge. Identify yourself and give us comfort for our destiny that shall land us in your Dark World." Hazel closed her eyes and leaned her head against the tabletop. She trembled. "We implore you, spirit. We beg you. Identify yourself. Let us know if you are friend or foe."

Buc shuddered. Lavinia almost giggled at his face that had become dead white.

"Spirit will out! We demand you identify yourself!" Hazel shot to an upright position, her dark hair flying.

"You call me? Me, you insolent wench?" A voice boomed from the direction of the darkened bedroom. Lavinia bit back a grin. Rawl was a genius when it came to ventriloquism and voice imitation.

Daisy gasped. Celene gripped her hand ever tighter.

In the shadows, Lavinia watched as Monty crept toward a large bookcase. His darkened form leaned against it and she could almost spy him dig at his shoe-heel. If all went as planned, he would leap from the shadows draped with the luminescent gauze on cue.

"Who are you, angry spirit?" Hazel pleaded, her eyes darting around the room as if she didn't know where the voice originated.

"Who do you think I am?" the voice echoed boldly.

Lavinia half caught herself believing it was real. Rawlings had outdone himself tonight. He did the imitation perfectly. But, of course, she had to remind herself, Rawl had heard the voice enough in past years to know it well.

"I know what you're up to, Lavinia, and I tell you this is not amusing." Edward started in his seat but the rope held him fast.

"You had the chance to leave, Edward, now let's hear what the spirit has to say." Lavinia looked to her sister.

"Spirit, give us your name," Hazel asked the darkness.

"You know my name!"

Daisy released a small cry. "It's Father. I'd know his voice anywhere!" She stared at Lavinia, then at Hazel as if she didn't believe it, but couldn't *not* believe it.

"Is that Wilhelm?" Lavinia finally interjected.

The spirit laughed. "Who else?"

"Why do you seek us out?" Lavinia asked calmly. She stared at Edward. Edward stared at her.

"I want sustenance," the voice seemed to echo from all corners of the room.

"Sustenance? Why, you had enough sustenance for ten men, Wilhelm. Your girth was large if I recall."

"Yes, but my spirit was starved, as it is starved now."

"For what?" she asked easily, her script memorized.

"For me," came a woman's voice in the direction of the bookcase.

In the shadows, Lavinia could just make out Monty's silhouette. The gauze had been dug out from his hollow heel and he held it balled in his hand. But instead of preparing to throw the sheer fabric over his head, he seemed distracted. His dark form was frozen, his gaze directed to the shadows on the ceiling.

"Who are you?" Lavinia asked, irritated. Rawl was not following the script and she thought she'd made it clear that it was important they not improvise.

"*I* am the sustenance he seeks and shall never find," the feminine voice rang out from the darkness.

"Oh, God," Cornelius moaned, his face held to the ceiling almost rapturously. "Is it you?" he seemed to whisper again and again as he unlocked his hands from the circle.

"Who do you wish to speak to?" Lavinia asked, wondering where Rawl was going in all of this. The séance was degenerating into chaos. None of this was planned.

"Edward," the voice pleaded.

"Who are you?" Lavinia asked, wondering if Rawl had lost his mind. She'd wanted Edward rattled by the séance, not driven to kill because of it. Rawl knew better than to taunt him with Alice. It was sheer idiocy.

"You goddamn bitch, stop this at once," Edward growled across the table to Lavinia. His rope still held, but his face, even in darkness, was terrifying.

"I don't want to talk to you, spirit, I want *Wilhelm*," Lavinia demanded. She waited for Rawl to come around. In the meantime, she nervously anticipated Monty to appear as the spirit, but he still seemed paralyzed beside the bookcase, his attention taken up by some mysterious spot on the ceiling.

"Wilhelm?" Lavinia prompted again. To her extreme disappointment and anxiety, Wilhelm did not return.

"My message is for Edward. . . ."

"We only wish to speak to Wilhelm," Lavinia said weakly, unsure whether she should unlock her hands and throttle Rawl, or let the river run its course.

"I've never left you, Edward," the voice said. "Never. Not when you were a babe, nor even now when you're a man full-grown and powerful."

Edward lowered his head. Lavinia could see his teeth grinding even from her position. He was fury incarnate. Every word Rawl spoke was like poking a wounded tiger.

"I'm proud of the man you've become. Proud, but . . . there's so much darkness, so much of *him* in you."

"Alice! Let me be with you now!" Cornelius suddenly cried out. He tried to get to his feet, but the rope held him down.

Edward's rage burst forth. He tore the rope from his chest with his hands and lunged across the table toward Lavinia. Hazel screamed. Monty darted from the corner.

". . . Don't become him, Edward. You're my son. My son . . . Remember me . . . remember me . . ."

"You bitch! To do this! I could kill you!" Edward lunged again. The candle on the table sputtered and extinguished.

"I did none of this!" Lavinia cried in the utter darkness. She stumbled backward, away from him, her heart torn apart. "I wouldn't!" she sobbed pitifully.

Rawl fumbled through the parlor and found his way to the lanterns. He lit them, shedding cruel light upon them all.

Cornelius released harsh dry sobs into his hands while Celene

tried to comfort him. Buc was alabaster white. Kylemore had somehow managed to squirm from his binding and held Hazel to him
as if protecting her from Stuyvesant-French.

All were silent save poor Cornelius.

"I didn't do this, Edward," Lavinia wept, her own breath coming
in quick, painful sobs.

"Liar," Edward mumbled, staring at her as if she'd just grown
horns. "Liar, fraud, cheat . . . whore." He threw the rope still in
his hands on the table.

"No," she whispered, not seeing anyone in the room but him.
She had to make him understand that it wasn't her, that somehow
Rawl had gotten it wrong, terribly inexplicably wrong.

"You've done your last séance, Countess." Edward looked down
at Cornelius. Celene shook her head as if to say, *I'll take care of
him.*

Edward's gaze returned to her.

She went toward him, her hands outstretched in supplication.
"I didn't do this, Edward. I wouldn't toy with you like this. I only
meant to teach you a lesson —"

The hatred burning in his eyes stopped her like a bullet.

"Stay away. Stay far away from me, you bitch." He kicked back
his chair and strode for the door. It slammed behind him.

Lavinia looked to Rawl as if to ask him why he had betrayed
her like this. With no explanation forthcoming, she ran sobbing
for her bedroom.

Chapter
Twenty-Eight

I can't bear to think of you sitting in the dark squeezing other people's hands.

—ELISHA KENT KANE TO MARGARET FOX, 1855

"How is he?" Hazel asked Celene.

"I left him resting. I think he'll be all right. It was a terrible shock for him to hear her voice. He says he remembers it so well." Celene accepted the tea Evaline poured. Buc and Kylemore milled around Daisy's parlor along with Monty and Rawlings. They made a strange midnight gathering in Daisy's parlor, but no one, servant or otherwise, seemed to dare retire until all explanations were out.

"So was it all a fraud, Hazel?" Celene finally burst forth, her hand trembling on her china cup.

"Rawl says he took no part in it. He had the Wilhelm script memorized and unless he spoke Alice's words without knowing it, then he swears he's innocent." Hazel looked at Rawl. The old Englishman seemed one hundred years older from his experience. To back up Hazel's explanation, he nodded furiously.

"And it was not you, Mr. Baillie?" Daisy asked softly, her gaze lit on Monty.

Monty shook his head. "Not me. I never left the bookcase. I was too startled by the voice. We were to produce Wilhelm, not a woman. Besides, the voice seemed to come from everywhere . . . and yet nowhere. When I heard it, I was perplexed, so much so that I forgot my part entirely."

"We're overlooking one important fact here," Celene whispered, the expression in her eyes distant. "The woman never identified herself."

"Edward recognized her," Daisy offered.

"But he didn't. He accused Lavinia of tricking him. Of playing with his emotions. I can understand his rage." Celene looked around the room at the faces now staring at her. "Besides, even if it was Alice, how would Edward know it? She died upon his birth."

"But it was Alice. It had to be," Daisy whispered.

"Indeed it was Alice," Celene confirmed, "or Lavinia's séance is the most brilliant fraud to ever be put on this earth, and do you know how I—how all of us—know this?" She again scanned the faces. "Because the only one who recognized the voice—and he recognized it instantly—was Cornelius. And Cornelius is the only one in the room who ever heard Alice speak."

Hazel sighed in despair. "But I understand he loved her so terribly. He wants to be with her. He told Lavinia all about her. If he wants Alice that badly, then it's been my experience he'll hear Alice whether it was Alice or not."

"There are, of course, other possibilities than the one I'm suggesting," Celene conceded.

"But none more convincing," Kylemore interjected.

"The only ones to know the truth are Rawl and Lavinia." Hazel looked again to the butler.

Rawl shook his head. "You know me, miss. I don't improvise. I never have. I did not perform Alice Stuyvesant-French this night or ever."

"I knew you would say that, Rawl." Hazel's expression turned dark. "I suppose it's the only thing you can say, because it is—I fear—the truth."

Edward ripped out of his jacket and flung it aside. He poured three fingers of brandy from the decanter on his desk and drank it in one gulp.

She'd really gotten to him. Maybe it was because she used his mother, a woman he'd never seen, never touched, but one whose very substance had created him, molded him into the creature he was now.

He poured more brandy, downed it, and poured again.

But Lavinia had him. He was all hers. She'd wound around his heart like a serpent, filling his thoughts, weakening his resolve. He was in love with her, but she didn't deserve it. Not that woman who'd played such a cruel trick on gentle Cornelius.

His hand trembled as he refilled his glass. He couldn't shake his anger. The sweet young woman he'd made love to on the porch in Bermuda was gone, replaced instead with a black-hearted mercenary who would do anything to impress those around her with her talents. And now he loved her.

"Bitch," he whispered, squeezing his eyes shut at the picture of her. She'd seemed so innocent as she'd denied conjuring Alice. Her expression had been so artless, so believable, so genuine. He had to hand it to her. She was a brilliant fraud. . . . *Or* . . .

No, he would not let his mind go down that path. It couldn't be. It wasn't true. Edward Stuyvesant-French had prevailed in a life headed for doom because he stayed fierce and yet logical. He wouldn't abandon logic now.

He opened his eyes. Maybe it was for the best. He wanted her as his mistress and now he could take her and have her any way he wanted and feel no guilt about it. He could treat her like the doll she was and know there was nothing inside her but sawdust.

He finished off his glass and moved to pour another one, but he paused. A long dark ribbon hung from his discarded jacket. He stooped and touched it.

It couldn't be, but it looked just like . . .

He pulled on it. The thick black velvet ribbon gave and a gold locket fell from his jacket pocket.

In amazement, he held it up. Indeed, it was his mother's locket. The one he'd given Cornelius.

He frowned. He didn't remember Cornelius giving it back to him, or rather, sliding it into his pocket. In fact he and Cornelius had never even shaken hands that night. He grabbed the jacket. It was one he hadn't worn once on the trip. Somehow, by strange coincidence, the locket had found its way into that particular jacket for him to find this night.

He ran his thumb over the locket's heavy gold embossing. It didn't ring right with him that Cornelius would give it back. He'd wanted it too shamelessly to sneak into Edward's armoire and tuck it back into his possession. Flipping open the lid, he expected to find the old tintype of Vanadder. Instead his breath choked in his throat.

A dozen tiny violet blossoms fell from the locket's interior. They floated to the floor and landed on the tip of his shoes.

Wordlessly he dropped to his knees and touched the blossoms. They were fresh. They couldn't have been in the locket for an hour.

He crushed one in his palm. Lavinia had to have planted the locket. She was the only one to know about the violets. She must have acquired the locket from an unwitting Cornelius, then had her minion Baillie somehow slip it into his jacket pocket.

It had to be that way, he thought, his anger rising. That was the only sensible answer. Because otherwise, he'd have to believe in ghosts. He'd have to believe his mother really had reached out from the grave to speak with him and that all she'd said was true; that she did love him; that she was proud of who he'd become.

He'd have to shove aside all logic and believe that it was she who planted the locket and the flowers inside. That she'd put it there as a sign. He'd have to believe the cosmos was made up of things he couldn't see or touch or make willful communication with. He'd have to believe all of that.

And he'd have to believe Lavinia.

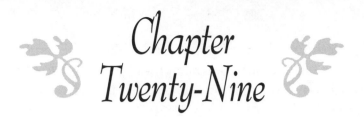

Chapter
Twenty-Nine

There were no more séances aboard the *Maritimus*. Lavinia kept to her suite and rarely ventured forth, even for a walk on deck. Hazel did likewise in an effort to avoid the duke and his veiled promises. Cornelius was often seen in the first-class lounge with Celene, having long morbid talks until the small hours of the morning. Daisy spent the rest of the time to herself. She didn't dare go about on ship. The thought of crossing paths alone with Monty was unbearable. Instead, she read, she did her needle-work, and wept.

The last night on ship should have been fraught with celebration, but Captain Stafford was occupied at the helm wrestling a nor'easter, and, unfortunately, the ship rose and fell along with the stomachs of many of the passengers. It was rainy, cold, and altogether a miserable night destined to make people think twice of leaving their snug cabins.

Monty, having nothing to do the rest of the trip, took to tippling with some of the stewards in the galley. It might have been depression on his part, he wasn't sure, but he was never much of a drinker, and it didn't take much these days to get him stinking. He was ripped pretty good by the time he decided to retire to his cabin. He shuffled along the passageways, hugging each wall in turn as either he or the ship took a tilt.

"*Oh, Bridget O'Malley . . . you left my heart achin' . . .*" he began to sing under his breath. It was an old Irish song his father used to belt out whenever he and his mother took to arguing. The tune was hauntingly beautiful, memorable even when in a drunk. But the words just weren't right tonight.

"*Oh, Daisy Vanadder . . . you left my heart achin' . . .*" No, that wasn't right either, he thought with a twist of guilt in his heart. She hadn't left his heart with any bruises at all. He'd been the one to do that. Her hurt had been so clear in her eyes the night of the séance, he couldn't bear to look at her.

But what the hell did she want from him? He'd done the upstanding thing and cried off just like her brother told him to do. Was it his fault she accepted her wounds like a sad-eyed doe? Was it his fault she appeared on the verge of tears even as all hell was breaking loose in that strange little séance Lavinia cooked up? It was not. It was all her brother's fault and Edward Stuyvesant-French had done the only thing he could. Why, he would have done the same thing if Daisy was his sister.

He swayed along the passage and threw open the door to his cabin. All eleven bunks were full of snoring or wretching men. Monty took one look around at the scene and shut the door in front of him. Even the damp passage would be a preferable bunk to the foulness of his own.

He slid down the wall and took out his bottle from his jacket pocket. The fabric ripped, but he no longer cared. The jacket had suffered one too many repairs already. It looked about as low as he felt.

"*Oh, Daisy Vanadder . . .*" He hummed the rest and took a hefty gulp from the whiskey bottle. As luck would have it, the stairs to second class and then up to first class were right in front of him. Her room was only two flights of stairs away but it might as well have been an ocean for all his ability to get to it.

". . . *I left your heart achin'* . . ." he improvised, his stare riveted to the display of steps that led up to where he really wanted to go.

"I didn't want to do it, damn it. I didn't want to," he grumbled drunkenly. He took another shot, then wiped his mouth with the back of his hand.

Those stairs just seemed to call out his name. Hesitantly he stumbled to his feet and clung to the wall for balance.

He should go and apologize to her; explain why he'd had to walk away. That might take the hurt from her eyes. Indeed, he should do that. Maybe a few soothing words and she'd understand. Maybe even he'd understand a little better.

If he got caught in her room Stuyvesant-French would throw him overboard and no one would be able to say he didn't deserve it. But he wasn't going to stay in her cabin. What he wanted to tell her, he could do it from the passage, nice and proper. He could tell her how good everything was going to turn out for her, what a fine husband she would have one day, and fine children who would look just like their father.

The very thought made his insides catch fire. He didn't want to think of her as someone else's, bearing the children of an as-yet-faceless man he already despised because that man was not him.

So he wouldn't tell her those things. Maybe the only thing left to tell her was the truth. She was too good for him, and she wasn't the one who should weep at their parting. He was the one who loved her. And he would tell her that, this last night aboard ship.

He found himself on the second-class landing, looking up the stairs to first class. He tipped the bottle again for sustenance, and then he took the rest of the stairs two at a time.

He straightened his jacket and ran his fingers back through his dark hair. The effort was of little use. He looked like hell. But what he had to say wouldn't take long. A man didn't like to take too long in wringing out his heart.

He held on to the brass knocker to regain his balance. Inhaling a breath, he knocked and waited.

It took a long time to answer the door. He expected the maid, but by this late hour he wondered if she were gone for the night.

The door opened slightly. He heard the sound of wheels, then the door opened fully and she looked up at him.

She said nothing. She was dressed only in a white batiste night rail and a challis shawl she'd hastily thrown over her shoulders. Her hair was unbound, a luxuriant mass of sable black that she'd obviously been in the middle of plaiting. He never remembered seeing her so fetching, so beautiful.

She returned his stare, taking in aspects of his appearance from his wretched jacket and unshaven jaw, to the bottle he still held in his left hand.

"I don't have much to say. It won't take long. I promise." He wondered if his expression was as pain-filled as hers.

She wheeled back and allowed him passage. He paused, unsure of whether he should enter her suite, but with her eyes offering mute invitation, he could no longer think of a reason why he should stay in the hall.

He closed the door behind them and leaned back on it.

She continued to stare. "You've been drinking," she said softly, only mild reprimand in her voice.

"It's the last night. I'll no longer be seeing you after we dock in London tomorrow."

"I'll see you on the stage, won't I, Montagu Baillie?" She wore that quiet, knowing smile on her lips that drove him crazy.

"I'm never going to be any great actor. I know it. Your damn brother knows it too." He tipped his head back and wished the room wasn't swaying so much. "No, I'll get to Londontown and do what I can to get a break, but in the end I'll probably take to driving a hackney cab again, or maybe Lavinia and Hazel'll let me carry their luggage through Egypt or some other such place. And that's the Baillie curse. Me father could never get good work either."

" 'Me father'?" she asked, lifting a dark eyebrow. "Are you finally admitting to being Irish, too, Mr. Baillie?"

He grinned. "Cheeky."

"Any other confessions?"

He felt his heart go to his throat. In a harsh, dark tone he whispered, "I love you."

She paled.

He shut his eyes to the sight of her. "It doesn't matter what I said the other day. It doesn't matter what I did, or what your brother did. It's all for the best that we part company because I'm no good and . . . and I love you."

"Oh God."

He looked down at her and saw her eyes fill with tears. Awkwardly she tried to get to her feet, but time and again, she failed.

"Don't," he said, pushing her back down.

"Let me stand—just one more time—hold me—" she gasped.

It was wrong to go to her, to lift her in his arms and embrace her.

But he had to because he was drunk and he was alone with her and it was the end and it was good-bye and, Jesus, he loved her.

"Don't leave me," she whispered tearfully before his lips met with hers.

The kiss was sweet and eager and bitter. He drew back only because his conscience was screaming at him. "I shouldn't be here like this," he whispered.

"I'll find a way to make Edward accept you. Please give me a chance to try. I'll get my money and then you can take me with you," she wept, holding on to his jacket with fists.

"It's not the money," he agonized, unwilling to let her back down into her chair, unwilling just yet to let her go.

"It is the money. I watched you walk away when Edward threatened to cut me off." She looked up at him with her beautiful tear-stained face. "If what you want is an heiress, then I'll make myself into that. I dreaded the idea before. I watched my mother pay the price for being such, but I don't care anymore. I want you. I love you. I'm so very rich and I'll get the money for you. I'll make Edward understand how much you mean to me."

"He'll never understand. I know his kind. He's made up his mind."

"Please give me the chance."

"Stop it!" He shook her. "Don't you understand? Even if he gave you his blessing I still wouldn't marry you. It's not the damned blunt that's holding me back."

"It must be," she insisted desperately, "because you said you loved me." She touched his cheek. "If you love me, then marry me. And if you won't, then it's either the money or . . ." Her gaze lowered to the wheelchair.

"It's not that. Definitely not that," he whispered.

"Prove it," she answered weakly.

"There's only one way for me to prove it."

She touched him. "So do it," she barely breathed, tipping her head up to his.

He kissed her, this time hesitantly. The whiskey was full in his veins now, but raging worse was his desire for her. He was losing his mind. Somehow he had to get it back and save both of them.

"Stay with me tonight," she whispered between kisses. "I'll never marry. We both know that. So who would cast stones upon me if I fell off my pedestal for one tiny moment in a lifetime of spinsterhood?"

He groaned. "Don't talk like that. Don't invite me. Don't even think it. This is madness. If I stay the night I'll have to marry you or prove I'm the biggest heel this side of America."

"You already proved the latter when you walked away from me and Edward." She looked up at him.

He kissed her, a full open-mouth kiss that left him hard and wanting. "You think it's only money I want from you, but I may prove you wrong," he gasped.

"Prove me wrong," she whispered before he picked her up and took her to the bedroom.

Chapter Thirty

"I haven't spoken to Kyle in weeks now," Hazel said glumly to Lavinia as they watched London harbor draw ever near.

Lavinia had no answer. The trip had ended despicably. She hadn't spoken to Edward for weeks, either, and guilt ran through her like a knife every time she saw Cornelius. In her mind she knew she hadn't been responsible for those words spoken in the séance that night, but though she might never get to the bottom of it, somehow she knew she was the responsible party anyway. It was she who had orchestrated the program and chosen the players, and when everything went awry, it was she who had inadvertently twisted Cornelius's heart and wounded him. She would never forgive herself; she'd grown fond of the old gentleman on the cruise. It would be her deep misfortune to lose him as a friend, but perhaps she deserved it. After all, she was nothing but a penny carnival act. She had no business manipulating people's lives and emotions.

Below the ship, the mighty waters of the Thames seemed to be only thick brown swamp banked on either side by ten thousand coal-burning chimneys. Mixed with the fog of early dawn, even Lavinia, who'd always thought of herself as adventurous and daring, was ready to head back to New York.

"Do you think he'll keep his promise?" Hazel asked glumly. "I didn't sleep a minute last night. I wanted so badly to get to London, but now that we're here, I think I might have been too hasty. What if he's been lying to me, promising things he didn't mean?"

Lavinia rubbed her own sleep-deprived eyes. "Buc asked us to spend the weekend at Kylemore House. If the duke is planning to sport his fiancée there and yet continue to make promises to you, he has another thing coming. I won't need to do another seance to scare him. I think I'll be pretty scary all by myself under those circumstances."

Hazel smiled. She linked arms with her. "You always stick up for me. If Kyle ever takes me down the aisle, you must promise that we'll find a fine husband for you. I don't want to think of you lonely."

Lavinia's thoughts turned to Edward. He was no woman's dream of a fine husband. He was black-tempered, suspicious and illegitimate to boot. No prize at all. But she loved him. Her very soul yearned for him.

With all her heart she wished he would think her worthy, but he did not think it. And now that Cornelius had been hurt, Edward would never think it.

She'd dreamed about Edward last night between fits of insomnia. He'd come to her ship's suite. They'd argued and he called her a whore. She tried to deny it but he grasped her nape and pulled to him, whispering that whore's mouths were best used in this way.

Even now she had to shut her eyes to the picture of it. He'd kissed her and murmured that there was but one other way she could use her mouth.

She hadn't wanted to perform for him, whore for him, but in her dream he'd paid his gold coin and she owed him. So she gave him his performance, because he demanded it; because he'd paid for it. She did everything he asked until she was on her knees begging him to stop, but all she found when she looked up was his face cast into a grimace of ecstasy. Ecstasy and triumph.

She opened her eyes. The sight off the ship rail was no comfort. She couldn't erase the picture of Edward's face, his dark, close-cropped goatee christening his features with the mark of the devil; his hands strong and demanding, seducing her with their very power. The nightmare had kept her awake until Hazel had appeared at her door unable to sleep also. Both had decided to go on deck and see the *Maritimus* make its dawn arrival in London.

Now she stared out across the London docks and suddenly realized the abysmal soot-covered tableau fit her mood perfectly. For the hundredth time, she cursed the séance. It had been a foolhardly endeavor to try to toy with Stuyvesant-French. Never in her wildest dreams did she think Alice would come out of Rawl's mouth, but what could she expect from a puppeteer who was old and forgetful, and who'd performed Alice Stuyvesant-French for Vanadder so many times he could probably do her in his sleep? Something like that should never have been attempted because she had had to rely on too many people, and the more humans, the more chance for human error.

There was, of course, the possibility that Rawl's mind hadn't failed him. The butler could have been telling her the truth, that he hadn't performed Alice that night. But then that would leave only the possibility that Alice's ghost had been summoned to her ship's cabin and that it was truly Alice who had spoken with her son. Lavinia was least susceptible to that explanation. There was no way for her to even entertain it when she knew all the tricks, all the methods, all the lies that were part of every spiritual encounter in which she'd ever been involved.

"Do you ever think about where we came from, Lavinia?" Hazel asked, seemingly out of the blue.

Lavinia reluctantly pulled herself from her dark thoughts. "What do you mean?"

"I mean, do you ever wonder who your parents were, what your family was like? Do you ever lay awake at night and wonder if you have brothers and sisters out there you don't even know?"

Taking a deep breath, Lavinia said. "I don't think about it. The name Murphy, it's unremarkable. I'm sure my parents were nothing special."

"But at least you know you are a Murphy. It's terrible to be like me and Jamie and Fanny. We went to the orphanage with no name at all. Just a blank slate with no writing on it."

"Murphy isn't much of an improvement to a blank slate."

Hazel shook her head. "You don't know what it means to us to use your name like we have. Jamie asked me one night in the orphanage what it felt like to have a father. I couldn't answer him. Now at least we do pretend there was a father there, a big jolly Irishman named Murphy."

"Yes, the kind who has 'Irish Need Not Apply' written all over him." Lavinia turned to her. "Why so pensive about this now? In truth, I hate thinking about where I might have come from. I see the poor women on the street and every one of them could have been my mother—and but for Wilhelm Vanadder and dupes just like him, there we would be ourselves. No, I don't wonder. I'm too much of a realist. I think I know all too well where I came from and I want to think about it as little as possible."

"That's why it never works for you, Lavinia. These séances. I think you really must believe a little bit in things you cannot see or they don't work."

"But they don't work." Lavinia sullenly turned back to the docks. "There are no such things as spirits and ghosts. We cannot talk to the dead. We wouldn't want to. How dreadful it would be to find out where you came from. You'd have no control over your heritage except the choice to disown it."

"Kylemore wouldn't want to disown his heritage. The dukedom is the very fabric from which he's made. I think it would be more terrible to have put him on this earth a blank slate."

Lavinia looked at Hazel, her features growing soft. "If you want a heritage, his is the kind you should have. Let the Kylemores do the writing on your slate. Then you'll never have reason to be ashamed of it."

Hazel nodded, a tear glistening in her eye. "I want that so much, not just for me. For Eva too."

Lavinia pressed her hand. "I know, and if there's any mercy at all, it will happen."

🌱 🌿

Edward heard the banging on his door as if it were very far away. The pounding permeated the thick dark tunnel of his hangover and finally wrestled open his eyes.

He stared up at the ceiling. He was on his bed, still in the clothes he'd worn last evening. The empty bottle had fallen to the floor. When he rose, he almost tripped on it.

"Confound it, Cornelius! What in bloody blazes is this?" He tucked in his shirttail and ran a hand through his hair. Finally, he got to the parlor door and threw it open.

Cornelius stood there with Celene at his side. They both looked shocked, perhaps more by Edward's appearance than with whatever news they'd come to bring.

"It's almost noon, my good man. The ship's been docked for hours. We've discovered they've already left!" Cornelius blurted out.

"Who's left? What are you talking about?" He turned to Celene. His head was pounding and his patience was nonexistent. "What's he talking about?"

"You look dreadful, Edward, dreadful. Like you were up all night drinking over a woman," Celene remarked in her usual subtle manner.

"What's going on here?" Edward growled. "Tell me this instant."

"It's Daisy—" Cornelius closed his mouth as if he didn't dare say more.

"Daisy?" Edward frowned, then he suddenly bolted for the passage as if on fire.

"She's not in her cabin, French. She's gone."

Edward stopped. He turned, a wild light in his eye. "What do you mean, she's gone? Gone where?"

"Gone with him, I'm afraid," Cornelius answered gently.

"What in hell are you saying?"

Celene obviously couldn't stay silent any longer. "She left with Montagu Baillie, the Murphys' servant. Captain Stafford married them early this morning and now they've departed the ship. We only just discovered it."

Edward felt as if she'd just punched him. The shock of it made him almost reel backward.

"Let's go back inside your cabin, shall we?" Cornelius took his arm.

"But I told him I would cut her off. Didn't he believe me? What a fool he is if he thinks to test me," Edward gasped.

Cornelius shrugged. "I don't think he's testing you, Edward. The thing is done. Daisy, according to the captain, is now legally and for all eternity wed to Mr. Baillie."

"How did this happen?" Edward demanded.

"They fell in love," Celene interrupted.

"They couldn't have. He walked away when I threatened him. He walked away! The money meant everything."

"But not as much as Daisy, apparently." Cornelius laid a strong hand on his shoulder. "I think you've got to accept it, Edward, they fell in love. The money just didn't figure in it."

"It will eventually." Edward stoked the vengeance in his eyes. "And he would be a fool to think I won't keep my word."

"Daisy won't ask for it. Her needs and wants were always modest, if I recall correctly. She has him now, and he must truly love her if he knows she's penniless. It's done, Edward. There's nothing you can do about it but give them their blessing."

"Like hell," he cursed, walking away from both of them.

"It's done," Cook repeated.

"Where are they? I'll see her found and brought back to the ship before it's too late."

"It's too late. Apparently Baillie gave that as reason for the hasty wedding."

Edward leaned his forehead against his fist. A surge of anger and bewilderment rushed through him. He hadn't even thought this a remote possibility—now it had happened. Daisy was gone, away from his protection forever. "Why? Why did she do this? I gave her everything," he whispered half to himself.

Celene walked to him. "She loved this man, Edward. She wanted him more than your approval."

"Was my approval, my *concern,* so bad, then?" he lashed out.

"No," she said softly, "I'm sure Daisy would still like to have it, if only you could see to coming around to Baillie."

"Never." He rubbed his jaw. It ached.

"Shall I notify the authorities so that they might find her for us?" Cornelius asked tentatively.

"No."

Celene gave Cornelius a despairing look. She whispered to Edward, "Don't cast her aside, dear boy. She's your only flesh and blood, and she loves you."

"I don't make threats idly. I'll carry this one out if it's the last thing I do. I'll make Baillie rue the day he ever looked upon my sister."

"How cruel you are. The ghost was wrong, Edward," Celene countered "you're not your mother's son. No indeed."

"Get out," he rasped, lowering his pounding head into his hands.

Cook nodded to Celene. She left Edward's side and they departed the cabin, leaving Edward alone with his demons.

"Have you heard the news? It's shocking! Just amazing!" Hazel burst into Lavinia's bedroom as Lavinia instructed Abigail and Rawlings on how best to pack for their arrival. The children were in the outer parlor playing games and reading but even they came around upon Hazel's dramatic entrance.

"Heard what?" Lavinia asked, her heart still heavy from a night of little sleep and wicked dreams.

"Monty's eloped with Daisy!"

Lavinia's eyes popped out of her head. Even Rawl looked shocked. "Monty?" she asked, not quite sure if she heard properly.

Hazel plopped on the bed. "Indeed. They asked the captain to marry them this morning and they left for London as soon as the gangway was down. Isn't that just the most romantic thing you've ever heard?"

"I didn't even know he knew Daisy," Lavinia said.

"Well, he must have met her sometime because according to Celene he and Edward had a row one time about it on deck. He threatened Monty and now Monty's just gone and thumbed his nose at Stuyvesant-French, for he and Daisy have left even though Edward has cut her off."

"How terrible. How cruel. He wouldn't," Lavinia sputtered.

"But he did. He won't even go to her. He's cut her off."

Lavinia turned around so the children wouldn't see the expression on her face. Worry mixed with hurt and fear. She couldn't expect much from Edward if he could treat his sweet crippled sister so heartlessly. So it was over for her. She had to erase her want of him entirely, or watch it come around and bite her like it bit Daisy. Inside her heart felt like it was cracking in two.

Hazel came up behind her. "I'm sorry, Lavinia. I know you and Monty were always friendly. I didn't think you would take his elopement like this."

Lavinia shook her head. She might have laughed if she wasn't so near tears. "No, don't be absurd. I love Monty. I want him happy. Daisy will make him happy." She forced herself to turn around and face everyone in the room. "Please don't think I'm upset. I'm thrilled they've found each other. In many ways I see now how compatible they are. I just never thought to put the two of them together."

"Do you want to be alone?" Hazel whispered, glancing toward Jamie, Eva and Fanny's faces stuck in the doorway as the children stared at them.

"No," Lavinia said adamantly. "I'm fine. Really. Of course, I'm shocked by Edward's behavior, but I don't know why. He's like that. Yes, just like that . . ." she said, her words drifting off. Catching herself, she looked at Hazel and plastered on a smile. "We have another wedding to think about soon, I imagine. So let us put our minds to our travels to Kylemore House, shall we? If the invitation still stands, I plan on taking you there."

Hazel just looked at her, a frightful gleam of hope in her eyes.

Chapter
Thirty-One

Edward fitfully rode in the carriage to Kylemore House with Celene and Cornelius. He shifted so many times, Celene stared at him as if he had a spider crawling in his pants.

"Is there something bothering you, my good man?" Celene finally asked.

Edward shot her a quelling look. The last thing he needed in his misery was an inquisition. "I'm fine."

"It feels strange going to Kylemore's without Daisy. I'm afraid we've become chaperons without a charge," Cook interjected.

"There are the Murphy girls. Edward is their chaperon. He can't shirk his duty just because his sister has gone and eloped—although Daisy's actions do make one wonder about the quality of her care. . . ." Celene gave Edward another probing, accusing stare.

Edward stared back. He knew the woman didn't approve of his harsh actions but Celene could be damned. He wasn't going to meet with Baillie until Daisy sought an annulment.

"Edward's just playing out this game of charades. He's not a chaperon for the Murphys. Sometimes I feel as if I have more regard for the Murphy girls than he." Cook finally said, "Why don't you cry off this social engagement, Edward? I can give Kylemore your excuses and Celene and I will be happy to look out for Hazel and Lavinia in your absence, if you care at all about that sort of thing."

Edward bit his cheek in an attempt to leash his anger. "I'm happy to do it."

Celene rolled her eyes.

Cornelius rambled on. "Of course, this little trip is going to require a lot of attention. Kylemore is sure to ask Hazel for her hand. We'll need to make a good impression. But once that's taken care of, then there's only one to go: Lavinia. What do you think of Buc for her, Celene? I myself believe the Earl of Spitzbergen would be ideal, and Kylemore tells me he'll be there this weekend."

Celene clapped her hands in glee. "Oh, delightful. Delightful. There's nothing more wonderful than playing matchmaker in your old age. Isn't that right, Edward?"

Edward only shifted in his seat once again, then obstinately turned his attention to the passing countryside.

⚜ ⚜

Lavinia walked through the grounds of Kylemore House, meandering in and out of the boxwood maze that centered the tulip garden. The weekend guests had all arrived and everyone seemed either to be resting or unpacking in their suites. She was too much on edge to read or nap, so she'd wandered downstairs and found the nearest door that led out into the tulips.

Behind her, Kylemore House loomed enormous. Built by the Kylemores in 1445, it had recently undergone a huge renovation and now boasted even the most modern comforts such as hot and cold running water. Kylemore's late mother had turned a medieval fortress into a château worthy of Fifth Avenue. Lavinia was quite impressed. If Hazel and the children lived out their days in this country idyll, Lavinia could think of no other place more perfect.

Tonight was to be the announcement. Kyle sent a note to Hazel's rooms that he'd offically broken off with Miss Carmichael. Along with it he sent a small posy of violets. Hazel adored them. Lavinia couldn't bear to look at them.

She reached the center of the maze and found Jamie inside it, perched on a marble bench, novel in hand. "There you are!" she said pleasantly.

Her face fell when he tried to hide the book from her.

"Not another one!" she said in dismay. Going to him, she read the title of the book. *These Untutored Bachelors of the Wilderness.* Rolling her eyes, she exclaimed, "Tell me, Jamie, does Mr. Coltrain not know the word 'Indian'?"

"Aw, I knew you'd find me!" Jamie scowled.

She sat next to him on the bench. "No, I'm not going to take it away this time. You've broken me. If you must read these things to the point of sneaking around, then go ahead and read them. What I don't understand is why Mr. Stuyvesant-French insists on giving them to you."

"Because he understands."

"Understands what?" she asked.

"Understand what it's like to be a boy. You'll never understand that."

A sadness crept into her heart when she looked at him, this young boy wanting so much to be a man. "I know Hazel and I can never understand. That's why we've come all this way. To get you a father."

"Is Stuyvesant-French going to be my father, then?"

She recoiled. "Why would you ask that? You know we're here to see Kylemore and Hazel wed. Then you and the girls will live here."

He looked around the boxwood maze, his face less awestruck than she'd expected. "I don't want to live here."

"But why not? This place is stupendous. Kylemore can see that you go to Eton and there you'll meet all kinds of boys your age."

"But if we live here with Kylemore, where will you be?"

The question took her aback. "Why, I'll be around. I might even let a cottage nearby just so you can come visit."

"It won't work."

"But why?" she asked.

He gave her a dark look. "Because Eva and Fanny think Hazel's their mother. They don't remember anybody else, but I was older when I got to the home. *I* know she's not my mother."

"But she's your family now and she would want you with the rest of the children."

"But you're my family, too, aren't you? So why can't I come with you?"

She felt as if he had both hands on her heart. "You could come with me, Jamie, but I'm a single woman. I've no man at all. Kylemore would be able to provide more male companionship than I ever could."

"You could marry Stuyvesant-French. He told me he treated you well when you got stuck out in the rain looking for me."

"He did?" she murmured. "Even so, that doesn't mean he wants to marry me."

"Do you want to marry him?"

The hand he had on her heart just got tighter. "If he had asked . . . Oh, I don't know . . . but he'll never ask. So we needn't think about it."

"So why don't you ask him, then?"

Her thoughts went back to the night in her parlor when she held the bouquet of violets to him and gave him her soul. "I—I did in so many words, Jamie. Mr. Stuyvesant-French declined, I'm afraid."

"But why? Why wouldn't he want to marry you? You're the prettiest girl around." Jamie looked utterly bewildered, so much so that Lavinia felt a stab in her chest.

"I'm really not his kind of woman, Jamie. I can't explain it better than that."

Jamie's expression turned stormy. A coldness crept into his eyes. His defense. "It's because we were orphans, isn't it? That's why he doesn't want us. He thinks we're just poor wretches of no account."

"No, it has nothing to do with that," she said.

He stood and clutched the book in his hands. "I'm going with you, Lavinia. I won't stay here in this place if you're not here. You'd be alone then."

"I can be alone," she pleaded.

He stomped away, retracing his path through the maze.

"Where are you going?" she called after him.

He turned briefly. "I'm going to give Mr. Stuyvesant-French his stupid book back. He's not my friend anymore. He hurt you."

"No," she lied, not wanting to see him hurt, too.

"Yes, he did. He did and I hate him now." Jamie turned and walked away.

"I shouldn't have told you," she whispered, watching him go.

Chapter
Thirty-Two

L avinia sat next to the dowager and watched the couples waltz
around the cavernous Kylemore ballroom. Hazel floated in
Kyle's arms. Lavinia had never seen her so happy, nor the
duke so content.

"He's in love with her. Look how he watches her. She can't
make a move that his eyes aren't lit upon her face in rapt fascination." Celene took the proffered glass of champagne from a steward
liveried in the Kylemore purple and gold, and handed Lavinia one.

Lavinia took it gratefully. At midnight Kylemore would make
the expected announcement. They had plans for a summer wedding
if the monstrous arrangements could be fashioned in time. She
never had known what it took to marry a duke. Everything was
grander and slower and more laborious than for the rest of the
world.

"Are you not speaking with Edward now that his sister has fled
him?" Celene watched her closely.

She felt a heat come to her cheeks but prayed she appeared

nonchalant. "Daisy's elopement is wonderful. I know Monty. He's a bounder but he's a charming one and, who knows, she might just be able to settle him. At the very least he'll keep Daisy amused, and she's sorely lacked that in her life. I can't help but think their union is good for them both."

"But he's a dark, stormy-tempered one, wouldn't you agree?"

"Monty?"

"No, no, dear. Edward. Why he's been absolutely peevish since we arrived at Kylemore's. It must be because of Daisy."

"Yes," Lavinia said hesitantly.

"But isn't that just the most romantic story, and now Hazel is to be wed. Why, you're the last one left. Is Edward going to take you on the rest of this tour alone?"

Lavinia looked at her. She never really thought about completing the tour now that Daisy and Hazel were gone from it. It was absurd to think of continuing because Edward wouldn't escort her, nor would she let him, given her weakness for him. "I—I don't think it's proper to continue, do you?" she answered lightly.

"Not continue? You must! You're the only one left unwed. How are you to find a husband, Lavinia, if you don't have your grand tour?"

Lavinia tried a smile. "This isn't a Jane Austen novel. I don't have to find a husband. In fact, when Hazel weds, I've been thinking I might stay here and look after the children for her."

"Yes, the children. Of course it's best that they stay here at Kylemore House than traipse around Europe like vagabonds." Celene leaned closer, a serious expression in her eyes, "But you know, dear, there's been a terrible rumor about those children. I'm sure you can guess what it is."

Lavinia brushed it aside. "People always talk like that. And it's not true. Why Hazel and I are too young to have had Jamie."

"But not the little girls." Celene frowned. "Hazel's going to be a duchess. It's important her past remain scandal-free."

"It is scandal-free." Lavinia refused to meet the old woman's eyes. "Besides, if I stay here and look after them, the rumors will be on my shoulders not hers."

"So you're already resigning yourself to being a spinster aunt who governesses for the children. I'm disappointed in you, Lavinia. I thought you'd go on to shock the crowns of all Europe with your séances."

"I'm through with those. Never again. I don't do them well. I—I am so sorry I hurt Cornelius." She looked at Celene, her eyes filled with contrition and pain. "I'll never forgive myself."

Celene shook her head. "You'll never convince him it wasn't Alice. I think it best never to mention it around him."

"I won't," Lavinia promised.

"And speak of the devil!" Celene smiled at Lavinia. "Look who's wandering our way. Why it's Cornelius himself with the dark knight Mr. Stuyvesant-French."

Lavinia held her breath. She glanced across the crowded ballroom aswirl in multicolored satin ballgowns, and met his gaze. Edward looked right at her, as an enemy spots another across a battlefield.

Her heart pounded. She felt the blood rush from her face. She hadn't seen him since the night of the séance and she didn't relish seeing him now. "I really must excuse myself. Hazel might need me to—"

"What, dear? Hazel is going to be a duchess. She'll have plenty of handmaidens without having to make her sister into one."

"No, I really must go. I've things to take care of—" Lavinia turned and found herself trapped on one side by the crowd and on the other by the sudden appearance of Cornelius and Edward.

"There you ladies are!" Cook bellowed good-naturedly. He kissed Celene's hand, then Lavinia's, and she felt ashamed because after what had happened to him, she didn't deserve his kind manners.

"Shall I have this dance, Celene?" Cook asked.

Celene laughed and allowed him to help her to her feet. "You would waltz with a woman in a turban?" she mocked.

Cornelius covertly bussed her on the cheek. "My favorite kind." Together they disappeared onto the ballroom floor.

In helpless silence, Lavinia watched them go. She refused to look at Edward, so she stood by his side, not speaking, not recognizing him until he took her hand and kissed it.

Her gaze flickered to him. She wanted to snatch back her hand and run, but she didn't dare make a scene, for Hazel's sake.

"Jamie sends his regards," he said coolly, his gaze locking with hers. "He threw Mr. Coltrain's latest literary attempt at me, then informed me how much he despised me."

She didn't know what to say. "He's young. He can't always control himself like we can."

"Do you control yourself?" Without waiting for her answer, he reached for her hand. "Dance, Miss Murphy?"

She didn't want to go with him, but to pull away and refuse would cause another ruffle of the gossips' tongues.

"The Emperor's Waltz" began. Edward gripped her waist; he held up her hand tantalizingly close to his cheek. They were off.

"You dance well, Mr. Stuyvesant-French," she said, looking up at him, her mind memorizing his features for fear she might never see him again.

"I've always enjoyed the feel of a woman in my arms." He locked gazes with her.

"Any woman?" she whispered, her heart wrenching.

"Are you any woman, Lavinia? You, with all your special talents for the parlor . . . and the bedroom?" The corner of his mouth tipped in a smile. He looked wicked with that dark goatee and those unforgivably green eyes. He was wicked.

Her depression deepened. He was never going to value her, and in some ways she could understand why. But in others, she never would. She wanted his love and she would return it fourfold, but she would starve to death this way, always taunted by him, never having him. "I'm no longer going to perform séances. I thought you'd like to know. Please tell Cornelius for me. I've given up being a spiritualist."

"What led to this? Surely not my pleas," he said dryly.

"I—I didn't want to hurt Cornelius. You may never believe me, but I don't enjoy doing such things and I've always tried to avoid them."

A coldness crossed his features. "Why didn't you, then?"

Hot tears sprung into her eyes. "Believe me. I didn't mean to do Alice. I just couldn't control it. Rawl is getting old, I suppose. I don't know what happened that night. . . ."

He stared down at her for a very long time, as if assessing her sincerity. Finally when they'd passed for the third time the doors leading out to the balcony, he abruptly quit their waltz and pulled her outside.

"What?" she gasped, half running to keep up with him as he dragged her to the balustrade.

"Tell me again that you did not wish to hurt Cornelius," he ground out, staring across the balcony to the moonlight hills of rye and flax surrounding the manor house.

"I did not wish to hurt Cornelius, because I only—I only—" Her voice dropped to less than a whisper. "Because I only wished to hurt you."

He looked at her.

She twisted in his grip, but his hands were like shackles binding her to him.

"You wished to hurt me. And you knew by hurting Cornelius, you'd hurt me."

"No, I wished to hurt only you. Only you," she said vengefully. Tears ran down her cheeks. "I gave myself to you with heart in hand. And you were laughing at me through all my confessions."

"No," he rasped, now barely able to look at her. "I was not laughing."

"You've treated me like a whore. Treated me like your father treated your mother." She swatted her tears with the backs of her hands. "You keep coming around, Edward, as if you want something from me, but then, all your accusations are of me wanting something from you. But I want nothing. Nothing, do you hear me?"

He bent toward her. Slowly he glanced around the balcony. It was dark; they were all alone. "You want nothing from me, Lavinia? Then prove it." In the darkness his gaze held hers. "Tell me our time spent together meant nothing to you. And when I try to kiss you as I want to now, turn your head and tell me of your hatred. Don't kiss me in return. Don't give me any more simple gifts that lead down treacherous paths. Then and only then will I know you want nothing from me."

She stared up at him. His arms went around her. He held her tightly as if afraid to let her go. "I want nothing from you," she whispered darkly, her instincts crying out for self-preservation.

"Turn away, then. Deny that you desired once to be with me, to stay with me. That once upon a time you desired to make me happy."

"I want better for my life than to be your mistress." She looked at him. Her very soul wept. The epiphany had come. She would either fully succumb to him and take what little he offered because she loved him so badly, or her pride would take over, and she would have to walk away, and know that no other man would ever give her soul sustenance as he could.

His features turned hard and cruel. "What don't you like about my offer? The fact that I'm not titled like your sister's duke over there, or the fact that I'm despicably from the same gutter that spawned you?"

"No," she cried softly and tried to break away. But his hand was on her wrist pulling her ever nearer to him.

"Show your true colors. Tell me I'm wrong about you. Tell me you're not just some kind of mercenary bitch prowling around here with all the cold motives of a businessman cutting a deal, ready to forsake love for a title."

"Let's finally speak of love, shall we?" she cried. "For whose love am I forsaking if I choose Buc for my husband?"

"You're forsaking mine, Lavinia. Mine," he whispered harshly, truthfully.

Her legs buckled beneath her. He caught her against him.

Hesitantly, his hand reached up and cupped her face. He murmured something almost like a curse, then he lowered his lips to hers, inch by inch, as if just waiting for betrayal.

But it never came. He placed his mouth over hers and broke into a fierce kiss unmindful of the packed ballroom only steps away. Shivering, she gave herself to him, her soul bursting with hope. Maybe she would never be this man's wife but maybe just being his would be enough. Perhaps he would give her all her heart desired, if only he would love her. Always love her.

If only.

Chapter
Thirty-Three

All Truths have their Martyrs.

—ROBERT RUTHVEN

T he clock struck midnight. As if the news had already filtered
through the guests, the crowd gathered at the dais where
Kylemore stood with Hazel and Celene on each arm. Lord
Buchanon stood behind them, grinning.

"Ladies and gentlemen, dear friends and honored guests, I've
invited you here tonight not only to share the hospitality of this
fine and noble house, but also to be the first to hear the news
which will change the fate of the Kylemores forever." Kyle looked
down at Celene. He released her from his arm and allowed her to
step in front of the crowd.

Holding up her champagne glass, Celene smiled at Hazel and
turned back to the crowd. "Dear guests, it is my pleasure to
announce a most happy union between my dear Kylemore and his
bride-to-be, Miss Hazel Mae Murphy of New York." She lifted her
glass to her lips and drank. The crowd reciprocated, then Buc struck
up a cheer.

"Huzzah! Huzzah! Huzzah!" the crowd followed.

Hazel began to weep tears of joy. Kylemore clasped her tightly to him, and Celene kissed her on the cheek.

Lavinia could barely watch. Her eyes filled with fresh tears and her heart felt as if it would burst with happiness. She looked up at Edward and said, "Perhaps fate is more kind than I thought." He squeezed her hand.

Kylemore tapped a spoon against his champagne glass for another announcement. The crowd grew silent.

"Today is especially rich in gifts, my friends. In our quieter hours, Miss Murphy, I, and the dowager," he nodded to Celene, "have discussed what shall become of Miss Murphy's younger brother and sisters. On our voyage across the sea from America, I, too, have grown fond of these children along with Celene. I would now like to announce my plan to adopt all three as soon as Miss Murphy and I have wed. It is not too soon for even a bachelor like myself to hear Kylemore House ring again with the laughter of children!" He laughed and raised his glass.

The crowd followed. It took several seconds for the boisterous crowd to hear the crash at the ballroom door.

Lavinia froze. She didn't know who the woman was who stood at the heavily carved double doors. Obviously neither did Hazel, but when Hazel searched the crowd for Lavinia, Lavinia knew there was only one person it could be.

"I will not be jilted by you for this woman and her bastards!" The woman pushed aside the hesitant liveries who flanked the door. By her expensive gown and jewels and perfectly coifed butter-blonde hair, even the servants knew she was someone with whom to be reckoned.

"Delia, get out." Kylemore looked like he was ready to explode.

The crowd—a hundred at least—fell into absolute silence.

"I will not get out!" Delia Carmichael began to cry. "I know about her! Everyone says she's a soiled woman! I will not rest until I've proven it!"

Hazel looked white as a sheet. She met Lavinia's gaze in the crowd.

Suddenly Lavinia ran to her.

"Stay with me, Hazel," Kylemore pleaded.

Hazel shook her head. Tears fell like a waterfall from her eyes.

Celene looked ready to fix Delia with the evil eye.

Buc just looked stunned.

"Come with me. Say nothing. *Nothing*," Lavinia whispered to her as she held her by the waist and led her to the back of the dais.

"Have you no honor, Your Grace? Are you so smitten that you'd be taken in by this crass American?" Delia stomped through the crowd that parted like the Red Sea. She stepped up onto the dais. "Why don't you ask if the children are really hers? That's what everyone is saying, so go ahead and ask her. Make everyone here witness to her denial." Delia turned her ugly expression toward Hazel and Lavinia. "Or are you afraid she won't deny it?"

"I curse you, Delia. You bitch," Kylemore said under his breath. His angry eyes were on fire.

Delia steeled herself. She crossed her arms over her chest. "Go ahead, dear. Ask her about the children. And she'd best tell the truth, because Father is even now writing to the United States to see if any Miss Murphys have whelped any bastards. And he will find out. You know Father."

"Oh God," Hazel moaned, sobbing into Lavinia's shoulder.

Lavinia stared at the woman, sickened. Delia Carmichael might be more devil than flesh, but she was only acting out of rage and rejection. Lavinia just wished they'd all been left alone. Delia would never know how much this wedding meant to Hazel. Lavinia was cut to the quick to think it would now all end in this terrible disgrace.

"We'll endure this. Say nothing," Lavinia warned her, putting up a strong front.

Edward stepped to the front of the dais. Cornelius went to Celene and held her, for she was beginning to tremble with rage.

"Stop this—these lies—" Kyle muttered to Delia.

Delia only pointed a cold finger at Hazel. "Make her deny it or confirm it. Either way, I will find out the truth and see this marriage—if it goes forth—annulled."

Kylemore lunged for her. The crowd screamed. Buc caught him by the arms right before he might have caused damage.

"Get out!" he cried, lashing at her.

"Make her deny it! To all these witnesses— Why isn't she denying it? Because it's true, that's why!" Delia laughed through her tears.

Slowly Lavinia spoke up, knowing her choice was ruinous, but seeing no way around it

"Your father, Miss Carmichael, needn't write to the authorities. Five years ago, there was an illegitimate baby to a Miss Murphy in St. Louis. That is the source of all these rumors, and that is the only thing your father will find."

Delia looked at Kyle, conquest and triumph in her eyes.

Lavinia knew tears were now streaming down her own cheeks. Her choice was fraught with peril. The Kylemores might have to shun her or risk the backlash of society. She could hardly bear the pain of never seeing Celene again, maybe even Hazel and the children, but she couldn't let Hazel pay the price. Not when Hazel had everything she'd ever wanted. And she, Lavinia, at best had the offer of being mistress to a rich, imperious man, and nothing more.

"The baby was mine, Miss Carmichael," Lavinia said. "Mine. I'm the fallen woman. Not Hazel. Never Hazel."

"No!" Hazel gasped through her tears, her expression filled with horror.

"Lavinia!" Edward exclaimed sharply, his face etched with disbelief.

"I had to," Lavinia whispered to him. "I had to," she wept,

hating the look on his face. He knew better than anyone how badly she was lying, but she couldn't stand by and watch her sister and her sister's child be destroyed. Hazel was the only family she had, the only family she might ever have. Lavinia couldn't stand by and not take the damage for her when Lavinia had no duke offering for her hand in marriage. When, in fact, she had no offers at all.

"This is madness," Edward said, finally at her side. He pulled her from Hazel and shook her. "What are you doing? They'll never accept you now. And I know how they'll treat you. They'll treat you just like my mother." His expression was filled with grief and rage, and, she hoped, just the tiniest amount of admiration.

"You can't do this! I won't let you!" Hazel cried. She ran to the front of the dais, but Kylemore caught her before she could even open her mouth.

"No," he commanded, dragging her back.

"I can't let her do this! I can't!" Hazel wept.

"But you must!" Lavinia burst out. "You can't wear the blame for something that was *not your fault*. You're not to blame here, Hazel. You are the *victim*. So take your duke and his fine palace. Take him. Take him. You better than anyone deserve this fine man. He loves you. Take him, I beg you. He's my wedding present to you. . . ." Lavinia broke down. She looked out across the crowd at the sea of shocked, horrified expressions. Society wanted women like her gone from them. She was happy to do it.

Buc went to Hazel to comfort her. Kylemore took Lavinia aside where the crowd could not hear them.

"She isn't to blame, I tell you. I'll take Eva away and we'll never darken the door of Kylemore House again," Lavinia promised through sobs.

"What? You would take a child from her mother just because you want Hazel to be a duchess?"

Lavinia stared at Kylemore. She was stunned. Shocked. "You— you know?"

"Of course I know. You think Hazel wouldn't tell me such an important thing? Especially when I've already consulted my attorneys in order to adopt Eva and the other two."

"And you still want to marry her? If the truth is known, you'll become pariahs." Lavinia hiccoughed.

"I'll take my chances. I'm not about to let you take Eva from her mother, society be damned."

Lavinia put a hand on his arm. "The truth will help no one, especially the children. We want them to grow up respectably."

"They will grow up respectably. I will be adopting them all legally and morally. This scandal will pass—"

"It will pass quicker if I'm gone. So let me take the burden of it away. I'm heading back to New York anyway. I can't stay. I don't belong here. And . . ."

She looked up and caught Edward's gaze. He stared at her as if she were the only woman in the room. She turned back to the duke. ". . . And I don't need a reputation like Hazel does. I'm just a parlor spiritualist and that's probably all I'll ever be." She kissed him softly on the cheek. Kylemore was made of sturdier fabric than she'd ever imagined and she was suddenly excruciatingly proud of Hazel for choosing such a noble man.

"You will visit us? She and the children won't go a day without thinking of you."

"Nor will I them, but now go and have your wedding, and don't let this get in the way of it. When the gossips have moved on to some other topic, I'll come back and see my family again." She smiled through her tears and left the dais. Unable to see anyone through her sobs, she ran to the entrance that Delia had used to ruin the night, and she ran up the three flights to her room.

Epilogue

He has now been nine years a medium. His family is broken up, and the wife, to whom he was a most worthy husband, is forsaken, he is travelling with his paramour who acts as his scribe . . . and, last Fall, bore to him what they call a spiritual baby—but of such sufficient materiality to counterbalance nine pounds.

—BENJAMIN F. HATCH, *Writing about John Spear, 1859*

A knock came to Lavinia's door. She didn't even bother to answer it. She was too busy packing her trunks to be gone from Kylemore House in the morning. Too obsessed with trying to save Hazel more guilt and embarrassment.

The door opened. She froze.

Edward stood there, arms crossed, that sardonic expression on his face, the one she knew so well.

"I'm shocked—shocked."

She shrugged. "How did you know what room I was in?"

"Kyle told me."

She ignored him. "Well, you better go or you'll ruin my already soiled reputation further. Besides, I've a lot to do before I return to New York."

He walked farther into the room. Behind him, the door and passageway lay wide open.

He took her hands in his. "You're not going back to New York.

I'll not have you performing two-bit acts in your parlor any longer. You said yourself you've done your last séance."

"I was hasty in my decision. In truth I really thought my future would keep me here at Hazel's side. Now I've got to buck up and reinvent myself. There's no place for scandal here. I've got to leave."

"To Egypt, with me, then."

She didn't look at him. Pulling her hands from his, she stuffed some more shawls into her trunk. "I know it wouldn't surprise anyone for me to go with you. But I—" Her heart suddenly felt so heavy she lowered herself to a nearby chair. "Oh, I know there's very little stopping me. I'm no debutante, that's for sure, but there are things to consider before I hook up with the likes of you. I could have a child, you know." She looked up at him, silent accusation in her eyes. "You have to think carefully about these things. Children need two parents. If I go with you and find myself in such a way— Oh, I couldn't do it."

"What you're saying, Lavinia, is that you don't trust me, isn't that right?" Edward's expression darkened. "You think I would abandon my child as easily as I would its mother."

"I don't know," she said wearily into her hands. "I don't know what to think or who to believe anymore. I just know that these things have consequences and it seems foolish for me to—to—"

"To trust me." He tipped her chin so that she would look at him. "So what you want is the law on your side. You want it all nice and legal and binding that I recognize any children of this union. Well, I'll do it. I'll have my attorneys draft the documents as soon as possible."

Dejected, she stood and began another attempt at packing. "I don't like lawyers. I think I'd prefer to do séances."

"Are you chasing me away, Lavinia? Are you forcing me to make the last choice available?" he thundered.

A stream of angry tears ran down her cheeks. "Say you love me! Say you want to make me your wife and keep me by your side always! And then do it, Edward! Otherwise, let me be." Her heart was cracking. "I can't let you keep throwing me back into the gutter. I can't let you do it." She broke down in sobs. She desperately wanted him to love her, marry her, honor her, but she knew she couldn't force him to do those things. Not with the will of iron he possessed.

"Shall I take the last available choice? I'll do it. I warn you," he said softly.

She paused. Tearfully, she looked at him and shook her head. "I don't want you to leave me. How can you even torture me with these threats when you know how much I love you?"

He took her in his arms and stared down at her, brushing away the tears. "And I love you." He kissed her softly on her trembling mouth.

She looked up at him and knew she would follow him anywhere, no matter the disgrace, no matter the pain. In the end, love was nothing but torment, but she would take it to be with him. The tears came again. "I'll go to Egypt with you. I'll live with you as your mistress. And if there's a child, I'll trust in you that you'll not abandon it."

He took her face in both his hands. "But I've made my decision. I'm taking the only choice left."

"No, don't leave me behind. I want to be with you. I must be with you," she begged, forsaking her pride.

"Then marry me. It's all that's left. Take my hand and my name and my love." His voice lowered to a whisper. "Please say it's the only choice left."

She stared at him, disbelief making her numb. It seemed so simple to propose, but these words didn't come from a man like Edward Stuyvesant-French. They were too humble, too wondrous, too deep, too moving.

Her hand went to her mouth as if she were afraid to answer. He was the life within her soul and now she could understand all the sad faces in her parlor who had longed to speak with a departed lover. If she were a ghost, she would find this man and be with him, even if he could never speak with her, or see her, or touch her. She would stay by his side and he would know she was with him, and she wouldn't need a two-penny medium to connect her to him.

"Shall you answer my pitiful proposal, wayward child, or shall I summon Celene up here to talk sense into you?" He stared down at her, a pensive hush in his voice, as if he weren't sure of her answer.

"Yes," she gasped, her eyes filling with another wellspring of tears. "I accept," she cried, wrapping her arms around his neck.

"Thank God that's over with, Cornelius. The suspense has been killing me!" Celene tramped in through the open bedchamber door, Cornelius right behind her, as if they lived there.

"Were you eavesdropping?" Lavinia said in amazement, her arms still clutching Edward.

"Of course! Do you think we Kylemores would let you flee when you and the rest of that Murphy brood are the best things to have happened to us in a century?" Celene took a nearby settee and Cornelius settled in next to her, smiling at Edward.

"Now, let's see," Celene ticked off her fingers. "Tomorrow you two and Kyle and Hazel will run off to London for a quick double wedding. Then you, my dear Edward, will fetch your Daisy and that fine, upstanding lad she loves so dearly, and you will *forgive them utterly* and bring them both back here for a wedding breakfast."

"Yes, dowager," Edward agreed humbly.

Celene smiled at Lavinia, the amethyst twinkling in her turban. "Then, you two silly gooses may rush off to Egypt or wherever, but at the first sign of a little Stuyvesant-French, you're to return here. I want all the children in this family born at Kylemore."

"Even Buc's?" Cornelius winked at them both. "He went baying after Delia the second she realized the game was up. She fled in tears and Buc's probably comforting her as we speak."

"It's a perfect union, unfortunately." Celene grimaced.

"Wounded feelings make even the sweetest women vipers," Cornelius quipped.

Celene tweaked his cheek. "Yes, my dear, you remember that, and we'll get along famously, even if I am a few years older."

"I'm trapped," Cornelius confessed.

"Join the club," Edward said, whispering down to Lavinia.

"You don't have to do this," she said, her heart in her throat.

"I must," he answered. "Alice compelled me to love you. You know. Lavinia, I never told you, but you're more talented than I ever gave you credit for being. I look forward to you stunning me again when you give me a son."

"And what if I give you a daughter?" She held her breath.

He kissed her. "As long as she has no penchant to speak with the dead, I'll be a happy man."

"I love you, Edward," she whispered.

"I love you, ghost girl," he whispered back, locking her mouth in a kiss.